Praise for M

"An inspiring and uplifting read about hope, faith, and perseverance. . . . To be captivated by such a compelling story, so much so I did not want to put it down, attests to the writer's storytelling ability."

Interviews & Reviews

"I really loved the story and the writing style of Jill Eileen Smith. She is a master storyteller of Bible stories and really keeps the reader captivated."

Life Is Story

Praise for *The Heart of a King*

"Smith uses poetic intervals to infuse the narrative with the sensuality and beauty of the ancient culture."

Booklist

"*The Heart of a King* was an intriguing, gripping look into the life of one of history's most famous kings."

Interviews & Reviews

Praise for the Daughters of the Promised Land Series

"Readers will appreciate that Smith infuses this well-known story with emotional depth and a modern sensibility not typically seen in historical novels."

Publishers Weekly on *A Passionate Hope*

"*A Passionate Hope* is a wonderful novel rich with historical detail about real people who suffer the heartache that comes from stepping out ahead of God, and the miracle of grace that comes when we cry out to Him."

Francine Rivers, bestselling author of *Redeeming Love*,
on *A Passionate Hope*

"Smith's fresh retelling of the story of Ruth and Naomi portrays these strong biblical women in a thoughtful and reflective manner. Her impeccable research and richly detailed setting give readers a strong sense of life in ancient Israel."

Library Journal on *Redeeming Grace*

"Rahab's story is one of the most moving redemption accounts in Scripture. *The Crimson Cord* perfectly captures all the drama of the original, fleshing out the characters with care and thought, and following the biblical account every step of the way. Jill's thorough research and love for God's Word are both evident, and her storytelling skills kept me reading late into the night. A beautiful tale, beautifully told!"

Liz Curtis Higgs, *New York Times* bestselling author
of *Mine Is the Night*, on *The Crimson Cord*

THE
PRINCE
AND THE
PRODIGAL

Books by Jill Eileen Smith

The Wives of King David

Michal

Abigail

Bathsheba

Wives of the Patriarchs

Sarai

Rebekah

Rachel

Daughters of the Promised Land

The Crimson Cord

The Prophetess

Redeeming Grace

A Passionate Hope

The Heart of a King

Star of Persia

Miriam's Song

The Prince and the Prodigal

When Life Doesn't Match Your Dreams

She Walked Before Us

THE
PRINCE
AND THE
PRODIGAL

JILL EILEEN SMITH

a division of Baker Publishing Group
Grand Rapids, Michigan

© 2022 by Jill Eileen Smith

Published by Revell
a division of Baker Publishing Group
PO Box 6287, Grand Rapids, MI 49516-6287
www.revellbooks.com

Printed in the United States of America

Library of Congress Cataloging-in-Publication Data
Names: Smith, Jill Eileen, 1958– author.
Title: The prince and the prodigal / Jill Eileen Smith.
Description: Grand Rapids, MI : Revell, a division of Baker Publishing Group, [2022]
Identifiers: LCCN 2021029331 | ISBN 9780800737634 (paperback) | ISBN 9780800741082 (casebound) | ISBN 9781493434183 (ebook)
Subjects: GSAFD: Bible fiction.
Classification: LCC PS3619.M58838 P75 2022 | DDC 813/.6—dc23
LC record available at https://lccn.loc.gov/2021029331

This is a work of historical reconstruction; the appearances of certain historical figures are therefore inevitable. All other characters, however, are products of the author's imagination, and any resemblance to actual persons, living or dead, is coincidental.

Published in association with Books & Such Literary Management, www.booksand such.com.

Baker Publishing Group publications use paper produced from sustainable forestry practices and post-consumer waste whenever possible.

22 23 24 25 26 27 28   7 6 5 4 3 2 1

To all those who long for reconciliation,
restoration, and redemption, remember—
the God who loves you wants them too.
Forgiveness is only a willing heart and a prayer away.
May this story give you hope in the God who redeems
even the most impossible situations.

TRIBES OF ISRAEL

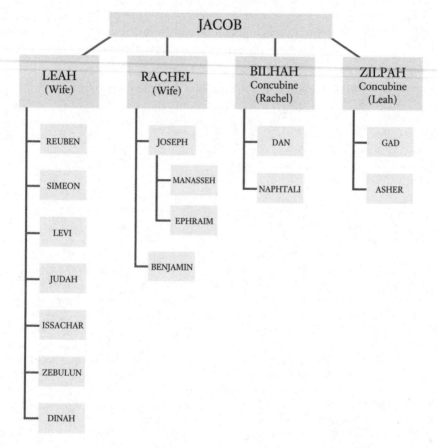

PROLOGUE

MAMRE, 1842 BC

Jacob paused at the outskirts of Mamre near Hebron, taking in the familiar hills and fields where he had spent the early years of his life. Memories filled him, along with an ache in his heart over the news that his mother had long ago passed into Sheol. Why had he been forced to stay away nearly thirty years? He closed his eyes against the glare of the setting sun, remembering his mother's tenderness, her way of speaking, her smile. If only things had been different. He should never have allowed his uncle Laban to keep him away so long. He should have been here for her.

His heart skipped its normal rhythm as anxiety flared with the memories. Would his father welcome him now? Isaac had spent years alone without wife or sons, with none but his servants to care for his flocks, his fields, his needs. Jacob should have been here for both of them. The moment he had wed Rachel, he should have made plans to return. But Laban had tricked him again and again, and the regret he felt gave way first to anger, then to acceptance. He had done what he had to do. There was no use in trying to change the past.

He slowly pushed his staff into the dirt and limped closer to the encampment, which spread far and wide before him, a testament to his father's wealth.

"Are you all right, Abba?"

The voice of Rachel's firstborn, seventeen-year-old Joseph, caused Jacob to turn and smile. How often had he thanked God for Rachel's oldest son? Every day was not often enough, but every day the thought of Rachel surfaced, and Joseph was his memory of her. He was so like her in looks and in spirit. So unlike his brothers. A better, wiser son.

Jacob patted Joseph's hand where he had placed it in the crook of Jacob's arm. "I am fine, my son. It has been a long time since I have laid eyes on my father. He will not see us coming, but he will hear us. And he will know my voice." He hoped. "My father will be pleased to meet you. Come. Let us not delay lest the sun sets before we arrive and the servants think we are strangers come to harm them."

Joseph glanced behind them, and Jacob turned his gaze as well. Their caravan of sons, wives, children, and animals would need more room than Isaac now possessed. Jacob would do his best to include Isaac in their home—to give him a family again.

He picked up his pace despite his apprehension and moved toward the black goat-hair tents, spotting the largest one in the center, right where his father's tent had been when he left it for Paddan-Aram. God had promised to be with him when he left, and now He had brought him home again. How fitting.

The thought pleased him more than he expected. And to know that he had finally set things right between himself and his brother still filled him with awe. God really could do the impossible.

He looked at Joseph once more, marveling again that Rachel had borne him after so many years of longing. Yet why did God take her upon Benjamin's birth? And why did Joseph's brothers so often look on his favorite son with disfavor?

Jacob shook the thoughts aside. "Come," he said again. "There is my father's tent. It is time for you to meet your grandfather."

Joseph followed obediently, and Jacob said no more as they reached the tent, where the flaps were lifted. Isaac sat in the doorway upon cushions with a young servant girl close by.

"Father." Jacob could barely choke out the word, and emotion suddenly overtook him. He knelt with difficulty due to his bad leg, drew up beside Isaac, and carefully touched his knee. "It is I, Jacob."

Isaac turned his head toward Jacob, his eyes unseeing. He cleared his throat. "Is that really you, Jacob, my son?"

"Yes, Father. It is really I. I have come with the wives and children and flocks that the Lord your God has given to me. I have come so that they can know you, Father." He paused, swallowed hard, and felt the strong grip of his father's hand in his. "I have come home," he said, this time letting his tears flow.

He leaned closer, and he and his father embraced as though they never wanted to part again. Isaac's tears wet Jacob's robe, and they wept together for all that had come between them. For all of the loss they had both suffered. And for the joy of coming home again.

1

1841 BC

Joseph walked the ancient path from the fields near Hebron to his father's tent beneath the oaks of Mamre. The shepherd's staff rested in his right hand, but his gait felt weighted, despite the brilliant colors of the setting sun and the cool whisper of the breeze in the trees above him. He wasn't sure he wanted the role his father had placed upon him. His brothers certainly would not approve.

The scent of roasting lamb wafted to him, and a moment later the cry of a child met his ears. He hurried closer as Dinah emerged from his father's tent, carrying his brother Benjamin.

"You are back," Dinah said, smiling above his brother's wiggling body. The boy was nearing his first birthday and did not often like to be held except by Joseph, though he seemed to tolerate Dinah above the other women in the family.

"Yes," he said, dropping the staff and reaching for Benjamin, who now tried to fling himself into Joseph's arms. "There you are, baby brother!" Joseph held him high above his head until Benjamin squealed with delight. They played their little game until Joseph finally set Benjamin in the dirt and held his hand to help him walk toward their father's tent.

"How did it go?" Dinah asked before he could walk away. "I

know it has not been easy for you of late. Our half brothers—
and my own brothers, for that matter—seem to consider you
a pest more than the grown man you are."

Joseph gave her an appreciative look. He lowered his voice
and leaned closer while trying to keep Benjamin from tugging
him away. "It's nice to know that someone understands. I fear
our father does not stop to consider that having me report to
him on their behavior will not help their feelings toward me.
He already favors me overmuch because I'm Rachel's son."

"Abba loves you, Joseph. He does not see clearly where you
are concerned—or that he puts you in difficult situations."
She touched his arm. "Perhaps I can speak to him about this
sometime."

Joseph shook his head. "No. Don't worry yourself over it.
If I have too much trouble, I will talk to Father."

Dinah lifted a brow, her expression dubious. "Sometimes
he listens to me better than to any of you. Keep that in mind if
you need me." She turned, then tossed him a smile and walked
off to her mother's tent.

Joseph chuckled as he led Benjamin to greet their father.
Jacob was sitting among his cushions just inside his large goat-
hair tent. The sides were up to let in the breeze, and Jacob smiled
as he saw them coming.

"Greetings, Abba. Did you rest well?" At over one hundred
years, Jacob often rested in the heat of the day. He no longer
had the strength to shepherd the flocks as he once did. Rachel's death seemed to have aged him, despite the joy Benjamin
brought to both of them.

"I did, my son." He motioned with a veined hand for Joseph
to come closer and sit beside him. Joseph did as he was asked.
"Tell me, how did it go in the fields today? Have the sons of
my concubines returned with you?"

Joseph glanced at Benjamin, who had picked up a wooden stick and was attempting to put it in his mouth. Joseph took the stick from him and offered him a small wooden toy he used to play with. He looked once more at his father. "They are taking the flock to greener pastures and staying in one of the caves tonight. They did not wish to return to camp just yet."

Jacob straightened, and his brows knit in a frown. "Was there good reason to travel away from the camp? Why not set out for greener pastures tomorrow? Did the sheep not find enough to eat throughout the day?"

"The sheep found plenty of green pasture to eat and rest in today. I told them we should bring the sheep to the pens tonight and set out elsewhere tomorrow, but they did not listen." Joseph did not enjoy bringing such a report to his father, but he withheld the things he suspected his half brothers were really intending to do this night.

"If they will not listen to you, send them to me. I will see to it they listen to you, my son." Anger filled his voice but quickly abated as Joseph held his gaze. "My son." He reached for Joseph's hand. "You always do what I ask. I never have to wonder or worry about you. What a gift from God you have been to me in my old age."

Joseph patted his father's hand and nodded. "Thank you, Father. I desire to please you, as I know this also pleases our God." Hadn't he known at his mother's knee that God watched over them, that it was God who had given Joseph to her after years of barrenness? That it was God whom they were to serve and obey, for He had created all things?

"You are a good son," Jacob said, attempting to stand. Joseph jumped up and helped his father, offering him his staff to steady him. "I smell something good—roasting lamb? Let us go now and meet your grandfather and let the women serve us."

They walked toward the tent door, Benjamin toddling unsteadily ahead of them.

"Do you know if Leah's sons will be joining us?" his father asked.

"I have not seen them. Perhaps they will send a servant to tell us."

Leah's sons rarely joined the family at mealtimes, even though it was one of the few times they had to spend with Isaac. They often took the flocks too far to return to camp in one day. He supposed Zilpah's and Bilhah's sons just did as they saw Joseph's other brothers doing. Though they often argued, they seemed to get along better with each other than they ever had with him.

Jacob led Joseph and Benjamin to the center of the camp, where stones were placed about a fire. "They always came home when we lived in Shechem. They should not stray so far here. How do we know the Canaanites will always be friendly toward us?"

Joseph sat beside his father and pulled Benjamin onto his lap. "I don't think you need to fear for Leah's sons, Abba. They are grown men, and so far the men of Canaan have never troubled us."

"They are young and foolish," Jacob spat, scowling as if remembering things Joseph wished they could all forget.

Moments later, Isaac's servants helped him walk to the central fire and settled him on a wide rock. A servant sat beside him to help with his food.

"Greetings, Sabba," Joseph said. He rose with Benjamin and walked over to kiss Isaac's cheek.

"Ah, my son Joseph. I know your voice. You smell of the sheepfolds."

Joseph chuckled softly. "That I do. I spent the day with the flocks, but now I am here."

"And you are well?" Isaac's voice sounded thin and reedy as though passing through little air.

"I am well, Sabba. And hungry!"

Isaac laughed. "Then I will not keep you from eating."

Joseph moved back to the rock beside his father and allowed Dinah to take Benjamin again. He listened to his grandfather and father speak for a few moments, until Leah stepped from her tent and brought food to Isaac. Bilhah and Zilpah also emerged from the tent and served Jacob, Joseph, and Dinah, who fed Benjamin from her plate.

Joseph smiled at his father, then wrapped a piece of lamb in flatbread and took a bite, grateful for the silence. He did not miss his brothers. The only one he longed to see daily was Benjamin. Though they had left his grandfather Laban and endured the death of his mother, coming back to Mamre had not brought the peace his father expected. Or Joseph had hoped for. The only thing he had found here that brought him joy was the chance to learn more about the God of his father from Jacob and Isaac. Both men had told him the tales of their encounters with the God of Abraham and repeated the history of their people. Even the deceit of his father and God's overwhelming grace afterward were not withheld from Joseph.

Joseph found great comfort in the stories. And in times when he lay awake upon his mat and stared at the tent above him, the comfort of knowing that God cared for him too kept him believing that one day things between himself and his brothers would improve.

ᴜᴜᴜ

The bleating of sheep met Joseph's ears as he climbed the low rise to the vast pens where his father's sheep were kept. Reuben and Judah called the sheep to follow from two of the pens, while the other four sons of Leah came behind, making sure none strayed as the men led the ewes with their young to the lush green pastures just over the rise.

Dan, Gad, Naphtali, and Asher took the goats and headed in the opposite direction without a single look at Joseph. Joseph tapped his staff into the dirt as he followed behind, wishing again that his father had not asked him to report on the actions of these sons of the concubines. Did they suspect his change in roles?

He glanced at the cloudless heavens, the place where God lived, grateful for the gentle breeze that offset the heat of the rising sun. His turban protected him from the glare as he searched ahead of him, where his half brothers seemed in a hurry to put distance between them. They were going to ruin the goats at that pace. The young could not travel quickly. As he watched, Asher struck one of the goats for lagging behind.

Anger flared, and Joseph picked up his pace. He hurried to Asher's side. "Why did you strike him?"

Asher waved Joseph away as though his words meant nothing. "You worry too much and have obviously not spent enough time with these ornery animals to know they need a firm hand. Forget about it."

"Our father would not appreciate you mistreating the goats." Joseph straightened, but Asher still towered over him and laughed at his concerns as if Joseph were a child to be coddled.

"It was merely a tap. The animal needed to keep up." Asher walked away, still laughing, as though their exchange was nothing more than a humorous spat.

Joseph stood still a moment, assessing the situation. His father had put him in charge of these sons because he did not fully trust their work. But they didn't know his position, and he didn't like telling tales on them. If only they acted as they should so that there would be nothing to tell!

He followed his half brothers again, determined to watch them and the goats, whether he spoke to them again or not. He felt the sacks at his side and the sling tied to his wrist.

When they came to a large field, Dan and Naphtali went in one direction while Gad and Asher went in another. Joseph knew neither group welcomed his presence, so he spent the day moving from one to the other.

He finally stopped where Dan's herd had settled and leaned against a large oak tree. He pulled a handful of almonds from one of his sacks and slowly chewed as he looked from one end of the field to the other. Dan and Naphtali were not together now—only Dan was visible against the rising sun's glare.

Joseph moved about, trying to locate Naphtali, but he had disappeared from view. Puzzled, he strode the length of the area where the goats had spread out. He walked toward where Asher and Gad had gone, but there was no sign of Asher either.

He glanced from Dan to Gad, debating whether to stay with them or continue his search for Asher and Naphtali. They couldn't have gone far. Or had they planned to go to the city or some other place all along?

He looked at Gad still sitting beneath a tree and occasionally looking at the animals. Frustrated, he looked back toward Dan, but he was no longer there. When Joseph came to the low rise in the field, he found no sign of Dan, and the goats were moving away from him. Where were they going?

Irritation spiked at the thought that they were purposely trying to avoid him or play some spiteful trick on him. To what end? What could they possibly be doing that they must keep secret?

He dug the staff into the dirt and hurried down the slight hill, shading his eyes to look in all directions. Had Dan known where Asher was and joined him there? They would weaken the herd and kill the young if they did not take care to go at the animals' pace. They knew this. Every shepherd knew this.

After a lengthy jog, Joseph found the goats near a row of caves. Naphtali was there as well, but this time Dan was missing. Joseph closed his eyes, telling himself to remain calm. They were toying with him, trying to upset him. Obviously they did not want to include him as they once did. But why? Did they not care what their father would say to them when he heard of this?

Suddenly Joseph wished he were anywhere but here. He did not want to care for the flocks with these brothers, with any of his brothers. They refused to treat him as their equal, and while they might have tolerated him in his youth, they had grown more frustrating with each passing year.

He walked toward the caves in search of a place to escape when he heard laughter coming from within. Female laughter. He stood still, listening. The distinct voice of each brother interrupted what could only be a liaison with women.

Disgusted, Joseph returned to the goats and approached Naphtali. "Is this how you care for Father's flocks and herds? By meeting with women and ignoring the animals?"

Naphtali shrugged. "What are you going to do about it? Run to Father and tell tales? We will deny what you say, so don't trouble yourself."

Naphtali waved him away as Asher had done, as though he were a troublesome gnat. Joseph looked him in the eye and then turned and walked off. He hated to disappoint his father, but watching his brothers was a waste of time. Surely there was something else he could do to help. Obviously he was not wanted here.

Of course, there was no way he could keep his brothers' actions from his father. They would soon like him even less than they did now. But what else could he do?

"You slept with women in caves while you were supposed to be watching my sheep?" Jacob's nostrils flared, and his voice rose so loud in the tent that Joseph was certain the whole camp could hear him.

Naphtali and Asher stood before their father, their heads bowed in proper respect. They did not even glance Joseph's way.

"We were with the goats," Asher said, his tone slightly sarcastic.

"That's what I said," Jacob bellowed. "You were supposed to be with the goats, but now I see that you paid no attention to them at all! You were hiding in a cave, sleeping with foreign women, ignoring my animals. They could have been attacked by lions in the forest or wandered off and gotten caught in the brambles. It is no wonder their skin is covered in scratches. If you had taken care of them all along, my flocks would be flawless, all capable of being offered as a sacrifice to the Lord my God. But *you*! You have done everything you can to ruin me!"

Joseph forced himself not to wince at his father's vehemence, and he worried more for his father's health than the animals in that moment. Veins showed in his father's neck, and his face darkened with rage.

Naphtali and Asher took a step back, obviously shocked by their father's harsh anger. They had taken their jobs as shepherds lightly, not caring that Jacob depended on these animals not only for milk, wool, and meat but to trade for things they could not make or grow themselves. Jacob's wool and goat hair brought a high price when his sons weren't mistreating his flocks.

"We are sorry, Father," Naphtali said, ignoring Asher's sullen expression.

"Sorry is not enough. You will listen to Joseph from now on.

There will be no more staying away overnight with the flocks. I will expect an accounting daily, and I myself will inspect the animals you return to my folds. I will not have you making a mockery of me!" Jacob crossed his arms and leaned back against the cushions, his gaze moving from one son to the other. "Do you understand me?"

"Yes, Father," they said in unison. They waited respectfully for Jacob's dismissal, which quickly came. "See to it you start obeying me today."

They said nothing more but merely nodded. Jacob waved his hand for them to leave, and they hurried from the tent. Joseph lingered, not sure whether to follow them to hear what they might say or to see if his father was going to be all right.

"Joseph, my son," Jacob said, motioning him closer.

"Yes, my father." He knelt at Jacob's side.

"It was right for you to tell me these things. Your brothers should be punished, but I see no way to do so. I cannot lock them away somewhere, and I need them to do what they are supposed to do." Jacob patted Joseph's hand.

"It is all right, Father. I am glad your God allowed me to discover the problem before more of the animals were harmed or lost. Shall I go now and follow after them?"

Jacob nodded, his expression suddenly sorrowful, as if Joseph's leaving brought him sadness. "Yes, go, my son. But come to me as soon as all of you return. Let us hope this evening's report is better than last night's."

"Yes, let us hope so." Joseph kissed his father's cheek and left the tent.

2

ONE MONTH LATER

Joseph rose earlier than his usual time, before the sun had even crested the ridge of sky. He sat up, his eyes adjusting to the dark, and looked to where Benjamin still slept. Normally he would wait for him to awaken and Dinah to come for him, but today he could not lie still. He donned his tunic and robe and crept from the tent.

He walked from the circle of tents to the sheep pens, where his brother Judah slept near the gate. The brothers took turns keeping watch against enemies of any kind, be they human or animal. Sheep were often preyed upon, and a gate alone could not keep out those who sought to harm or steal.

At his approach, Judah stirred. He squinted up at Joseph and rubbed the sleep from his eyes. "Is it morning already?" He glanced at the sky, which barely showed the predawn grays.

"Not quite," Joseph said softly. "I woke early and decided to join you."

Judah made a grunting sound and laid his head back onto the ground. "Go back to bed where you belong." With ten years between them, Judah had rarely taken kindly to Joseph. There had been a moment when Joseph's mother died that Judah attempted kindness, but since they had moved to Mamre, all attempts at friendship with any of Leah's sons had gotten Joseph nowhere. He was the favored, spoiled younger brother, and nothing he could do would shake the image they had of him.

Sometimes Reuben looked upon him with a hint of understanding, but perhaps that only came from his guilt for having slept with their father's concubine Bilhah when they were camped at Bethel. Their father had never forgiven Reuben for his disdain and his blatant attempt to show himself the future head of the tribe once Jacob rested with his fathers. All he had done was cause a deeper rift between Leah's and Rachel's sons, namely Joseph, for no one seemed troubled by Benjamin. Not yet.

How would they treat his little brother once he was grown? Joseph brushed the concern aside. Fortunately, Benjamin had time, whereas Joseph had already been favored for years by their father. What would happen if Jacob decided to declare him his firstborn and heir in place of Reuben?

Joseph moved past Judah and climbed over the wall into the pens, ignoring Judah's muttered protests. He wanted to see the sheep as best he could in this light. Most of them were sleeping, but a few stood to greet him. He moved toward them and ran his hands through their wool. They had been inspected the night before, but Joseph felt a keen desire to be certain his brothers had not overlooked anything. A small barb caught on his fingers, one so close to the skin they had missed it. He gently pulled to release it.

He refrained from showing his irritation lest Judah berate him so loudly he woke the camp. How many more had been inspected with so little care? Their father was a great shepherd and had taught his sons well. Why had they suddenly grown so lax since moving to live with their grandfather?

A ewe bleated, and Joseph gently stroked her to soothe her.

"Why are you here?" Judah's voice behind him made him jump. Obviously, his brother had not gone back to sleep. There was scorn in his tone.

"I wanted to be here. Is there a problem?"

"Do you think we did not inspect the sheep last night? Or do you think they somehow got full of brambles in these pens, where they are protected?"

Joseph met Judah's gaze as the sun began to lighten the sky. There was no mistaking the scowl on his face or his sullen glare.

"We know how to do our jobs. Or has Father now put you in charge of all of us without bothering to let us know?"

Joseph stood tall, but he did not meet Judah's height. He moved back a step with the ewe between them. "I am not ruler over anyone," he said slowly. "I am simply doing as our father requests of me." He rested a hand on the ewe's head. He had always preferred the sheep to the goats, but he went where his father sent him.

"See to it that you stay far from us. You will never be our leader. When Father dies, you will be last, not first. Even Benjamin will rise above you!"

Joseph blanched at the bitterness in Judah's tone. He held his brother's gaze, but a part of him wanted to flee. If he had ever hoped for a peaceful relationship with this brother, whose very name meant "praise," he knew now that he would never have it. Leah had praised the Lord upon Judah's birth, if the stories were true. But Joseph saw no hint of love for God in him.

"I have no desire to rule over anyone," Joseph said, kneeling down to concentrate his attention on the sheep. "I came only to be with the animals. I prefer the sheep and rarely have time with them."

Joseph felt the weight of his brother's glare but did not lift his head. He waited in agonizing silence until at last Judah's footsteps could be heard leaving the pen. The gate closed behind him. Joseph watched him walk toward the tents and released a long-held breath.

He didn't feel as safe in the presence of Leah's sons as he did the sons of the concubines, even though they were often upset with him. Though all of them were his seniors, it was Leah's sons who were the unfriendliest.

He lifted his gaze to the rising sun as he stood and walked among the flock toward the gate. The rest of his brothers would come soon to take the animals into the fields. He wished in that moment that he had not left his tent. This was not promising to be a good day.

⊔⊔⊔

Joseph sat apart from Zilpah's and Bilhah's sons as they congregated together to eat, while keeping an eye on the female goats. They'd not forgiven him for reporting their foolish deeds to their father, and in a sense he could not blame them. He had not wanted to tell his father of their behavior. He used to enjoy the company of these brothers when their boyhood held nothing more than who could shoot an arrow farther or who could run the fastest.

If only they had kept the friendliness of childhood and set aside the problems their father's favoritism had brought. If only his mother had lived to make all things right again.

His chest lifted in a heavy sigh, and he briefly closed his eyes. *Oh, God of my fathers, how do I make things right between us?* How often had he prayed such a prayer? He could not even share a love of Adonai with them, for they cared little for their father's God. They appeared at the sacrifices, but their hearts did not yearn for God the way their father's did. The way Joseph's did. How could one relate to another, even a blood brother, when the chasm of faith had become so wide that neither of them could cross it?

He glanced at the heavens, then looked toward the copse of trees where his brothers sat eating and laughing. They barely noticed the two male goats that were supposed to be kept separate unless the females were in heat, so Joseph turned his attention to them. They appeared to munch quietly on the thistle and shrub grasses, but a moment later they bounded out of sight.

Joseph jumped up and hurried after them. How fast they moved for animals that should be hungry and prefer to eat. But these two were always prone to wander and climb and get caught in difficult places. His brothers were supposed to take turns keeping the female goats from the males and should have paid closer attention. Apparently they'd decided that Joseph should be the one to traipse after the wayward ones.

He jogged his way over the hilly field until at last he caught sight of the two goats standing on a ridge at the edge of a precipice. He would never be able to get both of them to come away at once. If he called to his brothers, the goats might run off in fear. Though they were sure-footed and able to climb like the wild goats high into the hills, he couldn't let them get so far. Or worse, somehow tumble to their deaths.

He slipped a stone into his sling and hurried closer, attempting to keep from making too much noise in the brush. The staff would not be able to reach them, so with a flick of his wrist he whirled the sling, aimed to drop the stone just beyond the animals, and hoped to get them to step back. *Please, Lord*. If the stone landed in the wrong place, they could run farther away. The last thing he needed was to be blamed for the loss of his father's prized mating goats.

He let loose the stone, and the puff of dirt it created and the sound of its landing near the goats did as he had hoped. They backed away from the edge and turned to run in the direction from which they had come. Joseph ran up beside them and used his staff to guide them.

Heart beating fast, Joseph released a breath of relief when the rest of the herd came into view. His brothers stood, all of them looking at him. He drew closer, making sure the animals did not turn to wander off again.

"I suppose you will tell Father it was our fault they wandered away," Naphtali said. "How fortunate for you that you were able to save them."

"Yes, Joseph saves the day again." Gad sneered. "No doubt Father will somehow reward you."

Joseph refused to show them the hurt their words caused. "I only did what any shepherd would have done. There is no reason for reward." He walked away and returned to the tree where he had been sitting, wondering what he should tell his father, if anything at all.

3

Jacob folded his hands over his chest as he listened to Joseph's account of his day with the sons of the concubines. He leaned closer, assessing this son he loved with all of his heart.

"So you rescued the goats. Good. But you are not telling me everything, my son. I sense sadness within you. Do not withhold your thoughts from me." Jacob extended a hand, and Joseph took it and squeezed. They were alone in Jacob's tent, and Jacob pondered, not for the first time, what he could do to force his other sons to respect their brother. How would they ever follow his lead once Jacob rested with his fathers?

"It is nothing, Father. It is always the same, so why should I burden you with the relationship I have with my brothers? As my mother and Leah did not get along, so it is with Leah's sons and me." Joseph removed his turban and ran a hand through his sweaty hair.

"But the sons of my concubines—at least Bilhah's sons—should be amiable to you. Bilhah was Rachel's maid." Jacob scratched his beard, suddenly weary of his lot in life. Why had God not allowed Rachel to be his only wife? Why not give her many sons and let Leah and the maids be with someone else? But he could not change what was past.

"Bilhah's and Zilpah's sons desire the company of Leah's sons over me, Father. I cannot make them want my companionship. They are forced to be with me, but that is because of our arrangement. Perhaps I could do something else and let them shepherd on their own." Joseph's words came slowly, as if it pained him to speak them.

Jacob sat in silence a moment, considering his son's request. Bilhah's sons, of all of them, should treat Joseph with kindness. Bilhah had always been kind to Rachel. Until Reuben abused his place as firstborn and slept with her. The memory roused Jacob's anger, as it always did when he recalled the disdain such an action caused. Obviously Reuben did not think his father would live long, nor did he respect him. And Jacob had never punished him for it because he didn't know how to other than to strip him of his birthright.

He looked at Joseph, stroking his beard again, contemplating his words. "I will call Reuben to join us. I will fix this situation with your brothers, Joseph. And you will have your wish. I will not force you to oversee your brothers in the fields any longer. You will remain here as my household manager. Everything I have will be under your control. And Reuben will help to see that your life is better. I will make sure of it." He was not certain he could promise such a thing, but Reuben had better do as he said or worse things would come to him.

Joseph didn't respond immediately, as though he were taken aback by Jacob's words.

"Go and call my servant," Jacob told him.

Joseph went to the tent's door and called the man. He appeared at the tent's opening and bowed. "Yes, my lord?"

"Go to the fields and bring back my son Reuben. I would speak with him now."

"Yes, my lord." The man turned and ran off.

"Wait here, my son," Jacob said to Joseph. "You will see. I will make everything right for you. I failed your mother, but I will not fail you."

Joseph simply nodded and sat beside Jacob, hands folded in his lap.

"You will see," Jacob said again, rising to pace the tent. Reuben had better listen to him.

Reuben followed the servant's hurried gait toward his father's tent, his mind whirling with possibilities. What could possibly be wrong that he should be pulled from his duties with the sheep in the middle of the day? Was his father ill? Had someone been hurt? Was his grandfather in trouble?

His heart pounded as the camp came into view. He passed Bilhah's tent, the memories of his time with her heating his face. How sweet it had felt to steal her affection, and yet how ashamed he'd been as he bore his father's wrath.

As he approached his father's tent, he shoved the uncomfortable memories aside and stopped to catch his breath. He lifted the flap and entered the semi-dark interior. The sides of the tent had been rolled up to let in the cooler air, but no lamp was lit to brighten the shaded room. He glanced about, saw his father pacing with the use of his cane, his limp more pronounced.

Reuben stopped just inside the door. "You called for me, Father?"

Jacob turned to face him, then motioned for him to sit. Reuben waited for Jacob to sit first, then came and knelt before him. He would do anything to be restored to his good graces, though he doubted that would ever happen.

"I need you to do something for me, my son," Jacob said, hands folded in his lap.

"Anything, Father." He perched back on his heels, hands resting on his knees.

Jacob studied him a moment as if to ascertain his motives. Reuben forced himself not to squirm beneath his scrutinizing gaze. "I want you to convince your brothers to respect Joseph. I do not like the way they are treating him. I am making him my household manager since he is my firstborn heir, and I need to see this family come together in unity. Do you understand what I am asking of you?"

Reuben glanced from his father to Joseph sitting silently beside him, feeling as though he had been dealt a blow. Wasn't it enough to know his father had stripped him of his birthright? Must he now act as Joseph's servant and convince the others to treat him as better than they?

He met Joseph's gaze, assessing him, but to his surprise he did not see pride in his expression or an arrogant tilt to his head. Was the boy embarrassed by their father's request?

Reuben looked back at his father, though he felt in that moment a desperate desire to flee. The request was completely unfair. But his father's eyes did not leave him, and at last Reuben nodded. "I will do what I can, Father. I cannot force my brothers to be kind to the boy."

"Why not?" Jacob bellowed.

"They have never taken kindly to the favor Rachel's sons have had over them, Father. You know how our mother and her sister fought. We could not help feeling our mother's pain and angst over the favoritism." He spoke slowly, choosing his words with care. He didn't need his father growing angrier than he already was.

"Do not blame this on your mother or on Joseph's mother. Their struggles were not their fault, and all of you came to be because of the will of God. You are all my sons, and I would have you respect each other and speak kindly to one another. Including to Joseph and Benjamin."

Reuben closed his mouth against the words he wanted to say. No one had a problem with Benjamin because he was a child. They expected their father to dote on the boy. But Joseph held their father's heart and knew their father's plans. Things Leah's sons should have been privy to long before Joseph was old enough to care.

Reuben fisted his hands on his knees. "I cannot promise what the outcome will be, but I will do my best." He looked at Joseph. "You need not fear me, Joseph. I will speak to our brothers on your behalf."

"Thank you," Joseph said, inclining his head in a sign of gratitude.

"Thank you, my son," Jacob added as Reuben slowly stood.

"If that will be all, I will return to the sheep." He looked from one to the other once more.

"That will be all." Jacob dismissed him with a wave of his hand, and Reuben turned and walked from the tent.

He did not hurry on the return trip to the sheep. He could not imagine how he was going to convince any of his brothers to do as their father requested. How could he? Truth be told, they hated Joseph. And their father's defense of him only made things worse.

Judah looked toward his father's camp, wondering what was keeping Reuben. Had something happened? It was not like their father to call them away from their work unless something important had happened. Judah's thoughts swam with possibilities, but it did no good to speculate.

He turned to the flock of sheep grazing a short distance from him. His brothers were spaced about the large field, and some had taken part of the flock north of Hebron in the direction of Jerusalem and Shechem. He looked once more toward the camp and at last saw Reuben coming at a steady though rather slow gait over the rise and down into the valley.

"There you are," Judah said, coming up beside him. "What happened?"

Reuben rubbed the back of his neck and twisted his head from side to side as if trying to release the tension in his shoulders.

"It cannot be good if it has you aching like an old man." Judah gripped his staff harder and pushed it deeper into the ground. "Tell me."

"Father has requested that I convince all of you to respect Joseph. He is not happy with the way we treat him. And now Father has made him household manager. Joseph will know far more than any of us do and be ready to take over our father's affairs when he goes the way of all the earth." Reuben's disheartened expression matched the hurt behind his words.

"You are the firstborn. You should be the one who manages these things."

"You know that no longer applies to me." Reuben seemed resigned to do as he'd been asked.

"I know that. But Joseph is the youngest and the most spoiled among us. No one wants to take orders from a child!" Judah's anger rose swiftly, and he fought to tamp it down.

"I know that, but what was I to say? I don't think Joseph wanted Father to ask it of me. I think the whole thing embarrassed him." Reuben sank to the earth, and Judah sat with him. "I have to do what he says, and I need you to help me. Help our brothers to do as Father asks, at least in his presence. We can try to be civil to the boy. If we continue to provoke him or, as the sons of the concubines have done, completely disregard him, Father could do worse things than ask for respect."

"When our father rests with his fathers, who will protect Joseph then?" Judah did not like the direction of his own thoughts, but the very idea of Rachel's son having authority over them? Impossible.

"Before that happens, Father could do as Abraham did and send away the sons of the concubines, and even us, the sons of Leah, and give all of the land to Joseph and Benjamin—or at least all of his worldly goods. We don't actually own the land God has promised yet."

Judah scratched at a sudden itch on his arm. "Do you really think Father would send all of us away in favor of Rachel's sons?"

"Does that seem so impossible to you? It's been done before."

"That can't happen." Where would they go? They would have nothing! All of their hard work would be for naught. Even their father had bested their grandfather Laban before they left him and went away wealthy. He couldn't possibly send Leah's sons away. She was the first wife!

"It could happen if we don't treat Joseph better. You know it could." Reuben's gaze was firm. "Will you help me convince our brothers?"

"They will argue with us. They might even fight over it. You know how hostile Simeon and Levi can be." The massacre of the men of Shechem was never far from anyone's thoughts, especially when they interacted with their sister, Dinah. Simeon and Levi had murdered all of them because the prince had raped their sister.

"I know. Which is why I came to you first. Will you help me?"

Reuben's question did not sit well with him, but what could he say? At last he nodded. "I will do what I can. You know I don't like Joseph. But I will do it for Father and for you and hope that Father looks on us all with favor one day, as he does his spoiled son."

Reuben rose slowly. "I will go and find the others. We must tell them now so that by the time we return home tonight, they are amiable."

Judah stood as well. "I will wait here with the sheep. Do what you must."

Joseph sat beside his father around the central fire, listening to the distant sound of his brothers returning with the sheep. Voices rose and fell, and the sound was not entirely pleasant. They were arguing, as they usually did. But this time was he the cause?

He rose as his grandfather hobbled with the help of his servant to join them around the fire. The noise coming from the pens grew heated, but Joseph attempted to block out the sound. He approached Isaac and kissed his cheek.

"Greetings, Sabba. How good it is to see you tonight." Joseph took Isaac's hand and squeezed it, since his grandfather relied on sound and touch to connect with each person.

"Thank you, Joseph. I am well and glad to be able to join you again." He gripped Joseph's hand and released it, then made his way to his seat. Joseph returned to his seat just as his brothers entered the compound. Their voices had stilled, and one after another they approached first Isaac, then Jacob in order of age.

"Greetings, Grandfather," they each said. Isaac recognized each one by name, which Joseph noted brought a slight smile to their lips and seemed to ease the tension in the air.

When they approached Jacob, however, the tension heightened again. "Greetings, Father." Reuben spoke first, kissed his father's cheek, then nodded at Joseph and sat in his place. Each brother did the same, though many of them barely looked Joseph's way, and none spoke to him.

Food appeared at the hands of the wives and concubines and servants, and Benjamin bounced on Dinah's knee beside Joseph, cooing and making all manner of noises as she tried to feed him.

Joseph turned his attention to the boy and laughed softly at his insistence. Conversation among his brothers carried to him in a low tone, but Joseph could not make out the words above the sounds of Benjamin eating and flapping his arms in the air, waiting for Dinah to give him more. Dinah laughed at the boy and Joseph smiled at him, but a moment later he felt as though all eyes were watching him. The discomfort drained him.

"They are ignoring you," his father said softly, leaning close to his ear.

Joseph turned slightly toward him. "Yes. But that is no different than they always act."

"Reuben should have said something to them," Jacob said. "They cannot treat you with such disrespect."

"It is all right, Abba. Perhaps Reuben could not yet convince them. It may take them time to change old habits." Joseph touched his father's arm in a comforting gesture, then quickly removed it when he glanced up and saw every one of his brothers staring at him.

"I do not like it," Jacob said, lifting his eyes to meet the gazes of Joseph's brothers. His obvious disapproval caused them to look down at their food, silence descending on the group.

Joseph grew increasingly uncomfortable, despite Benjamin's playfulness. Even Dinah grew quiet and said only a few words to the boy. Were his brothers angrier than they had been because Jacob had forced Reuben to speak to them? If only their father could have simply let things be.

As Joseph left the group to return to his tent and put Benjamin to bed, he listened to the bickering begin again in the distance. Simeon and Levi raised their voices, and Joseph crept closer to the edge of his tent, straining to hear.

"What Father asks of us is unconscionable. We are not sons of a second wife, nor are we the youngest sons. We have rights that are greater than Joseph's." Simeon's voice dripped with disdain.

"Just because Rachel bore him shouldn't mean he usurps our place in Father's life. It is as though he has no other sons." Levi's deep voice carried obvious hurt.

"Father always loved Rachel best. You cannot blame him for favoring her children, especially with her loss," Reuben said.

"Nevertheless, it is our mother who has suffered because of his favoritism," Judah said. "Don't tell me you don't recall her many tears while Father spent the night in Rachel's tent."

His hostility stung, for it carried blame, as if Joseph's birth was his own fault. Joseph often wondered if Judah wished he had never been born.

"We can't ignore Father's wishes though," Reuben defended, raising his voice above the others.

They were going to disturb Father if they didn't quiet down, but Joseph did not dare go outside and ask them to keep their voices low. He moved away from the edge of the tent and lay on his mat, hands behind his head. Benjamin slept soundly, as most children did, innocent and unaware of the turmoil in their father's house.

Joseph wished in that moment that he could trade places with Benjamin—just for a short day—to live one day without strife. But no matter what his father might want, Joseph was not sure their household would ever be capable of such an impossible feat.

4

Joseph strode across the camp to the tent of his father's over-seer. Elkan looked up from bending over a tablet where he appeared to be calculating something. "Joseph. Good. You are here."

Joseph smiled, relieved once more to be away from the strife of his siblings. "Yes, and ready to learn."

"Good. Good." Elkan bobbed his head, his long, graying hair moving over his eyes. He brushed it aside. "I will show you my method of accounting for the wool your father sells and the price we get for each shearing."

"I am quite ready." Joseph came closer and followed Elkan to a table where tablets were spread out.

"I keep the tablets in different groups. Here we have a record of the servants—those born into the household and those purchased by your father." He pointed to a pile near the edge of the table. "This lists the amount of wheat we have on hand from your grandfather's fields." He pointed to another tablet. "Here is a stack that lists what the women and servants grow in the gardens. We rarely sell any of that produce."

Joseph knew all of this, but he simply nodded.

"Once a year, as you know, your father holds a sheepshearing.

39

Because of the number of flocks, it takes days to a week to finish the shearing, and the wool is washed and dried, then tied in bundles for sale."

"Except for what is kept for the household," Joseph said, leaning over the tablets. "Do we keep a separate column for those bundles and their weight?"

"Yes, of course," Elkan said. "See? Here are the columns of the wool that was purchased by the traveling merchants, and this is the column of what was kept last time for the women to use in weaving whatever is needed."

"What is this for?" Joseph pointed to a separate column that had a simple yod as the heading.

The servant straightened and put his arms behind his back. "I do not know." He glanced beyond Joseph, his look uncomfortable.

Was Elkan hiding something? "Why not? Don't you know all that goes on with my father's household?" Joseph's curiosity was second to his wondering what this servant might be keeping from his father.

"Your father has set that amount aside for something private. He alone knows the reason. I only know that some of the best wool has been separated for a special use." Elkan shrugged and then bent over the tablet again. "Here you can see that we sold more wool this last time than we did the year before. The women said they needed less wool for weaving, as they had a surplus from the year before." He moved to another list. "Here we keep the number of sheep and goats, how many were born, how many miscarried, how many died or were given in sacrifice."

Joseph took the list and studied it before handing it back to Elkan, and then they moved on to the next set of tablets.

"These show the amount of wine and raisin cakes, and this stack lists the baths of olive oil," Elkan said. "Over here we have a tally of the measure of balm, honey, gum, aromatic resin, pistachio nuts, and almonds."

Joseph took the tablets and examined them one at a time. He noted the way the servant had recorded each thing. If he had made these notations, he might have put them in a different order. But he was here to learn. One day, when he took over running the household, he would make this accounting more efficient.

"All looks good. What else do you have to show me?" Joseph smiled at the man and followed him from the open tent area to the pens where they kept the animals.

"We have many servants caring for the donkeys, but your father wanted you to see how we inspect them and where they graze." The servant gave Joseph an assessing glance. "Come this way."

Joseph followed the man, making mental notes of the conditions and cleanliness of the pens. As he watched the animals graze, he realized that he needed to learn more about their care. He would quietly tell his father and gain permission to construct better enclosures to keep the animals cleaner and safer at night. And find a servant who could teach him how to keep them healthy.

Joseph scooped Benjamin into his arms and carried him toward the sheep pens, where his brothers had returned and were inspecting the sheep. He hated to admit that he needed Benjamin as a buffer to keep his brothers civil, but he was out of other ideas.

Joseph greeted them with a smile. "Were you successful in finding good pastures today?" He addressed Judah, for he was the one standing nearest the sheep gate.

Judah looked up, surprise in his features, looking between Joseph and Benjamin. "The sheep found good pastures. You can tell Father that all is well."

Joseph did not miss the undertone of censure in his voice. "I did not come to report to Father. I simply wondered how things fared with all of you today." He gripped Benjamin a little tighter as the boy tried to wriggle to the ground. The child stilled as if he sensed Joseph's reluctance to let him go. Did he understand why?

Reuben stepped closer to Joseph and touched Benjamin's head in an affectionate gesture. "All is well," he said loud enough for all to hear. "But thank you for your interest."

Joseph lifted his gaze to Reuben's in surprise. He nodded, grateful that his oldest brother was making an attempt at respect.

But a moment later, Simeon moved between them. "You need not worry about us," he said. "We know how to shepherd—have done so longer than you've been living."

It wasn't the truth, but despite the scowl Reuben directed at Simeon, Joseph clearly heard the dismissal in Simeon's tone. He lifted Benjamin higher. "Of course you do," he said. "Thank you for telling me." He turned and walked away. No matter what he did, he was never going to gain the favor of his brothers.

ᘒᘒ

Jacob walked toward his father's tent. Enough time had passed since his talk with Reuben that his attempt to force his sons' attitudes to change toward Joseph should have shown by now. But they hadn't. Why was it so hard for them to get along? Even Leah and Rachel had become friends later in life. But men and women did not think alike, of that he was sure!

He moved slowly, his limp more pronounced today. He could

not walk without aid, not since that night when he had wrestled with the Lord and felt His touch near his hip. He would never be vigorous again or able to run as he had in his youth. It was the price he had paid for wanting God to bless him, and for thinking he could force God to do his will. Was he still doing the same thing?

He entered his father's tent and nodded to the servant to leave them. He came in slowly. "Father, it is I, Jacob. I have come to speak with you."

"Jacob. Come, come. Sit here and rest awhile." Isaac's voice had grown thin with age, but when Jacob took his hand, he found his grip still strong.

Jacob lowered himself onto a plush cushion and laid the staff on the ground beside him.

"Tell me, now, my son. What brings you to my tent in the middle of the day?"

"I need your advice." Jacob folded his hands in his lap and tugged on his belt. "I am having a problem with my sons and the way they treat Joseph. I want them to respect Joseph because he is my intended heir. When I die, he will be in charge of all I have. But his brothers treat him with disdain even in my presence, despite my insistence that they do not."

Isaac nodded, his white hair wispy about his ears and his beard hanging long and thick. "How well I remember," he said, his blind eyes looking into a distance that only his mind could see. "If I had listened to your mother and accepted what the Lord had said, that the older would serve the younger, you would not have faced Esau's hostility. We should not have favored different sons. Esau should have been taught from birth that you were my heir."

"Abraham faced the same problem between you and Ishmael," Jacob said, trying to soften his father's regrets.

"Yes, but my father sent all my half brothers away, including those born to Keturah after my mother died. I alone lived to inherit all that he had." Isaac faced Jacob and reached to pat his knee.

"But now I have twelve sons from four different mothers. I cannot send ten of them away and give all I have to Joseph and Benjamin. But Joseph will get a double portion. And he should be given the knowledge of how to run my estate. But even as I give him authority, my other sons do not recognize it. What can I do, Father?" Jacob did not expect to sound so desperate, but he did not want to see Joseph sent away because of the hostility of his brothers, as he himself had been when Esau's anger threatened his life.

"Why not show them outright that Joseph will receive the rights of the firstborn by giving him an object that sets him apart now?" Isaac said, his words coming slow and wobbly, as though he had already said more than he had strength for.

"An object? Do you have a suggestion?"

Isaac reached for the goatskin at his side and took a drink from it. He swallowed, silence falling between them. Jacob waited. He knew better than to grow impatient with his aged father.

"Perhaps give him your signet ring or your cords."

Jacob searched his father's face, wishing in that moment that they could make eye contact. "I don't know . . ." He wasn't ready to give those personal items to anyone. He intended to live a good deal longer before he gave such a blessing to Joseph. Hadn't his father done so too soon? How different his life could have been.

Then again, there was the coat he'd been planning, though he did not intend to give it to Joseph for some time yet. Not until he was older, married, with sons of his own. By then his brothers would have settled down, and perhaps they would all get along better. Surely he still had plenty of time for such decisions.

"Have you something else in mind?" Isaac asked, interrupting his thoughts.

Jacob glanced toward Elkan's tents where the wool was kept. "I have had something in mind, but I have not thought the time right."

"Tell me," Isaac said, turning to face Jacob, his expression earnest.

Jacob closed his eyes, envisioning a plan that had formed in his mind several years before. A plan he had thought foolish at the time. He wasn't really going to give in to it, was he? He drew a breath. What could it hurt to tell his father?

"I have been saving the best of the wool to have a colorful coat made for Joseph, one with gold threads woven within the fabric. But I did not plan to give it to him until he is older. Much older."

"It sounds like something a king might wear." Isaac's brows knit ever so slightly. Did he disapprove of Jacob's desire?

"I would not want it to be as elaborate as a king's cloak. Perhaps I should leave out the gold threads, but a robe that blends many colors . . ." He paused, not sure how else to describe what he imagined.

"Your other sons will be jealous, Jacob, no matter how long you wait. You know they will."

His father's words did not sit well with him. He had expected his father to support him.

"Was it not your idea to give him a symbol to set him apart? What better way to show it? My ring will be his when I leave this earth, but what good will my items of authority do him while I yet live? I should think those would be worse for Joseph than a simple coat." Jacob heard the terseness in his voice and drew in a breath to realign his thoughts.

"I suppose you make a good point. But I might caution you to not make the coat too colorful or too different from what his brothers wear. Just enough." Isaac smiled, and though his father couldn't see it, Jacob returned the gesture.

"Thank you, Father. I will see to it then. I will have to decide who to weave it for me. I cannot ask Leah, though her weaving is superb. It will have to be a servant, I think." He scratched his beard.

"Leah does make fine garments. Perhaps Dinah would enjoy the work."

Dinah. She already took care of Benjamin and was kind to Joseph above all others in the family. Yes, perhaps she could make it. Would he have to tell her why or whom it was for?

"I will think on it," Jacob said, slowly rising. "Thank you, Father. I must be going now, but your advice has helped me."

"It is always good to see you, Son." Isaac did not attempt to rise, so Jacob bent to kiss his cheeks, then bid him farewell again and left the tent.

He would not seek out Dinah. Not yet. His mind whirled with the conversation. Was a special coat a good idea? It pleased him, as Joseph pleased him, but still . . . what would Dinah say? Or Leah?

5

Joseph emerged from his tent to find Dinah approaching, Benjamin in tow.

"Peace be upon you today, Joseph," Dinah said, releasing Benjamin's hand, allowing him to run toward their father's tent. "He is anxious to see his father today." She smiled, though Joseph always found a hint of sadness in her eyes.

"And upon you, my sister." He took her hand. "I hope you are well."

She nodded and lowered her gaze. "I am as well as I will ever be." She looked up as he let go of her hand.

He searched her face, knowing of what she spoke, wishing again that he had gone with her that long-ago day. If only she had asked him. If only he had been able to help her since.

"You will always be my favorite sister. Never forget that." He smiled, and she laughed lightly.

"I am your only sister, Joseph. Of course you would say that." She straightened.

"Let us talk of better things," he said, taking her hand again and moving toward the central fire where the family gathered at mealtimes.

She pulled him toward a copse of large oak trees instead, away from the tents. He followed willingly, curious.

"I would rather not speak in such an open space," she said once they were in the shade of the trees. The wind whispered above them, and birds sang a mix of tunes in the branches.

"Something troubles you, my sister." He leaned against an oak and watched her beautiful face.

"I . . ." She paused as if searching for the words. "Our father seems overly anxious of late. Do you know what it is that troubles him?" She clasped her hands in front of her.

Joseph looked beyond her. "He concerns himself over the lack of camaraderie in our family. Particularly between my brothers and me." He held her gaze. "It is nothing to concern you."

"Everything our father does and feels concerns me, Joseph. He holds many regrets . . . as do I." She looked at her feet and sighed.

"You can't continue to wish the past could change, Dinah." He coaxed her to look at him, but his words did not erase the hurt in her gaze.

She glanced toward the fields where her brothers had taken the sheep. "My brothers always think they know best, but they don't. If Father had known they were going to kill all of those men that day . . . They didn't even ask his opinion, Joseph. And they didn't care at all what *I* thought. They were spiteful and hateful, and Shechem loved me." Her words came out in a near whisper, and her voice caught on a sob.

Why was it so hard for her to forgive after so many years had passed? But he did not live with her grief.

Joseph stroked his thinly bearded chin. What could he possibly say to encourage her, to help her see that God still cared about her? Surely the God of Abraham who cared for the servant Hagar cared for his sister.

He searched his heart for words that were difficult. "Dinah, your life is not over because of this. God still has a plan for all of us. I don't know what that is, but I know that with all our father has seen Him do, what he has experienced with our God, He has called our family out to be His own. We are His people, Dinah, and that means you too. No ill treatment by a foreign man, no lack of mercy from our brothers can change God's favor toward you. You did not sin, Dinah. They did. You cannot change what happened, but you can still do great things in life. God has not abandoned you." He touched her arm in a comforting gesture.

She nodded, moisture filming her large, dark eyes. "I want to believe that, Joseph. You are the only one who believes as Father and my mother do. I know your mother also believed in Him, but my brothers . . . they are always angry. It is like they hate the entire world and all that God made."

"They are jealous of me," he said softly. "Which is why our father troubles himself over it." He looked at his feet. He knew it deep down but had never voiced it to her.

She touched his shoulder. "They shouldn't be," she said, her voice firm. "You have lost so much. They should be grateful they still have our mother. Instead, they fault you for finding favor with Father. It makes no sense."

"I think it is more than that," Joseph said, looking toward the tents.

She stared at him, her dark brows lifted in question. "Explain yourself to me, please. I do not understand."

He cleared his throat and glanced briefly toward the heavens. "I believe in our father's God," he said. "Father and I often speak of Him, and Father teaches me about Him. So does our grandfather. Have you ever seen any of our brothers go into our father's tent or heard them ask him questions about our God?"

She slowly shook her head.

"Because they don't want to hear about Him. They are not interested in the things of the Creator as I am. As Father is. As Grandfather is. It is a connection I share with them that our brothers do not. They think Father favors me, and he does so not just because I'm Rachel's son but because I want to learn all that he knows of life, of God, of everything."

Dinah searched his face for a lengthy breath, then nodded. "You are right. They do not ask my mother such questions either. She tried to teach them—to teach all of us—about our father's God, but they wanted to run and play and now would rather work. They have little use for things they cannot see."

"But you do."

"Yes," she said, looking toward the heavens. "I talk about Him with my mother frequently. Not so much with our father. But then he doesn't seem to know how to talk to me on any subject except Benjamin."

Joseph laughed. "I think he struggles with having a daughter when he is used to mostly sons."

Dinah smiled, and this time he didn't see the sadness behind her eyes. "I will have to spend more time with him to show him not to be afraid of a daughter."

"I think having a daughter would be a wonderful thing." Joseph moved away from the tree. "I should get to work. Is there anything else?"

She shook her head. "No. I just wanted to give Benjamin time with Father. I will collect him now, and you go ahead and learn whatever it is you are learning."

He grinned. "I think I've already figured things out, but don't tell Elkan I said so."

She gave him a conspiratorial wink. "Trust me. I won't."

ᒐᒷᒐ

Dinah considered Joseph's words over the next few weeks. How hard it was to believe that her life held any worth after what she had done. After what had been done to her. If only . . . But her anger at her brothers, particularly Simeon and Levi, did her no good. They were quick-tempered and impossible to talk to. Not that she wanted to talk to them. If they had not killed Shechem, she might be wed and the mother of children by now.

She looked up from the loom where she worked in the common area with the other women, their voices a buzz in the background of her thoughts. Her mother sat opposite her and met her gaze with a lifted brow. Dinah simply shrugged. She did not want to discuss her feelings with anyone, not even her mother, for Leah would only defend her sons.

A deep sigh lifted her chest as she moved the shuttle, threading the weft through the warp. This tunic for Benjamin would be a little long on him, but he was growing so fast that he would outgrow it before she could make him a new one.

She suppressed a soft smile at the thought of Rachel's young son. If not for Benjamin, who would she have to love or to love her? Though she was not his mother, he still felt like a son to her.

"You're terribly quiet today, my daughter," her mother said, breaking into her thoughts. "Is something troubling you?"

Dinah lifted her head but continued to work. "I am fine, Ima. I was just thinking and concentrating on the weaving."

Leah's look said that her answer did not satisfy, but Dinah returned her attention to the task. Did God care about her the way Joseph said He did? What would she do with her life once Benjamin grew to adulthood, or even when he became old enough to tend the sheep with her brothers? Would they hate him as they hated Joseph?

She bit her lip and felt her shoulders tense at the thought.

Once Benjamin married, she would be alone. Her mother would not live forever, nor would the other women in Jacob's house. And she was not close to any of her brothers' wives.

The hobbling footsteps of her father pulled her out of her wayward thoughts. She looked up once more. "Abba," she said, smiling as he entered the women's work area.

"Greetings, Jacob," Leah said, laying aside her shuttle and rising. "Let me get you a cushion and something to drink."

Jacob waved her offer aside. "I did not come to stay," he said, giving her a look of mild affection. Dinah knew that her father would still favor Rachel had she lived, but he seemed to have made peace with Leah and spent time with her when the others were off doing other things. She often saw them together when she took Benjamin to Joseph's tent to nap.

"Why did you come then?" her mother asked, arms akimbo.

"I would like to speak to Dinah, if she can walk with me for a few moments."

Dinah let the shuttle slow, surprised at his request. "I can come, Abba." Though she was a young adult, the childhood endearment lingered.

"Good." He moved away from the enclosed area.

Dinah put the weaving aside, glanced at her mother, who seemed deeply puzzled by her father's request, then hurried to catch up with him.

They walked to the same copse of trees where she and Joseph had spoken. They stopped beneath the shade of a spreading oak. Jacob turned about and faced Dinah, searching her gaze.

"What is it that you wanted, Father?" She was shorter than he was by a handbreadth, so she tilted her head to better read his expression.

"I have a favor to ask of you. It is to be kept quiet for now. I don't want your mother or brothers or the concubines or your half brothers or even the servants to know about this yet." He ran a hand over his beard as if nervous.

Dinah nodded, wondering what could possibly need such secrecy. "What is it?"

"I want you to make a cloak. You are as good a weaver as your mother, and no one weaves better cloth than she does. She has taught you well." He paused, his gaze skipping beyond her.

"Is this for Benjamin?" If it were, why keep it a secret? The women wove tunics and cloaks and undergarments all the time.

"No," he said, looking down at her again. "It is for Joseph. It is to be a coat woven in many colors. I have had some of the finest wool set aside for this. I've wanted to have it made for him for a long time." His expression was earnest, yet she could not tell the reason behind the request. Each of her brothers already had a robe with his own color woven into a wide stripe and a matching one in his sash and turban.

"Why make Joseph's coat so different from that of his brothers?" Her brow furrowed, and she crossed her arms, feeling the faint hint of a chill though the air was warm. "What's going on, Father?"

Jacob rested one hand against the tree trunk and moved his staff to better steady himself. He normally twisted his body in this way when his hip ached. Was their conversation causing him pain?

"If you do not want to do this for me, Dinah, I understand. I will find a servant to do the work." He looked disappointed, and she couldn't bear to see the sorrow in his gaze.

"I will do it. Just tell me what you have in mind." How she would keep this a secret from her mother, she did not know.

He smiled and nodded. "Very good. Thank you. This is what I want."

He proceeded to give her detailed instructions, which she

pondered as she helped him walk back to his tent and then retrieved Benjamin from his nap. Joseph's coat was to have every color worn by her brothers and half brothers? Even Benjamin's? The thought deeply troubled her. The work would be tedious, as the dyeing process alone would take days for a single color. She would need twelve colors, one for each son—Joseph included.

Her heart beat faster as she headed toward the women's area, where she sat Benjamin to "help" her mother. He played with the wool left over from what she was now spinning into thread.

"What did your father want?" her mother asked the moment Dinah stepped beneath the awning and settled in front of her loom again.

She glanced at her mother, then focused on the weaving, unable to think straight. She must pick up the shuttle and begin again, or the tunic would never be finished in time to make the robe her father wanted.

"Dinah? Did you hear me?" Leah's tone carried concern rather than censure.

"Yes, Ima. Abba wants me to make a cloak for him." She flicked a gaze at her mother and then Benjamin, who gave her a toothy grin. She returned it and picked up the shuttle to work.

"Your father has a perfectly good robe. And why wouldn't he come to me with such a request? I am his wife!"

Dinah's heart pounded as she thought of what would happen once she finished the cloak and her father gave it to Joseph. When her brothers saw his favoritism and the way such a colorful robe would put Joseph above each one of them . . . what then?

6

Joseph took a circuitous route toward Elkan's tents, purposely avoiding the sheep and goat pens, where he could hear his brothers calling the animals to follow them. Since he began working with the chief steward, things had not improved with his brothers. If Reuben still attempted to bring some reconciliation or at least respect from them, he had failed, for the only attitude Joseph perceived from them was thinly veiled animosity.

He walked past the women's work area, where he spotted Dinah dipping wool through a hole in a stone tool into a baked earthen barrel of bubbling dye. He stepped closer, and she looked up at him.

"Shalom, Joseph," she said as she stirred the wool. "How are you this bright day?"

"I am well, my sister. Thank you. And what are you making?" He stepped close to the barrel and peered inside, but the liquid was too dark to tell what color it would be.

"I am dyeing wool for a coat Father asked me to weave." Her brows scrunched as though she was concentrating.

Joseph nodded. Father had a coat, but perhaps he intended to sell this one. "What color is that?" He pointed to the dye.

"This one is from the henna plant and should come out the

color of red orange if I got the dye dark enough. I have already dyed piles of wool." She inclined her head toward several baskets behind her.

Joseph walked over to look at them. Red, turquoise, blue, several shades of green, and a distinct white not the same as the sheep's own color. "These are colors my brothers wear. How many more will you dye?" He bent down to examine the wool. "This looks like the wool Father set aside for some special occasion."

"Yes," Dinah answered, still stirring the hot liquid. She lifted some strands to check the color and pushed them beneath the dye once more.

Joseph stood and walked back to her. "It looks like you are almost finished with the dyeing." How many more colors did she need?

She shook her head. "No. I have yet to do brown and purple and a few others. It is tedious work to find the plants and prepare the dyes."

"Then you have to spin the dried wool." He smiled at her. "I have watched your mother work since I was a small boy. I know this is a big job Father has asked of you. But why did he ask you and not your mother?"

Dinah scowled at him. "Are you suggesting I am not capable, my brother?"

He held up a hand. "No, of course not. You are as good a weaver as your mother."

"Which is why he asked me. He didn't want to burden her with it. I am young, and the work is easier on me than on her." She glanced at the pile of wool yet to be dyed. "Shouldn't you be off to whatever it is you do with the steward all day?"

Joseph laughed. "Trying to be rid of me, I see. I can take a hint." He kissed her cheek. "I am off to inspect the stores of wheat. Then we will visit the fields. Then I will see if the records match what I can see."

"You are becoming quite the manager." She smiled at him, and he returned it.

"I do enjoy learning." He left her with a parting wave. As he walked toward the tents of the steward, he wondered why his father had decided to use the finest wool for a coat that no one in the camp needed. It was not his business, Joseph told himself. What his father chose to do was his own.

Dinah at last had twelve baskets in a half circle near her loom. Each basket held one of the colors that defined each brother—their symbol of place given to them at birth. Red carnelian for Reuben, pale yellow green of chalcedony for Simeon, deep emerald green for Levi, turquoise for Judah, blue like lapis lazuli for Issachar, pearly white like moonstone for Zebulun, red orange like jacinth for Dan, a mix of light and dark brown for Naphtali, pale purple like amethyst for Gad, blue green like crystal beryl for Asher, shining black like onyx for Joseph, and olive green like jasper for Benjamin.

She admired her work, pleased that the dyes had come out so well. She could hold any one of the colors up to the robes her brothers now wore and find them a perfect match. A slight smile edged her lips. She had not felt such satisfaction in a long time. Her father was right to give her this task. It had pulled her from her melancholy as she aimed to do her very best for each batch of dye and wool.

She sank onto a cushion, took the red carnelian shade from Reuben's basket, and attached it to her spindle.

"Would you like some help with the spinning?" Her mother stood near, looking down at Dinah, an unreadable expression on her face. Was her mother still troubled by the fact that Jacob had asked Dinah to do this work?

Dinah pointed to Simeon's basket and nodded. "If you don't mind spinning with me, you can start with that one. I want to weave them in the order they are placed around me."

Leah's gaze moved over each color, her brow furrowing. "These are your brothers' colors."

"Yes," Dinah said, her heart skipping a beat in fear that her mother might again question why her father wanted this robe.

"Your father chose well then," she said, taking the wool and sitting across from Dinah. Her mother would spin the finest colors without knot or breakage, and Dinah was grateful for the help. The coat would be ready sooner if she didn't have to work alone.

"I can't imagine why your father needs such an elaborate coat though." Leah had the yellow green attached to her spindle, and her gaze rested on Dinah as she worked. "Is he doing this to declare that all of his sons are favored?" A look of pleasure lifted the wrinkled corners of her eyes, as if she realized she had figured out Jacob's intention.

Dinah swallowed, focusing on the red that began to spin beneath her hand. She couldn't tell Ima the truth, but to lie to her own mother . . . what could she say?

"You do seem distracted of late, Dinah." Her mother's brows turned downward again.

Dinah looked up. "What? Oh, I'm sorry, Ima. I was trying to get the thread right." She paused. "Abba didn't tell me all of his plans, but your idea is a good one." It was almost the truth. Though she did know the coat was for Joseph, perhaps she could change her father's mind and ask him to keep it for himself. So it wasn't exactly a lie. She smiled at her mother, hoping Leah couldn't see through her or somehow read her thoughts.

"I think it is one of the best ideas your father has had in a long time. He needs to do something to bridge the rift between his sons, and if he stops favoring Rachel's children by wearing something like this, it will help a little, I think." Leah began to whistle a tune. As his wife, she should be able to read his intentions, but Dinah knew that her father had not been spending much time with any of his wives of late. Benjamin and Joseph were with him more than anyone else.

"I hope things go as you say, Ima," Dinah said. Who knew? Perhaps her mother's idea would come to pass, if Dinah could find a way to convince her father that it was better than his own.

Jacob welcomed Dinah into his tent after his sons had left to tend his flocks and Joseph was off caring for his estate. She carried the robe he had requested over one arm and let the tent flap fall behind her.

"Dinah, you have finished! Now we can celebrate!"

She came close and stood at his side. "Yes, Abba, it is finished."

"Let me see it!" He hadn't been this excited in years.

Dinah opened the robe and held it up in front of her.

Jacob sighed. "Oh, my daughter, you have done magnificent work."

Dinah's smile did not reach her eyes.

"Do you not think so?" he asked. Who could understand a woman's moods? "Let me hold it." He reached for the coat, dismissing whatever caused her to look so somber on such a delightful day. He would rejoice, as would Joseph.

Dinah handed him the robe and knelt in front of him. "I want to ask you something, Abba."

He patted the seat beside him, offering her a place to sit. "Something troubles you, Dinah? Please, tell me."

He waited while she stared at the robe, then looked into his eyes. "I was wondering, Abba, if you would consider keeping this coat for yourself instead of giving it to Joseph."

Jacob tilted his head, assessing her. "Why would I do that? This is to show your brothers my intended heir. It is something I've had in mind for years, yet you would tell me to keep it for myself and not give it to my chosen son?"

Dinah looked about the tent as though she wanted to make sure they were alone. He drew in a breath, holding back his impatience.

"I am fearful of such a coat causing my brothers' jealousy to grow into hatred for Joseph instead of lifting him up as the leader you intend him to be." She paused. "But if *you* wore the coat that is woven with the colors of each of your sons, it would show them that you count all of them equally as yours and do favor them all, not only Joseph."

A heavy silence fell between them.

"Have you told anyone about my intention?" Jacob asked finally.

"No, Father. No one." Was she telling him the whole truth?

"This sounds like something Leah would say to me. Tell me, my daughter, that it was not your mother's idea or at least her assumption." He folded his hands over the top of his staff and leaned closer.

Dinah glanced toward the tent door. "My mother assumed this, yes. But I thought her assumption wise. It would do much good in our household if the coat is for you."

Jacob stared at her. All of his emotions and the joy he'd held on to for this day slipped away. He'd looked forward to the moment Joseph's eyes would light up and the gratitude he knew would come from the boy's lips . . . and now his daughter would deny him this pleasure? Keep the coat for himself?

He leaned against the cushions, defeat settling through him. Was she right? Would his gift cause harm instead of the good he anticipated?

"I do not mean to offend you, Abba. It is merely a suggestion that seemed wise." She slowly stood, but he remained seated, clinging to the coat.

The weaving was superb, the feel of the fabric exquisite. Not even he or his father had worn a robe so well woven. The colors would shine in the light of day, but even in the darker tent, they were easy to separate. Dinah had woven them in order of each son's birth.

"You have done an excellent job, my daughter," he said again after turning the robe over and over in his hands. He *would* enjoy wearing it, but that had not been his desire. How could he deny his heart's desire?

Neither of them spoke until at last Dinah took a step away from him. "If there is nothing else then . . ." She met his gaze, a question in her eyes. She obviously wanted to know if he would take her suggestion, but she wouldn't ask again.

"I will think on your request," he said. He laid the robe aside and pushed to his feet. He walked her to the tent door and kissed both of her cheeks. "Thank you."

She smiled. "I am glad you like it, Abba."

He nodded. He liked it more than he could say. He just didn't like her mother's assumption or their suggestion.

ௗௗௗ

A week later, once Joseph's brothers had returned from taking the sheep and goats and oxen to greener pastures, Jacob called them all together. They sat around the fire to eat as usual, but there was a festive feeling in the air, mainly because Jacob made it so.

Joseph sat beside Dinah while Benjamin played at her feet in the dirt. He watched the boy as Dinah coaxed him to eat between moments of play. What might his life be like without his brother? He dismissed the thought and focused on the stew still left on his clay plate. His father had killed two young goats for this meal, and wine flowed from the newest pressings of a month ago.

Laughter came from across the circle, and Joseph looked up to see Judah and Simeon slapping each other on the back. He could only imagine what they were laughing about. Not one of his brothers looked in his direction, but he pushed the hurt aside and again watched Benjamin.

Joseph turned at his father's hearty chuckle. "What has you in such a merry mood tonight, Father?" he asked. "It is not a new moon feast or some other celebration that I've forgotten, is it?" He glanced at Isaac, who also seemed in brighter spirits. What was going on?

"I have a surprise, my son." His father beamed at Joseph as though he could not contain his joy.

"I look forward to hearing what it is." Joseph searched his father's face but was not able to draw from his expression even a hint of what he was thinking.

"You will soon see, my son." Jacob smiled, then set his food aside and slowly stood and hobbled to the center of the group. Silence followed as everyone turned their attention to him. "For some time now I have wanted to designate my heir," he said. "I know that I may yet live many years, but since no one knows the day of his death, we must be prepared for one of you to lead the others. This does not mean that you will not all have your share in my inheritance. But the firstborn rights mean that he gets the double portion." He paused, looking from one son to another.

Joseph watched his brothers and saw their lips drawn in thin lines, their furrowed brows. They did not like the focus of his father's words.

"As you know, Reuben, the first show of my manhood, defiled my concubine some years ago and lost his right as firstborn son. That only leaves me one firstborn of a first wife to put in his place." He turned to face Joseph and motioned him to stand. "That man is Joseph." He glanced toward a servant, who held something colorful in her hands.

She came forward and handed the object to Jacob.

"I have had a robe of many colors—of all of your colors—made for Joseph," Jacob said. "This will show that he is my intended heir if I go to my fathers before I expect to. I want you to respect him and follow his lead should that be necessary. He will handle my affairs, as he has already begun to do. You will still rule over your own portions of land, once we have land to rule, but in the meantime, Joseph will be head of the tribes of Israel in my place once I am gone."

Jacob released a breath as though winded, then took the robe and draped it over Joseph's shoulders. "Put it on," he said quietly.

Joseph did as he was instructed, the heat in his face not coming from the central fire. He could feel the anger brewing all around him, but he put his arms through the sleeves and tied the sash. He looked down at the robe that fell to his ankles, a robe of near royalty, with colors that represented them all.

"Thank you, Father," he said, offering his best smile despite the sudden knot in his stomach. He could not disappoint the only one who truly loved him. No matter what his brothers thought of him, he could never hurt his father.

7

Judah strode from the central fire as soon as his father ended his speech and Joseph wore the offending robe. He would not sit and listen to another word. Simeon and Levi followed next, and soon all of his brothers and half brothers had fallen into line behind him. He bypassed his tent and left the compound, seething.

"It is an outrage!" Simeon said, hurrying to catch up with Judah's long strides. "And an insult to our mother! To all of us!" His words held venom as his voice rose in a near shout.

Judah stopped near the edge of a small forest and faced his brothers. "Keep your voice down, Simeon." He wanted to roar even louder, but they dared not let their father hear them. "We must talk, but we don't want word to get back to Father . . . or *Joseph*." He spat his brother's name like a curse.

"What are we going to do? We can't change what Father has done." Reuben moved closer to Judah. "It is my fault that he chose Joseph over me. You know what I did."

Judah stared at his older brother, certain that Reuben had made amends for his misdeeds often enough. He didn't need to defend their father's actions. "Father could have overlooked and forgiven your sin," Judah said.

"You know he would never do that," Issachar said. "Father has always favored Joseph. Why are we surprised by this?"

"It is as though he has made Joseph king over us!" Judah's tone hardened, and he tamped his anger down. "I will not be ruled by a selfish boy."

"No one is saying you will have to be. Our father is still in good health," Levi said, his arms lifted in appeal. "You know how long our grandfather has lived, and our father could live many, many more years. Joseph has a coat. What does it matter? We will still live our lives as we have always lived them."

"Father loves Joseph more," Naphtali said, a hint of sadness in his tone.

Silence followed the remark. They all knew it was true, but Judah hated the reminder, and the coat just added to that in a blatant way. "Well, let him. We don't need Father's approval. We don't need anyone's approval save our own. I for one am not going to pay any attention to what this night was meant to prove or disprove. Let Father celebrate what he thinks is good. We will show him that Joseph is not one of us. He will never be considered our brother."

Judah didn't expect the quick nods of agreement from each brother.

"We will treat him as we always have," Gad said, his words dripping with scorn.

"Or worse," Simeon agreed.

Laughter grew among them, and they slapped each other on the back. Camaraderie as they had not known before this night drew them together against a common threat. Joseph. He would remain their nemesis, and no matter what their father chose to do, they would not be dissuaded. Let him have Joseph. They wanted nothing to do with the boy—ever again.

ↃↃↃ

Joseph awoke with a start, blinking to clear his head. Benjamin still lay sleeping at his side and seemed unaware of his movement. Joseph crept quietly from the tent and hugged his arms to his chest against the sudden chill. The stars hung in brilliant patterns above him, with no clouds to hide them.

Adonai? What does it mean?

He'd dreamed of a field of wheat where he and his brothers had worked together bundling the crop—something they had not done together ever before. Why would he dream of something he'd never done? The servants harvested the wheat. His brothers handled the flocks. He managed the household. Something like that would never happen—or had yet to happen.

Was God showing him that they would one day come together and reconcile and work side by side? The thought warmed him, for he longed to be close to them—something he had rarely known. But why would his sheaf stand and theirs bow before it? Were his brothers destined to fall somehow? Was he going to be the only one left once his father passed from the earth?

Adonai, please don't let that happen!

Despite all of their faults, he couldn't bear to think of his brothers sent away or ruined or killed or having any harm befall them. The dream must have another meaning. Surely dreams meant something. His father had often told him of his dream of the ladder reaching to the heavens and how God had spoken to him after he'd awakened.

Do You want to tell me something?

Joseph stared at the heavens, but no thought came to him. No voice spoke, whether in a whisper or thunder. All was quiet and cold and peaceful. He would get no answers from God this night.

He returned to his mat and wrapped his old cloak around

him, for he could not bring himself to sleep in the new one. In the morning he would share the dream with his brothers. Perhaps God would speak to him through them.

ШШ

When Joseph awoke the second time that day, light spilled through the slightly opened door and Benjamin was no longer sleeping on his mat near him. Dinah must have come for him. How long had he remained asleep?

He hurriedly dressed, donned his sandals, and walked toward the central fire, where his brothers still lingered over a morning bowl of porridge. They would rush off now that he was here, so he glanced at his father and then approached them.

They did not look up from eating, though he knew they sensed his presence. He cleared his throat. "Listen to this dream I had last night," he said. "We were out in the field, tying up bundles of grain. Suddenly my bundle stood up, and your bundles all gathered around and bowed low before mine!" He clasped his hands in front of him. "I tried to make sense of it and thought perhaps you could help me do so."

Judah straightened, flicked his gaze over the others, then glared at Joseph. "So you think you will be our king, do you? Do you actually think you will reign over us?"

Joseph's jaw dropped, and he wondered why he hadn't seen what they would see. Had he been too tired in the night to think clearly? "I didn't think that," he said slowly, searching for more to say.

Before he could speak another word, Judah jumped to his feet, his brothers doing the same, leaving their bowls on the stones where they sat. Judah took one step closer to Joseph. "You will *never* rule over us," he said through clenched teeth. "Dreamer!" He stalked off, and the rest followed.

Joseph felt as if he'd been slapped. What a fool he had been. He should never have said a word to them. Defeated, he slowly turned around and moved to sit next to his father.

"What did you say to them?" Jacob asked.

"I told them my dream," Joseph said.

"Tell me."

Joseph shook his head. "It was nothing. Just a foolish dream." He stood. "I must get to work, Father."

"You've eaten nothing. Come, sit. Eat and talk to me." His father's pleading moved him, but he could not shake the sting of Judah's words.

"Perhaps later," he said, turning to go. "I'm sorry, Father. I just need time to think."

He hurried toward the steward's tent in the opposite direction of his brothers. Was it the way he had spoken? The tone in his voice? Or was he simply that naive not to think of the conclusion his brothers would come to? Why had he missed it?

Because you cannot imagine ruling over them. They will not be ruled by anyone.

The thought did not comfort.

ⅢⅢ

Light poured into Joseph's tent as he was in the middle of tying his sash. His father lifted the tent flap and let it fall behind him. "Tell me you plan to join us this morning. You cannot avoid your family forever."

Joseph averted his gaze and bent to tie his sandals. He'd spent the past several days eating alone behind his tent rather than sit with his brothers' silence. He looked up as the last strap was tied. "I don't want to avoid you, Father. But my brothers cannot speak a kind word to me. Rather than cause more discord, for now I would rather eat alone."

"But I miss you, as does your grandfather, not to mention Benjamin and even Dinah. Not everyone disapproves of you, my son. They are simply jealous. It will pass." Jacob motioned with his hand for Joseph to leave the tent ahead of him.

They walked together toward the central fire, where his brothers were finishing their morning meal. The women had gathered to collect their plates and then take their fill when Jacob finally took his seat.

Joseph greeted Isaac and sat beside his father. He did not look up or at his brothers until he heard them rise and leave the area. Not one of them looked back at him.

"How are you today, Joseph?" Isaac asked him once his brothers were out of earshot.

"I am well, Sabba. It is I who should be asking after your health." Guilt nudged him as he thought of how his absence of late might make his grandfather feel.

"My sleep was peaceful, Joseph. Though I ache a little more each morning. My time on this earth grows short, I believe," Isaac said.

"You thought the same many years ago, Father," Jacob said. "We cannot know how long God has for us."

"True, true." Isaac nodded, took a piece of flatbread, and dipped it into his porridge.

Jacob faced Joseph. "Tell me what is really troubling you, my son. I will speak to your brothers again if I must. There is nothing to fear from them. They are simply being stubborn because you are Rachel's son."

Joseph felt the pang of missing his mother all over again. He accepted a bowl of porridge from a servant. "Do I provoke them? Other than the fact of my birth, which I cannot change?"

Jacob stroked his beard a moment and looked over the compound. "Only you know what is discussed between you and your brothers when I am not near. I have not heard you say anything to make them angry, my son." He tapped Joseph's knee. "Do not fear. Come back to dine with us each meal and let them see that you are no threat to them."

Joseph looked into his eyes and wondered if his father was capable of seeing things clearly where anyone or anything connected to Rachel was concerned. "I will return, Father," he said. But he was not sure his brothers would soften their attitudes toward him, for the simple reason that he was not their mother's son.

8

A chill swept over Joseph, waking him in the middle of the night. He felt for his cloak to add to the wool blanket that covered his mat, then let it fall to the side as his dream came into clearer focus.

Another dream? *What are You telling me, Adonai?*

He rose and left the tent, wrapping his cloak around him, for the air was colder than it had been the month before when he'd had the first dream. Bright stars filled the sky and hung so low it felt as though he could touch them.

This time the dream had included the stars, the sun, and the moon. And they had all bowed before him. *I don't understand.* He gazed intently at the heavens, but God did not explain what the dream meant or even speak to him. Dare he mention this one to his family?

He shook himself, returned to his tent, and curled into himself for warmth, but sleep eluded him. The dream remained vivid in his mind's eye, and still it made little sense. The heavens bowed only to God, not to a mere human, and certainly not to him.

He pondered the meaning until the first sign of dawn filtered through the canvas. He rose and dressed before Benjamin awoke and walked to the central fire. He found Judah there warming himself. Joseph slowly approached to do the same, but he did not speak. This brother had been the most hostile to him.

Moments later Dinah joined them and greeted them both. "I did not expect to find the two of you here at the same time," she said, looking from one to the other. "And yet you are not speaking."

"There is nothing to say," Judah said, looking her way and avoiding Joseph's gaze.

Dinah gave him a scowl and turned to Joseph. "Is that your excuse as well? The least you could both do for our father is to be civil to each other. But none of you"—she looked at Judah— "can even say, 'Peace be upon you' to Joseph. I'm thoroughly disgusted with all of this childish behavior."

Judah glared at her, but he did not respond, for at that moment their other brothers and their father joined them.

"Isn't that perfect timing for you, my brother? Now you don't have to say a thing to Joseph." Dinah's scowl at Judah could have cut stone. "I do hope you will find some grace in your speech today." She left the courtyard to the sound of Benjamin's calls.

Judah turned away and sank onto his seat. The brothers did the same, and Joseph found his place beside Jacob.

"How are you, my son?" Jacob asked Joseph, as if he were the only son sitting near.

Joseph looked at his feet but took courage when Dinah returned with Benjamin and sat beside him.

"I had another dream last night," Joseph said slowly. The whispers of his brothers ceased as he spoke, and he felt the stares of each man without looking their way.

"You had one a month ago but did not explain it to me. So this time you must tell me," Jacob said, his eyes alight.

Joseph immediately wished he had not said anything, but it was too late now to retract his words. He swallowed, focusing on his father. "In this dream, the sun, moon, and eleven stars bowed low before me." He folded his hands in his lap, waiting for the onslaught from his brothers.

But it was Jacob who spoke. "What kind of dream is that?" he asked. "Will your mother and I and your brothers actually come and bow to the ground before you?"

"It was only a dream, Abba. I do not know what it meant. But it is not unlike the first one, and it causes me to wonder why I have them." Joseph glanced in his brothers' direction. Not one of them had a kind look in his eyes or said a single word to him.

"I do not know the meaning of such a thing," Jacob admitted at last. "Dreams that are repeated usually mean something, as we all know. But if God is not speaking to you as He did to me after the dream at Bethel, then you cannot know what it means. Best to forget it."

Joseph nodded, hoping his father's words would appease his brothers. Jacob was right. He would do well to forget such dreams. They could only lead to trouble if he continued to tell of them.

Judah led his brothers to a pasture far from his father's compound, the sheep following and grazing as they went. They kept the sheep and goats in the same general area, though not close enough to be in contact with each other. He needed all of his brothers to join him, and the fields were his most private place.

He climbed a slow rise in the hilly ground and turned to face them. "It has been weeks now since the *dreamer* has spoken to any of us, but our father is obviously considering the meaning of his dreams. And that cannot bode well for us." He crossed his arms and searched each man's face.

"What if Father gives Joseph authority over us before he rests with his fathers?" Simeon's scowl was familiar, and Judah could not deny similar feelings.

"Or sends us off to the land of our grandfather Laban," Naphtali said, stepping closer to the center of the group.

"Father would never do that. You remember the near fight he had with Grandfather at Mizpah." Reuben straightened and moved closer to Judah. "We've discussed this before. We have nothing to fear about being sent away. We can't let that rule our actions."

Judah faced Reuben as the others murmured among themselves, their voices growing louder. "You say so, but you can't know that. Why would you comfort us with something we cannot know for sure? Joseph could send us away once he is in power. Why would he want us near? We hate him and he knows it."

The men quieted at Judah's words, and he turned to face them again. "I think we need some time away from everyone."

His brothers exchanged looks but said nothing.

"We can take the sheep to Shechem for a while. We'll tell Father that the pastures here are thin and we need more space."

"What if Joseph tells him otherwise?" Gad asked, adjusting his turban over his unruly hair. "He was always running to Father to tell him wild tales about us when he was with us in the fields. Just because he no longer goes out with us doesn't mean we can trust him."

"We *were* wild," Dan said, laughing. "The boy wasn't lying. We just shouldn't have allowed him to catch us."

More laughter followed, and Judah listened to his brothers comparing things they had done in the fields while they were supposed to be watching the sheep. The sudden prick of conscience hit him as he considered what their father had taught them was right. None of them had actually followed God as their father and grandfather wanted.

But what could their father expect? Their mothers had not been raised to know Adonai, though his own mother believed in Him now. Still, following after a God they could not see when the nations around them had objects to worship and guide them made no sense. It was far easier to believe in something objective, something he could touch, and follow rules that made sense than to worship his father's God, who did not speak to men or give them direction often enough to know He was real.

That's why Father favors Joseph. He believes in Father's God.

The thought irritated him, sending away the guilt he'd briefly felt. He believed in his father's God. Just not in the same way as Joseph did. Joseph just wanted to please their father to gain his favor.

"So what are we to do? Are we really going to stay away indefinitely? Father will want to know when we will return," Levi said after the commotion had died down. He looked from Reuben to Judah.

Judah raised a hand high. "We will tell Father what we need to in order to appease him. We will head to Shechem tomorrow and then decide where to go from there."

"What if the people in the surrounding towns remember us? Things did not go well when we lived there. Remember what they did to Dinah." Simeon's dark brows furrowed as he crossed his arms over his chest.

"We killed the whole town and took the women and children. No other town will mistreat us. They will fear us," Levi said, lifting his square chin in defiance. He and Simeon had massacred the town of Shechem after their sister's rape, and his father had had to contend with sending some of the women and children to other towns, while others remained as servants. Their household had never been the same.

"What if Father doesn't want us to go back there or take the sheep so far from him? They are his flocks, after all." Reuben stepped higher up the rise in the ground to stand above his brothers. "As firstborn, I think we need to be cautious with this. Father will think we are doing something he wouldn't like. And so soon after Joseph's dreams."

"Don't even speak his name!" Judah growled. "The *dreamer* can remain in the dark about our plans. We will wait until we can speak to Father alone and assure him that we know how to keep his flocks. He will listen. He has to. He cannot act as if we don't exist, even if he wants to flaunt his favorite son." Anger bubbled within him, and he felt heat rise in his face. His hands clenched of their own accord. If Joseph had been standing there, he knew without a doubt he would have knocked him to the ground.

"All right," Reuben conceded, meeting Judah's gaze. "We will do as you suggest, but we leave it to you to tell our father. You want to go as soon as tomorrow?"

Judah glanced at the sky, then looked from brother to brother. "Yes. We will go tomorrow. For now, take the sheep to their normal pasture. I need time to consider how I will counter any objections our father may raise." He stepped down from the rise and passed through the crowd of brothers, who began again to all talk at once. "And pack enough to last a while," Judah said over his shoulder. If he had his way, they would be gone for a long time.

ꭟꭟꭟ

Joseph walked through the quiet camp, feeling a sense of loss. Except for Dinah and Benjamin, none of his siblings remained in the camp. Some of his brothers had wed a few of the women of Shechem, but the women rarely came anywhere near him. Even though he had had nothing to do with the destruction of their city, the women and even a few of the older children of Shechem seemed to hold the same hostility toward Joseph that his brothers did. And most of them still clung to their gods, though Jacob had commanded everyone to be rid of them before they had traveled to Bethel.

The evening meal had ended hours ago, and the sun nearly touched the edge of the horizon, showing off its glory in a blaze of orange, red, and yellow hues. Joseph stopped near his tent and startled when Dinah emerged and nearly bumped into him.

"Joseph!" She whispered his name and held a finger to her lips. "I just got Benjamin to sleep. Perhaps wait a little longer before you go in there."

He nodded. "I can walk around the camp for a time." He couldn't hold back the sorrow in his tone.

"Would you like company?" She gave him an empathetic look. "I'm a good listener."

He nodded and moved toward the trees where they had often spoken before. She followed in silence. Once far enough from his tent, he turned to face her. "I wish there were some way to change things. Our family will never be united or civil to each other if I can't do something to change the way our brothers think of me." Joseph ran a hand through his hair, dislodging his turban. He left it off and held it.

Dinah's gaze skipped beyond his as if trying to find an answer in the foliage or the trees. "I know it is hard for you, Joseph," she said at last. She searched his face, her expression filled with compassion. "I would help you if they would listen to me. But even when I try to appeal to them—even when my mother appeals to them—they raise a hand to stop our words and stalk off. They accuse us of favoring you and our father over them. It is their anger that we cannot appease, and I do not think they are simply angry at you or Father."

Joseph gave her a curious look. "There is no one else and nowhere else to direct their anger to. What do you mean? If they are upset with my mother or that I was born, they have no cause to hate the dead."

Dinah shook her head. "Dear Joseph, don't you see? You, who love our God as our father and grandfather do, who counseled me the way I am counseling you, should realize that our brothers' real hatred is against our God. They are rebellious in many ways that have nothing to do with you or me. They have not embraced the ways of the God of Israel."

Joseph slowly nodded. In the silence, crickets chirped and the wings of night owls flapped in the branches above them. Joseph looped Dinah's arm through his and walked them a little closer to the camp. "I just want to do something, anything, to make this right."

"But you can't, Joseph. Surely you can see that." Dinah gripped his forearm.

"Why not? What if I appealed to them? Apologized for the dreams? Gave away the coat Father gave me? Would they not see that as an act of reconciliation?" He scrunched his turban, his mind whirling as it often did, especially since his brothers had left the area with the sheep. He knew they had gone to Shechem because of him. There was no other reason for them to leave.

"None of that would do any good," she said. "They would ask you if you no longer believed the dreams happened. And to whom would you give the coat? You would hurt Father if you refused to wear it. He is already sad when he does not see it on you every day."

"He's never said so." Joseph stopped walking just out of earshot of his tent now.

"He wouldn't. But I can see it in his eyes when he watches you enter the central court without it." She patted his hand.

"I can't wear it all the time. It is too fine a cloak, and I don't want to ruin it." He searched her face, trying to make sense of her words and his conflicting feelings.

"I know it is a fine cloak. I made it, remember? Our brothers do not appreciate that fact, so if it is any consolation, they are not happy with me either." She smiled. "But they will get over their pouting moods. Wait until they return and have had time to think about their actions. They will miss our family, and they will stop blaming you for things that are beyond your control. You need to do the same." She paused. "As you have told me I also need to do." She lowered her gaze.

Shechem would always represent the worst time of Dinah's life. For her brothers to take the sheep there had to have upset her as much as it did their father. Had they done so on account of their hatred of him? Or of God? Or of something he could not see?

What are You doing, Adonai? Will our family ever come together in harmony?

They had never been a close, loving family. His grandfather Laban had made sure it did not begin that way. And the rivalry between the women had filtered down to their children. If only there was something Joseph could do to change it.

9

As the sun splayed an array of yellow and pink hues like fingers spread wide, Joseph wore his multicolored coat while joining the others around the central fire. The wives of Jacob had prepared food for them, and the servants offered it to each one in turn.

The women spoke among themselves, and his father was engaged in conversation with his grandfather before turning to him. "Joseph, my son, I am glad to see you wearing the coat I gave you. It makes me proud to see it."

His father's loving smile warmed Joseph's heart. He would wear the coat more often if it gave his father such joy.

"I am happy to please you, Father." Joseph took the plate of hot bread and fruit from the young servant and held it on his knee. Benjamin's high-pitched voice mimicked words Joseph did not quite understand as Dinah fed him.

"I'm glad to hear it," Jacob said, pulling his attention back to their conversation, "for I have something to ask of you."

His father's words caught the attention of those nearby, and silence settled one by one over the small group.

"What is it, Father? I will do whatever you ask." Perhaps he wanted Joseph to do some new task with the overseer today or help him walk the length of the land he rarely walked alone.

"Your brothers are still pasturing the sheep at Shechem," his father said, his dark eyes never leaving Joseph's face. "Get ready, and I will send you to them."

Joseph finished the bit of bread he had broken off and swallowed hard. Go to his brothers? Was this God's answer for him to make amends with them? A little thrill ran through him. Surely God's hand was in this. He knew Joseph's heart. Perhaps He was making a way for Joseph to fix the brokenness in his family.

"I'm ready to go," he said, his heart beating faster.

"Good. Go and see how your brothers and the flocks are getting along," Jacob said. "Then come back and bring me a report."

Joseph nodded. "I will leave now."

"But take a few servants with you," his father said as if in afterthought.

Joseph saw his father's furrowed brow and the sudden concern in his gaze. "I will take them if you want me to, Abba, but there is no need. The Lord will be with me, and you need the servants here." He touched the pouch of nuts at his side. "I will take my sling and staff, and you know I am strong. You need not fear for me."

He waited a breath until his father nodded his assent, then gathered food to put in a second pouch and another skin filled with water. He went to his tent to grab his staff and looked about the room to see if he should take anything else with him. No. He would not be gone long. Shechem was not such a long walk. He added his sling and sack of stones to his belt for protection from wild animals, then left the tent, satisfied with what he had.

He returned to his father, kissed Benjamin goodbye, and then kissed his father's and grandfather's cheeks. "I will return soon," he promised.

Dinah touched his arm as he was about to leave the central area of the camp. He looked at her, and she pulled him close. "Be careful, Joseph," she whispered in his ear.

"I will," he said, pulling back and smiling into her eyes. "Perhaps this is the answer we spoke about. Perhaps God will give me the chance to bring peace between us all."

"I will pray that this is so." But her brows were drawn low, and worry filled her beautiful eyes.

"Thank you," he said, not wanting to dwell on her fears. All women worried about their men, and Dinah had been his closest friend all his life, sister or not. "It shouldn't take long to find them," he added, then turned to head north toward Shechem.

ᴜᴜᴜ

Joseph walked with a light step, moving closer to a town he had never expected to visit again. He'd been young, barely a man, when his father had camped outside the gates of Shechem. Dinah, two years his junior, had been but thirteen when she fell prey to the prince of the land. The thought brought with it the weight of sadness, but he could not dwell on what he could not change.

He glanced at the multicolored coat he'd worn to please his father, hoping against hope that the object would not incite wrath in his brothers. His dreams comforted him when he thought of their anger. God had surely shown him that one day they would respect him. But would they really bow to him?

He looked at the clouds skipping across the bright blue sky. Sunlight poked between their cumulous layers, and it seemed as though the lights of heaven had broken out just for him.

Though he'd pondered the dreams for weeks, he could not see any possible way his brothers or his father would bow to him. Even when he became head of the clan after Jacob rested with his fathers, there would be no cause or reason for such a thing. Brothers did not bow to brothers just because one was their leader.

He focused again on the road ahead, using his staff to make the way steady. Walking alone through the hilly country did not cause him fear, for he had been alone with the sheep as a much younger lad. And he felt the strength in his arms and legs and knew he could handle himself. Still, sudden doubt rose within him. Would it not have been wiser for him to bring a few servants as his father had suggested? What if he was attacked along the way? Even with his sling and stones and shepherd's staff to fend off wild beasts, what would he do against a band of men?

His heart missed a beat at the thought, and he swallowed the lump in his throat. Should he go back and gather servants and perhaps a donkey to take provisions to his brothers? By now they might be in need of food, and he could have appeased them with a gift. Why had he not thought of it? Why had his father not insisted and suggested a gift?

You were simply sent to check on your brothers' safety, not to gain something from them.

That was true. But the more he thought on it, the more he considered turning back. He had not gone so far that he could not make it home by nightfall.

He glanced heavenward again. *Do I fear for no reason, Adonai?* He knew God wanted his trust. It was a lesson he had learned from his parents, Leah, and his grandfather. Perhaps he'd learned the most from his grandfather, who had suffered much agony during his youth. It was a trial Joseph could not imagine facing. To have your own father offer you as a sacrifice with no one to stop him but God.

Whenever that story came to mind, he shuddered inwardly. His father could not have done what Abraham had. And Joseph was certain he could not have submitted as Isaac had. Did that make him a man of lesser faith?

But he believed in his God. His faith was sure, even when his brothers disdained him and refused to speak to him. And one day God would show them how wrong they were and elevate Joseph in their eyes to the place he belonged.

As he continued toward Shechem, his faith was renewed, and he began to hum a hymn of praise. He had been right to refuse the company of others. God was with him, and alone he could better commune with Him. Besides, didn't God control the wild beasts and protect from the hands of men?

ᴜᴜ

Two days later, Joseph came to the place where the town of Shechem had been. The grass was green in some spots and brown in others. He wandered from the ruins of the city to the pastures where his brothers once kept their father's flocks. From the amount of recent animal dung and short-cropped grasses, it was obvious shepherds had been there.

So where were they now? Had they left Jacob's camp to set up their own?

The thought was ludicrous and he knew it. Some of them had wives they would not have left behind, and they would not steal their father's livestock.

He looked from left to right, turned in a circle, and looked more. He spotted a man walking toward him, probably from one of the neighboring villages that lay in the shadow of Mount Gerizim.

"What are you looking for?" the man asked as he came within earshot of Joseph. He was dressed in the manner of those who tended livestock, though he had no animals following him at the moment.

"I'm looking for my brothers," Joseph said, straightening to his full height. The man did not intimidate him, but he had learned from his dealings with his brothers that it was always better to show confidence. "Do you know where they are pasturing their sheep?"

"Yes," the man said, looking Joseph up and down. "There were ten of them?"

"Yes, ten men with many sheep and goats."

The man nodded. "They have moved on from here, but I heard them say, 'Let's go on to Dothan.'"

"Dothan?" That was only another day's walk north and west. He could be there by early tomorrow.

"Yes," the man said. "They seemed eager to leave this place." His look told Joseph that he had recognized his brothers from their years of sojourning here. Perhaps they had feared to stay in a place where the inhabitants of the neighboring towns had long memories and unfriendly faces.

Joseph assessed the man, wondering if he had intimidated his brothers into leaving. "Thank you for your help." He touched his head in respect and waited for the man to do the same.

"You looked like you needed some. Glad to be of service to you, my lord." The man turned and walked away, his words catching Joseph off guard. *My lord?*

He glanced at his robe. Had the man thought him a prince? And yet, why else would he address him in such a manner? Joseph waited until the man was some distance beyond him, then turned and began his journey toward Dothan.

10

DOTHAN

Judah looked up from examining one of the lambs that had gotten caught in a bramble bush and peered in the direction of Shechem. They'd been in Dothan for over a week now, and no one from the area of Shechem had followed them. He had rested more easily last night, knowing they were safer here.

But sudden movement like a dark shadow caught his eye, and he lifted a hand to shade his view. Someone *was* coming from the area of Shechem. Had he grown comfortable too quickly? Yet it was not an army of men who approached but a lone figure.

Judah straightened and sent the lamb back to join the others while he strode slowly closer to the person walking toward them. He blinked twice as his vision grew clearer, and his ever-present anger rose within him. *Joseph!* He would recognize that coat from any distance.

What was he doing here?

Judah whirled about and walked toward his brothers. Most of them had spread out to watch the flocks, but he motioned with a wave of his arm for them to join him.

"What is it?" Reuben asked once they had gathered.

Judah turned and pointed toward Joseph, who grew closer and more visible. "Here comes the *dreamer!*" he said.

"What is *he* doing here?" Simeon asked, his tone harsh. "Come to check up on us so he can tell Father everything we are doing wrong?"

"Maybe he wants to join us so we will bow to him!" Asher laughed, but no one else joined him.

"We should rid ourselves of him for good!" Dan said, eagerness in his gaze.

"Yes, let's kill him!" Naphtali said. "We can kill him and throw him into one of these cisterns." He pointed to a dry well a short distance away. "We can tell our father, 'A wild animal has eaten him.' Then we'll see what becomes of his dreams!"

"No!" Reuben fairly shouted. He lowered his voice. "Let's not kill him." He was clearly attempting to remain calm—and keep them all calm. "Why should we shed any blood? Let's just throw him into the empty cistern here. Then he'll die without our laying a hand on him."

Judah studied his oldest brother. There was something more to his suggestion than he was letting on. Perhaps Reuben intended to rescue the boy before he perished in the pit. It would put him back in the good graces of their father, especially after he'd been so foolish to take their father's wife as though she were his own.

Judah shook his head, and a murmur of conversation erupted.

"Do you disagree with Reuben?" Levi asked. "I do! I say kill him and be done with it. Father will think he perished on the way if we return and make no mention of having ever seen Joseph."

Judah held up a hand. "No. I do not disagree with Reuben. It is better for us not to shed the boy's blood. How would we ever be free of bloodguilt even if our father never knew? Better to let him die in the pit."

One by one the brothers slowly nodded in agreement. They spread out again to make Joseph think they were simply tending the sheep and goats. But the moment he arrived in their camp, Simeon and Levi grabbed him, while Dan and Judah stripped him of his robe. Then the four of them, with Reuben watching nearby, carried Joseph, screaming, toward the cistern and threw him into it. They walked away without a backward glance.

ມມມ

Joseph's whole body trembled. He felt his head where it had hit the sides of the cistern on his tumble to the bottom. Blood smeared his fingers, but the gash did not seem to drip onto his tunic. He removed his turban, still shaking so badly his teeth knocked together, and felt more blood where his head began to pound.

He could barely see in the darkness in this depth, but he noticed rips in his tunic and felt the sting of scrapes on his shins and knees. He closed his eyes, still reeling from the rush of anger that had exploded against him once he set foot in the camp. His brothers had sprinted toward him from all directions, and their hands had grabbed him so quickly that he'd had no time to use his staff in defense or even consider whipping a stone into his sling.

As his ears cleared from the pounding in his head, he heard laughter in the distance and the voices of his brothers growing louder. As if they were giddy over what they had just done to him.

Had they left him here to die? He tried to move in the narrow cistern and finally managed to get his legs beneath him to stand. He leaned against the cool dirt wall, chest heaving and body shaking from the effort. He willed his limbs to obey him again as his mind whirled with a thousand questions.

Why would they do this to him? In his wildest imaginings he would not have thought them capable of such hurt toward one of their own flesh and blood. Toward others, yes. Hadn't they destroyed the town of Shechem? But they'd been angry over Dinah's rape. And on some level, he understood why. But sinners or not, people made in God's image should be treated with respect.

Did they hate him as much as they'd hated the men of Shechem?

He lifted his face toward the heavens, his heart crying, *Adonai, please help me!*

He closed his eyes and drew in a deep breath. "Help me!" he called, hoping one of his brothers was near enough and would take pity on him. "Please! Don't leave me here. Whatever you want from me, please let me have the chance to do it."

He heard their continued laughter. Had they heard him? Were they laughing at his plight or over something else? But he knew. Deep in his spirit, he knew they were laughing at his expense. They did not care what became of him or they would not have done this.

The realization that not one of his older brothers cared for his life hit him like a fist to his gut. That bone-crushing feeling of loss could never be erased. Even if he should live through this, he would never look at them again with love, not even with compassion. They had always hated him. Hadn't he known it deep in his soul?

Numbness settled over him. Though he continued to cry out, he knew they would not answer.

Սսս

Reuben glanced at his brothers where they sat on stones they'd placed in a circle and ate the toasted grain and handfuls of dates and nuts they always carried when they traveled with the flocks. He longed to join them, to watch them to make sure they didn't harm the boy more than they already had. But he'd glimpsed two of the lambs wandering away from the group, and someone had to go after them. He should send one of the younger brothers, but they hadn't seen the direction the lambs had gone, and he knew these lambs better than most, as they had been in his care since their birth.

Joseph's cries from the nearby pit felt like someone had punched him, but Reuben could not have stopped the frenzied taste for blood his brothers had any other way. Throwing the boy in the pit was better than killing him. But walking away even for a moment worried Reuben. Surely Joseph would be safe in the pit for the short time it would take him to rescue the two lambs.

He approached Judah, whose laughter had just erupted at a crude joke Simeon had made about Joseph. Reuben held back a grimace. "I'm going after a couple of the sheep that wandered off. Don't do anything foolish while I am gone." He met Judah's gaze with a stern one of his own. He might be the disgraced firstborn of Jacob, but he was still the oldest and they needed to listen to him.

Judah waved his hand in a dismissive gesture. "Don't act so worried, Brother. Go after the sheep. Joseph isn't going anywhere." He laughed again, with all of his brothers joining in.

Reuben turned and headed off in the direction the lambs had gone. His brothers had better listen to him. But by Judah's response, he had no confidence that they wouldn't do something more to hurt the boy before he returned. He quickened his pace, searching, nearly praying that he would be swiftly successful.

Judah heard the camels and noise of a caravan before his brothers did. He looked west toward the road to Egypt when the sound of the caravan coming from the north finally caught the attention of them all.

"Who do you suppose is coming?" Levi asked after taking a drink from his flask and wiping his mouth on his sleeve.

Simeon stood and held a hand to his eyes. "Looks like Ishmaelite traders. They're probably making a trip to Egypt."

Judah watched as the caravan grew closer, his mind spinning. Where was Reuben? He glanced behind him in the direction of the sheep, but there was no sign of his brother. The lambs he sought must have gone farther than he'd expected.

The bells on the camels' harnesses rang louder the closer they came, and the sound of male voices with foreign accents grew more distinct. Slaves in chains were attached to the camels with a length of cord, forcing each man to either run with hindered steps to keep up or fall and be pulled by his neck the whole way. The traders risked death to their captives, but perhaps they didn't care. Shackles bound the slaves' ankles.

What if the brothers sold Joseph to the traders? It would answer all of their problems! They wouldn't have to kill him, and he wouldn't be able to return to their father—should someone come and rescue him—and tell him what they had done to him. Jacob would be furious with the way they had treated his favorite son. But if he didn't know, he couldn't punish them for treachery.

Suddenly, guilt hit him square in the gut, and the rashness of their act against Joseph caused his heart to pound. Panic filled him. What would their father do to them? Reuben had lost his position as firstborn for sleeping with Bilhah, but if they were to

harm Jacob's heir, the son he intended to lead the rest of them
. . . would he send them all away or strip them of any inheritance?

Judah looked again at the caravan as his brothers talked among
themselves.

"We should have just killed him—could still kill him," Dan
said, as though he had also realized the state they were in. "If
we don't, he will surely tell Father what we have done."

"He will die of hunger in the pit," Asher said. "Why think
of killing him when we already know he will die?"

"What if someone comes when we leave this place and res-
cues him and returns him to Father?" Levi asked. "You know
we will pay dearly if that happens."

Judah turned from the caravan, which was nearly beside them
now, to his brothers. "What will we gain by killing our brother?
We'd have to cover up the crime. Instead of hurting him, let's sell
him to those Ishmaelite traders. After all, he is our brother—our
own flesh and blood."

As the words left his lips, he was not prepared for the swift
agreement from his brothers.

"That's exactly what we should do. Then we will be free of
him without shedding his blood," Levi said.

Judah stood, glanced again in the direction Reuben had
gone, and still saw no sign of him. He smoothed his robe and
walked toward the Ishmaelite traders, waving them down.

The caravan slowly came to a halt, and the leader of the clan
approached.

"Where are you headed?" Judah asked, hoping the man understood him.

"We carry gum, balm, and myrrh to sell in Egypt and in
other stops along the way." The man's words carried the deep
accent of the Ishmaelites, who lived in the wilderness of Paran
and bore Egyptian blood.

"And these slaves?" Judah nodded in the direction of the closest bound man.

"They were sold to us to sell in the markets of Egypt. Why? Are you in need of one?" The man laughed. "They will cost you." His wide smile showed even, white teeth in his tanned face, and his clothes spoke of wealth. Obviously this man had done well in his travels.

Judah returned his laugh. "No, no. I do not need a slave. But I have a man to sell to you if you are interested. He is young and strong."

The man sobered. "Let me see this 'young and strong' man." He rubbed his bearded chin.

"Let me get him." Judah hurried to where his brothers waited, motioned for Simeon and Levi to join him, grabbed some rope they used to rescue the more wayward sheep, and returned to the pit, where Joseph had grown quiet.

At his approach, Judah heard Joseph's cries of "Help me!" coming from below. He looked toward the caravan master, who had turned his attention to speaking to another man.

The Ishmaelites would not be coming to help Joseph. Hope flared that Judah might finally be free of his nemesis. Ignoring the guilt that accompanied that thought, he lowered the rope to the pit, unwilling to imagine what fate awaited this hated little brother.

11

Joseph slowly calmed as he adjusted to the dark, cramped surroundings of the pit. He strained to listen, but his brothers' laughter had faded, and their voices were too dim to hear. Rumbling in the distance shook the ground, and the faint sound of bells wafted down to him. Was someone coming? Should he call out to them for help?

He waited, for his voice was hoarse from yelling for his brothers. The bells and the tramping of animal hooves grew more distinct. A caravan? He closed his eyes, trying to remember the roads that passed this way. He was not far from a main thoroughfare that led southwest toward Egypt. Traders from across the east even as far as Mesopotamia traveled this way. His father had purchased rare items at one of their stops closer to Hebron. Perhaps if he caught their attention, they would rescue him and return him to Hebron on their way back or even let him go. He could find his own way if he could avoid contact with his brothers.

Then he would tell his father all that had happened. No more would he protect these sons of Leah, Bilhah, and Zilpah from their father's wrath. Let them taste the bitter cup they'd dealt him. He could not imagine what his father would do to the sons who would treat his favorite son so cruelly.

The bells' jingling grew louder, and now the sound of a caravan was clearly evident. He drew in a breath and lifted his voice. "Help me! Help me! Help me!" He stopped. Listened hard.

At last footsteps drew closer. Someone had heard his cries! Someone was coming to his aid.

He lifted his gaze to thank Adonai as a rope was lowered down to him. He grabbed the rope and used his legs to push against the sides of the cistern to help his rescuer pull him out. But when he reached the top and the sun illuminated the faces before him, it was Judah, Simeon, and Levi who glared into his eyes.

"He doesn't seem too banged up." Simeon looked him over while Judah inspected the gash on his head.

"Put your turban back on to cover that wound." Judah examined the rips in Joseph's finely woven tunic. "We won't get as much for him with these welts, but it will be enough to be rid of him."

Judah's words rocked him, and he not only felt his brother's hatred but saw it in his eyes.

"Be rid of me?" Joseph glanced beyond them to the caravan of men. They had stopped moving as if they were waiting for something.

Simeon and Levi grabbed Joseph's arms, and Judah tied them behind his back.

"What are you doing?" Joseph's voice rose, emotion coming to the surface. "Let me go! I won't even tell Father what you have done. Just release me and let me return to him."

"Do you actually think we would trust anything you say?" Simeon's strong grip grew painful. "We want to be rid of you, *dreamer*! You're going on a little trip to Egypt!"

Judah led the way while Simeon and Levi pulled Joseph along toward the waiting caravan. Joseph dug his feet into the dirt, trying to stop them.

"Don't make me carry you," Simeon hissed in his ear. "Walk politely or it will go worse for you."

Joseph still tried to wrestle himself free of their grasp, but their hold only grew more painful until he could no longer resist them. They stood before the caravan master now. Bile rose in Joseph's throat, and he barely choked it down.

"Here is the young man I spoke about," Judah said, handing the end of the rope to the man.

The man looked Joseph over as though he were a product to purchase. "Open your mouth," the man commanded.

Joseph obeyed, only to have the man stick his finger along his gums as if to check his teeth. Was he a camel that he should be treated this way? He longed to bite down on the man's finger but restrained himself. Making things worse would not be wise.

"Twenty pieces of silver." The man pulled a pouch from his belt and counted out the coins, placing them in Judah's palm.

"Done," Judah said, smiling.

The caravan master took the rope and tugged Joseph closer, then handed him off to another man, who forced him to sit. The man put shackles on his ankles and an iron collar around his neck, then removed the ropes from his hands. He took the end of the long chain connected to the collar and attached it to a waiting camel's saddle.

Joseph fought the urge to resist the taller, stronger man, all the while fighting a greater urge to cry out. Sweat beaded his face and trickled down his back. His heart pounded as if he'd run the distance from Hebron, and his whole body began to shake again. He needed to tell these men that he was a prince and his brothers had kidnapped him. Thoughts of what his father would eagerly pay flitted through his mind. Surely someone would listen to him! His teeth knocked together, his panic rising. The collar tightened with every swallow, and he fought for breath.

"Move out!" the man shouted in the direction of the caravan master, startling Joseph. The animals began to move, and Joseph's feet were forced forward. He nearly fell to the earth, but by some unseen mercy, he managed to remain upright as he shuffle-ran behind the smelly beast.

He could not turn his head to glance back at his brothers, for the collar nearly choked him. But he could fairly see their faces and their utter lack of compassion. It was the last expression he would ever remember of them, unless by some miracle God set him free.

Sweat poured down Reuben's back, and he cursed under his breath as he attempted to free the second lamb from the brambles that had her stuck fast. He needed to get Joseph out of that pit before he died of thirst. What if he'd broken a bone on the way down? He must return Joseph to their father personally.

But what if Joseph told Jacob what they had done to him? The thought added to his utter frustration with the wayward lambs, and he tugged harder, catching his tunic on the barbs and hearing it rip as he freed the second lamb.

He released a pent-up breath. Finally! He lifted each one and moved toward the path he had taken to find them. He couldn't carry them both, so he released them and used his staff to prod them along.

At last he saw the large flocks appear in the distance, and he stepped in front of the lambs and called their names to hurry them faster. His heart pounded as he pondered what he could possibly say to their father about why they had put Joseph in the pit. Their father would never forgive them.

But he must return the boy. If Joseph died, Jacob would never recover from his loss. And Reuben would bear the blame as firstborn for the rest of his life. Jacob might even cast him out.

Fear coiled in his middle, and he quickened his pace, still urging the lambs to follow. At last they entered the larger flock, and Reuben caught sight of a handful of his brothers. They no longer sat about eating and seemed to have returned to their work. Good. He could retrieve Joseph and perhaps even take the boy home, or send him home before his brothers knew what had happened.

He undid the length of rope he carried to lower it to Joseph and lift him from the cistern. Glancing about, he saw no sign of Judah, Simeon, or Levi. They must have taken the goats someplace apart from the others, for he saw only the sheep not far from the pit.

He would deal with them later. He half ran the rest of the way to the cistern. Looking down, he opened his mouth to call to Joseph to catch the rope, but the light shining from the angled sun showed the cistern to be empty.

He straightened. Did he have the right cistern? Of course he did. There was no other this close to where they kept their flocks.

He walked around the pit, looking at it from every angle, but his eyes did not deceive him. The pit was indeed empty. Fear twisted his gut. Had they killed him? A deep cry of despair pushed past his lips, and he grabbed the neck of his tunic and tore his clothes. This could not be! He had told Judah not to do anything foolish regarding the boy.

What had they done?

Angry now, heart pounding harder than before, he went in

search of Judah. He found the three brothers huddled together behind a copse of trees.

"What have you done?" he demanded, facing Judah down. "The boy is gone! What will I do now?"

Judah held Reuben's hot gaze with a cool one of his own. "We sold him to a caravan of Ishmaelite traders. He is on his way to Egypt as we speak." Judah shook the pouch at his side, and Reuben heard the clanking of coins. "We couldn't kill our own flesh and blood. But we couldn't have him running back to our father and telling him we had thrown him into a pit either, now could we?"

Reuben stared at him, then looked to Simeon and Levi, whose smug faces told him they had agreed with the plan. They had probably all agreed.

"I cannot face our father without the boy," Reuben said. "What are we supposed to tell him? Have you even thought of that? You know when we return he will ask if we have seen Joseph. Do you just plan to lie and have him send servants to search for him? It would consume him the rest of his days." Reuben drew in a breath. "And what if he sends men to Egypt and they find Joseph there? Then when Joseph returns, things will go far worse for us than you can even imagine!"

At Reuben's words, his brothers' expressions sobered. Judah cleared his throat but did not speak.

"Well? What are we supposed to do?" Reuben paced before them, barely tamping down his fury.

"Let's kill a goat and dip the boy's coat in it," Simeon said. "One of us can take it to our father so he is prepared before we return. Or we'll pay a messenger and have him say, 'Look at what we found. Doesn't this robe belong to your son?'"

Reuben halted his pacing and studied Simeon's calculating gaze. This brother was the most ruthless among them all. No doubt he would have killed Joseph and done exactly what he was suggesting now.

But the plan was a good one as long as they could keep the truth from ever coming to their father. Let him think the boy dead.

Reuben nodded. "Let it be as you've said." But he knew he would live to regret this day more than he regretted sleeping with his father's concubine. More than anything he had ever regretted in his life.

␢␣␢

Joseph breathed a sigh of relief when the caravan stopped for the night. A young man removed the rope from the camel and led him by the neck to a place near a fire where other prisoners attempted to sit with their feet bound. The man thrust a bowl of some type of mushy grain into his hands. He had no bread to dip into it, so he tilted the bowl to his lips and did his best to get some of it into his mouth.

Moments later, another servant tossed some dry bread at him. It landed in the dirt, and Joseph reached with shaky hands to grab it. Tears wet his cheeks, and he could not stop them despite his efforts. He could not cry aloud. Not here. He had seen others who attempted to even talk to the masters receive blows to the face for opening their mouths.

So Joseph remained silent. But he could not stop himself from looking toward the heavens and crying out to God. *Adonai, why is this happening? Where are You?*

But as he lay in the dirt without a covering beside a dying fire, still in chains, God did not answer his continual silent pleas. Not even the insects chirped to distract him from the desperate cries coming from his broken heart.

12

Judah licked his fingers, tasting the last of the goat meat, and moved to the front of a cave where they had sheltered the sheep for the night. The robe with the animal's blood on it rested on a protruding rock in the cave, to protect it from wild animals that might steal the only evidence they had to convince their father of Joseph's death.

His heart beat with a mixture of relief and guilt, and he could not erase the memory of Joseph's neck snapped into an iron collar and attached by a chain to a camel far taller than he was. The boy would not fare well trying to keep up with the animal, especially with his feet also shackled.

What have I done?

He rolled onto his side, facing the cave wall. *Don't think about it.* He and his brothers would head back to their father with the sheep, and once they drew near, they would find a servant to take the coat to Jacob with the message they had decided on and then show up in time to comfort him. It was a good plan. Once their father was over his grief, life could return to normal.

But Joseph's cries from the pit, his fighting against them, his pleading for his life, rang in Judah's ears the whole night. Dawn could not come soon enough, and he rose from a restless half slumber and called to his brothers.

"Wake up, all of you! Let's get going."

Grumbling met his ears. Apparently some of them had actually slept, but then, it hadn't been their idea to sell Joseph.

He turned and headed out of the cave, calling his part of the flock by name. Reuben, Simeon, and Levi soon followed him, and before the sun crested the eastern ridge, they were headed from Dothan back to Hebron.

The journey took several days, as the animals could not move quickly. But at last they were within a few hours of their father's camp. Judah walked to where his donkey was tethered to a cart with Joseph's robe draped over the side. He called to Gad, "Come!"

Gad moved at a pace that seemed purposefully slow. "What is it?"

"I want you to run ahead until you reach one of the servants in the fields and give them the robe and the message. Tell him we will be along soon." Judah took the robe from the donkey's side and handed it to Gad.

"Why do I have to do this? Pick someone else." Gad crossed his arms, his stance defiant.

Judah glared at him. "You are the quickest among us. Don't act like a child. Just do as I say!"

Gad held his stare, unmoving. "You are not lord over us. Do you think you will take Joseph's place?"

The words unnerved Judah, and he felt like he'd been struck. The weight of the silver suddenly seemed heavier at his side. He reached into the pouch and retrieved a coin. He placed it into Gad's hand. "Just do your part, please." He held the coat out again.

Gad turned the coin over in his hand. At last he accepted the coat as well. He took off at a run without another word, and Judah breathed a deep sigh.

Reuben drew up beside him. "We should be home in another hour or so, by the time the sun hits the midpoint in the sky."

Judah nodded. "We should probably try to get there sooner if we can. I don't want to see our father's reaction, but if we are not there, things could be worse. We need to make sure the servant follows through with what we want him to do."

"Agreed." Reuben stepped away to tell the rest of their brothers to quicken their pace.

Judah felt his strength fade, and an acrid taste filled his mouth the closer they came to Hebron. But what was done was done now. They had all agreed to the lie. Now it was up to each man to keep it.

HEBRON

Jacob sat with Isaac in the shade of Jacob's tent awning. A soft breeze blew through the open sides, cooling the air. It was a pleasant time of year, one where a man could feel warm yet not overly so.

"Joseph should be returning soon with news of his brothers," Jacob said to his father. "Perhaps his brothers will come with him." It would be good to have his family all around him again.

"I look forward to hearing from all of them," Isaac said, "though I particularly enjoy Joseph's company. He is the most interested in learning about the things of the past." A slight smile lifted the corners of his mouth, and Jacob wished not for the first time that he had returned home with his family far sooner than he had. If his children had grown up around his father instead of Laban, how much different might their lives have been?

But some things could not be changed.

The sound of someone running into the camp caught his attention, and he shaded his eyes to see one of his servants approach.

"My lord." The young man fell to his knees at Jacob's feet. In his outstretched arms he presented a cloak to Jacob. "My lord . . ." He paused, seeming reluctant, and Jacob looked more closely at the cloak, his mind reeling with recognition. "I received this with a message from your sons, asking if you recognize this as your son's coat."

Jacob's body suddenly shook with violent force. He could barely lift his arms to take the coat from the servant. Tenderly he pulled it closer and saw the rips in the fabric, the dark stain of blood down the front of it. He rocked back and forth, unable to move or breathe. As though a deep pit opened to swallow him, he sensed that he was falling . . . falling . . .

"No!" He dropped the coat and raised shaking arms to grab the neck of his tunic. He pulled down with all of his strength, ripping the garment in two. "*Joseph!*" His voice sounded like the cry of a wounded animal. A thousand scenarios filled his mind. A lion or a bear must have mauled Joseph.

"What is it, my son?" His father's voice came from some distant place.

Jacob turned his head, trying to make sense of his words. He stared at the servant as if in a dream. "You say my sons found this and sent it to me? Are they on their way?"

"Yes, my lord. They are coming quickly."

Jacob stared at the lad, not really seeing him. "It is my son's robe," he said, his tone flat, as lifeless as he felt. "A wild animal must have eaten him. Joseph has clearly been torn to pieces!"

"What?" Isaac cried out, and Jacob realized his father was still sitting there hearing everything. "Impossible! Our God was with him. He would have protected him."

Footsteps and the voices of women drew his attention from his father, and Dinah rushed to his side. "Abba! What is it?" She quickly turned her head away from her father's exposed skin, jumped up, and hurried into his tent. She returned with the burlap he had worn for Rachel and covered him.

Her hand on his arm caused him to look into her teary eyes. "What happened, Abba?"

A guttural cry escaped his lips in response. "Joseph! My son, my son! If only I had died instead of you."

He continued to weep and refused food and drink. Dinah did not speak again but sat beside him and took his hand, sitting in silence. Leah and his concubines also joined him in wearing burlap and sat in a circle of grief, each putting ashes on their heads.

No one spoke as Jacob continued to rock back and forth, his heart torn as if someone had ripped it from his chest. He drew breath, but it did not relieve the hard lump in his throat. *Joseph! Joseph! Why, Adonai?*

Time seemed to stand still, and he barely noticed his sons as they entered the camp. When at last they joined the circle with his wives, Jacob summoned his raw voice to ask, "Did you bring his body? I need to see his body."

Reuben shook his head, but Judah spoke first. "We did not see a body, just the coat. We looked, but there was no sign of him." His glance skipped from his father to his feet. Was he ashamed or embarrassed?

A thousand thoughts flitted through Jacob's mind, but he could not land on one that made sense for why they could not find his son's body. He wanted to give his Joseph a proper burial.

Of course, he couldn't, because the animal probably left nothing to bury. The thought brought another deep moan from within him, and great sobs wracked his body.

"Abba," Dinah said near his ear once his sobs had subsided and he managed to calm. "Joseph is with God now, Abba." Her voice was a mere whisper. "We can take comfort in that, can't we?"

"There is no comfort in this," he said, looking into her large eyes and her tear-soaked face. "I will go to my grave mourning for my son." He did not think he had any tears left within him, but they came again, and he could not stop the anguish that kept rolling over him in waves. If only he could lie in the dust and join Joseph and Rachel. Maybe Sheol would give him comfort.

13

EGYPT

Joseph's ankles grew raw from rubbing against the iron shackles, and his eyes stung from the dust and tears he could not stop as he shuffle-walked the many miles to Egypt. At last, the Nile Delta came into view, and the atmosphere of the caravan of men lightened. They arrived at the marketplace, and one by one the men halted the camels and Joseph could at last stand still.

He looked around him, heard the sound of a strange tongue, a language he did not understand. The caravan master approached him after what seemed like hours and at last released him from the camel's side and removed the shackles from his feet. He did not remove the iron collar, and though Joseph was strong and might have fought to free himself, he submitted instead. It would do no good for him to flee. He would die before he could ever reach his home in Hebron.

"This way," the caravan master said, tugging not so gently on the chain and forcing Joseph forward.

They moved through the stalls of wares, the likes of which Joseph had never seen, and came to a stone platform. The other slaves, led by other men from the caravan, were being forced up the steps, and Joseph soon followed.

A crowd of men, soldiers, and well-dressed businessmen, among others, surrounded the platform while the caravan master spoke to them in their language. Joseph would be sold to one of these men as his slave. The thought was not new to him, as he'd considered it from the moment Judah had sold him to the Ishmaelite traders.

But he hadn't expected what lay before him now. He watched, wary, his gaze moving from one man to another. *Please, Adonai, let the man who purchases me be kind.* If he were forced to do manual labor, he would do it. But he hoped they didn't beat their slaves for failing to meet standards they could not know. How would he know what was expected if he could not understand their language?

A tall, well-dressed soldier, with no beard beneath the strap of his helmet and dark hair just visible above his brows, approached him and looked him up and down. He wore many gold and silver decorations, telling Joseph that this man was one of renown. Joseph kept his gaze averted, as he expected servants did. The man touched Joseph's chin and forced his gaze to meet his. Joseph looked into his eyes, unwavering. The man walked around him, looked him up and down again, and at last said something to the caravan master. He then handed the man a pouch and retrieved a key from him, then took the chain attached to the collar around Joseph's neck and led him down the steps.

The man handed the chain to a servant, who followed behind his master's precise, quick steps. Joseph nearly matched the long strides and might have overtaken him if not for the collar.

Is this my life now, Adonai? Am I to be held captive in Egypt the rest of my days and never see my family again?

The thought brought intense anguish, and with it came the

memories he could not shake, the utter disdain in Judah's eyes. Perhaps he could have accepted the hatred from the others. But Judah . . . Judah had befriended him after his mother died in childbirth. Judah, like Dinah, had been kind—though his kindness had lasted for only a brief moment. Still, Joseph had felt somewhere deep within him that Judah had cared.

Obviously he'd been very wrong.

The noise of the city drew his attention away from his melancholy thoughts, and he darted glances where he could, all while trying not to trip over the cobbled streets. They walked on for what seemed a long time, but soon they turned onto a lane with a locked gate, which the master quickly opened. The lane led to an estate where manicured foliage lined the path and a large Egyptian house appeared in the distance.

As they came close to the estate, the likes of which Joseph had never seen, he noticed outbuildings that could house slaves or animals and fields and vineyards that stretched beyond.

The servant followed his master to the main doors, where he abruptly stopped. The master climbed the steps to the door, but the servant waited at ground level. The master turned and tossed the key to the servant, who missed and had to pick it up from the dirt. Joseph watched the master enter the estate while the servant walked him to the back of the estate to one of the outbuildings.

Joseph was led inside the dark interior, shown a mat on the floor, and forced to face the servant. The man put the key in the lock and removed the collar from Joseph's neck. Relief swelled through him. He drew a deep breath but did not release it as fully as he would have if he were alone.

"This is where you will sleep," the Egyptian said in the Hebrew tongue.

"You speak my language." Joseph stared at the young man

who seemed more like a boy, but he was probably older than he looked. Without a beard, which Joseph was used to seeing on all the men in his family, even the master seemed a younger man. But who could tell?

"Yes. I was sold to Egypt several years ago from Mesopotamia. Our tongues are not very different, and I learned to speak your language when my master needed me to interpret the words of other slaves for him. I learn quickly." He took a step back and assessed Joseph. "My name is Hamid. If you work hard and obey Master Potiphar, things will go well for you here. He is a kind master, but he is also the captain of Pharaoh Amenemhat III's elite palace guard and in charge of the king's prison, so he is quick to punish when he needs to. Be on your guard and do your work well, and you will find your needs met here."

He turned to go, then looked back with a passing nod. "Do not try to escape. Those who do . . ." He let the sentence die, and Joseph could imagine what these people might do to those who attempted to disobey them. Was there no hope, then, of ever going home?

"I was kidnapped," Joseph dared to say. "I don't belong here. I am the son of a wealthy man who would gladly pay for my return." Should he have said so—trusted this man so easily?

Hamid's look held empathy. "Many of us were kidnapped from families who would want nothing more than to find us. But if I were you, I would not mention this again to anyone. If our master or any of his high officials find this out, they could hold you for ransom and your family could face extortion. I say this as a friend."

Joseph nodded, searching his gaze. He'd been a fool to open his mouth. This "friend" might be one to tell the captain, and then Jacob could lose all he had to the man.

"I won't tell anyone then," Joseph said. "I trust you won't either."

Hamid laughed. "No one would believe a slave's word. Trust me, I would gain nothing in betraying your confidence." He turned and walked to the door. At the entrance, he touched the doorframe and spoke one more time. "I will send a servant to take you to the bathhouse and get you dressed in the way of the Egyptians." He pointed to his chin. "They will shave your beard and clean you up before I present you again to Captain Potiphar."

He walked away as Joseph touched his dusty beard. He'd only begun to grow it a year or so ago, but he had never trimmed it. His father's beard was long and gray, and his brothers all had full beards. He would look nothing like them after today.

He tried to imagine that this was a good thing.

Hours later, as the sun began its descent toward its resting place in the west, Hamid led Joseph into an antechamber in the house where Captain Potiphar lived. They waited in a cool, intricately designed alcove where blue and white tiles lined the floor and colorful tapestries hung from light brown stone walls.

Joseph had spent the day enduring a cleansing dip in the Nile River, a branch of which flowed some distance behind Potiphar's house. Another slave, one of lesser rank than Hamid, had helped Joseph wash his body and hair and cut off his beard, trimmed his long hair, and shaved even the mustache from his face. He was dressed now in a white linen half tunic that covered him only from the waist down, with a matching belt to hold it together. No robe covered the tunic, and Joseph wondered what would cover him as he slept on the thin mat at night. Memories of the coat his father had made for him surfaced. His heart ached as his mind filled with images of the day his father had given it to him so proudly. But the more vivid memory of his brothers ripping the coat from him came swiftly, replacing the joy of that day.

He studied his feet and the ground beneath him. Footsteps caught his attention, and he looked up to see the captain enter the alcove.

The captain spoke to Hamid in words Joseph could not understand. Hamid turned to Joseph. "He asks your name."

"Joseph ben Jacob," Joseph responded.

Hamid passed the information on to the captain, who nodded. More words were exchanged with the captain and the servant, and at last the captain gave Joseph a brief nod and left.

"He said that you are to work in the vineyards to start. He wants you to help with the pruning," Hamid said. "You do know how to prune, don't you?"

Joseph nodded. "Actually, I know livestock—sheep in particular—better than vineyards, but I've been trained to know how to care for and account for vineyards, grain fields, and animals. I was in charge of my father's affairs."

Hamid crossed his arms. "Keep this information to yourself. As you prove yourself to our master, he will see that you can take on more, and you may rise to power—even over me—in this house."

Joseph raised a brow. "I don't expect to rule over anyone or rise in rank, especially in this place. My only hope is to one day regain my freedom and return to my father."

"Keep that to yourself as well," Hamid reminded him. "Right now only I can understand your tongue, but one day you will be fluent in Egyptian and have no need of an interpreter. The less you say, the more likely the master will look on you with favor."

"I will do as you say," Joseph said.

They left the estate and moved to the servants' quarters for the night. Joseph could not foresee a day when he would be in charge of anything. His dreams of ruling over his family were meant for Hebron, not Egypt. So why had God allowed him to be sent here?

14

HEBRON

The wind whistled in the trees above Judah's tent as if a storm was headed toward the camp. A month had passed since they had left Dothan and returned home. A month of agony for him, and the looks he got now from his brothers were more than he could bear.

They blamed him. Their father was still inconsolable over Joseph's loss, and when his brothers took the sheep and goats to the fields and hills nearby, they would barely speak to him except for Reuben. When he joined them for a meal, all conversation ceased.

"Do they think it's my fault Joseph is gone?" he'd asked Reuben a few days ago. "They wanted to kill him! I saved the boy's life."

Reuben had looked at him with a somber expression. "I had planned to rescue the boy and return him to our father. If you had waited for me to return, we would not be living with this dark cloud of constant grief."

So even Reuben hated him for selling Joseph to the Ishmaelite traders.

Judah folded a spare tunic and stuffed it into a goatskin sack, along with every other item of clothing he owned. In another sack, he added raisins, nuts of various kinds, and a great round of cheese wrapped in cloth on top.

He rolled up his mat and would take down his tent once he loaded his belongings onto the donkey. He couldn't stay here. Not another moment. The atmosphere nearly strangled him, and the hatred and bitter blame seeping from his brothers was more than he could bear. How could he ever forget Joseph if they constantly reminded him with a single look? How could he ever feel welcome near his father, when the man still wore sackcloth and wept every day? Without a body to bury, there had been no closure for Jacob. Perhaps they would have been better off if Joseph was dead. Maybe he was. Who knew what had happened to him once he reached Egypt? The traders might have slain him along the way.

The thought brought a kick of guilt to his gut. He had to get away from this place. He retrieved a male donkey from the pen, grabbed a sack of feed, then covered the donkey's back with a blanket and tossed his sacks over the side.

An hour later, the tent was dismantled, his belongings ready. His brothers had gone to the fields, thinking he would follow, and his father's tent was some distance from his, so they would not immediately notice he was gone. It was just as well.

But as he turned and headed toward Adullam, where he planned to stay—far from his father's house—Dinah approached him, holding Benjamin.

"You're leaving us." She looked from him to his belongings, her dark eyes somber.

Judah faced her. His one regret was leaving his mother and sister behind, for neither of them had ever treated him with disdain or unkindness. "Yes," he said. "I cannot live in a house of grief."

She tilted her head, giving him a curious look. "Father will not grieve forever. Where will you go? You cannot simply leave your family." She patted Benjamin's back in rubbing motions, and he rested his head on her shoulder, his eyelids drooping.

"I'm going to Canaan. I have a friend in Adullam that I met when we were tending the goats there. Don't tell Father or our brothers. I don't want to be followed. You can tell our mother, but only if she promises to keep my secret." He tugged on his beard, feeling conflicted about having told her.

"Thank you for telling me," she said, touching his arm in an affectionate gesture. "Please don't stay away long, Judah. Whatever happened to Joseph was not your fault. You must learn to forgive yourself and forgive Father for such extended grieving. I know it troubles all of you that he favored Joseph, but Joseph never wanted the favor. He was a good brother and one we will all miss. But life will go on, and we cannot let the past destroy us." She leaned forward and kissed his cheek. "I will miss you, Judah."

Emotion rose up to clog his throat, but he swallowed it back. "Thank you. I will miss you as well." In a moment of weakness, he pulled her into a half hug, careful not to disturb Benjamin. "I'm sorry for what happened to you. Please take care of Ima and yourself. I will try to send you word from time to time."

"I would like that." She pulled back, and he held her at arm's length. "Be safe, my brother."

He saw the sorrow in her gaze, but he could not let her pain talk him into staying. He must go. He must.

"I will," he said, turning to take the donkey's reins and head toward Adullam. He did not look back, lest he break down and tell her everything to relieve his terrible guilt. But he could not do that. If he did, she and his mother would never look on him with kindness again.

ᴜᴜᴜ

EGYPT

Joseph crouched beside the wheat, looking across it as he examined the field that stretched far beyond him. Hamid stood beside him, tanned and bare-chested, wearing the now familiar mid-waist skirt that all Egyptian servants wore. The clothing had felt strange at first, but the Egyptian sun was hotter than the air in Hebron, and the fewer clothes the better.

"What do you think?" Hamid asked. Joseph had pruned Potiphar's vineyards, and Hamid had been so impressed with his work that he had moved him to examine the wheat, which was not doing as well as it had in years past.

"I see tares among this wheat," Joseph said. "Someone has gotten into the fields, and when the first planting went in, they sowed the tares among the wheat."

Hamid bent down to examine the short stalks. "It is very hard to tell the difference, but I see what you mean." He stood, Joseph with him. "We must begin to pull out the tares immediately," he said, authority in his tone.

Joseph shook his head. "I don't think that is wise." He rubbed a hand along his now bare chin.

Hamid lifted a dark brow. "And why not? The servants are used to keeping the weeds from the grain, though they usually clear the field before we plant. What harm can it do to weed as it grows? If we leave the tares in, they could weaken the wheat."

Joseph glanced again at the wheat, which was about knee-high and blowing slowly in the breeze. "The tares are too similar to the wheat." He bent down again and pointed out the difference. "Do you think the servants will be able to tell them apart? At this stage of growth, they are too similar, but let the wheat grow to its full height and it will become apparent then which is wheat and what is not."

Hamid stared at the stalks, squinting against the glare of the sun. He pulled a few apart, then plucked a few from the ground to examine them more closely. He held out his hand to show Joseph the stalks. "You are right. I could not tell while they remained in the ground, but now I can see. The wheat would be destroyed along with the tares." He tucked the grain in a pouch at his side. "I will show this to the master. He will make the final decision."

Joseph nodded, then looked out over the sprawling field. "How did the tares become sown among the wheat in the first place?" His mind whirled with possibilities, but it made no sense unless an enemy of Potiphar had done this.

"Our master is lord over many men," Hamid said. "He is captain of the pharaoh's guard and is in charge of the king's prison. I suppose he has made enemies over the years." His voice trailed off. "Though . . ." He stopped and glanced at the grand house.

"Do you think someone who works for the master did this?" Joseph could not imagine someone wanting to risk the wrath of the captain of the guard. Something like this could cost the enemy his life.

Hamid turned to face Joseph, glanced about the area, then pulled Joseph farther from some of the servants who were tending the field close enough to hear them speak. Though the two of them spoke Hebrew and the others did not, Hamid was clearly worried.

"I will tell you this, though I do not know why I trust you when you have been in Egypt such a short time. But it might be wise for you to be aware. In case." Hamid glanced again at the house and ran his hand over the back of his neck.

"In case of what?" Joseph's curiosity was heightened now, and he could not help but wonder why Hamid seemed to fear the captain's house.

"The captain's wife," Hamid said, lowering his voice and leaning close to Joseph's ear, "is not faithful to the master. Many of the servants have fallen prey to her desire to draw them to her bed."

Joseph's heart skipped a beat, and he couldn't stop his eyes from growing wide. "Why would she risk that? Would this not make the master angry?"

"She thinks he does not know, but we believe he does. He simply does nothing about it. She is the daughter of a priest of Neper, a god of grain in Egypt, and the master does not want to accuse the man's daughter publicly. At first, I'm told, Potiphar was possessive of her, and no one dared look at his wife without consequences. Now he is distracted with too many things, so he ignores her and her . . . ways." Hamid's color heightened as he spoke, and Joseph wondered if he had also bedded the woman.

"So do you think one of the servants who did as she asked did this to the fields? Might she have encouraged such a thing, given her father's role?"

"There is one servant she shunned," Hamid said. "He is not as attractive as she likes, so she never invited him to join her." His words came out slow, as if he were trying to frame each one correctly. "That man wanted her, so he assumed she would want him. He had seen the others called to her rooms when the master was away, so he expected he would also receive a summons. When he didn't get one, he approached the mistress. She shunned him in front of two other servants. He was humiliated." Hamid crossed his arms, then uncrossed them and turned to lead Joseph to another field.

"Does that man still work here?" Joseph glanced around,

wondering which man had so offended or displeased the master's wife.

"Yes. The mistress could not tell the master, for then she would have to give a reason for why she wanted him sold or sent away. And she wants to keep her secret." Hamid stopped near another row of wheat far from the first one. "Let us check this row, and every row, to be sure the tares are among them all. I will let you handle this, as I have other business to attend. When I return, I will expect a full report."

Joseph dipped his head in respect. "Of course. I will do as you say." He wanted to ask so much more, but it was not his place to know what Hamid's duties were or where he intended to go next.

Hamid turned to walk toward the cattle stalls, then turned quickly back. "Tell no one what I have said to you. I have trusted you. Don't let me regret that trust."

"You have my word." Though Joseph did not yet speak well in the Egyptian tongue and so had little ability to share secrets, he offered Hamid a slight bow to show his honorable intent. Hamid seemed pleased, for he turned again and headed off to his next task.

Joseph bent to examine the next row of wheat, working backward from where they had started. Every row was littered with tares and impossible to weed until they were grown. Perhaps half of the harvest would be ruined. The master was not going to like that information. But what would he do to the person responsible? And could anyone prove the man's actions?

What more might this enemy do, given the chance? What might the master's wife do if she were found out? Joseph didn't want to explore the answer to those questions.

15

CANAAN

Judah walked the fields with his new friend Hirah, inspecting the man's flocks and offering advice as they walked.

"You know much about shepherding, my friend," Hirah said, his thick accent carrying admiration. "Don't you think it is about time you join me in a partnership and we raise sheep together? You can provide your knowledge where I lack, and I will provide the animals." He laughed merrily, and Judah's heart lightened.

"I have so little to offer you. I have knowledge, but I could not even come to you with flocks of my own. My father would not have divided his sheep for me."

A sense of sadness filled Judah at the thought. If he'd asked, he surely would have been refused, wouldn't he? His father had never offered to divide the sheep with his sons, and after losing Joseph, he would not have considered such a request had Judah made it. Still, by now Jacob knew he was gone and not returning. Might he have sent Judah away with more than his tent and clothes? Or was he secretly glad to be rid of him? Did his father suspect him?

Hirah touched his arm, jolting him back to their conversation. "I will give you a third of my flock if you can increase our stock by a third within five years. Then we will share the increase, and you will soon have many animals to provide for a family."

"I will need a wife to begin a family." The thought brought Shua's daughter to mind. Shua was a wealthy man with a good family, and his daughter was inviting to look upon. Judah flushed as he remembered the way she had glanced at him when she served them the day Hirah included him in an invitation to Shua's home. "Though I can think of one I would like to wed."

"I will be your go-between to ask for her," Hirah said, sounding certain that he would be successful. "Who is she?"

"I don't know her name, but she is the daughter of Shua." Judah's cheeks heated as he imagined their wedding night. He could have taken any of the women of Shechem years ago when Simeon and Levi had killed the men there and taken the women and children captive. But most of them had ended up as servants, and he had not found any of them appealing. Perhaps he'd simply been too young to want a wife.

Now, however, Shua's daughter seemed most appealing.

"I will speak to Shua on your behalf," Hirah said, his grin wide and his eyes carrying a spark of knowing. "We will have a wedding soon!"

"I have nothing to give the man as a bride-price." Judah thought of the items of gold and silver his father owned and of the priceless robe he had made for Joseph, but Judah had no such luxuries. If only he had asked for some type of inheritance.

"Shua will understand," Hirah said, calling to the sheep and leading them toward an area beneath the trees along a slow-moving stream. "You will pay him once you earn your wages by working with me."

Judah searched Hirah's face for any hint of manipulation but saw only sincerity in his gaze. "It will be as you say." He gripped Hirah's shoulder, and they kissed each other on opposite cheeks as a sign of their friendship and covenant.

Judah returned to his tent that night with the promise that Hirah would speak to Shua on the morrow. Soon he would be sleeping beside a wife, and she would bear him children. And no one in his entire family would be there to celebrate with him. He was fairly certain that his father would not approve of his Canaanite choice. But in that moment, he determined that he would forget his family and begin one of his own. It was time to move on.

ᎶᏃᎶ

Kaella entered Judah's tent three days later amid the biggest gathering of people and the wildest flowing of food and drink Judah had ever seen. Even his grandfather Laban had not entertained so many people. But Shua was a prominent man in the town, and Hirah was a close friend. His influence had gotten Judah exactly what he asked for.

And now she stood before him, the bridal tent dim with a few lamps, while the drum beat and the music played outside as though the entire town waited for them to become one.

Judah approached her, the first chance he'd had to even speak to her, and took her hand. "You are more beautiful than I remembered," he said as he unwrapped the veil from around her face and neck, then continued to remove one garment after another. He leaned close and kissed her cheek, then let his lips travel over her face, her neck, until his mouth captured hers.

She did not speak, but he heard a little gasp of what he hoped was delight as he pulled her close, and when he kissed her, she responded in kind.

He held her at arm's length and searched her face. "Do not fear me, Kaella. I will never hurt you." He tugged her to his bed and set her among the cushions he had managed to purchase, then swiftly removed his clothes.

She gazed at him for a lengthy breath, then glanced beyond him, her cheeks turning a deeper pink. He couldn't push her. It would be wrong to treat her as Dinah had been treated. But she was his wife. He'd placed the corner of his garment over her and had promised to protect her. Still, he wanted to hear her speak.

"Will you say nothing?" He wanted to know her, but should he talk to her first?

She smiled shyly and placed her arms slowly around his shoulders, drawing him to her. "We can talk after," she whispered, as though she feared breaking the intensity of the moment. Surely she felt the charged air between them as he did.

And as soon as she spoke, he laughed. The drums outside spurred the blood pumping through his veins.

When he later emerged from the tent, cheers erupted, and he smiled as he joined the other men. Kaella remained secluded from the watching eyes of onlookers. She was his now, and his she would remain.

ᴗᴗᴗ

EGYPT, 1840 BC

Joseph looked up from the table in the outer portico, where he worked on a list of items recently purchased by Hamid. Joseph had risen above Hamid in Potiphar's eyes, which often made him wonder if Hamid held animosity toward him.

But Potiphar had insisted that Joseph check to see if Hamid had recorded everything correctly. So Joseph obeyed. Hamid was thorough, and though Joseph never found a mistake, Potiphar still seemed unwilling to fully trust his steward. Could it be because he knew Hamid had been with his wife and therefore Potiphar had lost faith in him? But if he knew, would he not have thrown the man in prison or had him killed?

Joseph glanced across the vast estate to the blue sky and the few clouds that fringed the tops of the tall, swaying palm trees. The time since he had entered Egypt seemed both short and long, and he was grateful for work to keep his mind off all he had lost. Though he could not forget what his brothers had done to him, God had blessed him.

He turned at the sound of footsteps on the tile floor coming from the inner court. Hamid appeared, carrying a scroll.

"Greetings, Hamid," Joseph said, smiling.

Hamid bowed, and Joseph tried not to squirm. "My lord," he said, handing Joseph the scroll. "Here is another list from the master's storage keeper."

Joseph took the scroll. Potiphar would want an accounting of this too. "Thank you." He placed the scroll on the table beside a pile of others.

"The master also has asked to see you tonight when he returns from his duties. He said to come to his private quarters." Hamid's lips thinned into a straight line, and Joseph was not sure how to read his expression.

"Is something wrong?" he asked, resting an elbow on the table and setting the reed writing utensil in its holder.

Hamid shook his head, then looked at his feet. At last he met Joseph's gaze once more. "May I speak freely?"

"I wish you would. I have few in my life that I can trust, considering I could not even trust my own flesh and blood." Joseph crossed his arms, searching Hamid's dark eyes.

"I have been with the master many years now." Hamid

glanced about as if to make sure no one could overhear him. "I thought one day the master would raise my position to personal attendant. But that is not to be."

"You don't know that for sure," Joseph said, extending a hand toward him. "The master's personal attendant may one day leave or be given a different job, and you will take his place."

Hamid nodded. "This was my hope. But I believe the master is going to give that job to you."

Joseph raised a brow. "I have not worked here long enough for that."

"But it is clear the Lord is with you, and everything you touch is blessed. Even I can see that, and it is not hidden from Potiphar that you are blessed of the gods." Hamid glanced about again.

"If I am blessed, it is the Lord, the God of my fathers, who has blessed me. If Potiphar is blessed because of me, I am grateful, but that is not of my doing." He touched his chin, a thousand thoughts running through his head.

Hamid remained silent for a few moments, then straightened and stepped a little closer. "I believe you are blessed of your god, not the gods of Egypt. They do not bless a man, and our master knows this. You will go far in this land as long as your god is with you. And I will not because my favor comes from the master's wife more than it does from the master." He twisted the sash at his waist, his face darkening as if he was embarrassed to admit it.

"I hope you will rise along with me, if that is God's will for me, Hamid. I trust you, and I hope we will work long together." Joseph stood and bowed to the man, though it was not proper protocol to do so.

Hamid bowed in return, still seemingly embarrassed. "I would be honored to serve you, my lord."

"Please call me Joseph when we are alone. I am not used to 'my lord.'"

"Joseph. When we are alone." Hamid smiled, and Joseph prayed the smile was genuine. How easily was he deceived? He had trusted his brothers, and they had betrayed him. Was he being foolish to trust a man whom he had surpassed?

Adonai, please give me wisdom.

Later that evening Joseph answered a summons to Potiphar's private chambers, where few were ever invited. Joseph entered the ornate room with gold trim along the tops of the walls and gilded couches placed in a half circle. Blue and green tiles that shimmered like glass were placed in intricate patterns along the floor. Tall pillars lined the walls, made from the best cedars from Lebanon and also plated in gold.

Potiphar was already seated on one of the couches when Joseph arrived. Joseph came close and bowed with his face to the ground.

"Stand, Joseph. I would speak with you face-to-face." Potiphar no longer needed an interpreter, as God had given Joseph a quick understanding of the Egyptian tongue.

Joseph stood and looked into Potiphar's kohl-rimmed eyes. "Yes, my lord. How can I serve you, my lord?" He glanced at his feet, then thought better of it and kept his gaze steady.

"I know how successful I have become since you came here. Everything you have done has multiplied my earnings beyond what I have ever seen. Therefore, I have decided you should become my personal attendant and be in charge of my entire household and all that I own. I'm entrusting it all to you." Potiphar studied him, and Joseph knew he expected a pleased reaction. Hadn't Hamid warned him this would happen?

"Thank you, my lord. I am most honored to serve you in this way." He bowed low again to show his understanding that Potiphar still ruled the household whether Joseph was in charge of things or not.

"Good," Potiphar said, tenting his hands. "You will start tomorrow. And from now on you will sleep in a room in the house where the household servants sleep, rather than with the field-workers. I've had the room prepared for you." He clapped his hands, and a servant appeared. "Take Joseph to the room I have set aside for him." Potiphar looked once more into Joseph's eyes. "Continue to work as you have done, and you will do well in my household. Egypt will be blessed because of you."

Joseph dipped his head in a nod. "Thank you, my lord. I am pleased to serve you." He followed the servant to his new sleeping quarters. The room was spacious, like nothing he had seen before, with a raised bed and table and a clay lamp. There were scrolls in niches along the walls, apparently for Joseph to read at his leisure, should he have any. He could work and sleep here if he so chose, but he would work in the area already assigned to him.

The servant left him, and he lay on the cushioned bed and put his hands behind his head. He glanced at the wall where more tunics and an ornamented robe were displayed on pegs. The robe could not match the one his father had given him, but the sight of it brought the memory sharply into focus. He closed his eyes, acutely missing his father, unable to stop the sudden sting of tears.

He would avoid that robe if he could. A simple robe was less of a distraction, but if Potiphar demanded it, he would obey. He lifted his gaze to the ceiling and wished for a view of the stars instead. He knew God was with him, and perhaps one day God would right the wrongs done to him. One day he would be free of the memories he could not shake. For now, he would be grateful to have Potiphar's trust and hopefully Hamid's friendship. He could be happy here. Couldn't he?

But a part of him knew better than to believe that. Nothing could make him care for this land as he did his father's camp. If God allowed him to leave this place, he had no doubt that he would take the fastest way home.

16

CANAAN

Judah wrapped his cloak about him and left his tent. Kaella greeted him and offered him flatbread, cheese, and dates to break his morning fast. "How are you this day, my husband?" she asked, sitting beside him in their small compound.

"I slept well with you by my side," he answered, smiling into her beautiful eyes.

She looked shyly away, her cheeks flushing dark.

"Don't tell me you are still embarrassed by my compliments after more than a year of marriage?" He took a bite of flatbread, some of the best he'd ever tasted.

She shook her head. "It's not that." She took his hand, her smile growing. "It is just that I have news for you, and I hope you will like it."

A soft glow seemed to surround her as she spoke, and he tilted his head, giving her a quizzical look. "Tell me."

"I am with child." Her smile widened, and her delightful laugh filled the area.

"With child?" Judah stared a moment, then stood and lifted her in his arms. "How could I be anything but delighted?"

Her look held joy, but then her expression suddenly sobered, surprising him. "The men in my village prefer sons over daughters." She glanced beyond him as if remembering something painful. Had she felt unwanted because she was female? "Sometimes they sacrifice the girls and spare the boys. Sometimes, when times are hard or fear of famine strikes, they choose a boy." She looked into his eyes. "I don't want to sacrifice our children, boy or girl."

"Never!" he fairly shouted, then lowered his voice. "Our God does not condone the sacrifice of children. I promise you, this will not be the fate of our sons and daughters."

Her smile returned. "Thank you. I would give you both—if the gods allow. Perhaps we will have both at once. Twins are not uncommon in my family."

He kissed her nose and ignored her reference to the gods, thinking how blessed indeed he would be to have two children at once. He hoped that someday Kaella would embrace the God of Israel. He just had to give her time. After all, he hadn't been one to insist she believe in someone he wasn't sure he believed in himself.

They sat again, and he chewed the flatbread, watching her as she ate. "When are we to expect this little one?" Surely she suspected a time for the birth. His mother had always known these things.

She looked at the cheese in her hand, then met his gaze. "I suspect in about six months. At least that is what my mother has told me."

He nodded. He knew little of the ways of women except that his mother had continually carried a new child and gave birth to one after another. Would Kaella do the same? How many children might she bear? His mother had stopped bearing after four, then began again. But he could not imagine himself the parent of twelve sons or even six sons and a daughter, as his father and mother were.

"I'm going to be in the eastern pasture today," he told her, tucking the rest of his food into a pouch at his side. He would eat it along with the food already there at the midday meal. "I will be home tonight." He kissed her cheek.

"I will have your supper waiting when you come," she said, walking with him toward the sheep pens.

When Hirah appeared, she backed away and let him go. Judah nodded her way, and she smiled her farewell. He wondered why Kaella always shied away when Hirah drew near, but he did not question her behavior. His wife was shy with many people, and likely she preferred the company of her mother and sisters over that of men, whether she or her father knew them or not.

"Ready to go?" Hirah asked as he opened the gate and began calling the sheep. He glanced at Kaella's retreating back and gave Judah a knowing look. "She pleases you, I see." His smile warmed Judah.

"She is with child."

Hirah's eyes widened. He clapped Judah on the shoulder and laughed outright. "At last! May the gods give you many sons by her, my friend."

"Thank you, Hirah. I, too, wish for many sons, though not as many as my father has!" He chuckled, and Hirah joined him.

"Perhaps five or six would be enough for such a man as you." He encouraged a straggling lamb to follow the others, and Judah prodded one of the goats with his staff.

They walked toward the eastern pasture while Judah pondered Hirah's words and Kaella's news. A father. He was going to be a father now. Perhaps having his own children would better help him to forget his brothers, particularly one. But as he watched the goats graze along the crags of the hilly land, he could not stop the images of his brothers doing this very work. And the cries of Joseph still called to him as if from beyond the grave.

ᴜᴜᴜ

EGYPT

Joseph stood on the highest step of the portico, taking in the vast length of Potiphar's land. How many years had it taken this man to rise to such a level of wealth? Or did he inherit these lands from his father, as Joseph would have inherited his father's wealth and blessing one day?

The image of his father passed before his mind's eye, and he blinked, forcing the memories to wait. He would think about his father another day. The more he shoved the memories aside, the better.

He shook himself, took the steps two at a time, and headed for the enclosures where the cattle were kept. A field bordered the pens, a place for the cattle to graze. The animals were a good distance from the wheat fields that were visible from the house. Potiphar did not want the stench of his animals anywhere near his grand estate. Joseph sent a silent prayer of gratitude that God had allowed him a place in the house instead of the fields. Perhaps he was becoming far too used to the Egyptian way of life.

He reached the pens just as the servants were leading the cattle to the fields. Several men were spread out to watch that none of the cattle ran off or were frightened by wild beasts.

Joseph stopped at the small hut where one servant kept watch each night and met Hamid there.

"Greetings, my lord," Hamid said as all of the servants bowed to him.

"Greetings," Joseph said as each man straightened and awaited his instructions. "You may go about your work. I simply came to inspect the cattle. Hamid tells me you have a female that is sick?"

"Yes, my lord," Hamid's servant Lateef said. "If you will follow me." The man turned and led Joseph to the far corner of the pen, where a cow walked about as though she were drunk. "Her name is Masika, and as you can see, she cannot walk properly, has lost all ability to give milk, and has little appetite."

"Do any of the others show the same symptoms?" Joseph asked as he felt the cow's shoulder. "She is cold." He had seen this in his father's cattle, but normally it affected more of the herd.

"Yes, my lord. We are beginning to see others stumbling as they are led out to pasture."

Joseph patted the cow in a comforting gesture, then walked to the field to observe. Nearly half of the animals walked on unsteady feet as though they were drunk or weak.

He walked back to the pen where Lateef and Hamid waited. "Move the animals to a different pasture. This field is making them sick."

"But they always graze in this field. It is the one Potiphar allotted to his herd," Hamid said.

Joseph looked from the men to the animals, remembering this same weakness. Moving his father's herds had been the cure. "This tends to happen when the fields are greenest. I've seen it before. Potiphar will be happy to find healthy animals no matter where they graze." He walked away with one glance over his shoulder. "Give me a report by day's end and again at the end of the week. If there is no improvement, we will reexamine them then."

He headed toward the house, memories again surfacing of

the training he'd received from his father's steward in all of the household care, including that of the cattle and grain fields. Without that knowledge, would he be as aware of what to do here?

He lifted his gaze heavenward. Had God allowed him to be taught in his youth so that he could survive a future he could never have foreseen? He paused near the wheat fields and gazed at the house. He had accounts to manage and reports to fill out for Potiphar tonight. But as he stood on the outskirts of one of Egypt's finest homes, his heart's burning questions rose within him as he studied the puffy clouds.

Why, Adonai? Why am I here, and what are You trying to teach me? Will I ever see my home again, my father or grandfather or Benjamin or Dinah?

But the sky was as silent as always beneath the Egyptian sun. He lowered his gaze to the earth and his surroundings and headed to do his work. At least he had work to help him forget. Though forgetting was something he could probably never do.

17

Judah walked from the sheep pens, staff in hand, feeling a sense of elation he hadn't felt in all his life. Kaella had given birth to a second son earlier that week, both boys barely a year apart. Er, his firstborn, bore the name he had chosen, but Kaella had given their second son the name of Onan.

It was a good name, he supposed, though he liked his choice better. But then the firstborn carried a special place in his heart, the first sign of his manhood. *You are beginning to sound like your father.* The thought did not sit well with him. He must not allow himself to show favoritism to Er as his father had done with Joseph. Not even Reuben had enjoyed the favor of the firstborn as Joseph had. Judah would not make the same mistakes as his father.

He shook his head to clear it and headed toward his tent. He couldn't visit his wife during this period of uncleanness, but he would visit his sons once they were in the care of the nursemaid. He must circumcise Onan as he had Er in a few days, though Kaella did not understand or agree with his insistence on keeping the covenant of his fathers. Just because he wanted nothing to do with his family did not mean he wanted to be cut off from the promises given to Abraham. Not circumcising Onan would be a foolish decision.

He was using his staff to help him climb the steep incline to his tents when a voice called to him. He turned. "Hirah. I thought you had gone home."

"You must come," Hirah said, his breathing labored. "Something has happened to Shua."

Judah hurried down the slope, and the two half walked, half ran toward the house of his father-in-law. "What happened?" Judah asked.

"He was wounded when he attempted to free a lamb from the mouth of a lion." Hirah glanced Judah's way. "They don't have much hope for him."

A lion? Shua was no longer a young man. "Did he not use a sling to attack the animal from a distance?"

Hirah shook his head. "I do not know. Shua is a proud man, and he thinks himself still young enough to do what we can do."

The house, where a crowd of relatives had already gathered, came into view. Judah slowed his pace to match Hirah's. They drew closer and approached his brother-in-law Majid.

"How is he?" Judah asked, his heart beating too fast. He would have to tell Kaella, who would want to come at once. But should she leave her tent so soon after childbirth?

"He is not well," Majid said. "He tried to pry a lamb from the mouth of a lion, and the lion got hold of him. He wasn't quick enough to scare it off with his staff, and he couldn't grab his knife to kill it. The animal pinned him to the ground and bit his shoulder before running off with the lamb."

"Is the bite deep?" Hirah's face had paled, and a lump formed in the pit of Judah's gut.

"The cat did much damage. If he lives, Shua will not have use of his arm again." Majid walked into the house when someone called for him.

"You should go with him," Hirah said, touching Judah's arm. "Kaella will want to know everything, and you can't tell her what you do not see."

Judah nodded, though he moved slowly toward the house, then shouldered his way past Shua's relatives. The house began to grow darker as the sun set in a blaze of color. He looked about for a servant he could instruct to light some lamps but found himself pushed along to the door of Shua's bedchamber instead.

Soft weeping came from Shua's wife, Farida, and his sons who lived on his property, now gathered about his bed. A local physician bent over Shua, applying a poultice, and when he lifted his head, his expression was grim.

He motioned everyone out of the room and to another part of the house where the crowd was thin. "He will need these poultices applied three times a day. I gave him something to help him sleep. But I must tell you that I do not hold out much hope that he will recover. It may be that the gods will show him kindness and allow him to live. But the wounds cut deep and some of the flesh is gone. If he recovers, he will not be the same."

Judah's mind whirled. He had never seen a man attacked by a lion or bear, though he had killed a few of those animals from a distance with his sling, as had his brothers. Like Judah's own father, Shua should have left the care of the animals to his sons and sons-in-law.

Farida began to weep again, and her daughters-in-law surrounded her and drew her away to a private bedchamber. Majid walked back to the crowd and sent them away.

Judah slipped outside with Hirah following. "What will you do?" Hirah asked.

"I'm going home to tell Kaella." He did not look forward to breaking such news to her.

Hirah nodded. "I will go home then and have my wife prepare food for Shua's family. She will insist, and you know how impossible it is to keep a woman from doing what she wants to do."

Judah's laugh held no mirth. "I do indeed."

They parted ways as they reached the bend in the road, and Judah again climbed the hill to his tents. His gut churned as he considered the best way to tell Kaella about her father. She was Shua's youngest daughter, and the two were close. He clenched his staff until his knuckles whitened, wishing this day were any other.

⊔⊔⊔

"Judah!" Kaella said, surprise in her voice. "You are not supposed to enter my tent for many days yet." She studied his face, concern etched across her brow.

"I had to come." He stayed in the doorway, longing to approach her and hold her in his arms, yet uncertain what to do in such a situation. When his mother birthed children, his father stayed away from her tent for at least a month, and Dinah's birth kept him away two months. Judah didn't understand why his father thought this important, but like the covenant of circumcision, he tried to keep the traditions he knew.

"What's happened?" Kaella's voice drew him out of his musings.

He took one step closer and held out his hands to her. "I have news. It is not good."

Her face paled. "Tell me."

He swallowed the lump in his throat, still unable to process what had happened. "Your father . . . he was with the sheep and tried to retrieve a lamb from the mouth of a lion. The lion tore his shoulder. He lost much blood."

Silence fell between them as she stared at him as if unable to accept his words. "Yet he lives?"

Judah nodded. "A physician attended him and he sleeps, but there is little hope he will recover."

Shock seemed to paralyze her for a moment, then she leaned against her cushions and closed her eyes. Onan nursed at her breast, and she leaned close and kissed his forehead. She looked up and met Judah's gaze. "I must go to him."

"You just gave birth. You should not go out yet." Judah crossed his arms and gave her a concerned look, but her eyes suddenly sparked anger.

She sat up. "If my father is dying, right or wrong, I am going to see him before it is too late."

Onan pulled away and began to cry at their raised voices. Kaella stood and walked with him, patting his back. Judah took a step closer to the door. He looked on helplessly as the baby's cry grew louder. He left the tent, uncertain what to do. Did he have a right to keep her from leaving her tent when her need to do so was so great? How would he keep her home when he took the sheep to the fields?

He walked with weighted steps to his tent, letting the flap close behind him. He should light a lamp, but he had no desire for light. His world had just shifted, and he wasn't sure how to go on. Shua was more than his father-in-law. He was a business partner and friend. His loss would mean Judah would be forced to work with his brothers-in-law along with Hirah. He had no choice but to do so until he had earned enough profit to have a flock that was his alone.

He sank onto the cushions and thought of many different ways they could divide the responsibilities. He must make sure his brothers-in-law did not try to cut him out of the profits he had worked so hard to earn, much like his grandfather Laban had cheated his father out of his earnings year after year. Judah would not let that happen to him.

ᴜᴜᴜ

EGYPT

Joseph stood at the head of the first wheat field and watched as the servants began harvesting the crop. This time there were no tares in the crop. Potiphar's investigation into the matter had found the servant who had betrayed him, and the man had been swiftly executed. Memories of that ordeal during his first year in Egypt still caused a hint of fear to rise in Joseph whenever he was forced to bring bad news to Potiphar. Thankfully, bad news was a rare occurrence since God had begun to bless the work of his hands.

A threshing floor stood on a rise to the west of the fields, and once the men had finished the harvest and threshed the grain, Joseph expected a great yield. Potiphar would be pleased.

Satisfied that the work was well in hand, Joseph turned and walked back to the house. Potiphar met him at the top of the stairs.

"My lord," Joseph said, bowing low. He rose and faced his master as Potiphar took a moment to look over his fields.

"All goes well?" Potiphar rarely asked such questions, but this time concern etched his brow.

"Yes, my lord. I will keep watch on their progress, but for now all is well." Joseph briefly placed a hand over his heart.

"Good." Potiphar's gaze shifted to Joseph. "I'm going north with my men to settle an uprising. I am leaving you in charge of everything, as always. This time you will also check on the prison. Make sure the chief jailer, Joba, has everything he needs.

The servants who don't obey you, take to the prison until I can return and assess the situation." He paused a moment and glanced behind Joseph. When he seemed satisfied that no one was about, he leaned closer. "Ignore my wife, should you come into contact with her. Ignore anything she does or anyone she invites to visit. If you see her doing anything she shouldn't, you can give me a full report when I return." He rubbed a hand along his jaw.

Joseph nodded, surprised at this personal request. Aneksi, Potiphar's wife, was not someone Joseph often saw. Other servants had gone to her rooms, but she rarely left the suite of rooms Potiphar had built for her. Why would Potiphar suddenly take an interest in what his wife might do or whom she might entertain?

"Of course, my lord," Joseph said. "I will do everything you have said."

Potiphar did not smile, as smiling was not in his character, but his lips twitched as though he wanted to. "I knew I could count on you. Don't make me regret my decision to do so."

"I won't." Joseph watched the man turn on his heel and walk away. He was used to being in charge of the household, but these added duties made him the most powerful man in Potiphar's house. Was this part of the fulfillment of his dreams? Had God put him here to have Potiphar's servants and not his brothers bow to him?

He shook his head as he moved to his table of accounts, certain he was mistaken. The dreams were simply the working of an overanxious mind—one that wanted connection to his brothers. And maybe he had also wanted to hold something over them because of the way they had always treated him. The dreams were just selfish longings of a foolish young man's heart. His life here was not the life of a ruler. He was still a slave, high-standing or not. He would do well to remember that fact.

18

1833 BC

Joseph startled awake and sat up in his bed. He blinked in the darkness, a sliver of the moon still visible. Another season of fruitful harvest had made Potiphar so completely at ease with his work that he seemed to care only for the food that went into his mouth. His closeness to Aneksi had obviously diminished. Yet Potiphar continued to succeed.

The thought faded as another hit him. He slid to the edge of the bed and put his feet on the tile floor. A servant would come to dress him, but Joseph did not wait for him or for dawn to fully rise. Today would have included a big celebration in his father's house now that he was twenty-five years old. Full manhood and perhaps a wife would be his, and he could have taken his rightful place in charge of all his father's affairs.

But he'd been a slave in Egypt instead for eight years.

That reality, along with missing his father—did he still live?— and Benjamin, who would be nine by now, caused a deep ache in his gut. Did Dinah still watch over his brother? Did Benjamin go to the fields with Leah's sons to learn the ways of a shepherd, or did his father keep him close to home? The boy was still young, but not so young that he couldn't learn.

The food quietly left by a servant suddenly held no appeal to Joseph. He looked over the room, knowing that he should be grateful for what he had here. But how hard it was to praise God when the very things he loved the most had been ripped from his hands.

He brushed an unexpected tear from his eye and left the room. A deep breath of the warm Egyptian air did little to help other than remind him that he was alive. God must have a reason for allowing this to happen. And if God allowed it, surely He would use it for Joseph's good.

He moved slowly about the large palace complex, almost longing for a dip in one of the many lotus pools Potiphar kept. Birdsong welcomed the dawn, and the rustle of palm leaves sounded high above him.

"My lord." Hamid interrupted Joseph's musings. He climbed the steps from the servants' quarters, where he remained in charge of the other servants. "How are you this fine morn?"

Joseph smiled. "Warm, as usual this time of year. I am not sure I will ever be used to Egypt's heat, but at least we know what to expect."

"I wonder if you have your assignments for me." Hamid lowered his head, and Joseph again felt that Hamid belonged in this position, not him. Why had he been chosen?

"I thought we could inspect the prison together today. Potiphar likes a monthly check on conditions there. I could use your help." Joseph wasn't sure he wanted the company, but he decided he could use the distraction.

"I would be glad to help, my lord. Thank you." Hamid's smile warmed Joseph.

They walked together through the main halls of the estate

toward the back of the large lot that housed Potiphar's many buildings. The king's prison was a long walk from Potiphar's estate, but the path was worn from constant use.

They moved in silence, though Joseph felt Hamid glance his way now and then as if he wanted to speak but did not know what to say. Joseph's mind could not stop focusing on his family.

As the view of the prison came into sharper focus, Hamid spoke. "You are quiet today, my lord. Does something trouble you?"

Joseph looked at Hamid for a brief moment. "I am well. There is nothing wrong." He heard the lie on his tongue and immediately regretted it. "That's not entirely true." He stopped walking to face Hamid. "Today in my hometown among my family, we would be celebrating the day of my birth. I was reminded of the date and began to wonder how they fare." He swallowed and looked beyond Hamid. "Even after eight years, I miss them."

Hamid's expression held sympathy. "Of course you do. I did not know. You are right to grieve, just so the master does not know it."

Joseph had heard the same warning since the first day he arrived here. He wondered why Potiphar cared nothing for where his servants and slaves had come from. But Potiphar seemed concerned only with his own needs. Why would he concern himself with the stories of other people?

Joseph turned and walked on. "It does little good to grieve. I will soon forget again. Now come, let us see what the prison master needs and inspect the places where the prisoners are kept." Potiphar would want those places clean. Other prisons might be foul pits, but the king's prisoners were not treated the same.

Hamid nodded. They entered the low door of the prison,

where the chief prison master, Joba, met them, and Joseph explained why they had come. For the next hour, he and Hamid moved through the large building, Joseph putting to memory the things he saw.

The place was dark, and the prisoners, though they were given food and water and a clean mat to lie upon, could do little during the day without more light to see. More lamps were needed, and after securing one from Joba, Joseph saw that the floors were in need of sweeping. He gave the necessary commands and left with Hamid.

"I would not like to live in such conditions," Joseph said, running a hand over his face.

"Nor I," Hamid agreed.

They walked back toward the house, Joseph more troubled than he had been, not only by what he had seen but by the memories of home that again assaulted him. He had to stop thinking of home. He couldn't go back, at least not now. Perhaps someday Potiphar could be persuaded to allow him to leave Egypt.

ᒐᒐᒐ

CANAAN

Judah kissed Kaella and patted the heads of his three sons, Er, Onan, and Shelah. Three boys in his eight years of marriage, and he wondered at the toll their births had taken on his wife, for she no longer seemed to want children. She pushed him away when he needed her, as if she feared another pregnancy.

"I will take Er to the fields with me tomorrow," he told her as he walked toward the tent door. "He is seven now, and though he's young, he can learn how to treat the sheep."

Kaella bristled at his words. "My father died because of those animals. I won't have my sons put in danger."

Judah stared at her, though he should not have been surprised by her anger. She still grieved her father's death though it had been many years ago, and she barely tolerated the mention of sheep, even though the profession of shepherd had been in their family for generations. Kaella had never been completely consolable after her father's loss, and Judah did not know what to do with her.

"You can't actually expect our sons to learn no trade," he said, keeping his voice low. She could not hold their sons back or keep them from learning because of fear.

"They can learn to be potters or something else. Something safe." Her arms crossed like a shield between them.

"I am a shepherd, Kaella. I own large flocks of sheep and goats, and I will not pass them on to a stranger when I go the way of all the earth. Or would you rather I give them to Hirah?"

Her relationship to Hirah had also confused him. They had been betrothed as children but had broken the relationship as they matured. Still, though Hirah was married with a family of his own, Kaella sometimes acted too friendly with him and other times looked upon him with disdain. Judah had wondered how to broach the subject with her, but every time he tried, she turned away and refused to answer him. He'd walked away in disgust.

But these were his children, and she was not going to pamper them and keep them from learning the ways of men.

"Well, they will have to wait until they are much older and strong enough to kill any predator," Kaella said. "Er is not even able to wield a sling or handle a small sword. I will not put him in such danger. Even with you watching him." She stood firm, both feet planted as if she would defend her sons against their own father. He wasn't a beast who would hurt his children!

His cheeks burned, and he fought his rising anger. "They

will come with me when I say they will. I will not let you shield our sons from proper work at the right age to begin to learn."

She glared at him but said nothing.

"Seven is old enough to handle a sling." Tamping down his indignation, he whirled about and stormed out of the tent.

His wife was becoming more frustrating by the day. Since Shelah's birth, she had taken to visiting her mother often, when she should be at home caring for her family's needs. But what was a man supposed to do about that?

As he approached the sheep pens, he saw Hirah calling his sheep in the adjoining field. He couldn't discuss this with his friend as he once had. He waved in greeting, opened the door to the pen that housed his flocks, and called each one to follow him. He would go to a different pasture than Hirah, as they rarely found a valley large enough for their many animals.

He noticed Hirah's sons in the distance, already leading some of the goats in the opposite direction of Judah's animals. He released a deep sigh. In times like this, he often missed his brothers and the camaraderie they'd shared as they worked together. He even missed his mother and father and especially Dinah. But with the memories of his family, Joseph's face always filled his mind, and with that came a deep sense of guilt. He could not bear the guilt.

Shaking his head, he barked at the sheep to move them along. He didn't need solitude, he needed distraction. But he doubted being alone with his sheep would give him much of that.

19

EGYPT

The sun had begun its descent toward its midafternoon spot in the cloudless blue sky. Joseph had worked alone today and now climbed the steps to his station in Potiphar's house. The house servants seemed to be elsewhere, except for a few of the men who kept the artifacts polished and the floors free of dusty footprints.

He drew in a breath, his mind whirling with the state of the crops and the things he would record for Potiphar, though the man had come to trust him so much that Joseph wondered if he even looked at the records. Nevertheless, he would do his work and hopefully be found blameless should anyone ever question him.

He picked up a reed, dipped it in black ink, and began recording the state of the wheat. The crop had more than doubled in the years it had been under his care. A surprising sense of gratitude filled him at the thought. Only by God's blessing could Potiphar's crops have done so well and his animals remained so healthy. Even the cattle had multiplied since Joseph had taught the servants to vary their grazing areas. Everything he touched seemed to increase in his hands.

He did not care as much that Potiphar noticed, though his favor had allowed Joseph many freedoms. He cared far more about pleasing his God, for he knew now that God was with him even though his father was not. He had not abandoned Joseph in this foreign land.

Footsteps interrupted his musings, and he looked up, expecting to see Hamid, who often stopped to talk with him or give him a report on something. To his surprise and alarm, Aneksi, Potiphar's wife, approached. Her sheer robe was draped low over one arm, exposing her shoulder, and her white tunic revealed too much of her female form. She tilted her head and looked at him with an expression he had never seen. And yet he knew it was seductive. His heart skipped a beat.

"Can I help you, my lady?" He pushed his chair farther from her and stood, keeping the table between them.

She leaned closer, and Joseph's face heated. He could almost feel her breath. "You can do much to help me, dear Joseph." Her voice reminded him of the purr of a large cat, and he imagined a lion ready to pounce on him.

He straightened and backed farther away. "Tell me how, then," he said, knowing he had at last become her object of desire. Had she tired of everyone else? If only Potiphar had been enough for her.

Her tone turned demanding. "Come and sleep with me."

He stared at her, his mind whirling, as he sent a silent prayer heavenward. *Help me, Adonai.* The prayer seemed to give him strength, and he knew no matter what happened to him, he could never go against the laws of his God.

"Look," he said, "my master trusts me with everything in his entire household. No one here has more authority than I do. He has held back nothing from me except you, because you are his wife. How could I do such a wicked thing? It would be a great sin against God."

She reeled back as though he had struck her. "A sin against god? Which god?" She laughed, but the sound held no humor. "I have given you an order, Joseph. Do you really think my husband cares what I do with my time or whom I sleep with? He is never home and doesn't care. I do what I please and I get what I want. And I want *you*!" She reached out as if to grab him, but he stepped back again until he was on the other side of the table and could flee to the fields if he needed to.

"I'm sorry, my lady. My God would be offended if I took another man's wife. It would be my sin, and I cannot sin against my God." He held back the fact that she was also a sinner, an adulterous woman whom God would likely punish one day if she did not repent. He did not want to raise her ire. She was a danger to him here, and he now realized just how much.

"You put too much faith in the gods," she said. "No god has ever punished me for what I do. I suffer no malady other than disinterest from my *husband*, who cares more for his work and his food than his wife!" She leaned closer. "Do not ever accuse me of sinning against some *god*! I have every right to live my life the way I want to, and no servant is going to tell me otherwise." She had lowered her voice to a mere whisper, but every syllable held menace.

Joseph held her gaze. She glared at him, but then in an instant her features changed and she returned to the seductress she had been.

She pointed a finger at him. "You will change your mind. You will see." Her chin tipped up, and she whirled about and left him, heading toward her rooms.

Joseph watched her go and didn't release a breath until she

was out of sight. He glanced about, but the servants who had been cleaning the house had disappeared. He was blessedly alone. Yet he did not feel safe. He would need to keep his guard up in this place.

ᴜᴜᴜ

CANAAN

Judah led his family toward Hirah's home, passing the golden wheat fields and carrying a young goat in his arms. Hirah had planned a great feast for everyone from the town of Kezib where they lived, not far from Adullam. Kaella came behind him holding Shelah's hand, while Er carried a basket of food. Onan kicked at stones along the path. The celebration was an annual one to a Canaanite god, and Judah realized the closer they came that this could be the exact thing he needed to remove his guilt. The gods of Canaan did not fault a man for standing up for his rights. Was there a gift he ought to give to cover murder? Had Joseph died on the trip to Egypt?

He couldn't know that, but he still fought the fact that it was he who had suggested Joseph's sale into slavery. He simply had to get over this constant battle in his heart.

The sounds of a large crowd grew louder, and soon they were surrounded by nearly the entire village. Kaella took Shelah and joined the women who were preparing the food while Er and Onan ran off to join the young children. Judah joined Hirah and Shua's sons and sons-in-law.

"This is going to be a good day," Hirah said, patting Judah on the back. "Once the food is almost ready, we will offer the sacrifice to Molech and then feast the night away." He laughed, and the other men joined in.

Judah smiled, but laughter would not come. Molech. Why had he expected it to be any other god?

"One day you must join us in offering to Molech, my friend," Hirah said, placing an arm about Judah's shoulders. "Usually we give the firstborn, but perhaps your next child."

Judah shrugged away from Hirah's touch and stared at his friend. "You know that I worship the God of Israel. I will not offer one of my sons on Molech's altar."

Hirah took a step back, assessing Judah. "Is it your father's god you worship, or has Kaella convinced you she would not abide losing a child as she lost her brother?"

Judah flinched.

Hirah smiled. "She has not told you then. It is why we never married, my friend. I believe in the sacrifices and she does not. She was close to her brother as a child and was inconsolable, even though her father implored her to understand. I'm surprised after all these years that you did not know." He slapped Judah on the shoulder. "Never mind. Come and enjoy our festivities anyway. Perhaps you will change your thinking."

Hirah moved away, and Judah stared at his retreating back, dumbstruck. Shua had sacrificed Kaella's brother to Molech, one of the most prominent and ruthless gods of the Canaanites? How could she even want to come to these celebrations then? Why had she never told him?

Judah looked about at the faces of the men all standing in groups, talking and laughing as if nothing momentous was about to happen. Which one of these men would be giving up a child to the bronze arms of the god? Did they not care to lose a child?

A feeling of revulsion swept through him, and he slipped away from his friend and brothers-in-law and moved through the group, listening. He searched faces but could not find even one man among them who seemed distressed with the upcoming offering. Why had he ever thought a foreign god could help him? Must he sacrifice his firstborn for the sake of his sin? How would killing Er bring Joseph back?

His father's God had never commanded child sacrifice. Even the test Abraham had undergone when asked to offer Isaac upon God's altar had been abruptly ended with the shout of God. Their God, Jacob had said, would never abide a people or nation who killed another person and called it a gift to Him. And God detested the offerings of these people.

A drum began to beat, startling Judah, and the men gathered in the central courtyard. The women came from the house and remained on the outskirts of the circle. Children ran to stand behind their mothers. A solemn stillness fell over the group, as if they had done this all before and knew exactly what to expect. Judah, in all of the years he had been in Canaan, had avoided such gatherings while the children were small. But now that Shelah was old enough to come, he could no longer stay away and still remain in Hirah's good graces.

He glanced across the courtyard, spotting Kaella still holding Shelah's hand. Er and Onan stood behind her as if they were trying to hide behind her skirts.

"We have the great honor today," Hirah said, drawing Judah's attention, "of giving a great sacrifice to our god Molech. Nadeem, come forward, please."

Nadeem stepped into the center of the courtyard, carrying a newborn babe in his arms. A sob came from the women, and Judah looked in their direction. A woman about Kaella's age stood with three girls clinging to her, while she held a hand over her mouth. One of her daughters looked about Er's age, and her wide dark eyes were filled with horror. But not one of them moved to join Nadeem or try to dissuade him from what he was about to do.

"Let us go to the high place where Molech awaits us," Hirah said, turning to lead the men some distance from his house.

The women did not follow, and Judah stood torn, longing to do something to stop this but forced along by the crowd of men to follow. He glanced back as the men stepped beyond the courtyard and saw that the women had surrounded the mother and her daughters. Loud weeping began, and the chorus of their voices pierced his heart.

He moved ahead as if in a dream, and at last they approached the high place. There on a large round stone structure stood a tall bronze statue with arms reaching forward and toward the sky. A fire smoldered from the bowels of the metal beast.

Nadeem moved up the steps to the statue while the rest of the men stayed behind, waiting at the base of the high place. Judah caught a glimpse of Nadeem's tortured face, but a moment later he unbound the child, a boy, and walked forward. The child began to cry, but the man continued forward as though pushed there by an unseen hand. He placed the boy on the bronze arms, and the boy rolled into the flames, his cries silenced.

Bile rose in Judah's throat, and his head pounded as he stared, unable to pull away from the unimaginable scene. Had Nadeem just sacrificed his only son? Did every man in the group have a similar experience? Of course they did. This was Canaan, and these were their beliefs. If they could appease the gods of their people, perhaps they would be prosperous. It was a pervasive belief that swept the land where Jacob had traveled since leaving Laban. And even Laban had his household gods. Until Abraham had heard from the Almighty, no one knew any different.

But Judah knew better. He just hadn't wanted his father's God to rule his choices.

Your choices have brought you here.

The thought pressed in on him, and he felt smothered by the smoke, by these men, by all of it. Yet could he remain here and not accept their customs? Even if he didn't believe them, he could still live among them.

Hirah was wrong though. Judah would never participate in such a thing. His sons would not be brought up to believe such lies.

But as he headed back to Hirah's home and saw the food laid out and the women no longer weeping, he could not force his family to leave this celebration, though what they were celebrating he would never understand. Somehow he had to forget what he'd seen. Somehow he had to make peace with this culture yet keep his distance. That would probably mean another conversation with Kaella and with Hirah. Which would lead to confrontation.

Or he could keep his mouth shut and ignore it all. Fleeing was better than fighting.

20

SIX MONTHS LATER

Judah and Hirah walked the dusty road to the outskirts of Kezib to meet traveling merchants. Er skipped along ahead of them, continually dropping out of Judah's sight. He should have left the child with Kaella. She had spoiled him to the point that he'd become nearly incorrigible.

"He will mature," Hirah said as they approached the caravan master. "You should betroth him to a future wife, so he will know that one day he needs to become a man."

Judah shook his head, trying to keep his mind on watching Er and wondering if this caravan master was the same one who had purchased Joseph. It had been years since that awful day, but . . . could these Ishmaelite traders be the same men he'd dealt with back then?

"Did you not hear me, my friend?" Hirah interrupted his musings. "You are terribly distracted today."

Judah glanced at Hirah, then searched for Er, who had again disappeared from his sight. "Er!" he called, his voice rising. He strained to see, catching a glimpse of him too close to one of the camels. He stalked off and reached his son before the camel driver noticed him. He grabbed the boy's arm. "You are going to get hurt standing too close to these beasts! What's the matter with you? Stay with me or you will not come with me again."

Er squirmed and complained as Judah dragged him back to Hirah.

"You think this child is ready for betrothal?" Judah scoffed. "You were betrothed young and broke the contract. This boy is nowhere near ready to present to some father as a potential husband to his daughter." Judah released Er and commanded him to sit in the dirt and not move.

With a deep scowl at Judah, Er silently obeyed.

Hirah laughed softly and patted Judah's shoulder. "And fortunate for you, Kaella was free to marry you, my friend." He glanced at Er. "You make a good point, but these things are done this way in our land all the time. You could do worse if you wait. I know of a man with three daughters who might be willing to settle things early."

Judah glanced beyond Hirah and noticed a group of boys who had been at Hirah's house on that awful feast day. He touched Er's shoulder. "You may go, but do not stray from that group. And come when I call you!" Er jumped up and ran off while Judah turned his attention back to his friend. "And who is this man?"

"Nadeem. You remember him from our last feast to Molech." Hirah spoke as though the incident with Nadeem's only son should not bother the man or his family. As if Nadeem would be ready to part with another member of his family, even if it was only a daughter.

Judah opened his mouth to speak, but no words would come out. He had never been able to stop the memories, first seeing Nadeem place his son on brazen arms leading to the hunger of the flames below, then hearing Joseph's pleas for help from the pit.

He shook himself. He needed to leave this caravan of Ishmaelites. The whole place was going to drive him mad!

"You are unusually pensive today, my friend." Hirah ran a hand over the markings of a decorative jar, one of the many wares set out for purchase. "Let me set up a meeting with Nadeem. He has a daughter near Er's age. She is quite comely for a child."

Judah stroked his beard. He glanced again at Er, who was fully engaged in a game of throwing stones in an attempt to hit a tree. A copse of trees edged the area, and children often played beneath the branches.

"He is too young, but if we set a wedding for seven years from now, he will be ready. But not with Nadeem's family. I will not give my son to the daughter of a man who would kill his only son."

Hirah tilted his head and gave Judah a curious look. "My friend, nearly every man in Canaan has offered a son or daughter to Molech. You will not find one with daughters who has not."

"Then I will look elsewhere." He set his jaw as the caravan master approached.

"There is one I can think of," Hirah said. "Let me talk to him. He has many daughters."

Judah nodded. Recognition hit him the closer the Ishmaelite came. He was the man who had purchased Joseph. Judah's stomach clenched as though a fist had dealt him a hard blow.

"How may I help you?" the man said as he stopped and faced Judah and Hirah.

"I have changed my mind," Judah said, walking quickly toward Er. He should not have come. The market in town carried enough items. He had no need of balm or spices or pottery or anything else these men carried. For all they carried were memories he could not escape no matter what he did.

He called Er, who surprised him by coming at his first request. Perhaps the boy was ready to betroth to a young girl, as long as the marriage came seven years from now. But Judah wondered if even seven years was enough time to help his spoiled son mature into the man Judah hoped he would be. A man better than he was.

 unn

EGYPT

Joseph stood near the bronze fire pit that sat in front of one of Potiphar's columns, warming his hands. The air held a slight chill as the sun set, and he drew in a breath, relieved that this long, busy day was at an end. Potiphar was gone again, this time to the southern part of Egypt, due to some concern over thieves.

Joseph glanced about and noted guards posted along various pillars that bordered a grand open space. Sleeping rooms, cooking rooms, weaving rooms where the female slaves created the garments for the household, and visiting areas all opened toward this main portico.

The house was more like a small city, for Potiphar did not even bother to purchase his pottery but had a place far from the house where he employed potters to make whatever was needed. Cooks and bakers and wine tasters made Potiphar seem nearly as wealthy as Pharaoh Amenemhat III himself. Yet Joseph could tell from his limited walks through the city that the king's palace far outshone any other house.

He moved from the open fire and headed toward his rooms. The weavers' shuttles were silent now, and all of the servants had returned to their sleeping quarters away from the house. He passed Aneksi's rooms, thankfully some distance from his, and breathed a relieved sigh that the door was shut.

As he rounded a bend in the hall to his room, however, he heard laughter coming from her rooms. His curiosity was piqued as he wondered which slave she had seduced this time, but he pushed the thought out of his mind, until her door opened just as he was about to open his.

He turned back and walked stealthily along the smooth floors. He glimpsed Hamid hurriedly retreating along the wide hall, past the guards and down the steps to his rooms away from the palace.

Joseph stood watching, a feeling of sorrow overtaking him. He knew Hamid spent time with Aneksi but had never caught him leaving her rooms. Should he report this to Potiphar?

He whirled about, returned swiftly to his chamber, and shut the door. A servant greeted him, and for a moment Joseph wondered why the man stood there with his nightclothes over one arm. Nothing was right about this night. Nothing was right about anything in this place. He was not supposed to be here. *Why, Adonai?* But he had asked that question without response for too long.

"My lord, is everything all right?" the servant asked him.

Joseph mentally shook himself. "Everything is fine," he said, offering the servant a smile. "But if you do not mind, tonight I would like to dress myself."

The servant nodded, though he seemed disappointed. "Yes, my lord." He laid Joseph's garments on the bed, bowed low, then discreetly left the room. Joseph had eaten no dinner, and food was laid out on a table in one corner of the room. He looked at it as though it were some foreign thing. When had he grown accustomed to the foods of Egypt? He missed the taste of roasted lamb in a lentil stew. He missed the flatbread made by his sister's hands.

He sat on the edge of the bed and untied his sandals. He

trusted Hamid, but now he wondered if he'd been a fool to do so. Potiphar didn't seem to care whom Aneksi spent time with, so was it really his place to tell the man that his third-in-command was bedding his wife? Potiphar likely already knew in any case.

Joseph removed his cloak and hung it on a peg, then draped his tunic over another and slipped into his nightclothes. Stretching out on the bed, he placed his hands behind his head and stared at the same spot in the ceiling that reminded him faintly of the stars he loved.

The scent of the fire, the baaing of sheep, and the delightful laughter of Benjamin filled his mind, and he could not stop the tears from slipping to the pillow that cradled his head. He rarely cried. He had told himself it would do no good. All of his cries for help from the brothers who were supposed to care for him had done him no good. Egyptians considered tears to be a sign of weakness. Not to mention they would not want to mar their painted faces.

But Joseph had no need of kohl for his eyes—at least not yet. Though he dressed as an Egyptian, he did not mingle in circles where he needed to impress anyone. And still he did not allow himself to publicly express the emotion that slipped out now and then in private.

Oh Adonai, why am I here? I have no one I can truly trust. I have no friends, no wife, no place to call my own. I do not belong in a foreign land, and I miss my family, hatred and all.

He wasn't sure he meant that last part, for he could not decide which was worse—betrayal at the hands of his brothers or seduction by the master's wife. In the world he once thought good, he would have had none of this.

A bitter taste filled his mouth, but he swallowed it down and rolled onto his side. He'd been a slave in Egypt for eight years, and though he had it better than most, he was not free to go home. He was not free to choose a wife and marry. Here he was lost, forgotten, unwanted, unloved. Useful was the best he could be.

He wanted so much more.

᠋᠋᠋ᏞᏞᏞ

Potiphar returned home the following week and called Joseph into his audience chamber. On the way, Joseph passed the weaving rooms, where he glimpsed Heba, a beautiful young woman close to Joseph's age, bending over the loom. She was new to Potiphar's household, and Joseph had been unable to keep himself from feeling an attraction to her.

Of course, he could not befriend her or grow close to her. Potiphar's slaves could not marry each other, could they? What kind of life would they have? And what would happen to any children she might bear? Potiphar could sell their children, as any master could. Joseph could not live with yet another family loss.

More female slaves surrounded Heba, their looms spread in a large circle. Behind them in another part of the large space, spindles and distaffs whirled as younger slave girls spun the linen to be made into cloth.

What would happen to these women? Were they safe in Potiphar's house? Memories of Dinah's rape in Shechem those many years ago surfaced. That coupled with Hamid's liaison with Aneksi, and he couldn't help but wonder what would happen to the beautiful Heba.

He shook his head, reminding himself it was not his concern, then hurried past the rooms before she could look up and see him. Potiphar sat waiting on his raised dais as Joseph entered the ornate chamber moments later and bowed before his master.

"Joseph," Potiphar said as Joseph straightened to meet his gaze, "tell me—how have things fared while I was away?"

Joseph clasped his hands in front of him and reported all that had gone on in the fields, the household, and the prison. Potiphar nodded with interest, but his mind seemed to wander as his gaze shifted beyond Joseph. Was someone else waiting in the chamber? Joseph did not turn to look.

Potiphar returned his attention to him when he had finished and asked, "And what of my wife?"

Joseph had not expected this. Normally Potiphar did not concern himself with Aneksi, so why ask about her now?

"I'm not sure what you mean, my lord. She has been here as always. She remains mostly in her rooms as far as I can tell. I am not always in the house to know." Joseph fought the desire to twist his belt.

Potiphar nodded again. "No doubt she has had visitors while you were not near to see."

Joseph swallowed. He did not want to give away Hamid's secret and silently prayed that he would not have to. "It is possible, yes," he said at last.

Potiphar studied him. "You are an honest man, Joseph. I trust you with everything, even with my wife because I know you are the one person she cannot have because you will not allow it."

How Potiphar could know this or even address the subject caught Joseph off guard. "Yes, sir. You can most assuredly trust me. I would never do something so offensive to you or to my God."

Potiphar leaned away from him and rubbed his chin. "You have never spoken of your god."

"It was not a subject to discuss until now." Joseph's heartbeat quickened as he watched this powerful warrior sitting there with his sword at his side, dressed in his military garb, one eye twitching.

"This god you worship. Which one is it? We have many gods here, and I am glad to know that you believe as we do." Potiphar smiled, showing the deep lines along his mouth. This man had known a hard life despite his wealth.

"If I may explain freely?" Joseph asked, silently praying for wisdom. How much should he tell of his past? Hamid had warned him to keep his history to himself. Adonai was part of that history. He glanced at his feet, then met Potiphar's gaze once more.

"Yes, please. I wish to know." Potiphar intertwined his fingers and rested them under his chin.

"I believe in Adonai, the Creator God. He alone is God, and I ascribe allegiance to no other god." He bowed. "He forbids me to take a woman that is another man's wife, so you can be certain I will never betray you."

Potiphar's look grew intense, but a moment later he nodded. "This is good. I knew I could trust you."

Joseph thought the conversation at an end until Potiphar cleared his throat. "Would your god hold it against me if I took another woman who is not my wife? I ignore Aneksi's actions because her father is a priest of Neper. If I brought charges against her . . ." He leaned closer and lowered his voice. "Let's just say that she comes from a powerful family. She married a powerful man, but the priests hold more sway with the pharaoh than his guards do—even a guard such as I."

It was more than Joseph ever expected to hear him say, and he wasn't sure how to answer. *Adonai?* "I understand your concern. It is unfortunate that your wife feels the desire for anyone other than you, my lord." Had he said the right thing?

"So for me to take one of the slave girls to my bed would be no different than what she has done to me." Potiphar looked beyond Joseph again, and Joseph did not know if he expected a response. What slave girl did he have in mind?

"Would your wife's father cause you trouble if she found out, my lord?" Joseph asked, suddenly fearing that the woman he wanted was Heba. The very girl Joseph felt protective of, though he had no reason to feel thus.

Potiphar startled at the question. He glanced down, then looked over the room as if wanting an answer from its decor. "I do not think her father can say a word against me when I can prove to him that his daughter is less than faithful to me." He spoke with a hint of anger.

Words failed Joseph. He could not condone the man committing adultery simply because his wife did. And though his own father had married several women, Joseph knew from his grandfather that in the beginning God had not designed marriage to include many wives or many husbands. One man and one woman, Isaac had taught him, was what God always intended. But how could he explain that to this foreign man?

"But you are right," Potiphar said, interrupting his thoughts. "This is something I must give consideration to. My reputation matters more than hers does. Still . . ." He looked away, his mind obviously churning.

"Perhaps think on it, my lord," Joseph said, not certain how far he should push the man.

"Yes." He looked once more into Joseph's eyes. "I will think on it. You are dismissed."

Joseph left the audience hall, his thoughts whirling. Potiphar had never seemed the type to seduce a slave. Was Heba's presence the difference? Why would such a comely woman be sold into slavery?

Perhaps for reasons not so different from his own.

He passed the weaving rooms without a glance inside. He couldn't risk his feelings or his fears for Heba or any other woman in the house. Potiphar had an unwritten rule to protect his servants. But what if that had all changed? What should he do then?

21

Two days later Joseph met Hamid in the fields to inspect the grape harvest. Servants worked the rows, pulling the grapes from the vines and dropping them into wooden buckets to be pressed into wine.

"Things are going well, my lord," Hamid said as he approached Joseph and bowed slightly.

Joseph nodded and walked with Hamid over the length of the vineyards. "I want to speak with you, Hamid," he said. "Come with me to a quieter place." He motioned to the edge of the field where no workers stood and no one could see them behind a copse of trees.

Hamid followed.

Joseph drew in a slow breath and released it, searching Hamid's face. "I saw you the other night coming from Aneksi's rooms." He paused, letting the meaning of his words sink in.

Hamid's eyes widened. He looked down and moved the dirt with his toe. "You knew of our relationship years ago, my lord. Did I not tell you this was likely why Potiphar chose you over me when he made you overseer so soon?"

"You did. And I have often wondered if you have resented my

168

position." Joseph clasped his hands behind his back, straightening to his full height.

Hamid shook his head. "No, my lord. I do not resent your good fortune. As I told you once before, everyone knows your god has blessed you and Potiphar's house because of you."

Joseph nodded. "I wonder if my God will also bless me with your friendship, Hamid. If you do not resent me, that is. I would like to think we could befriend one another."

"Of course, my lord. You honor me to ask." Hamid smiled.

"Then return to calling me Joseph. I did not tell Potiphar of your liaison with Aneksi, though he asked if she had visitors. I did not mention your name, but if he ever asks me outright, I cannot lie."

Hamid nodded. "I will be more discreet then." He cleared his throat. "Thank you for keeping our secret. She is impossible to resist, and I fear she will have me killed if I ever refuse her. Though . . ." He paused. "It is you she really wants."

Joseph had sensed this was true, for she had now attempted to seduce him on several occasions. He had managed to slip away from her and stay out of her area of the house as often as he could.

"I am aware of her desires. But I cannot give in to them." He looked beyond Hamid for a long moment, suddenly longing for home and wishing this trial and temptation had never arisen. "Can I still trust you, Hamid?" Joseph held his gaze.

Hamid's expression softened, reminding Joseph of the man who had befriended him from the start. "I must be loyal to the master, as must you, but there is no reason we cannot share a bond as we began to when you first came here. You can trust me."

Joseph allowed a small smile. "I would like a friend in this foreign place." He would also like to know that should God ever get him out of Egypt, perhaps Hamid could return to Hebron with him and be free as well.

"You have my friendship and my allegiance as much as we both can give," Hamid said.

Joseph touched Hamid's shoulder. "Thank you. And I will keep your confidence. Perhaps Aneksi will stop pursuing me as long as she seems pleased with you. Though I wish Potiphar would give his affection to her so she does not sin with other men."

Hamid gave him a curious look. "Sin? Do you think of me as one who sins then?"

Joseph swallowed, wishing back the words. He had spoken the truth, but had he just undone what he was trying to do? "We are all sinners in the eyes of my God. If you could avoid her, she would remain guilty, but you could stop. My God values turning from sin to Him."

Hamid shook his head, then offered Joseph a smile. "I cannot stop her now, Joseph. I guess I will simply die a sinner then."

They walked back to the vineyards to inspect the progress, but Joseph's heart was heavy. How he would love to convince Hamid to believe in and obey the true God, the Creator God. But Egypt had no real concept of sin—only ways to appease the various gods they worshiped. They had no idea how great was the God they denied and did not know.

Perhaps one day they would see.

⊔⊓⊔

CANAAN, 1831 BC

Judah gently prodded a straying lamb with his staff, encouraging her to rejoin the flock. Er and Onan worked with him, but too often Judah had to remind them to watch the animals rather than run off to play. They were not yet men, but at nearly ten years old, Er was definitely old enough to be responsible. Judah had watched entire flocks on his own by that age.

Kaella had continued to spoil their sons, and though he tried, he was unable to undo her influence, especially when she fought against him in front of them. A deep sigh filled his chest. Perhaps Hirah had been right. Might it be time to choose a bride for Er to marry when he turned fifteen or sixteen? The young girl Tamar had caught his attention at the last feast. She was not Nadeem's daughter but that of another man with seven daughters he must find husbands for.

He rolled the thought over in his mind, his gaze moving from the sheep to his sons. Er was tall for his age, and sometimes Judah had to remind himself that he was still a child. But he also couldn't deny the fact that sometimes fathers arranged marriages far in advance of the actual wedding.

Did Er have an interest in girls yet? Should he ask the boy's opinion of Tamar before making the decision? Judah balked at that thought. Er would have to accept his choice for him whether he liked it or not.

Yes. It was a good plan. He hadn't been ready to admit Hirah was right a year ago, but if Judah secured the boy's future, he would have a sense of rightness . . . and ease. If anything happened to him, he wanted Er to have a good woman to marry.

Judah led the flock toward a brook to drink, all the while making plans on how to request such a thing of Tamar's father. And to convince Er this was a good choice.

ᴌᴍᴌ

The next evening, Judah closed the sheep in their pens and headed south toward the home of the young Tamar. Hirah had agreed to meet him there, though Judah had yet to tell Kaella what he intended to do. She had no way to stop him or to go against his choice. True, most men consulted their wives in such matters, but Judah was weary of fighting with Kaella, and this time he would make the decision.

The glow of the setting sun lit his way. The house was not far, and he lifted his head to see Hirah walking toward him.

"Are you sure you are ready for this?" Hirah asked, nodding in the direction of Tamar's house.

"It was your idea. Why would you ask me if I have doubts?" Judah fought a sense of irritation.

"I simply want you to be sure. Yassib has many daughters. True, Tamar is closer to Er's age, but she is older. I believe she is thirteen and could wed a man who wants her now. You might consider taking one of the younger daughters, that's all." Hirah lifted a brow, watching him closely.

Judah slapped Hirah on the back. "If you have known this, why did you not tell me sooner?" He scratched the back of his neck and faced away from his friend. Was he doing the right thing? He should have asked Kaella, but something in him still fought the idea. He lifted his chest and turned back to face Hirah. "Tamar is the one I will request. If Yassib denies me, then we will know." He walked on, Hirah at his heels, silent.

They came to Yassib's house and heard many female voices coming from within. Judah glanced at Hirah, who simply smiled.

Judah knocked on the door. Hurried footsteps came from inside, as if all of the women had run off to escape him. He knocked again and called, "Yassib! It is Judah ben Jacob."

The door opened, and Yassib stood in the entry. "Judah! And Hirah! What brings you to my humble home this night? Please come in."

The two followed Yassib and removed their sandals. A ser-

JILL EILEEN SMITH

vant hurried to wash their feet, then Yassib led them to a sitting room.

"Now, tell me why you have come," he said after they were settled on plush cushions. This man, though he had no sons, was wealthy enough to have a servant and such furnishings? How much would he want in payment for his daughter?

"I have come to seek an alliance with you—a betrothal of my oldest son, Er, to your daughter Tamar," Judah said, hands clasped on his knees.

Yassib studied him. "Your son Er is still a boy, not a man. My Tamar is young but is old enough to wed."

Judah nodded. "True. They are three years apart in age, but many girls wait until they are fifteen to marry. Could she not also wait a little longer until Er is ready?"

Yassib looked as if the request was absurd to him. "How ready?"

"I thought in five years, when he is fifteen." Judah's hands grew clammy as he looked at himself the way this man undoubtedly looked at him. He was a fool to think such a thing would be good. He should have consulted Kaella.

Yassib stroked his lengthy beard. "How much are you willing to pay to secure my daughter for so long a time?"

Judah hid a smile. The man was not so against an agreement as he had thought. "What do you require for her?" he asked.

Yassib glanced from Hirah to him, then back to Hirah. "And you are in agreement with Judah? Or are you here to convince him against it?"

Hirah lifted both hands in a gesture of ignorance. "I only told Judah that you had many daughters and that perhaps you would like having one betrothed soon. It may be hard to find so many men once they are all of marriageable age."

"I have already betrothed two of them, and another has

approached me about Tamar, though I have not given him a response yet." Yassib drew a hand over his dark, bushy beard and looked at something beyond Judah. "And yet, I find your suggestion reasonable. If you will pay me each year that she waits your two best ewes and your finest male goat, then I think we can arrange something."

Judah covered his mouth with one hand as he pondered the man's request. At last he nodded and smiled. "It is a reasonable request." Though he would lose his best mating animals for at least five years, he had secured a wife for his son, and that mattered more. "I agree. Let there be a contract between us, and when the time is right, I will send Er for Tamar."

Yassib took a cup of wine his wife offered him, as did Judah and Hirah. The woman had slipped in unnoticed and disappeared to a back room as quickly as she had come. Kaella would hear the news from these women if he did not hurry and tell her first.

"Bring your seal, and we will stamp the ketubah I have had waiting for her betrothal." Yassib set the goblet on a low table and stood. Judah followed, while Hirah remained to the side to witness the event.

Yassib pulled a leather scroll from a niche in the wall and unrolled it on another low table. He lifted a lamp so Judah could read it. Yassib added the agreement of ewes and goat as payment for waiting, then both men affixed their seals to the thin leather.

"It is done," Yassib said, reaching for Judah's shoulders and pulling him into an embrace. Both men kissed each other's cheeks and laughed and said all of the welcoming words Judah had heard when he wed Kaella.

"Five years," Judah said. "Our family looks forward to the day when we can fulfill this contract."

"As does ours," Yassib said.

They spoke a little longer, then Judah suddenly felt an urgent need to return to his family and tell them the news. Kaella . . . how would she react? And Er was so young. Doubt assailed Judah. He truly hoped he didn't live to regret his decision.

22

EGYPT

Joseph moved through the halls of Potiphar's house. The sounds of many servants had dimmed as the sun began its descent. He passed the weaving rooms and glanced inside. Heba was bent over a basket, where she appeared to be arranging her threads for the next day.

Joseph paused. He had spoken to her now and then, especially since Potiphar had suggested he might take one or more of the servants to his bed as his wife did with many of the servants. Had he taken Heba?

A familiar protective feeling filled Joseph, not because he thought of a future with her anymore but because she seemed so much like Dinah in their younger days. He poked his head into the room. "Greetings, Heba."

She straightened and whirled about. At the sight of him, her tenseness seemed to flee. "My lord Joseph. I did not hear you walk by." Her dark skin flushed in the fading light of eventide.

"I did not mean to startle you." He stepped inside. "I was simply checking the rooms on my way to my own. I thought you would be at supper with the others by now." Why was she still here alone?

Heba glanced at the floor, then lifted her head, but her large, dark eyes did not meet his gaze. "I was late today. Sometimes it is best for me to wait until—" She stopped abruptly and looked beyond him.

Joseph turned to see Potiphar standing there. Joseph lowered his head in respect. "My lord. I did not hear you." He moved farther into the room, allowing the master to enter.

Potiphar remained outside the door. He shifted his gaze from Joseph to Heba. Joseph glanced at Heba as well. Her color had heightened even more, and she did not look up.

"Are you ready?" Potiphar said to Heba.

She nodded. She smoothed her hands on her tunic and walked slowly toward him. Joseph watched in despair as Potiphar took the young woman's hand in his and led her toward his rooms. Joseph quietly moved to the room's entrance and watched them go. Heba said nothing as Potiphar moved his hand to the small of her back.

The feeling of falling threw Joseph off-balance. He should protect Heba. He longed to run after them and wrench her from Potiphar's hold. Instead, the helplessness he'd felt the day he was thrown into the pit resurfaced. He had no power here to stop this evil, just as surely as he could not stop Aneksi's adulterous behavior.

Feeling ill, Joseph abruptly turned back and headed toward the stairs that led to the fields. In the open air, God felt closer, and he found a secluded spot where he could watch the stars pop onto Egypt's black celestial canvas. What good was his life here? Why would God allow him to be sent to a place where men and women weren't free and were at the mercy of those who owned them? He was a prince in Israel!

But he was not. Not anymore. He was simply a slave with a high rank who had no power to help anyone. Not even a beautiful, helpless young woman who needed him.

ЛЛЛ

The next day and into the following week, Joseph could not pass the weaving rooms without a deep feeling of guilt filling him. One glance in Heba's direction and he felt the resignation and even despair emanating from her. He did not stop to speak with her. What could he possibly say to make things right? This was worse than Dinah's situation when Shechem raped her. This was unstoppable abuse from a powerful man. At least Dinah had had a way out, even if it was brought about in the wrong way. Their father could have saved her.

But he can't save you. The thought caused him to stop near the steps leading to his work area. He stared at the wide steps and toward the room filled with papyrus and numerous records he kept for Potiphar.

A sigh escaped. The heavy weight that had landed on him the night he discovered Heba's plight would not abate. But that could not stop him from doing his work. He drew in a breath and climbed the stairs. The sun stood at its midpoint in the sky, a time when the workers took a rest from the heat.

He moved into the house, where it was cooler, and sat at the table in his work area. He glanced at the work from the day before and picked up a clay tablet to record what he had seen thus far today. It gave him a small sense of relief knowing that Potiphar had left again for a few days to travel south in Egypt. At least Heba would be free of his abuse for now.

He picked up a reed utensil and wrote his findings in the hieroglyphic markings he had learned well in the years he had served here. He bent forward, intent on getting the amounts correct, and did not sense another's presence until he felt a soft touch on his shoulder.

He jerked away and pushed his chair from the table. Aneksi. She had the same look in her eyes that he'd seen more times than he could remember. Always her pleading tone was the same.

This time, however, as he glanced beyond her, he realized there was no one else working at this hour of the day. The other servants were resting on their pallets. He was alone in the house with her.

Determination filled her gaze, and she came closer. She grabbed a fistful of his cloak in her hand. "Joseph," she purred. "Come now. You have resisted me long enough."

He shook his head. "You know that I cannot do such a thing."

The coy look turned to a cunning scowl. "You cannot refuse me! Come on, sleep with me!"

Joseph would not end up like Heba or Hamid. He would not disgrace his God with this woman.

He tried to pull away, but she clung to him. He pulled harder, but she used both hands until she held half his cloak.

"You will come," she seethed, her anger palpable.

Fearing that she would pounce and push him to the floor despite his stronger frame, he tore himself from her grasp, leaving the cloak in her hands. He ran toward the servants' quarters with only his tunic on. But the cloak showed his symbol and rank. There would be no mistaking it as his, and she had it now.

As he hurried toward the fields, Aneksi's screams followed him. He stopped and turned to watch from a hidden place behind one of the servants' buildings. Her guards came rushing from other rooms. And not only her guards but all of the men who worked beneath him on Potiphar's estate. Even Hamid.

"Look!" she said. "My husband has brought this Hebrew

slave here to make fools of us! He came into my room to rape me, but I screamed. When he heard me scream, he ran outside and got away, but he left his cloak behind with me."

The men surrounding her said words he couldn't hear, as too many were talking at once.

The clamor of voices dimmed, allowing Joseph to hear Hamid clearly. "What do you want us to do, my lady?" he asked.

Had his friend spoken loudly as a warning to Joseph? Or was this friend also going to betray him?

"You are my witnesses against him. When my husband returns, I will tell him what happened. You will back up my words." Aneksi let out a bitter laugh. "Now find Joseph. He will be held in Potiphar's guardroom to wait for my husband."

"Yes, my lady," one of the guards said.

Joseph slipped toward the copse of trees out of sight of the house. Should he run and try to leave Egypt? Would Potiphar believe her? He knew Aneksi slept with the servants. He could not possibly believe such an accusation against Joseph. Could he?

Joseph sank to the earth, head in his hands. They wouldn't find him quickly. And he desperately needed time to think, to plan, to pray.

Oh, God of my fathers, come to my rescue. Save me from this evil woman who would have me betray You.

Surely God would protect him. But He had not stopped Joseph's own brothers from betraying him. Why should he expect God's help to keep him from betrayal at the hands of foreigners?

ᴜᴜᴜ

The sun sank until it rested on the edge of the horizon. Joseph stood and brushed the dust from his tunic, glancing toward the house now illumined with lamps. Potiphar would return soon. Tonight. Tomorrow. No one knew when. But Joseph had heard the servants moving through the fields and saw some near the sleeping quarters, searching from room to room.

He was well hidden here, but not so well that Hamid couldn't find him. Hamid was aware of many of Joseph's hideaways, where he came to pray or escape the pressures of being overseer. Should he find Hamid and allow him to take him to the house to await Potiphar's judgment? Or wait for Hamid to come to him?

His stomach growled, and he realized how long it had been since he had eaten. Darkness deepened, but he could not return to his rooms to sleep. Must he sleep in the dirt, nestled beneath the sycamore trees?

Heavy footfalls caught his attention as they crunched twigs. He peered from behind a tree and saw Hamid's unmistakable build illumined by the light of the moon. Defeat settled over him. He could not hide from his friend. Would Hamid help him escape if he asked him? Or should he cast himself on Potiphar's mercy?

"Joseph?" Hamid whispered, his voice closer now.

Joseph stepped into the swatch of light. "I am here."

Hamid glanced behind him and drew Joseph back into the shadows. "You know Aneksi has forced us to look for you, do you not?"

Joseph nodded. "I heard her shout her order as I fled here. She has done a great wrong, Hamid. She accosted me and grabbed my cloak until I had to let it slip from my shoulders into her hands. I could not give in to her demands to sleep with her."

Hamid took Joseph's measure. "You are a better man than I, Joseph. I could not refuse her as you have."

"Little good it will do me now," Joseph said, clasping his hands in front of him. "So what will you do?"

Hamid drew a hand along his jaw. "I would hide you and help

you slip away from here, but you know Potiphar would have my head if he found out. And Aneksi would not defend me."

"I know that. You cannot help me flee. Where would I go regardless? I have no money to take me home again. And I will not steal from Potiphar to finance such a trip." God would not want him to steal to escape, would he? Fear and confusion fell over him, and in that moment he had no idea what to do except to surrender to Hamid and wait for Potiphar. "Take me to Potiphar's guardroom," he said at last, though he still hesitated to take a step forward.

Hamid's dark brows furrowed, and he frowned, his gaze sorrowful. "If I am allowed, I will put in a good word for you," he promised.

Joseph nodded, then stepped into the light and motioned for Hamid to lead him. He would not be bound, as he had been that day when his brothers betrayed him. He would go willingly. Though he seriously doubted whether the outcome would be any different.

23

Potiphar arrived home two days later. Joseph heard the commotion through the thin walls of the room where he was being held. This small guardroom was not meant to house a prisoner, so there had been no bed to lie upon. He could not have slept even if he'd tried.

Servants moved quickly through the halls, a horde of rushing feet, until at last he heard Aneksi's whiny voice nearby. They must be in Potiphar's audience chamber, where Joseph expected to be called soon.

"What is all of this nonsense I hear from the servants?" Potiphar's voice boomed, his anger obvious. "Where is Joseph? I don't believe a word of this!"

Hope rose for a brief moment, until Joseph heard Aneksi's voice again. "You must believe me, my husband," she said. "See this cloak? Do you not recognize it? That Hebrew slave you've brought into our house tried to come in and sleep with me. But when I screamed, he ran outside, leaving his cloak with me!"

Silence followed her remark, and Joseph's heart raced with dread.

"Why should I believe you when I know you seduce the servants to your bed whenever I am gone?" His voice sounded as though he was barely containing his fury.

"Have I ever run to you with such a tale? If I have called others to my bed, it is because I wanted someone and you would not have me! But this man, this *Hebrew*, nearly forced himself on me! Why else would I have his cloak? What I might give freely to some, he would have taken by force. You cannot allow him to live, my husband. He has mocked you by mistreating me. You must do something!"

Potiphar let out a string of curses, then slammed something against the wall. "Bring Joseph to me now!"

"Yes, my lord," one of the servants said. It was not Hamid's voice Joseph heard. Was he standing near?

"You will send him to the executioner, won't you, my husband? My father would not be pleased to hear this tale." Aneksi's tone held an almost gleeful menace.

"I will decide what is to be done when I hear what Joseph has to say. Your father does not make my decisions."

"But—"

"Go! I will deal with Joseph alone."

The sound of many steps filled Joseph's ear until they drifted away and he was left with silence. A moment later the door to his inner prison opened to the light spilling from the audience chamber.

"Come," the guard said, allowing Joseph to precede him.

Joseph walked into the chamber where Potiphar sat on his raised dais. He bowed low as he usually did, waiting for Potiphar's permission to stand.

"Leave us," Potiphar shouted to the few guards who remained. "I will call you when we are finished."

The guards moved to the exits until at last all was silent.

"You may stand, Joseph." Potiphar's voice had gentled, surprising Joseph.

He stood, hands clasped in front of him, but he did not cower or lower his gaze.

"These are serious charges my wife brings against you, Joseph. And after you assured me you would never—could never—do such a thing to me. What do you have to say for yourself?" Potiphar searched his gaze.

"Would my lord have me speak truthfully?" Joseph asked, not certain Potiphar wanted to know.

"Have we ever spoken anything but truth to each other? I've trusted you with my entire household. And I know my wife. Tell me. Does she speak the truth?" Potiphar rested his arms on the seat, his expression open.

"She does not, my lord. She has come after me many times when you were away. I did not tell you because nothing came of those times. Either I slipped away from her or she turned about and returned to her rooms when I refused her. But she is persistent . . ." He paused, weighing his response.

"Go on."

Joseph cleared his throat. "It was noon, when I returned to my work to record the day's yield, that she approached me again. I was alone in the house, and though I stood and moved away from her, keeping the table between us, she came around and grabbed my cloak with both hands. She grew insistent. So much so that I knew only trouble lay ahead. I slipped away, only this time I had no choice but to leave my cloak with her, as I could not have pried her fingers from it. I ran toward the trees, but I was not far from the house when I heard her scream and call all of the male servants to tell them I had tried to force myself on her. She ordered them to find me so she could keep me confined until you returned."

Potiphar rubbed the back of his neck, looking beyond Joseph as though trying to determine what to do. "Why did you not leave? You could have fled my household and even Egypt, yet you allowed them to find you?" His brow scrunched and his eye twitched.

"Where would I go, my lord? I have no funds to pay for my escape or to return to where I come from. And when you found me, it would surely have been worse than if I stayed." Joseph forced himself to remain still, watching Potiphar.

"I believe you, Joseph. I know my wife, and I know she is lying to me. But you realize that I cannot allow you to remain in my employ. I cannot do nothing when the entire household is aware of her claims." Potiphar's expression held empathy. "But I will not have you executed. You will be confined to the king's prison on my estate. And may your god have mercy on you and release you one day, but I simply cannot." Because of Aneksi's father, no doubt.

"I understand," Joseph said. "You have a duty to uphold. Thank you for sparing my life." He bowed low again, touching his forehead to the tiles.

"You are a good man, Joseph. I deeply regret that this has happened to you."

They exchanged a look that reminded Joseph of the days when he had been in this man's favor. It was followed quickly by a look of deep sadness from Potiphar, something he rarely showed.

"Stand up," he ordered, his tone now that of master of the house. "Guards!" he shouted, and his personal guards came running to his side. "Take this man to the king's prison. Put him under the care of Joba the jailer. And send for Hamid. He will now be my second-in-command."

Potiphar stood and left the room, while the guards took

Joseph's arms and led him toward the back entrance of the house, down the steps, and across the grounds to the prison.

"We will miss you, Joseph," one guard said when they were some distance away. "We know you are innocent."

The others nodded their agreement.

"It is enough to know that you see the truth." Joseph looked at each one. "I will miss you all."

Moments later Joba met them and escorted Joseph to a small room, closed the door behind him, and locked it. Joseph's only light came from the moon shining through a window high in the wall. A window too small for any person to fit through. But at least he could see.

The prison was swept clean, and no mice or other rodents were evident. Suddenly the weight of it all hit Joseph, and he sank onto the thin mat and put his head in his hands. *Why, Adonai? What have I done to deserve such treatment? I obeyed Your laws. I served You faithfully. Yet I am here, worse off than I was when I first arrived in Egypt.*

Emotion rose within him, and silent tears fell to the earthen floor beneath him. No one wanted him. Not even his family, except Dinah and Benjamin, and his father, who probably thought him dead by now. If he didn't, he would have sent a delegation to find him. But his brothers' deceit coupled with his father's inability to think beyond grief would have caused Joseph to be forgotten.

Rejected. That was the one word that kept playing through his thoughts. His family had rejected him, and now his master had done the same. Even God seemed distant here.

Joseph removed his sandals and lay on the thin mat. Sleep was a long time in coming.

24

HEBRON, 1829 BC

Dinah walked with Benjamin to the sheep fields, sensing the boy's desire to rush ahead and be on his own. He was on the cusp of manhood at thirteen and loved to care for the animals, but their father had refused to let Benjamin go anywhere unless he or Dinah accompanied him. Dinah knew Benjamin chafed at the restrictions, but she allowed him enough leniencies that he went willingly with her nearby. She didn't particularly enjoy these treks to find her brothers, but she knew they were close today, so she had said yes when Benjamin begged to go.

"They're just over that ridge." He was two steps ahead of Dinah and glanced back so she could hear. "I'm going to run up the hill. Don't fret over me. I will wait for you." He paused long enough to see her nod her approval, and then he was out of sight.

A sigh escaped. She understood her father's need of Benjamin. He had lost everyone else connected to Rachel. His heart had become so bound up with Benjamin since Joseph's death that she often wondered if he would die if something happened to this son too.

She climbed the ridge and saw Benjamin kneeling beside one

of the lambs in Reuben's care. Reuben walked about, prodding the flock with his staff to remain in the open field. Some were so prone to wander. Like Judah, who had not shown his face or returned home since he left twelve years before.

She really should go to Adullam and search for him, tell him of the things that had gone on in the family since he'd left. Had he married? Did he have sons and daughters? No news had come and gone between them, and she ached for the chance to see him again. Aside from Joseph, Judah had been closest to her. But for all of his promises to send word, none had come, and despite Dinah's wishes, she couldn't simply wander off by herself to find him.

The desire to go, however, grew as she watched Benjamin move from one lamb to another, his gaze darting to Reuben now and then.

"Dinah," Reuben said, coming alongside her. "I wish you would convince our father to let Benjamin come with me. You know I would not allow anything to happen to him. Especially now."

She shook her head and glanced at Benjamin in the distance. "You know Father would never allow it. You travel too far to find good pastures. Benjamin could be at risk from animals."

"If he stayed by my side, he would be safe," Reuben protested, though he did not demand. They both knew his request would never come to pass.

"I think it is best that you teach him when you are close to home," Dinah said. "Father would not really want Benjamin to grow up knowing nothing about shepherding, but he cannot bear to have the boy too far from his sight."

Reuben nodded and scratched his beard, his expression filled with regret. "I wish our father trusted me, but I fear he trusts no one but you and our mother."

Dinah searched Reuben's face, pondering his expression. Her brother would always bear the mark of having provoked their father by sleeping with Bilhah, but something in his eyes told her his regret had a greater cause. Yet she did not ask him for answers. There was constant strain between all of the brothers, and she didn't want it to come between her and them as well.

"He seems so happy here," she said, pointing to Benjamin. "I wish Father would allow him to be the man he is meant to be."

"Father would die if something happened to the boy."

"He is almost a man." Dinah straightened and turned her head at the sound of someone calling in the distance. "Do you hear that?" She faced Reuben, then looked behind him. A servant rushed toward them from the direction of the camp. "Something has happened," she said, a sudden feeling of dread filling her.

Reuben seemed to sense it as well as Dinah called to Benjamin. He came to her with reluctance and arrived just as the servant did.

"Mistress Dinah," the young man said. "You must come at once."

"What has happened? Tell me." Dinah saw sorrow in the man's gaze, and her dread grew.

"Your grandfather Isaac. His servant went to bring him food for the morning meal and found that he has gone the way of all the earth. Even now the camp is in mourning, and your father has sent word to his brother Esau. He would like to get word to Judah as well, but he doesn't know where Judah has gone."

"Sabba is gone?" she asked. Isaac had lived with them a long time since their return to Hebron.

"Yes, mistress." The servant waited as if he wanted her to instruct him.

"Tell my father that we will spread the word to his sons and return to camp quickly." She turned to Reuben as the servant ran off the way he had come. "Go and tell the others to return with the flocks. And find wood to build a bier. Father will want to bury Sabba in the cave of Machpelah before nightfall." She glanced at Benjamin. "You must come with me to comfort Abba."

"Will Esau arrive so soon? It is nearly halfway to midday as it is," Reuben said. But he did not wait for her response as he hurried off to find their brothers.

Dinah and Benjamin half ran to the camp, Dinah's heart beating with sorrow. They slowed their steps as they arrived to the sound of the women weeping. They reached Isaac's tent, but the room was already filled with the wives of Jacob and other servants attending to their grandfather's body.

She looked at Benjamin. "Go to Abba. He needs you." She looked toward the fire where Jacob sat slumped forward, head in his hands.

She opened the tent flap and pushed her way inside. "I must see him," she told her mother, who was busy washing Isaac's limbs.

"You should be with your father," Leah said, but her tone held no censure.

Dinah knelt at Isaac's side, staring at his lined face. His white hair hung limp, his cheeks were sunken, and his once pink lips were tinged with blue, all evidence of life gone. A sob rose within her. "Sabba!" She touched his veined hand but recoiled at the cold fingers. She had not touched a dead body since Rachel's death, for Joseph's body had never been found.

"He has gone the way of all the earth, my daughter. One hundred and eighty years is a long life, and we should be glad of it. God gave him a good life, even if he could not see." Leah, always the practical one, gave Dinah a compassionate look. "I know how you loved him. We all did."

"Perhaps we will meet again one day." Dinah did not know what happened in the afterlife, but she had always believed that God would not abandon their souls to the grave forever. Perhaps even now Sabba could see again and was reunited with Rebekah, his only love.

"Perhaps," Leah said, her tone hopeful.

"Is there anything I can do?" Dinah could see that the women had things well in hand, but she could not just stand there and weep.

"You can go and keep watch for Esau and your brothers. Once they arrive, we will make the trip to Machpelah." Leah turned back to washing Isaac, and Dinah left the tent.

She found her father and Benjamin consoling each other near the campfire. "I'm so sorry, Abba. I know you loved him." Dinah knelt at her father's knee and touched his arm. "Will it take Uncle Esau long to get here?"

Jacob patted her hand and then held it. "I have sent my fastest riders to find him. If I know my brother at all, he will not delay."

She nodded, glancing in the direction of Edom's mountains. Was that a trail of riders coming in their direction already? "I think they may be coming."

Jacob stood, using his staff to aid him, and shaded his eyes to look toward the mountains. "Esau is swift. He will be here soon. I had warned him the time was near, so no doubt he was prepared to come."

Dinah watched the distant road. If only she could also get word to Judah. But how? She couldn't travel to Adullam or wherever he lived now to search for him. She could send a servant, but would they know where to look? And even if they found him, would he come?

She already knew the answer to that, and a feeling of defeat settled over her. No. Judah had left them with no intention of returning. Twelve years was so long. By now he could have moved even farther from where he first intended to go. And she couldn't ask it of servants to search high and low. Judah would not be able to make it home by evening for the burial in any case.

Deep sorrow filled her in that moment as she pondered all she had lost. First her innocence. Then Rachel, whom she dearly loved. Then Joseph, whose loss still brought a profound ache to her heart. Then Judah, who left for reasons he would not say. But she knew he was running from some guilt unknown to her.

And now Sabba. She felt the tears spill over her cheeks and did not try to stop them. Life was like this, she told herself, even if she didn't want to face it. Someday she would be bereft of her mother and father and even more of her brothers. And one day she too would go to the land of Sheol, where she might be reunited with her loved ones.

The realization brought some measure of comfort.

᠊᠊᠊

The cave of Machpelah was large enough to bury many family members. The bones of Dinah's great-grandfather Abraham and great-grandmother Sarah were here, along with her grandmother Rebekah. And now Sabba Isaac would rest in peace beside her.

Dinah looked about and recognized her uncle Esau standing near her father, the two of them speaking softly, while her brothers rolled the stone from the cave's entrance. She searched the crowd that had gathered, though it was hard to see well in the moonlit dark. Many carried lamps to light the way, but daylight would have made the whole ordeal easier.

She took Benjamin's hand and squeezed. Their father would not want him to get caught up in the crowd. She peered northwest beyond the trees, hoping to see Judah yet knowing it was an impossible wish. But when she started to look away, a shadow caught her eye. Or was it two people standing near the trees?

Again she searched the crowd, counting off each brother, and realized Reuben was not among those who had rolled away the stone. She lifted her gaze to the tree line again and definitely saw the silhouettes of two men. Silently she begged them to come closer, but they did not move.

Slowly, as her father and uncle said words over Isaac, she pulled Benjamin with her and made her way to the edge of the crowd, close to the trees. And then she saw him.

"Judah!" she whispered.

Judah turned, appearing startled, and Reuben placed a hand on his arm. Was he trying to keep Judah from fleeing again? Dinah hurried closer, not wanting him to slip away. In the darkness, it was hard to see the features of his face. But she knew in her heart, despite the different cut of his beard and the gray hairs near his temples, that this was her brother. She released Benjamin's hand and threw herself into his arms.

His arms came around her slowly at first, then he held her tight. "Dinah," he whispered against her ear. "How could you see me from this distance?"

"I hoped you would come. I did not expect Reuben to look for you or know where to look, but I am so glad you are here. Will you see Father before you return?" She lifted her face to read his expression.

Judah held her at arm's length. "I don't know. I had only planned to come see Grandfather laid to rest."

"Father would so love to see you. He has missed you more than you know." Dinah clutched his arm, afraid he would disappear again before she had any chance to talk to him.

Judah looked at the earth and kicked a few twigs away from

where they stood. "I don't know if I can, Dinah." He looked at her, then glanced at Benjamin. "Is this little Benjamin? You are a grown man already!"

Benjamin beamed at the praise. "I am thirteen," he said, standing tall.

"You are older than my son Er. He is twelve. Has Father betrothed you yet?" Judah seemed anxious as he asked the question.

"You know our father would wait until Benjamin is much older," Dinah said, searching his face. "Is your son already betrothed?" Er was a child, but perhaps the people of Canaan did things differently. They certainly allowed girls to marry far younger than her mother had.

"I betrothed Er to a girl two years ago. When he is fifteen, they will wed." Judah looked from Reuben to Dinah, then again at Benjamin.

"Father won't let me go out with the sheep without Dinah near," Benjamin said. "I am not ready to think of marriage."

For one so young, he seemed wiser than Judah. Why was Judah so concerned with a bride for a child?

"Please come back to the camp and stay a day or so to talk with Father. It would mean so much to him." Dinah studied every feature of his face, from his dark brows and eyes to his prominent nose and thick beard. How had they lived so long apart? *Oh, Judah, come home!*

"Dinah is right, Judah. We all miss you. Your wife and children can survive without you for a few days, can they not? And didn't you say you have a friend who is caring for your sheep?" Reuben put an arm around Judah, as though he too would not let their brother go.

Judah remained silent for a lengthy breath, looking from one to the other, then glanced in the direction of his home in

Canaan. Their father and uncle had finished speaking, and the sound of weeping began again as their brothers rolled the stone in front of the tomb, forever encasing Isaac inside.

"Please, Judah," Dinah said one more time, but she was quickly losing hope that he would do as she asked.

He faced the crowd below, but their father's back was to him. "I can't." He did not move to leave, but once the crowd turned to go back to the camp, Dinah would have to take Benjamin with them.

"But you only just arrived. Surely you could at least spend the night?" Reuben said.

Judah moved from foot to foot as Dinah glanced at the weeping crowd now retreating. "I can't," he said again. "But give Father and Mother my condolences." He turned and hurried away.

"You knew where to find him?" Dinah asked Reuben.

Reuben nodded. "We have kept in some contact when I've taken the sheep in that direction. But it is not often. I did not know about Er's betrothal."

"But you knew he has sons? How many? What is his wife's name?" He should have stayed so she could have asked him such questions.

"I think he has three sons. I can't remember his wife's name." He started walking with her to join the crowd, Benjamin in tow.

"How can you not know their names? They are family." She shook her head. Brothers!

"It's not like I saw him often. We don't chatter on like women, you know."

Dinah darted a glance at him. His face lay in shadow, half hidden by the moon.

"Humph." She would never understand men, not even these brothers who shared the same mother as her. Joseph would have asked.

The thought came so suddenly that she staggered, missing him all over again. Perhaps she was simply grieving Sabba so much that she missed Joseph as well.

She slipped her arm through the crook of Benjamin's, and together with Reuben they joined the others. She wept as the other mourners did. But she wasn't sure whom she wept for most—Sabba or Judah or Joseph or her entire fractured family.

25

EGYPT

Joseph awoke to the sound of the prison's heavy door opening and chains dragging along the floor. He rubbed sleep from his eyes and walked to the open door of his cell. Six months had passed since Potiphar had sent him to this dismal place, but at least he was allowed the freedom of coming and going from the small room where he slept.

He moved through the hall, taking a lamp from its niche to light the way. Potiphar had put him in charge of helping Joba since his first weeks in this place, for which he should be grateful. *Oh, Adonai, forgive me. I try.* But he struggled with his purpose in life.

Surely God had a reason for allowing him to take this path. Surely the God he knew, the God of his fathers, would not completely abandon him.

He reached the main door to the prison, where Potiphar stood with two men dressed in fine linen, as though they had come from a wealthy home or the king's palace. Joba emerged from his room, hurrying to Joseph's side. Both of them bowed before Potiphar.

"Joseph," Potiphar said, "these men are close officials to the pharaoh. This is HeQaib, his chief cupbearer, and Baufra, his chief baker, and they have greatly offended the king. I want you to be the one to attend them." Potiphar handed their chains to Joseph along with the key, and Joseph nodded his acceptance and led the men toward an empty cell.

"Joba," Potiphar said, "see to it that these two men are the only prisoners in Joseph's care. Once they are released or executed, you may allow Joseph to resume his normal duties for you."

"Yes, my lord," Joba said. Joseph imagined his bobbing head and clasped hands, the posture he always took in Potiphar's presence.

"Good. See that you do all that I say." Potiphar's footsteps receded, and Joseph glanced behind him at the man's retreating back.

It was rare to see Potiphar since coming here, and even more infrequently did he personally deliver new prisoners to this place. His guards usually did that for him. These men must be important indeed.

Joseph opened the door with a barred window near the top, undid the men's chains, and motioned them inside. "Tell me why you are here," he said before turning to a servant he heard passing by. "Bring fresh food for these two men. They are the king's officials."

The servant bowed and hurried away while Joseph focused again on the two men.

"I am HeQaib, chief cupbearer to Pharaoh Amenemhat III," the first man said, "and this is Baufra, Pharaoh's chief baker. Tonight as I served the king, a commotion came from the baking and cooking rooms. Someone shouted about a plot to kill the king, and suddenly more than half of the understaff were taken to the main prison while Baufra and I were brought here."

"Somehow the pharaoh thought the two of you were involved," Joseph said, easily imagining how chaotic a large group could become. He'd seen problems arise even at Potiphar's social gatherings, where the people drank too much wine and the Egyptian heat caused tempers to flare.

"Yes," HeQaib said. "Though I have no idea why I was included. Most of those who were taken to prison were from the king's bakeries."

Joseph looked from one man to the other. "I am sure the king will get to the truth, and then you will both know. Meanwhile, give me a list of your needs, and I will do my best to see that they are met. Though you are prisoners, as am I, we come from high positions, so the king's captain of the guard sees to it that we are well treated."

The men glanced at each other, then at Joseph. By their curious looks it was obvious that they had no idea who he was or the esteem the captain once had for him.

"I will tell you my story another time," he said to appease them. They both nodded, and Joseph retrieved a clay tablet and writing tool and wrote down what the men requested.

As he walked away sometime later, he pondered their story. Was the pharaoh often threatened? Were both men part of the plot? To be betrayed by those closest to him . . . was the pharaoh angry? No doubt, as Joseph himself had been. Angry. Hurt. Betrayed. Rejected.

He wished in that moment that he could comfort the pharaoh. But who would comfort him?

ꀍꀍꀍ

Joseph woke with a start to the sound of someone groaning. No, not groaning. An outright cry had awakened him. Was someone hurt? As he closed his eyes and listened, his body longing for a few more hours of sleep, he heard nothing more. Perhaps he'd had a dream?

He drew in a breath, listening. Nothing. At last he drifted to sleep again, but what seemed like only a moment later, dawn broke through his window. Had he slept at all?

Rubbing his hands over his eyes, he stifled a yawn and rose. He made his way to where water and a pitcher sat near the jailer's rooms. After scrubbing his face and grabbing a few dates to stave off his hunger, he hurried to the prison cells to check on his two prisoners. Had he truly heard a cry in the night? Had it come from them? If he had not been so weary from his work the day before, he would have risen in the night to check. Perhaps it was nothing.

He looked into the cell where HeQaib and Baufra had spent the past four months and saw that they were both sitting on their mats, legs crossed, looking worried and sad.

"Why are your faces so sad today?" Joseph asked as he unlocked the door and stepped into the room.

"We both had dreams," HeQaib said, wringing his hands, "but there is no one to interpret them."

Joseph looked from one to the other. Baufra said nothing, but he could not hide his fear. "Do not interpretations belong to God? Tell me your dreams," Joseph said. Though God had never explained his own dreams, he silently prayed that perhaps He would grant Joseph insight into theirs.

HeQaib stilled and looked into Joseph's eyes. A spark of hope replaced his sorrow. "All right. In my dream I saw a vine in front of me, and on the vine were three branches. As soon as it budded, it blossomed, and its clusters ripened into grapes. Pharaoh's cup was in my hand, and I took the grapes, squeezed them into Pharaoh's cup, and put the cup in his hand."

Joseph closed his eyes, praying again. *Adonai, please give me*

Your wisdom. What does this dream mean? He waited several breaths until peace settled over him.

"This is what it means." Joseph searched HeQaib's face, smiling. "The three branches are three days. Within three days Pharaoh will lift up your head and restore you to your position, and you will put Pharaoh's cup in his hand, just as you used to do when you were his cupbearer. But when all goes well with you, remember me and show me kindness. Mention me to Pharaoh and get me out of this prison. I was forcibly carried off from the land of the Hebrews, and even here I have done nothing to deserve being put in a dungeon."

HeQaib clapped his hands and then covered his face, laughing. He stood. "Thank you, Joseph. I will be sure to remember you to Pharaoh at the first opportunity!" He grasped Joseph's arms and kissed him on each cheek as though they were meeting for the first time. "Thank you, thank you!" He moved in a little dance about the small room while Baufra sat watching.

"Because you have given HeQaib such a favorable answer, I too will tell you my dream," Baufra said to Joseph. His expression held such hope that Joseph silently prayed he would have good news for him as well. "On my head were three baskets of bread. In the top basket were all kinds of baked goods for Pharaoh, but the birds were eating them out of the basket on my head." Baufra leaned closer, grasping Joseph's hand. "Please, what does it mean?"

Joseph felt his stomach dip. How he hated giving bad news. But he could not lie about the message he sensed from Adonai.

"This is what it means," he said. "The three baskets are three days. Within three days Pharaoh will lift off your head and impale your body on a pole. And the birds will eat away your flesh."

HeQaib stopped his happy dancing and faced Baufra. Baufra's face paled, and his body shook. In three days the man would die. Did that mean he had been found guilty, part of the plot to kill Pharaoh? He'd seemed so innocent whenever Joseph spoke to him. And HeQaib seemed to trust him too.

Baufra buried his head in his hands, his weeping growing louder by the moment. Joseph stood quietly and motioned for HeQaib to follow him. When they were outside the room, Joseph shut and locked the door. He led HeQaib to a different cell. "I do not want him to harm you in his grief," he said. "You will stay here until Pharaoh calls for you."

As he locked HeQaib in his new quarters, Joseph's own hopes rose. Perhaps the man would keep his word and speak to Pharaoh on his behalf. If Pharaoh knew the story of all that had happened to him, surely he would let him go free. Wouldn't he?

ການການ

Three days later, Joseph walked the length of the prison and back again, waiting, wondering. Had he heard God correctly? But the day was young. Perhaps they would not know until evening.

As dusk deepened, Potiphar entered the prison and met Joba near the door. "Send to me the chief cupbearer and the chief baker. Pharaoh is celebrating his birthday with a feast, and he wants both men there."

Joseph stepped out of the shadows. "I will get them." Earlier that day he had provided water and soap so the men would be cleaned and shaven just in case Pharaoh called for them, as his dream had predicted. He brought them to Potiphar, and along the way he whispered in HeQaib's ear, "Please don't forget me."

The men left the prison with Potiphar, and Joseph sank onto his mat, feeling suddenly bereft. The next day, news reached him that his interpretation of both men's dreams had come true. The baker had been executed and the cupbearer restored.

But as the weeks continued to pass and then months turned to a year, Joseph knew the cupbearer had not kept his promise to remember him.

26

1827 BC

Bright light like that of many lamps shone in Joseph's face, forcing him awake. He held a hand over his eyes as he sat up, blinking. "I'm awake! Please, remove the lamps." He squinted as Joba and a servant set the lamps in niches about the room.

"Good. You must get up quickly," Joba said, motioning for Joseph to follow him. He held a fresh tunic over one arm, and Joseph noticed the servant carried a basket of ointments and a razor.

"What is this about?" Joseph asked as he followed Joba into his personal rooms. "It is the middle of the night!"

"It is past dawn, and Pharaoh has summoned you." Joba looked him up and down. "I can't send you to Pharaoh Amenemhat III looking like a prisoner, now can I?"

The servant pulled the tunic from Joseph's head, and he blindly allowed several slaves to wash and shave the beard that had grown during his years in prison. "But why does the pharaoh ask for me?" It had been two full years since the cupbearer had been restored to work for the king, and Joseph had never been released or called during that time.

Joba pulled a fine linen tunic over Joseph's head and tied a belt at his waist, then looked him up and down. "There. You are at least presentable." He moved from his rooms and motioned Joseph to follow. "I do not know why you were called. I only know that when Potiphar tells me that Pharaoh wants you, you must go."

Potiphar stood outside the gate, where Joba halted and gently pushed Joseph forward. "Now go! Do whatever is asked of you and all will be well."

Joseph blinked, feeling as though he was in the midst of a dream, like the dreams of old when he thought the sun, moon, and stars would bow down to him. How foolish he had been as a child. How arrogant to tell those dreams to his father and brothers. What had he thought could possibly come of them?

Potiphar studied him a moment. "Jewels would have helped, a chain or something about your neck or arms, but there is no time. Come."

Joseph fell into step behind Potiphar, but Potiphar called him forward. "The king had a dream last night—two, in fact—and none of his magicians or wise men can tell him the meaning. The dreams frightened the king, and the last thing we need is a pharaoh who is afraid. Then the cupbearer told him that you had interpreted dreams for him and the baker, so that is why you are being summoned. See that you don't disappoint the king." Potiphar gave Joseph a sidelong glance. "You can interpret dreams, can't you?"

Joseph swallowed hard. "God alone knows the meaning of dreams, my lord. If He gives me their meaning, then I can tell the king what he needs to know. But I will not know that until I hear what he has to say."

"Pray your god gives you that wisdom then, or you may not live to see another day." Potiphar grew silent, and Joseph prayed as they climbed into Potiphar's chariot and he drove them to the palace.

Joseph walked through grand doors and along gleaming tiles that outshone anything in Potiphar's estate. They traveled several halls until they came to one of the king's many chambers. This one seemed small, no bigger than Potiphar's, and must be one of the king's private rooms.

Many men dressed in rich, flowing robes stood along the walls, while the king sat on a dais surrounded by attendants. His expression was troubled.

Potiphar led Joseph close to the king and bowed low. Joseph did the same.

"Rise," the pharaoh said.

"This is the man the cupbearer spoke of, my lord," Potiphar said. "He is Joseph, a Hebrew, but has lived in Egypt many years. Perhaps he can help you." Potiphar stepped back while Joseph remained, hands clasped in front of him, looking beyond the king.

"Look me in the eye, Hebrew." The pharaoh did not sound pleased.

Joseph complied.

"I had a dream, and no one can interpret it," the pharaoh began, "but I have heard it said of you that when you hear a dream you can interpret it."

Joseph again sent a silent prayer heavenward. He waited a moment, and when peace settled over him, he knew God had heard his prayer. "I cannot do it," he said, "but God will give Pharaoh the answer he desires."

Pharaoh studied Joseph as if wondering whether he should believe him, but apparently knowing he had no one else to ask, he spoke again. "In my dream I was standing on the bank of the Nile, when out of the river there came up seven cows, fat and sleek, and they grazed among the reeds. After them, seven other cows came up—scrawny and very ugly and lean. I had never seen such ugly cows in all the land of Egypt. The lean, ugly cows ate up the seven fat cows that came up first. But even after they ate them, no one could tell that they had done so. They looked just as ugly as before. Then I woke up."

Pharaoh took a deep breath, his brows drawn low. He ran a hand over his fake beard. Even this early he had dressed as king, though the kohl beneath his eyes did not mask his lack of restful sleep.

"In my next dream," he continued, "I saw seven heads of grain, full and good, growing on a single stalk. After them, seven other heads sprouted—withered and thin and scorched by the east wind. The thin heads of grain swallowed up the seven good heads. I told this to the magicians, but none of them could explain it to me."

Joseph held Pharaoh's gaze, nodding once. "The dreams of Pharaoh are one and the same. God has revealed to Pharaoh what He is about to do. The seven good cows are seven years, and the seven good heads of grain are seven years; it is one and the same dream. The seven lean, ugly cows that came up afterward are seven years, and so are the seven worthless heads of grain scorched by the east wind. They are seven years of famine."

Joseph paused a moment. Pharaoh's attention remained on him.

"It is just as I said to Pharaoh," Joseph continued. "God has shown Pharaoh what He is about to do. Seven years of great abundance are coming throughout the land of Egypt, but seven years of famine will follow them. The abundance in the land will not be remembered, because the famine that follows it will be so severe. The reason the dream was given to Pharaoh in two forms is that the matter has been firmly decided by God, and God will do it soon."

He paused again, allowing Pharaoh to interject, but the king remained silent. Joseph drew in a breath and released it. His suggestion to the king could prove wise or foolish, but he sensed God prompting him to give it.

"And now," he said, "let Pharaoh look for a discerning and wise man and put him in charge of the land of Egypt. Let Pharaoh appoint commissioners over the land to take a fifth of the harvest of Egypt during the seven years of abundance. They should collect all the food of these good years that are coming and store up the grain under the authority of Pharaoh, to be kept in the cities for food. This food should be held in reserve for the country, to be used during the seven years of famine that will come upon Egypt, so that the country may not be ruined by the famine."

Pharaoh looked to his advisors, who drew near the king's dais and nodded their heads.

"He speaks wisdom," said one.

"Yes, we agree," said another. "Who else in all of Egypt has such wisdom as this man?"

At last Pharaoh spoke to the many officials filling the room. "Can we find anyone like this man, one in whom is the spirit of God?"

Everyone nodded and murmured their agreement, and a collective sigh seemed to spread over the room.

Pharaoh smiled into Joseph's eyes. "Since God has made all this known to you, there is no one so discerning and wise as you. You shall be in charge of my palace, and all my people are to submit to your orders. Only with respect to the throne will I be greater than you."

Joseph blinked, not wanting to stare. Could this truly be

happening? For Pharaoh to trust him so quickly . . . He did not know Joseph or whether his words would come true. Joseph's heartbeat quickened as he saw in his mind's eye the pieces of his life falling into place. Had this not also been his dream as a young man, in which men and women would bow to him? Had God been using this time in slavery and seclusion to prepare him for such a time as this?

"I hereby put you in charge of the whole land of Egypt." Pharaoh pulled the signet ring from his finger and stepped from his raised seat, took Joseph's hand, and placed the ring on Joseph's finger. He summoned servants to bring a fine robe and jewels.

Joseph focused on the servants, who draped a striped collar about his neck along with a multicolored belt about his waist. The cloak that covered his bare shoulders also bore, to Joseph's shock and amazement, the very colors that were once woven into the coat his father had made for him. Not wanting to stare overmuch, he looked up at Pharaoh as the last golden bracelet was placed over his right arm.

"There. Now you are a prince in Egypt, second only to me. I am Pharaoh, but without your word no one will lift hand or foot in all Egypt. You must have a wife of Egypt as well." He clapped his hands and summoned another servant, who hurried to do his bidding.

"I give you the name Zaphenath-Paneah," Pharaoh said. Turning to another servant, he commanded, "Ready a chariot." To Joseph he said, "You will ride through the streets of Egypt as my second-in-command."

Pharaoh, surrounded by guards, left the room, and Joseph followed the servants, still reeling from his quick turnaround from prisoner to prince.

Pharaoh mounted his chariot, which led the way. Joseph's

chariot gleamed in the sunlight, and Joseph stepped into it, his confidence slowly growing.

Crowds lined the streets, and the people shouted, "Make way!" as Pharaoh's driver expertly guided Joseph through Egypt's streets from city to city, until they returned to the king's palace near midday.

"We will eat," Pharaoh said as they alighted at the palace gates, "and then you will meet your wife. Tomorrow we will celebrate your wedding, and you will live here in the governor's quarters of my palace. The palace is grand, and while one half is for my personal use, there are many rooms and gardens and pools and places for my personnel, courtiers, scribes, and advisors to meet. You will be head over all, second only to me. You will live in the best of rooms in the palace."

Joseph bowed low, again overcome.

A few moments later, as they sat together at a table overflowing with food, Pharaoh asked, "Is there anything you would like me to give you to make your home the way you want it?"

Joseph shook his head. "I am overwhelmed by all you have already given, my lord. How could I ask the king for anything else?"

Pharaoh studied him as he plucked a ripe olive from a golden tray. "But there is something you would like. Your eyes tell more than you know."

"Pharaoh is an astute king," Joseph said, careful not to refer to him as a god as so many people did.

"Ask me for anything," Pharaoh said.

Joseph ran a finger around the golden cup, then met Pharaoh's gaze. "There is one thing. When I served in Potiphar's house, I met a man who is a fine steward. His name is Hamid. I would like him to work for me."

"Consider your request granted." Pharaoh smiled and spat the olive pit into a bowl.

Joseph smiled back. He would ask for nothing more, though he would one day look for a way to also free Heba from Potiphar's house. To ask for her now might make the pharaoh think he had a personal interest in her, which could upset his new wife. Perhaps she could become Hamid's wife in the future, but for now, Joseph had done what he could. He could trust Hamid, and the man would make an excellent addition to his house. It would be fair justice on Aneksi, who no doubt still held the man captive to do her will.

27

Asenath stood at the window in the opulent rooms of her father's estate. The sky still held a pink tinge, as Ra had not yet fully crested the ridge in the east. How quickly her life had changed! Was it only three days ago she was called to her father's chambers and told she was to marry a foreigner on Pharaoh's orders?

Zaphenath-Paneah. An Egyptian name, but her servants had quickly discovered that this man, a Hebrew, had just come from the king's prisons and risen to second-in-command over all of Egypt. And she was to be his wife.

This was no doubt her father's doing. He held the highest rank as priest of On, worshiper of the sun god, Ra, and was nearly as powerful as a prince in the land. Priests held special favor with Pharaoh, and because she was the next daughter in line to wed, her father had surely told Pharaoh that she was available.

But marriage to a Hebrew? She had always expected to wed an Egyptian prince, one of Pharaoh's sons or the son of another of On's priests. What was this man like? What if he did not please her?

What if he is not happy with me?

She turned away from the window at the sound of her door opening. Her maidservant Jomana bustled into the room, her arms laden with a tray of bread, garlic, onions, leeks, and grapes, while another servant followed bringing a gilded white robe, along with jeweled sandals that were more delicate than her everyday wear.

"There you are. Up already," Jomana said. "And it is a good thing too. The wedding is set for noon today, when Ra hits the exact midpoint of the sky. You must hurry if we are to be ready on time."

Asenath looked at the food Jomana placed on an ivory table and felt her anxious stomach turn over. "I'm not sure I could eat a thing," she said.

Jomana gently pushed her toward the dais, plucked grapes from their stems, and placed them on a golden plate. "At least eat some fruit. If you do not eat, you will become faint, and you do not want your new husband to think you are weak. Royal women are not weak." She placed a cup of honeyed barley beer beside Asenath. "Drink," she commanded, as she had been doing all of Asenath's life.

Asenath scowled at her maid but ate as she was told. The fruit and bread, what little she could handle, did revive her. She dabbed her mouth with a piece of fine linen, rose, and followed more servants led by Jomana into her adjoining bathing chambers.

A few hours later, she had washed, shaved all but the short hair of her head, and oiled her scalp, and now she smelled of rose petals.

Jomana hurried to the window to glance at the sky. "The sun is nearly there. We must finish your makeup, dress you, and go."

All fear slipped away as Asenath allowed her servants to paint her face and eyes, complementing the intricate henna designs on her hands, then they put a sheer white tunic over her head and a pure white robe over the tunic. Jomana tied a golden sash at her waist. Asenath sat gingerly on the raised bed and allowed a young girl to tie the delicate sandals to her feet.

At last she stood, accepting the jewels draped over her neck and the veil placed over her black wig.

"You look exactly as a princess should," Jomana said, smiling. The maid looked her up and down, turned her around, and finally pronounced her ready. "And now the chariot awaits you."

They walked the halls to the wide doors of the home on the temple grounds. Asenath could have easily walked the distance, but not on this day. Today she would ride in the gilded chariot her father used when he moved throughout the city.

The driver helped her with the step and seated her behind him, then slowly drove her past waiting crowds of men, women, and children. They all tossed palm branches and lotus flowers along the path, scenting the air and reminding Asenath of how many times she had done this very thing for her older sisters.

And now it is I who rides in splendor to meet my prince. Thoughts of him sent a fresh wave of anxiety through her. She had not even seen this Zaphenath-Paneah yet. The servants from the palace proclaimed him quite handsome. They said that he spoke fluent Egyptian, and looking upon him, no one could tell he was anything other than a prince from Egypt.

The chariot stopped at the temple doors, and the driver helped her alight. Guards lined the steps as she took each one slowly. The doors opened, and she moved into the familiar chamber where her father and Pharaoh waited at the end of a long hall. A strange man who must be her intended stood beside Pharaoh, showing him to be of high ranking in Egypt indeed.

Asenath drew in a small breath, unwilling to release a deep sigh lest someone hear and assume she feared this day. She must remain strong. She was the daughter of Potiphera, priest of On, and equal to this man who would be her husband.

But was she equal? Women were held in high regard in Egypt and priests had great authority, but as she drew closer to Zaphenath-Paneah, she knew by his clothes and Pharaoh's signet ring on his hand that she was marrying a man of higher status than her own father. What protection could her father give her if this man proved to be unworthy?

A sliver of fear moved through her as she stopped at last near the dais where her father and Pharaoh sat. Zaphenath-Paneah stepped close to her. Her father also rose and came to stand before them both.

"I have chosen Zaphenath-Paneah to be your husband, Asenath," her father said. "Though he has no gifts of his own to bring us, the pharaoh has generously given this man great power and many favors. You will share his life and these ouroboros rings, which you will give to each other. They mark this promise of life's circle that has no end and show that you will stay together your life long. Zaphenath-Paneah will marry no other but you."

Her father held an embroidered blue pillow out before them. Her groom took the ring intended for her, grasped her hand, and placed it on her second finger. Asenath looked at the golden serpent, the head with sapphire eyes eating its tail of diamonds. She met Zaphenath-Paneah's gaze, her pulse quickening at his touch. She told herself to breathe as she lifted a matching ring from the pillow and placed it on the second finger of his left hand.

"Now," her father said, "let us go to the banquet hall of Pharaoh's palace to celebrate your union."

Asenath felt her husband's fingers grasp hers. He lifted their hands high and walked slowly, dignified, through the hall, down the steps, and into a chariot.

Asenath's senses heightened at the spikenard wafting from

him as their driver took them on a long, circuitous route to the doors of the royal palace. Her father and Pharaoh came in separate chariots, Pharaoh before them, her father behind.

When the horses came to rest, her new husband leaned close. "When we are alone," he said, "I want you to call me Joseph."

"Joseph?" A strange name to her ears, but she nodded.

"It is my Hebrew name, and I do not wish to forget who I am." He took her hand and helped her to the ground, then played the part well of newlywed husband escorting his bride to their feast.

"Joseph," she whispered so low he did not seem to hear her. She liked the sound of the name on her tongue.

ᘁᘁᘁ

The day turned swiftly to night. Joseph watched his new bride mingle among the women, sit sedately in her pure white robe with the golden sash, and laugh freely, though he could not tell whether she was laughing for joy or if her nerves betrayed her. His own caused his heart to beat harder.

When the sun set below the horizon, Hamid touched his shoulder. "It is time, my lord. Our custom is for the groom to take the bride in his chariot to their home at sunset."

Joseph knew that, for Potiphera had made sure he knew exactly how to treat his daughter this night and for the rest of his life. Though Joseph held a higher position now than anyone but Pharaoh, he could not deny that Asenath's father would always want to protect her. Much like Aneksi's father intimidated Potiphar.

He rose from the seat where he'd been speaking with one of Pharaoh's advisors and walked the length of the room. He came up beside Asenath and took her hand, drawing her away from her suddenly giggling friends.

"It is time, my love." Joseph said the prescribed words and led her smoothly toward the waiting chariot.

The crowd followed them, tossing lotus petals toward them and singing love songs that faded into the night.

Once up the steps to the newly refurnished rooms of a previous favorite of Pharaoh's, Joseph guided Asenath inside ahead of him. He turned her to face him and removed the veil. "What color is your hair beneath your wig—or do you shave your hair as most women do?"

"I do not shave my head," she said, glancing beyond him, her cheeks darkening.

He smiled, lifted the wig from her head, and saw short, silky black hair in its place. "Ah," he said. "Black as night but shining like the sun."

She smiled, though she would not hold his gaze. Was she afraid of him? Or simply quiet?

He lifted her chin to force her gaze upward. A little gasp escaped her lips, telling Joseph what he needed to know. She found him acceptable, and as he kissed her and drew her farther into the room, tossing their fine clothes to the floor, he sensed that she also desired him as he desired her.

A feeling of coming home filled him, and for the first time in more years than he dared count, Joseph felt that his life finally held purpose. He would make a life with this woman, and he hoped she would know and love him. As he wooed her and they came together as husband and wife, he sensed that she would be all he had hoped for in a wife and much more.

28

Joseph allowed his servant to apply the final touches of kohl to his eyes, then donned his headdress and the robe and belt of many colors and took the golden staff in his hand. He had done his best not to associate this Egyptian garment with the cloak from his father. Had God chosen these colors to match those of his brothers for a reason?

Asenath poked her head into his room and nearly took his breath as she walked barefoot across the tiles in a filmy white nightdress.

"You are out of bed early, my sleepy wife." Joseph kissed her upturned face as his servant slipped away.

"And you are off again to inspect the crops while I must sit alone in the house all day waiting for you." Her slight pout made him smile. What an ardent lover she had proved to be, a surprise for a woman so much younger than he. She clutched his arm and leaned close. "You know you want to stay with me."

He wanted nothing more! "You tempt me, dear wife. But how can I ignore the work Pharaoh has appointed for me? We have spent a month together. It is time I began to work again, now that the crops should be pushing their heads from the black earth." It was too early to harvest what he was certain would be Egypt's first year of plenty. But he would inspect the growth of the crops just the same.

Asenath offered him a coy smile. "It is a wife's job to tempt her husband." She touched his cheek. "My only love."

She'd taken to calling him that when he told her of his false imprisonment and the behavior of Potiphar's wife.

"She should have been punished," Asenath had said.

Joseph nodded. "In a world where justice rules, she would have. But Potiphar feared her father. So they lived in a loveless marriage and found pleasure in other people—slaves who had little choice but to obey them."

"Would you fear my father as Potiphar feared hers?"

Joseph started at her question. He rose up on one elbow and ran his fingers through her hair. "You have nothing to fear from me, beloved. Never. So, no. I would not fear your father because I would never do anything to hurt you." He looked so intently into her eyes that she leaned into him and sighed.

"And I would never do anything to hurt you, dear Joseph. I will admit that on the day of our wedding, I feared that your power over my father would make me vulnerable, because who but Pharaoh is greater than you? You must admit that at least Aneksi had her father's protection if the captain had been cruel to her and not the other way around." She traced a finger along his bare arm.

"And she needed his protection because she was not faithful to Potiphar. Potiphar could have done something, but I daresay he did not love her. Perhaps he once did, but there was little kindness between them while I lived in his house." He held Asenath close, remembering the many times he had trusted people only to be betrayed by them. He would not do that to her, he vowed. He would protect her with his life. "There is one thing I would ask of you," he said, looking again into her luminous eyes.

"Anything for you, Joseph."

"I never did as Aneksi asked because I would have offended my God. While I know your father is a priest of On and that Egypt worships many gods, in our house, while raising our children, I want them taught only of the one true Creator God. They can learn of the others, of course, for the sake of their culture and history, but they must know that only Adonai is God. There is no other."

She had stared at him in disbelief for a long moment. Even now he wondered how much she grasped of a faith in one God when she had been raised to sacrifice to so many. And to believe as he did would mean giving up the faith of her father. Had he asked too much?

Yet he could not allow any children born of their union to be uncircumcised Egyptians. They would be Hebrew. He would make sure of it.

As he kissed Asenath one more time with a promise to return as early as possible, he wondered if she still struggled with his request. Was she at least trying to accept his faith in the God of his fathers?

He hurried down the many steps to his waiting driver. Guards stood before and behind him, ready to run with his chariot as he traveled to every city, every field in Egypt. He'd lived in Egypt for fourteen years and had gone from slave to prisoner to prince.

Even the dreams of privilege he'd had in his youth could not compare to this experience. He could not have predicted it and would not have chosen it. But he was beginning to accept it.

ᴜᴜᴜ

1826 BC

Joseph rode to the city of Giza, where the first set of granaries stood. Pharaoh's workers had already threshed the wheat from

221

the harvest and were now pouring it through a large opening in the top with baskets drawn up by ropes. Two granaries were already full, and this third one would barely hold this year's yield.

"Circle the area, then take me to the land outside of the city," Joseph told his driver. With six years ahead of them, they would never be able to keep all of the grain in one city.

They drove closer to the granaries, and Joseph hopped down. Hamid stood near the third granary with clay tablet in hand, calculating how much wheat they'd already stored.

"How many more stacks of wheat are yet in the fields?" Joseph asked as Hamid looked up and smiled.

"According to my men, there is double the amount of wheat they usually produce each season. I would say they are in the process of threshing at least fifty more stacks, and I don't think this container will hold it all. I've given orders for another granary to be built, and quickly!" Hamid scratched his chin with the end of his bronze stylus.

"Good," Joseph said, taking in the scene with one sweeping glance. "I am going to choose more cities to hold the grain. If we have six more years of this yet to come, we will need six to twelve more cities to hold it all." He placed his hands behind his back and walked the length of the area, inspecting the work that had already been done. A short distance away, workers had begun bricking a cylinder-like storage bin to hold the rest of this year's crop.

Hamid hurried to walk with him and showed him the number of bushels of wheat he had calculated so far.

Joseph nodded. "God has been very good to Egypt. I must admit I underestimated just how good He can be when He chooses to bless us. This is far above what I had imagined." He turned back toward his chariot. "When you are finished, I want to discuss a new assignment for you." He stepped into the chariot and sat behind the driver. "Come to my home at eventide, and we will discuss these things then."

Hamid gave a slight bow. "I will be there."

Joseph nodded once as they drove off, hoping he hadn't caused the man to fear change. Hamid's skills were good, but any of the other head servants could keep track of the wheat in one city at a time. He had other plans for Hamid and hoped the man was up to the task.

Later that evening, Joseph's servant ushered Hamid into his private banquet chambers. A servant offered both men goblets of beer and a tray of various nuts, olives, and cheeses. Joseph looked at his friend, hoping his faith in this man would never be misguided. He needed people he could trust, as even the pharaoh could be a target of ill will.

"This is very good beer, my lord," Hamid said after taking a sip, following Joseph's lead. "Made from wheat, not barley? And I taste ginger?"

Joseph nodded. "From the best of Pharaoh's storehouses." He lingered over the cup, then ran his finger along its rim. At last he looked up and studied Hamid a moment. "I have two things to ask of you, Hamid," he said, tenting his hands and resting his chin on them.

"Anything, my lord." Hamid set his drink beside him on a low, intricately carved table and clasped his hands in his lap. "You took me from slavery to a woman I came to despise. I could never feel anything but gratitude to you. How may I serve you?"

"You can start by calling me Joseph again. Zaphenath-Paneah when we are in public, but not when just the two of us are talking or around Asenath, should she join us."

"Very well," Hamid said. "Joseph, thank you."

Joseph lifted his cup toward Hamid in a gesture of approval. He would never get used to his Egyptian name, but then again, he'd only had it a year. Perhaps one day it would fit him more. "I have decided to place you as my right hand to oversee the people in my household, from my chief steward to the lowest slave. You will also oversee your replacement in charge of counting the wheat. You are far more useful to me here than out in the field alone. I also want you to be my spokesman and interpreter for those who speak in anything other than the Egyptian tongue, but you will pass everything by me and I will give you a decision."

Hamid looked both awed and taken aback by Joseph's request. It was a lot of responsibility to work as Joseph's right hand. Even holding such a position for Potiphar did not come close to the responsibility he would have now. Nor the power he could wield.

"You do me a great honor, Joseph. I know that of all men, I do not deserve your respect in this way." He looked at his hands before meeting Joseph's gaze. "My past—"

"Is behind you," Joseph interrupted. "You have shown me that you are loyal, and I need loyal men in my service. You of all men know where I came from. I was born a prince in my family, but I am not Egyptian. I would like you to help the people never doubt that I am of Egypt now. Pharaoh has made me such, and I am ready to let the memory of my people go."

Hamid leaned back in his chair and gave Joseph a curious look. "I never thought I would hear you say so. What of your father and brother?"

Joseph could not deny the kick of longing at the mention of them, but he did not show his feelings. "My father could be in Sheol by now, and one day, if God allows it, I may send men to find Benjamin and bring him to me. I will make him an Egyptian as well, if he wants it. I would protect him, in any case."

"But you can forget them?" Hamid picked up his goblet again.

Joseph smiled. "I do believe God has made a way for me to do that, yes." He leaned closer. "Asenath is with child. When she delivers, I will know that God wants me here to stay."

Hamid laughed and slapped his knee. "With child! How wonderful! When do you expect this birth?"

"In about four months. We said nothing except to her father until she was far enough along. Of course, her father wanted to give her all manner of amulets to keep bad things from happening to her, but she refused them all for my sake."

"She believes in your one god then?" Hamid's eyes widened as though he never would have expected such a thing.

"She does. And if she doesn't, for my sake, she has agreed she will try. I hope someday you will do the same."

Hamid looked beyond Joseph. "I respect your faith in your god, Joseph. I have seen the way he has blessed you, and I know those things don't happen by chance. I fear I have been in the teachings of Egypt so long . . . it is hard to consider that none of the gods we worship are true." He cleared his throat, and Joseph watched him closely. "For your sake, I will try to understand your god. I hope that is enough for you."

Joseph nodded, though his heart longed for more. "It will have to be, now won't it? I cannot give you faith, Hamid. One day perhaps you will see my God do something so amazing that your doubts will flee. In the meantime, it is enough that you seek. It is in seeking Him that we will find Him."

Hamid sipped from his cup again but said nothing more.

Joseph took a bite of one of his favorite cheeses. "There is one more thing I would like you to do for me."

"Anything," Hamid said.

"This one is something you may decline if you wish. I would not force a man to marry if he does not want to."

Hamid's brow furrowed. "Marry, my lord? Who would I marry?" Hamid lifted his hands.

"I have requested Heba be released from Potiphar's house to serve Asenath. My wife understands how Potiphar and his wife treated you both. I would offer Heba to you in marriage, if you so desire." Joseph leaned back in his seat.

Hamid's eyes widened, and a smile slowly spread across his round face. "Joseph, you do me great honor! I thought my life would never include a wife or family after what happened with Aneksi."

"Well, now you have the chance to begin again, as I have." Joseph lifted his cup and nodded toward Hamid. "I will have Asenath and her servants arrange a wedding for you, my friend."

Hamid laughed, and Joseph joined him.

When Hamid left later that evening, Joseph returned to his rooms, pondering his life. While he had never expected to be in this place, he found satisfaction in knowing he had helped someone else find joy and freedom. When Asenath gave birth, his life would be complete.

29

FOUR MONTHS LATER

Asenath awoke with a start. Pain pierced her back, not like the nagging ache she had endured during the day but stronger, a fierce grip on her spine.

"Safiya!" she called, her voice barely able to rise above a whisper. "Hurry!" She leaned against the pillows, forcing her legs over the side of the bed to pace and hopefully make the babe kick her in a different place. But was it kicking she felt?

Her mother had told her that birth pains came across a woman's middle, not her back, but Asenath could not deny that something was either terribly wrong or she was in labor.

"Safiya!" Her voice rose to a shout this time. She rubbed the small of her back as she walked.

"I'm here, mistress," Safiya said, her breath coming fast as if she had run a long distance, though she slept in a small room near Asenath's chambers. "Is it time to send for the midwife?"

"Yes. I think so." Asenath winced as she drew in a breath. "But gather the women quietly. I don't want anyone to wake Zaphenath-Paneah." There was no sense in waking her husband when the child could still take hours to come. "And don't call on anyone who performs charms or brings amulets with them. I am not going to give birth with the gods of Egypt looking on." Not that they could see, as Joseph had told her many times, but she didn't want them in the same room with his child.

"But Bastet watches over the lives of mothers, my lady. Don't you want her likeness near to protect you?" Safiya's mouth curved into a frown, her expression clearly troubled.

"Joseph's God will protect me." But she still struggled to know what she truly believed. Joseph's God was so far above them and impossible to understand. If He watched over Joseph, why had He allowed him to be sold into slavery by his own brothers? A shiver worked down her spine. Her children would never be so jealous of one another. She would not allow it.

Another pain gripped her, and she bent forward, groaning. Safiya rushed to the door and called on the guard to send for more servants. She would wake the entire household with the way she barked orders, but Asenath no longer cared. The pain was too great. How could she bear it?

She felt Safiya's presence beside her moments later, taking her arm and guiding her about the room. "It helps to walk, my lady. The babe will shift and get into the right position if you can stand to keep walking."

"How do you know so much? You have not given birth." Asenath did not want to sound so harsh, but Safiya did not seem to notice.

"I have sisters. They talk about such things." The girl patted Asenath's arm and began to speak soft, encouraging words. "The midwife will be here soon. Do not fear, my lady."

A knock sounded on Asenath's door soon after. A young servant girl answered it. Asenath looked toward the door and winced at the sight of Joseph standing there, hair rumpled, rubbing sleep from his eyes.

"Is it time?" he asked, not making a move to enter her rooms.

"I believe so, my lord," Safiya answered for her.

Asenath could not have spoken if she had tried as pain gripped her again. When the agony subsided, she looked at her husband. "My back ached all yesterday, but it woke me with a start a few moments ago. The midwife is on her way." She knew a man should not be near a birth, but for this brief moment she took comfort in seeing him there. "You should be sleeping. I'm sorry we woke you."

Joseph shook his head. "I am glad to know. I slept enough." A yawn overtook him and she doubted his words, but his smile warmed her. "I will go to my rooms and pray for your safe delivery, since there is nothing I can do to help you, my love."

"I am grateful for your prayers." Another wave of pain came on her slowly, gaining in strength until she could not stop the cry that came from her lips.

Joseph's brows drew down, and she knew her misery troubled him. He hesitated in the doorway, but a moment later the midwife bustled down the hall and he stepped back to let her into the room. Asenath watched him turn toward his rooms.

Please, God of Joseph, let this baby come swiftly and be a healthy boy for Joseph's sake. And please let me live through it to raise him.

It was the first prayer she had uttered to Joseph's unseen God, but she meant every word. And suddenly his God did not seem so far from her. She felt a heady sense of peace fill her, and the pain in her back, though intense, became manageable.

"Let me see how far you have come," the midwife said, interrupting her thoughts. The women helped her onto the bed, and the midwife checked to see if the baby was ready to come. "He appears to have his feet coming first instead of his head. I will attempt to turn him if you will let me." She glanced at

Asenath, who dreaded the intense discomfort she knew would come from such an action. Yet the peace of Joseph's God remained. She nodded her assent.

The midwife pushed on Asenath's belly and had her turn this way and that, until at last she felt the baby move. "I felt something," she said, daring to hope.

The midwife checked her again, then pushed and prodded the apparently stubborn child until at last the babe turned. "There!" the midwife said with triumph. "He is in position. Now bring the birthing bricks."

Her servants helped her to squat on the large bricks while the midwife moved into position to catch the child. Another wave of agony washed over her, but this time it came over her belly, not her back. Relief would come soon. Joseph must be praying for her as he had promised.

Moments later, though it seemed much longer for the pain she endured, a baby's cry pierced the room. The midwife laughed and held up a healthy boy still covered in the blood of birth.

Asenath drew in a breath of relief, then pushed once more to complete the delivery. Safiya took the child to wash and wrap him in cloths, while the servants worked to clean and change Asenath into fresh clothing. At last the boy was placed in her arms.

"Someone must go and tell his father," Asenath said as the infant's mouth found her breast to suckle. The feeling of love that flowed through her at the sight and smell of this beautiful boy, her son, was unmatched to any feeling she had ever known. Tears filled her eyes. To know such love . . . She knew Joseph loved her and her parents loved her, but this helpless child . . . she could give her love to him most fully.

The door opened again as she focused on the child, and she

looked up to see Joseph enter the room. He came close enough to see the child but did not touch her.

"You have a son, Joseph," she said, stifling a yawn. She removed the boy from her breast to show him. "What will you name him?"

Joseph looked on the child with an expression of awe. "A son," he said softly. "A beautiful son." He wiped a tear from his eye, and she wondered if he had been weeping as he prayed for her. "He is Manasseh. It is because God has made me forget all my trouble and all my father's household." Joseph looked long at him. The boy's mouth continued to move as though he were searching for his mother's milk.

"Manasseh," she said, pulling the boy back to her breast and looking into Joseph's grateful gaze. "I hope he proves to do for you exactly as his name implies."

He nodded but did not speak for a moment, as though words would not come. "In eight days we will circumcise him after the custom of my fathers," he said.

She had always known this was his intention. "In eight days," she murmured, nodding, though she could barely keep her eyes open.

"I will leave you until then." He turned to go, then looked back. "Thank you, Asenath, for my son."

She smiled. She had made him glad, but he could not know that her joy was even greater than his. He had given her a son to love. And she intended to pour her life into doing just that.

30

CANAAN, 1825 BC

Judah stood at the tent's door, peering into the endless gray sky. The rains had been steady during this season, causing his crop to grow greater than he could have imagined. This, the third harvest, had been as plentiful as the first. He'd never seen wheat fields yield so well. Surely God's hand was in this. Perhaps He had forgotten what Jacob's sons had done to Joseph, and all the other things they had done. Why bless them if He had not forgiven?

Judah ducked into the tent again, troubled that he still thought of the boy—for that was how he remembered him. His own son was nearly the age Joseph had been when they sold him to the Ishmaelite traders.

He glanced at Er still asleep on his pallet. At fifteen the boy should be rising with the dawn, even if dawn was hard to see for the clouds that blocked the sun. The goats needed to be milked, and both sheep and goats needed pasture, rain or not. Judah couldn't handle his large flock alone. Would a wife help to keep Er responsible? The time had come when he needed to fulfill his promise to wed Er to Tamar.

The thought rested heavily on him. Tamar had grown into a beautiful woman, yet Er was still half man, half child. He had never taken kindly to his father choosing a wife for him years before he was ready. Was he ready now?

Judah walked across the room and shook Er's shoulder. "Er! Wake up!"

The boy grumbled and moaned, and Judah shook him again.

"I wish you would let him rest, Judah," Kaella said as she mixed her ground wheat with water. "The scent of the flatbread will awaken him."

"He needs to learn to awaken long before food is ready to break his fast." Judah took hold of Er's shoulders again and forced him to sit up. "Wake up, Er. We have much to do."

Onan and Shelah stirred and rose, and at last his eldest son blinked hard and stretched. "What is so urgent? The goats can wait a little longer."

Judah tamped his rising anger. Er had been a problem for most of his life, and now he was nearly hopeless. Would he ever change? The thought troubled Judah.

"The goats cannot wait to be milked, and we also have a wedding to plan," Judah said, shoving his frustration aside.

"A wedding?" Kaella spoke before Er fully shook himself awake.

But the words must have penetrated at last. "Whose wedding?" Er asked, rising. He walked to the clay basin and dipped his hands in the water to scrub his face.

"Yours," Judah said. "It is time we keep our agreement with Tamar. With the plentiful harvest, we will have more than enough food and wine to entertain many guests." He smiled at the thought, reminded of his own wedding.

Er whirled around and stared at Judah, wide-eyed. A hint of . . . was that hesitation or fear or something else in his gaze?

"What if I don't want to marry her?" His dark eyes narrowed, and his tone held a defiant edge. "My friends don't have to marry someone they don't want."

Judah's mouth opened in shock, but he quickly clamped it shut. Kaella lifted her gaze from the griddle, and she also looked surprised by Er's comments.

"I thought you liked Tamar. Any young man would find her good to behold." Judah rubbed the back of his neck and felt a sudden need to pace the length of the tent. "I cannot back out of an agreement with Yassib. I would never be able to make an agreement again. Your brothers would be unable to find a suitable mate." He glared at his son, whose obstinacy had not abated. "You will marry Tamar at the end of harvest, and I won't hear another thing about it. We will build another section to the tent so you can have privacy with her."

"I want my own tent, not one that is just part of yours." Er walked toward his mother, skirting around Judah. He knelt near the griddle and snatched up one of the flat cakes. "I'll marry her if I can live in my own house or tent. Though I would rather have a stone house. It's what she is used to, after all." Er gave Judah a smug smile, as though he had been planning such a thing for a long time. Had he?

Judah stepped out of the tent into the misty rain and cursed under his breath. Though he owned a sizable piece of land here, his family had always lived in tents. The women had tents of their own, as did Jacob's sons. But they could all gather in their father's tent should he want to speak with them there.

Er was too young to live apart from them, though he was old enough to sire children. Marriage would settle him. Make him into the man Judah had always wanted him to be.

He shielded his eyes from the mist and turned in a circle, looking for a possible place to raise another tent or . . . did he dare give in to the lad and allow him to build a stone house? If he did, Kaella would want a house of stone like her father had owned. No. He would not become completely like the Canaanites. Shepherds lived in tents, and despite the other crops he cared for, he was a shepherd first.

He turned and moved back into the tent, brushing the water from his shoulders and hair. "You may have your own tent if your mother agrees to make it for you," he said to Er. "You may not have a house of stone. And you *will* wed Tamar at the end of harvest. I don't want to hear another word about it." He picked up some dates and flatbread and took a bite of the bread. "Now hurry up. Onan and Shelah, you will come too. Rain or not, the sheep must eat."

He stuffed more food into a pouch at his side and grabbed his goatskin of water and his staff where it lay near the door. Without a look back at his family, he marched toward the sheep pens. The boys would follow, sulking every step of the way. But at that moment, Judah did not care what his children thought or what went through his wife's mind. He would keep his word. He would honor the covenant he had made with Yassib. He would not betray Tamar as he had Joseph. He lived with enough regrets.

ᴜᴜᴜ

Tamar walked with her friends, who giggled and laughed as they all followed the bridegroom and his brothers to Judah's property, where a large feast awaited them. Legally she had been Er's wife for five years. And her father grew richer for every year she was forced to wait.

But to marry Er . . . the idea had troubled her from the beginning. She was three years his senior and should have married at fifteen as her sisters had. She felt as though she was marrying a child, for it was no secret that Er did not act like a man. Not like the men in her family. Even thirteen-year-old boys behaved more as men than Er did.

And now she would find out what it was like to live with this man, her husband. A shiver worked through her. She did not realize how nervous she truly was until they approached Judah's property.

A large fire blazed in the central court area. Judah's family lived in tents, so they had no brick courtyard as houses in the towns did. Tamar looked at the tents that surrounded the large fire pit, torches lit outside of each one. Judah was said to be a wealthy man, for in the years he had been in Canaan, he had amassed many sheep and goats, enough to allow him to hire men to farm his fields. But the area where they lived seemed crude to her. She was too used to her father's sprawling house of stone.

Living in a tent wouldn't be so different, would it?

The shouts of the people in Judah's camp greeted them as Er led their procession, with the men immediately following and Tamar leading her maids behind them. Her thoughts whirled as she and Er were led to a hand-carved bench and food and drink were placed before them, while the rest of the crowd ate in various places around the fire.

Judah and her father said a few words, but Tamar's heart beat too fast to pay attention to them. She knew what awaited her, for her sisters had been happy to tell her every detail. What she couldn't imagine was how Er would treat her. She glanced at him now, laughing with his younger brother Onan. She listened, trying to make out what had brought on their laughter, when she felt a touch on her shoulder.

"Tamar, my daughter, welcome to our family." Er's mother, Kaella, took a seat beside her. "I am so glad to finally have another woman to talk with about . . . things women do." Her comment brought Tamar's thoughts into clearer focus. Had her mother-in-law intended to say something else? By the look she gave Tamar, she could only wonder.

But life would go on here, like it did in her father's house. The only difference would be her status as Er's wife and some-day mother to his children. She would still work in a family, just alongside this woman instead of her mother and sisters.

"I look forward to working with you, to serving you," Tamar said, longing to please the woman she did not yet know well.

"We will have plenty of time to grow close," Kaella said, glancing at Er with an expression Tamar didn't understand. But he was her firstborn, the first to marry, and perhaps her thoughts moved in the direction Tamar's had as she imagined her new life.

"Ah," Kaella said, standing. "I hear the drumbeat rising." She looked at Er, who seemed not to have heard the change in the beat or the beckoning call it signaled to draw the bride and groom to their tent. "Er," Kaella said when his hesitance grew embarrassing, "it is time to take your bride."

Er turned at his mother's comment, then looked at Tamar as if for the first time. He stared for a moment, then reached for her hand and raised her to her feet. She hurried to keep up with him as he fairly marched across the compound to a lone tent some distance from his father's tent. They were to have their own home? She felt a sense of relief at not having to share their space with her new mother-in-law, father-in-law, and brothers-in-law. She would have a place to come to escape them all if she needed such a thing.

"Welcome," Er said as he led her inside. He moved ahead of her, then let down the tent's flap, enclosing them in semi-darkness save for one lone clay lamp set on a low table.

She glanced around but decided she would make out the furnishings better in daylight. The sun had long since set, and Er yawned as he moved to the bed in the corner. He removed his robe and sandals, then lay down on the bed.

Tamar stood in the center of the room, watching him, her heart beating even faster than the drum, if that were possible. Were they not supposed to come together as man and wife?

"Er?" she said softly.

He lifted his head. "What?"

"Are we not supposed to . . . the bridal sheet . . . the proof for my father." She stifled a sob. He was not acting as a groom but as though she were a servant or a sister.

Er sat up and stared at her. "I suppose you are good to look upon." His tone held a slight sneer. "Let me see you without the wedding clothes."

Heat filled her cheeks, and she struggled with the headdress as though she had forgotten how to undo the wrapping. At last she dropped the headscarf and undid her hair, and still Er did not move closer, nor did he show much interest in her, as his gaze kept skipping beyond her toward the door. She fumbled with the belt of her robe and stood before him, shivering despite the warmth of the night.

He looked her up and down as though inspecting an animal. "Come to bed," he said.

She hurried to lie beside him, expecting him to touch her, to kiss her, to do what all grooms did when they had finally gained a bride. But a moment later, Er turned on his side, his back to her, and pulled a blanket over his body.

She lay atop the sheet, tears dripping onto the linen beneath her, until at last she reached for part of the blanket and pulled it close to her shoulders.

She slowly turned her back to Er and soon heard his even

breathing. Perhaps he had simply had too much wine to drink. But the gossips had never given her such a tale as this one.

She dared not weep, lest someone hear above the drum still beating in the distance. Would Er awaken and go out to them as though they were now one? What of the bridal sheet he must give her father? Would he ever be man enough to want her?

The night deepened, and the drums stopped beating. The noise of the crowd grew silent, and still Er did not move, his loud breathing filling the tent. Sleep eluded her, and she could not escape her humiliation.

What was she supposed to do in the morning when her father demanded the proof of her virginity? Would Er deny that she was a virgin? But he would be wrong. What was so displeasing about her that he did not want her? Tormenting questions plagued her.

Just as dawn approached and she finally fell into a restless sleep, Er jostled her shoulder and turned her toward him. He was not gentle or kind, nor did he say a word to her as he fulfilled his duty to her. He then forced her up, told her to dress, and handed her the sheet to give her father. Rolling onto his side again, he acted as though she were nothing but a prostitute.

She stood at the door of their tent for a long time as her cheeks burned and her tears fell, until she could compose herself and walk toward the area where her father was just awakening in a tent Judah had set up for his use. She tossed the sheet at his feet but did not answer the unspoken questions in his eyes. She could not have answered them even if he had asked.

31

Judah walked about the camp at the end of Er's wedding week, bidding the last of the townspeople farewell. Yassib met him near the central fire and walked with him toward the trees that led to the path to Yassib's home. The rest of Tamar's family had left just after dawn.

"My daughter is in your care now, Judah," Yassib said as they stopped where the road went in different directions. "I must warn you, treat her well." He rested a hand on Judah's shoulder. "I do not think your son will do so unless you force him to."

Judah's mouth went dry. He had feared his son was still too immature to be a husband, but he could not admit that. He lifted his hands. "I have seen nothing to show me that Er has been unkind to Tamar. Of what do you speak?" Er wouldn't mistreat the girl just because she wasn't his choice, would he?

"Tamar brought the bridal sheet to me the morning after the wedding, Judah. Er should have brought it himself the night of the feast. She was not smiling, nor did she say a word to me, but I know my daughter. She was not happy."

Yassib's troubled expression caused Judah a pang of worry. He had paid dearly for this girl, and Er should be grateful that her father had agreed to the marriage. To his deep regret, he knew that his sons were not obedient. He should have been firmer, stronger, with all of them. And now he had this to deal with?

"I cannot imagine that Er would have done anything to trouble Tamar, Yassib. But I will speak to my son and see to it that he treats her with kindness. She deserves nothing less." Judah patted the man's shoulder. "Do not worry, my friend. Your daughter is safe in my household."

Yassib merely nodded, but Judah sensed what he did not say. Yassib would not stand by quietly if he discovered his daughter was being mistreated in Judah's home.

He parted ways with Yassib, promising to meet again soon, then whirled about and headed back toward the camp. He would speak with Er and set things right. His own reputation hinged on the behavior of his sons. He would not allow this child to ruin that.

ⴖⴖⴖ

Several weeks after her wedding, Tamar left the tent she shared with Er and stepped gingerly over the rocky ground toward the area where Kaella ground the grain. She braced herself for any questions her mother-in-law might send her way, silently praying to any god who might be listening for help. She could not let them know the way Er forced himself on her morning after morning, with nothing but a primal need to satisfy his urges. He never kissed her, never spoke kindly to her, and she had yet to engage him in much conversation other than responding to his barked orders to feed him or serve him in some way.

Emotion swelled within her, and she swallowed hard, making herself walk straight and keep the tears at bay. They came too often when she was alone, waiting for Er to finally return to her.

A shiver ran down her spine as she spotted Kaella motioning her to hurry. She picked up her pace, forcing herself to smile instead of wince at the pain she still could not get used to, and sat beside her mother-in-law to work.

"Good day to you, Ima Kaella." She looked into the woman's astute dark eyes and saw a hint of compassion there.

"It is good to see you up and about, Tamar. How well I remember my first days as a wife. Judah was . . . an ardent lover. A woman can take time to adjust to such . . . things." Kaella searched Tamar's face as if trying to read her thoughts.

Tamar nodded, emotion rising again. She would not cry. She would not betray Er to his mother, for how did she know that his mother wouldn't take his side? "I'm sure that is what we are experiencing as well," she said, knowing Kaella expected her to respond. "I am not used to Er's . . . ways."

Kaella laughed softly. "You will soon adjust, dear girl. Er can be immature and spoiled, but he's a good boy at heart." Her expression changed as though she were still thinking of her firstborn as a young boy.

But Er was no longer a youth. He was a man who acted like a youth, and Tamar did not know how she was going to cope with it all.

She took up the mortar and pestle and poured some of the wheat into the clay bowl to grind for the flatbread the men would want to soon eat. Er would go off with his father and brothers to care for the sheep since the harvest was now past. Soon she would begin to spin wool into thread to make clothing for Er and perhaps in time for a child who would come. Not a child of their love, but perhaps a child whom she could love.

"I'm sure things will grow easier as we get to know each other," Tamar said, willing it to be so and telling her heart that this had to be all that was wrong. Once she understood Er's ways and why he acted as he did, she could avoid his anger, which seemed too quick to spark toward her. She would learn to appease him, if not please him. In time, perhaps he would care for her.

But as she worked in silence beside his mother, she wondered if anything in her own heart could change enough to make her care for him.

ᴌᴜᴌ

Months passed, and Tamar thought she saw a softening in Er's attitude toward her, so she decided one evening, with Kaella's permission, to prepare a meal for him in their tent and do all she could to make him feel like the man she hoped he could be.

She stirred the stew that sat warming over the coals outside the tent, checked the flatbread and fruit and nuts that would accompany the meal, and longed to sample the pistachio treats she had lovingly created from her mother's best recipe. A hint of hope stirred inside of her as she looked up to see Er walking with his father toward the central fire. He stopped there, but when Kaella pointed to his tent and apparently explained that Tamar had made a special meal for him, he turned and headed across the compound. He stopped near the door and looked down at her as she knelt to stir the stew once more.

"Welcome, my husband," she said, offering him a tentative smile. "I hope you are well."

Er stared at her, lifted the flap, and went inside. Did he expect her to bring the food into their small living space when she had so carefully arranged it all in front of the tent beneath the awning? She assumed that was his intent, and picked up the clay pot and moved into the tent. She hurried to carry each item into the tent and arrange them in front of the cushion where he sat, legs splayed in front of him.

"Close the flap," he commanded once she had finished.

She obeyed and came to stand before him.

"What made you think I would want to eat with just you? We eat with my family. We eat the food my mother prepares. Not you." He swept his arm over the food she'd so carefully prepared. "How do I know you will not try to poison me with food made only by your hand? Do you think I don't know the way you look at me? How you despise me because I don't love you or give you what you want when you want it? You are a selfish creature, and I never wanted to marry you."

Tamar began to shake inwardly from the shock of his words. She swallowed twice, then said, "I thought it would please you. I wanted only to please you, Er."

He jumped to his feet and closed the distance between them. "Please me? You will never please me. You are no better than a prostitute to me. You are someone my father chose, not me. You are worthless to me."

Tears trickled over her cheeks as he towered over her, his gaze filled with hatred.

"My father was a fool to choose you!" he fairly shouted.

She opened her mouth, though she could think of nothing to say. His hand connected with her cheek so fast she stumbled backward, face burning, and more tears blurred her vision.

"Have you nothing to say?" He sneered at her.

"I never meant to anger you," she managed, holding her burning cheek with one hand.

"Well, you did. You can never be a wife to me. I would divorce you if I could." He turned to leave the tent.

Tamar watched in horror as he fell face forward to the earth. Had he tripped?

But when he didn't move, Tamar crept closer. Was he playing one of his games? She held her breath as she came alongside him and knelt. She slowly touched his shoulder. He did not move. She tried to roll him onto his back but still feared he was pretending to be hurt.

She must do something. If he was playing a trick, let his father deal with him. She rose and ran through the tent door toward the fire where Judah's family sat eating.

"You must come," she said, standing before Judah. "Something is wrong with Er." Her shaking grew, and she could not stop her teeth from chattering.

Judah jumped up and ran toward her tent, and she followed at his heels. "What happened?" he yelled, his long legs putting him far ahead of her.

"I don't know. He turned to walk out the door when he fell to the ground and didn't get up." She put her hands on her knees to catch her breath.

Judah brushed past her into the tent and fell to his knees at Er's side. He rolled Er onto his back, but still he did not move. His lips held a bluish cast, and his face had paled.

Judah shook his son. "Er!" he cried. "Wake up, Son." But Er's limbs fell limp, and Tamar saw the look of death in his eyes.

Kaella shoved the tent door open, nearly knocking into Tamar. She quickly scooted toward the back of the tent, away from Er's family, who descended on her small home, all wailing and crying over their son and brother.

"He's dead," Judah said with defeat in his gaze. He turned to Onan and Shelah. "Come, help me make a bier to carry him to a cave for burial." They quickly left the tent, leaving Tamar with Kaella and Er's body.

Kaella's gaze shifted to her, and Tamar could not tell whether there was any kindness in her or not. "You will help me prepare my son's body."

Tamar nodded. She stepped closer and did as Kaella told

her, gathering linen and spices and water to wash his body. A body she should know well after many months of marriage, but she hardly recognized this man in his unmoving, silent state. What had killed him? He hadn't touched her food, so no one could accuse her of poisoning him. He was young. Too young to just . . . die.

Kaella worked alongside her as they washed and anointed the body, one moment grieving and the next looking on Tamar with questions she did not raise. Would Er's family accuse her of his death?

But she hadn't killed him. She had simply withstood his angry, cruel words. Could words kill a man?

32

Judah paced the entire length of the camp and back again. He stopped before his tent, stared at the door, and marched off again. Anger fueled his steps, and along with it a healthy sense of fear. God had surely killed Er. And it was his fault. If he had taught the boy how to be a husband, how to love his wife . . . Had his son truly treated his bride so poorly? If so, why?

"Tell me again how it happened," Judah had said to Tamar for the third time, days after they had buried Er.

Tamar shivered as though she were cold and wrapped her arms about herself. "I had prepared a special meal for him. He grew angry that we were not eating with the family and wouldn't touch the food." She scratched the back of her neck. "I have told you twice before."

"You said that he yelled at you. Did he curse you? Did he curse God?" he asked.

That thought had haunted Judah in the month of mourning that had recently passed. Tamar had haltingly answered his questions the same way every time, but Judah sensed that she was not telling him what mattered most. Had Er abused her? He couldn't bring himself to ask. Still, Er must have said cruel things to her. Hadn't he done the same to his own mother a time or two?

Judah turned back and finally stopped pacing in front of his tent. One thing was certain. Tamar had not dishonored his son by accusing the dead. Whatever happened had to be from God. Only God held the power of life and death.

The image of seventeen-year-old Joseph flashed in his mind. *Did You take my son because of what I did to my brother?*

But he found no answer in the heavens or in his heart. That didn't mean he shouldn't do the right thing. He drew in a deep breath, pushed open the tent flap, and looked at Onan's pallet. Onan sat upon it, legs crossed. By his disheveled appearance, he had obviously just awakened, and it was long past dawn.

"Onan," Judah said, walking across the room to stand above him. "Get up! Your brother did not provide Tamar a child or himself an heir. So go and marry Tamar, as our law requires of the brother of a man who has died. You must produce an heir for your brother." He pulled his son to his feet and shoved him toward the basin of water. "Wash up. After you eat, you are going to marry your sister-in-law."

Onan looked at Judah, eyes wide. "What if I don't want to marry her? Er wanted to choose his own wife. I want to do the same, and it's not her!"

"Why do you find her so distasteful? You must raise up a child for your brother." He walked closer until Onan began to wash his face and wet his hair.

Judah watched him, then decided it was better to make him thoroughly wash in the creek. Onan complained the entire walk there, and Judah wondered if any of his sons were ready to marry. Perhaps he had hurried things along too quickly. But Onan could wed, and he must keep the traditions of his fathers.

Onan crawled up the bank a short time later and dressed

in the clothes he had not had his mother wash in over a week. Judah noticed and knew Tamar deserved better, but he would waste no more time.

"Come," he said when Onan had tied his sandals. "I will take you to her tent now."

Onan said nothing, but Judah did not miss the scowl on his face. They crossed the pasture and climbed a low hill until at last the tent Kaella had made for Er and Tamar came into view. Judah spotted the girl outside, squatting over the fire and stirring something. She had taken to eating alone since Er's death, and Judah could not help but think that the reason had to do with the way Kaella acted toward her.

But Er's death wasn't the girl's fault, no matter what his wife might think. He had questioned her, and he knew by what she did not say that she was innocent. His heart told him this was true.

They came to the tent and Judah stopped near the fire, Onan standing sullenly at his side.

Tamar looked up and quickly stood. "My lord, what can I do for you?" She offered him a slight bow, hands folded in front of her.

"We have a tradition," Judah said, looking at Onan. "When a man dies, leaving no children, that man's brother must marry the widow to raise up a son for him. I am here to give you Onan as a husband to raise up a son to carry on Er's name." He placed a hand on Onan's shoulder and urged him to step closer to Tamar.

Tamar's eyes grew wide. She looked from one man to the other as if both had lost their senses. Had she not heard of this tradition? But of course she would know of it. Though it did not happen often, her people had practiced it for generations.

Her silence lingered as she looked at Onan, who did not meet her gaze. She closed her eyes briefly, then lifted her head, acceptance apparent in her expression. "I am my lord's servant," she said softly. She let her hands fall to her sides.

"And I declare Onan, my son, to be husband to Tamar, daughter of Yassib, to carry on his brother's offspring." Judah fairly pushed Onan closer and took each of their hands. He placed Tamar's hand in Onan's, and Onan finally lifted his gaze to the girl and gripped her hand.

Judah released his hold, said a quick blessing over them, and told Onan that this was his home now, with Tamar. Onan did not argue or give Judah any complaint, to Judah's great relief. Instead, he led Tamar inside the tent.

Judah turned to walk away. Onan would fulfill the vow and all would be well. It had to be. How could he face the men of the land and especially Yassib if his own sons could not give them both a grandson? He and his generation would die without grandchildren, like Joseph, who could have no kin to carry his name.

Guilt over Joseph, over Er, over his life, followed Judah to the sheep pens.

LrLrLr

Tamar felt her whole body go numb, barely sensing Onan's hand holding hers or him leading her into the tent. What had just happened here? He was barely old enough to be anyone's husband. If Er had been childish, Onan was more so. She had seen his selfish attitudes, had heard the taunting and insulting words they both used, all in the name of humor. And now, just when she was free of the one, she found herself bound to the other.

The tent flap closed behind them, and she heard Judah's footsteps fade in the distance. Onan let go of her hand once they entered the tent. The porridge would burn over the fire if she did not attend to it, but what could she do? He had pulled her inside, and she was captive to do what he wanted.

He turned to face her after a lengthy silence and looked her up and down. "I didn't want this," he said, his tone irritated. "My father gave me no choice, but be very clear, I will marry the woman I want to marry and have my own children. If you think you can come into our family and kill my brother and then acquire a child from me, you are mistaken."

Tamar took a step back and crossed her arms, shielding her heart, which now pounded in her chest. Were both brothers so cruel? "What of the law?" she asked softly, hoping her expression showed humility and not the disdain his words evoked in her.

"You care about the law?" He laughed. "All right then. Come." He reached for her hand, which he had to pry from her clutched arms, and dragged her toward the bed she had shared with Er.

Light spilled through the sides of the tent where she had lifted them slightly, exposing more than secluding them. He shoved her onto the mat without removing her clothes. Like Er, he did not treat her with kindness but forced his way upon her.

Tamar closed her eyes, her cheeks heating with shame, silently begging the God of Judah to look on her with kindness. Let this time be enough to give her a child so she never had to endure this man again.

But when it came time for him to implant his seed within her, he pulled away and spilled it onto the dirt beside the pallet. His breath came fast as he knelt above her, laughing at her shocked look.

"What have you done?" she asked, feeling as though she were falling into some kind of abyss.

His hand connected with her mouth like his brother's had,

and she did not see it coming. She cried out and shielded her face, fearing another blow, but Onan stood and walked out of the tent, leaving her alone.

Tamar buried her head in the pillow and wept.

ᘉᘉᘉ

Judah drew a breath and at last felt the world would be kind to his family again. Onan and Tamar seemed to be doing well, though there was still no sign that she carried a child. Onan's attitude had lifted from sullen to pleased, if Judah understood his son's expressions, but Tamar's eyes held a hollow sadness, perhaps even despair. Surely Onan treated the girl better than Er had.

He pondered that thought but did not let it linger as he walked beside the sheep where they fed in fertile fields. The rains had been plentiful and the crops and fields ripe in each season, in greater quantity than Judah had ever seen. He would make a hefty profit from the sale of the wheat and barley and the wool once they held their annual shearing.

He whistled a tune he had learned from his mother as he thought of the good things that had come to him even since Er's death, though he would never get over the loss of his son. How did a father ever forget a child? He'd felt so blessed when the boy was born, and to lose him . . . he had never imagined such a thing could happen.

He looked up as Onan walked toward him, a smile on his tanned face. Did his son have news for him? Was Tamar finally with child?

"Father," Onan said, using his staff to aid him. "I want you to give me some of the sheep and goats to start my own flock. If I'm to be a husband, I must also be able to care for my wife."

And children? "Everything I have is yours already, Onan,"

Judah said. "When I am gone, you and Shelah will share in my wealth. You know this. You have no need of it early. You have plenty to care for a wife and many children."

"Tamar will not be having children. My next wife may, but Tamar will not." Onan's grin held a hint of menace, and Judah felt his knees weaken.

"What have you done?" he managed to say through a suddenly dry throat. He held his son's gaze with a commanding one of his own.

Onan offered Judah a bold look that told him everything. In his mind, he was doing his "duty" by Tamar on behalf of Er, but he had no intention of giving her a child.

"What you are doing is wrong, my son. God will not be pleased with this disobedience. What is so wrong with giving Er an heir? The next child she has will be yours." Judah had to make Onan see the sense in it all. Fear that this son was also angering God rose within him.

"I don't care what your god thinks, Abba. I want to pick my own wife and have my own children. Nothing you say can change that." He walked away, laughing.

Judah felt a sense of dread rush through him. Was Tamar a curse on his household that two of his sons should disdain her so? She was a beautiful young woman from a good family. Why couldn't his sons have been content with that?

He turned back toward the sheep, catching Shelah's gaze. His youngest was two years behind Onan, and Judah would have to find a wife for him in the next few years. He briefly thought of Yassib and his many daughters but quickly dismissed him. Tamar was difficult enough.

Was she the reason his sons treated her so poorly? Was he wrong to think her so innocent? Surely his sons were better men than that.

A scream pierced the air and reverberated through the field, causing the sheep to startle. Judah and Shelah used their staffs to keep them from running off in fear. The cry was like that of no animal Judah had ever heard before. And yet it didn't sound entirely human either.

"What was that, Abba?" Shelah asked, coming closer. "Should we investigate?"

Judah looked in every direction. "Let's take the sheep to the pens, then we can search." He dared not risk hearing that sound again and sending the sheep into a panic. "Let's hurry."

Between the two of them—for Onan had left them to do the work—they managed to coax the sheep and goats to follow them back to the pens.

"You examine them and close them in," Judah said to Shelah. "I'm going to see if I can find the animal lest it come and attack them when we are not here."

Shelah nodded, and Judah trudged toward home in the direction of the sound, his staff holding him up as his thoughts whirled with Onan's revelation. What could he do or say to make his son see that he needed to do what was right?

The midafternoon sun beat down on him as he walked, and he slowed his pace as he reached the copse of trees near his camp. Something lay among the underbrush, and as the light filtered through the branches, he saw the form of a man. He crept closer, recognizing the cloak, the sandals . . . the form of his son. Blood drained from his face as he drew close and turned his son onto his back, memories of doing the same for Er flashing through his mind.

Onan. With his mouth wide open as if he were still screaming, his eyes vacant and staring at something Judah could not see. Something that had terrified him? Had something scared him to death?

Judah looked around, high into the trees and through the low-hanging branches, but saw no movement, no animals prowling, as they were more apt to do at night. He looked again at the prone form of his second son, gone. Had God killed him, as Judah perceived He had killed Er? Or was Tamar really the one to blame? Was the woman cursed?

Confusion and grief engulfed him, and he bent, weeping, over his son. At last he lifted Onan's body into his arms and carried him home. The crowds would come, and the boy would be laid to rest in the same cave as his brother.

How could he bear it?

As he entered the camp, he glimpsed Tamar standing at the door of her tent, watching him. He could not see her expression, but his heart beat faster as he grappled with another grief linked to this woman. How could he ever give Shelah to her? He could lose all of his sons and gain nothing but a widow to care for.

No. He dared not risk it. He knew the law and what he should do, but Shelah was young. Tamar could wait for him. Yes, that was what he would do—send her back to Yassib until Shelah was of age. Then he would send for her again.

Though as he heard Kaella's cries and looked once more into the face of his son, he was not sure he ever wanted to see Tamar again.

33

Joseph watched the sun dip below the surface of the Nile, a view he found relaxing after a day of moving through a fourth of the cities and fields in Egypt to make sure the grain was counted and collected. Hamid had told him that the numbers were growing too high to count, but Joseph insisted they continue keeping track of the amount to show to Pharaoh for as long as they could.

Now he stood on the roof of his house and let the stress of the day flow from him. He could never have imagined he would find himself in this place or this position of power. Sometimes his whole life felt surreal, as if he was in the middle of a dream more impossible than those he'd had in his youth. *Was this Your plan all along, Adonai?*

The sun's last rays, splayed in fingers of orange and red, set the Nile on fire on its way to the other side of the world. Or, as the Egyptians taught, to die and rise again each dawn.

Joseph could not accept such teaching, even though God did not always seem close to him here. Hadn't God blessed him in everything his hands had touched? Hadn't He given him a wife he had come to love and Manasseh, his precocious two-year-old? The boy was smart and already speaking in long sentences, surprising in one so young.

He turned at the sound of voices behind him in the house. Manasseh's nurse held him as he wiggled to get down. "Abba!" the boy cried.

Joseph smiled. He opened the doors leading to the house. "Let him come," he told the nurse.

She placed Manasseh on his feet, and he ran toward Joseph, who scooped him into his arms, laughing. "And what have you done today, my son?"

"Salma took me to play." He touched Joseph's ornamented robe. "Are you leaving again, Abba?"

Joseph rubbed the boy's head. "Not today."

Manasseh clapped his small hands, and Joseph carried him into the house to his private rooms, where he removed his Egyptian garb each night. The boy bounced on Joseph's raised bed while Joseph's servant helped him return to a normal Egyptian rather than a ruling one.

Manasseh ran to him once he wore his plain tunic and the robe and headdress and makeup had been removed. Joseph tossed the boy into the air and caught him again, bringing on delighted giggles. He let Manasseh lead him into his room, and Joseph knelt onto the floor to play with him.

An hour passed, and Joseph expected the nurse to return to put Manasseh to bed when the noises coming from his wife's rooms grew louder. Was it time?

Asenath was due to birth their second child any day, but she had shown no signs of labor when they spoke before he left for the fields. He lifted Manasseh into his arms again and walked the length of the hall toward Asenath's rooms. Manasseh's nurse appeared, and Joseph kissed his son's cheek, then handed the boy to her.

He poked his head into his wife's sitting room, but the obvious rushing of midwives and servants caused him to walk back the way he had come. He traversed the halls of his large estate, every now and then hearing Asenath's distant cries.

Please, Adonai, be with her. Deliver to her a safe and healthy child.

He almost asked for another boy but decided those things were up to God. He would be happy with a daughter as well as a son.

As the night waned and he stood again on the balcony overlooking the Nile, a baby's cry pierced the air. He turned and hurried down the halls toward Asenath's rooms. This time he entered the outer room and waited. The midwife came at last with a wrapped bundle and placed the child in his arms. He glimpsed his wife through the door, saw her smile his way.

"You have another son, my lord," the midwife told him.

Joseph looked into the face of the child and felt an overwhelming sense of wonder. He walked with the boy to the threshold of Asenath's bedchamber. "He is Ephraim," he said, looking from the boy to her. "It is because God has made me fruitful in the land of my suffering."

"Ephraim," she said, sounding groggy, as she had with her last delivery. "It is a good name."

Love for his small family rose within him, and he watched his son's mouth move as if he was looking for his mother. Joseph laughed for joy. He handed Ephraim to the midwife to give to Asenath, then quietly watched as she nursed the babe.

God *had* made him fruitful and blessed him in the land of his suffering. He had made him forget his betraying brothers. He had given him better than he had known before.

Joseph knelt, raised his hands toward the heavens, and worshiped.

 பாப

Asenath held Manasseh's hand while Safiya carried Ephraim to the inner courtyard gardens of their vast estate. Months had passed since Ephraim's birth, and she had taken to bringing them to this favorite place. Manasseh loved to run between the rows of bushes and often brought her bouquets of flowers he'd picked from the clay pots or flowering trees.

The sun had risen to the midpoint of the sky, so she chose the bench in the shade and sat. Taking Ephraim from Safiya, she held him to her breast to nurse. "Keep watch of Manasseh," she told the girl, knowing how easily the boy could lose himself in the maze of greenery. The gardeners had created a place of immense beauty here, following Joseph's instruction and her design. She smiled as she gazed at it all, remembering Joseph's approval and the light in his eyes as he agreed to her final choices.

"What brings such joy to my dear wife's face?" Joseph asked, coming up behind her.

She startled at hearing his voice so early in the day and turned to greet him. "You are home early, my love. Is everything all right?" She patted the seat beside her, beckoning him to sit with her.

He obliged and leaned back against the stone bench, stretching his legs and crossing them at the ankles. "All is well. So well that they cannot keep up with the building of granaries. Hamid has his hands full overseeing the placement of these storehouses, but the amount of harvest is nearly too much to count. And we are only beginning our fourth year of plenty."

Asenath lifted Ephraim to her chest and rubbed his back,

waiting for him to burp, and looked at her husband. "That is good news, is it not? More is better if the famine to come is going to be as bad as you have said."

Joseph nodded. "It is good. It is just a lot to keep ahead of. We should have anticipated more when we saw the yield in the first year. As it is, we are only one step ahead of each harvest, whether it is grain or fruit from the vine. God has blessed it all."

Asenath studied her husband's face, saw the lines along his brow, and wondered if the work Pharaoh had him do was all that filled his mind. But before she could ask, Manasseh came running through the maze of plants, straight for Joseph.

"Abba! You are home!" he cried.

Joseph sat up straight and reached for the boy, who flung himself into Joseph's arms. Their mingled laughter filled Asenath with a sense of deep delight. How blessed she was to have been given to this man. How good his God had been to all of them.

She listened to Manasseh chatter about his exploration in the garden and saw his little hand open to reveal a beetle in his palm. Asenath flinched and leaned away from the bug, but Joseph took it in his own hand, and the two of them examined its large body and small head.

"This is a scarab beetle," Joseph said. "The Egyptians consider this beetle to be sacred or special. But why don't we put it back into the garden so it can do what my God created it to do?"

Manasseh nodded, his face suddenly solemn. "I didn't crush it, Abba. I did as you said and held it gently."

"I know you did," Joseph said, patting his back. "You did well." He kissed the boy's forehead and set him down to place the creature back into the garden.

Joseph watched him with an expression Asenath had not seen before. "Something is on your mind, my husband," she said softly, while Manasseh crouched low to watch the insect and Ephraim nursed at the other breast.

Joseph faced her, his dark eyes open and sad. "He looks just like my little brother Benjamin. My only full blood brother. I cannot know what Benjamin looks like today, of course, but the last time I saw him, he was still a young child, barely more than an infant in arms. Manasseh has nearly all of the features that Benjamin had then. When I see our son, I also see my brother. Sometimes it is harder than at others." He looked away, his gaze on Manasseh once more.

Asenath sat in silence beside him, struggling with how to respond. Joseph had rarely spoken of his family of origin. He'd been in Egypt, spoken in the Egyptian tongue, and looked Egyptian for so long that she sometimes forgot he was Hebrew. Did he miss the family that had betrayed him? That much he had told her. She thought Manasseh's birth had caused him to forget them. Obviously not.

"Tell me about Benjamin and your mother and father," she said at last, hoping the question would not cause him undue pain.

Joseph did not take his eyes off Manasseh, who now walked with Safiya to examine the lotus blossoms and the pool in the center, where he was not allowed to go without an adult by his side. Joseph's silence lingered, but after a time he drew in a lengthy breath and released it. "My father and I were very close. My mother, Rachel, died with Benjamin's birth, so he never knew her. I knew her well, and I'm afraid she probably spoiled me. Both my mother and father favored me above all of my brothers, even above Benjamin, for my father struggled with the grief of my mother's loss."

He swallowed and glanced at her. "I have not seen my father or Benjamin in seventeen years. And while I know God is with me and has helped me forget most of my family since He gave me you and our sons, there is always the reminder that part of me is missing, especially when I gaze on our firstborn. He does not bring me sadness, Asenath," he said, looking at her with kindness. "He simply brings back the memories."

"But those memories of your brother are good ones," she said, hoping it was true.

Joseph nodded. "Yes. They are good ones. I only wish I could have known him and watched him grow up and taught him how to be a man of character, and taught him of our God."

"Surely your father will do those things for him. It is what fathers do." She lifted Ephraim to her shoulder and again patted his back in a slow, circular motion.

"My father will teach him of our God, but I do not know if he will teach him all he needs to know. And I do not know whether Benjamin will receive the teaching as I did. My brothers do not trust in Adonai as my grandfather, my father, and I do." Joseph rubbed a hand down the back of his neck. He was still in the garb he wore when he went into the streets of the city.

"One day Benjamin will believe as you do, my husband. He is your blood kin. God will reach out to him, and he will know the truth of all that has happened to you. Perhaps then all of your brothers will believe." It was wishful thinking, for who could know the mind and heart of another? But she had to give him hope.

Joseph smiled and cupped her cheek. "You are good for me." He leaned closer and kissed her, then kissed Ephraim's head as well. "But I must be getting back. I wanted to see you all, so I slipped away." He glanced at the sun. "Pharaoh wants to meet with me to hear the progress of all we are gathering."

Asenath nodded. "Then of course you must go. And we will be waiting with your favorite foods to eat when you return tonight." She stood with him as he called Manasseh and held the boy once more.

"Abba will be back soon," he said, tickling the boy's belly. Manasseh giggled and squirmed, and Joseph hugged him close then released him. He smiled at her and walked back into the house.

Asenath watched until he was out of sight. What mysteries lay beneath her husband's thoughts besides these few he had shared with her? Would she ever know?

34

CANAAN

Tamar sat at the loom in her father's house, dressed in widow's weeds. She should be used to her life by now, but to be widowed twice in less than a year . . . She still fought nightmares and could not seem to find a sense of peace. That Judah would send her back to her father was even worse.

"Go back to your parents' home and remain a widow until my son Shelah is old enough to marry you," he had said.

She'd stared at Judah, sure she had not heard him correctly. Return to her father? "But I belong to your household now. How can I return to my father? Such a thing is a disgrace to him and to me."

How bold she sounded even to her own ears. But Kaella's scowl and teary, red eyes only added to Judah's insistence. "I will speak to Yassib," he said. "Do not worry. It will only be until Shelah is old enough to take a wife."

He had sounded so reassuring. So caring.

The cloak she was weaving held colorful threads, and she imagined herself wearing it if she could ever put off the black garments she was forced to wear until she remarried.

Would she marry again? Would she bear children and have a family to surround her? Or would she live here until her parents passed into the next life and she herself died alone? A deep ache settled inside of her where warmth and love once lived.

I just want to love someone. To be loved in return.

But Er and Onan had never loved her. They had used and abused her. Yet her father-in-law had acted as if their deaths were her fault. Not at first—not with Er. But when Onan died . . . Judah had sent her back to her father three days after they buried him.

The thread knotted in her hand as she wove, forcing her to stop the shuttle and pull the knot through the other strands. Her weaving used to bring her father a goodly sum at the markets, but since returning home she found everything tangled. Her threads. Her thoughts. Her life. She rarely left the house except to draw water, but even there the townswomen barely spoke to her.

Tears threatened, but her emotion was interrupted by a loud knock on her door. "Tamar? Come out of there. I have news."

Her sister Donatiya poked her head in the room, and her expression softened as she looked into Tamar's eyes. Tamar never had been very good at hiding her pain. She stood, leaving the knot, and followed her sister into the courtyard, where her mother sat grinding grain.

"There you are," her mother said. "I wish you would come out of that room more often. You grow paler by the day. Just because you are a widow doesn't mean you should wither away by yourself."

"It is hard to move the loom, Ima," she said, to give an excuse that her mother might accept.

"Then we will have your father move it."

Apparently Ima would not be so easily convinced. Tamar

had spent far too many days alone, and she felt the sadness of it grow by the day. She needed the company of family. She just hadn't planned on it being with her family of birth. Marriage had not turned out to be at all what she had imagined.

"That would be nice," she said. "Now what is this news that is so important I must stop my work?" She glanced at her sister.

"Judah's wife Kaella has died," Donatiya said, a frown creasing her brow. "Some say she never got over the deaths of her first two sons."

Kaella gone? Tamar sank onto a stone ledge, for her knees had weakened too much to hold her steady. "When?" She looked at her mother, who had surely been the one who first heard the news.

Ima stopped her grinding and brushed the dust from her hands. "Two days ago, though the news only reached us this morning at the well. The nerve of Judah to keep that from us! We are family, after all."

"There is nothing tying us to him except me, Ima," Tamar said. "I'm sure he is in shock and grieving." He had only Shelah left to comfort him. A sense of sorrow filled her, not only for Kaella to lose so much that it apparently took her life but also for Judah to lose so much. Did he blame her for Kaella's death as well?

"You know, Shelah has been of age for you to wed for months. Judah should have called for you by now."

Her mother's words did not surprise her. Tamar had kept track of the months until a year had passed. Plenty of time for Judah to bring her back to his family.

"I don't think Judah intends for me to marry Shelah," Tamar said softly. She twisted her hands in her lap, looking at calluses she had acquired from working the threads each day.

"He would be breaking the contract with your father if that

is true," her mother said, her tone holding the disgust she had often shown toward the man since Tamar's return.

"I can't force him, Ima." She couldn't very well walk into Judah's camp and insist she marry Shelah. It wasn't her place. And her father had made no move to act on her behalf. Did he also believe her cursed because of the deaths of Judah's sons? If he did, why not get her out of the agreement and allow her to marry another?

A deep sigh came from her mother. "I know you can't, dear girl. The gods know I have tried my best to get your father to speak to the man on your behalf, but now . . . he will never go and ask such a thing with Kaella so soon in the grave."

"He didn't even tell us so we could mourn with him," Donatiya said, coming to sit beside Tamar. She placed a hand on Tamar's shoulder. "Don't worry, my sister. Something will change for you soon. You cannot lose hope."

Donatiya was always the cheerful sister, and Tamar forced a smile to appease her. But her heart still carried the weight of sadness. If she had remained in Judah's camp, she might have given Kaella some hope. Then again, if both Judah and Kaella blamed her, she might have brought about greater pain for them.

"If only Father would break the contract. Perhaps someone would have me, widowed or not." Tamar knew she now carried a stigma that would never leave her. She would die alone and childless, just as she had feared back in her room. She rose slowly. "Thank you for telling me about Kaella, Ima. I will mourn for her. Perhaps in time, Judah will see that calling me back to marry Shelah, once the time of mourning is past, is the best thing he can do." She turned to walk the short distance to her room.

"I will be surprised if that man ever changes," Donatiya said in an uncharacteristically bitter tone.

Tamar tried to ignore the words. Unfortunately, her sister

was right about one thing. Judah was a stubborn man, not unlike his sons. His sons were evil whereas Judah was simply obstinate. Maybe she truly was better off without them.

ᒐᒐᒐ

EGYPT

Joseph stood patiently as his manservant finished placing the gold chains about his neck and the thick bracelets on his arms. He'd at last grown used to being dressed by another, though he often wondered why he needed such help. But if having servants do the work for him allowed them to earn food to eat and clothes to wear, so much the better. He would not deny a man his wages for his work.

"There," Ahmed said. "You look as royal as Pharaoh, my lord. Well, almost as royal," he amended.

"Thank you, Ahmed." Joseph smiled. "You have done well." He walked through the halls, poked his head into Asenath's rooms to bid her farewell, and strode toward his chariot. Normally he would travel to a few cities, then meet with Pharaoh to discuss what he'd found. But this morning Pharaoh had requested his presence in the audience hall, and he was not one to disobey.

He hopped into the gleaming gold and white chariot with red stripes along the sides and sat behind his driver. The man bowed to him, then took the reins and led the way through the streets of Memphis.

Pharaoh's palace was just a turn of the corner from Joseph's connected estate. Joseph loved the way it caught the rays of the sun, the gold glimmering like a glassy sea in early morn. Blue and gold and a small mix of red and green made up the bricks of the building.

The chariot stopped in front of the wide white doors, and Joseph alighted and took the grand steps to the portico that surrounded the building. Guards stood watch holding tall spears, dressed in military garb. They stepped aside at Joseph's approach and allowed him entrance with a bow.

The great hall that led to the throne spread out before him, and he glimpsed Pharaoh sitting there waiting for him. Joseph walked forward, head held high, and came to kneel before Pharaoh.

"You may stand, Zaphenath-Paneah. Come, sit beside me."

The pharaoh was younger than Joseph, which always struck Joseph as strange. He felt like a father to the man, though he was actually more the age of an older brother. The king had reigned as co-regent with his father, then on his own before Joseph came to Egypt.

"Thank you, my lord," Joseph said, climbing the steps and taking his seat next to Pharaoh.

"I trust things are still going as my dreams suggested? We are securing a great quantity of grain as before?" He glanced at Joseph but did not hold his gaze.

"Yes, my king. The numbers are recorded at each granary, and we are still building new ones. In only three years, we already have enough grain to feed all of Egypt. Should the famine begin early, your people will not go hungry." Joseph still felt a sense of awe every time he inspected the yield and spent nights with Hamid trying to find new places to house it all.

"We will be able to feed the rest of the world if your god continues to provide at this rate," Pharaoh said, this time holding Joseph's gaze. "I expect the famine will strike more than just Egypt. When that time comes, we will gain the wealth of all the nations around us."

Joseph nodded. He had considered this. "We will charge

them as we will the Egyptian people. I would imagine that the years of plenty are happening in other lands as well, but God revealed to Pharaoh His plan to save many people when that time comes. We cannot know whether He revealed that same truth to the leaders of other lands."

"If He did, then I hope they are as wise as you are. If not for your wisdom, even Egypt would not have thought to preserve during these times of prosperity." Pharaoh clapped his hands, and two servants appeared with a gilded box and placed it in his hands. He shifted in his seat and handed the box to Joseph. "This is for you. My thanks for what you have already done."

Joseph took the box. "My lord has already given me more than I deserve."

"Nonsense. You deserve much more. You have preserved my life as well and that of my sons."

Joseph saw the gratitude in Pharaoh's eyes. "Thank you, my lord." He lifted the lid, peered inside, and pulled out an intricately carved silver chalice.

"Use it to drink wine or to divine the future. It is good for both," Pharaoh said.

Joseph turned the chalice to look at it from all angles. The cup was exquisite. He lowered his head in respect. "I thank you again. I will treasure this and keep it in a place of prominence in my house."

"And use it, I hope." Pharaoh offered Joseph a rare smile.

"And use it too," Joseph said, placing the cup back into the box.

"If there is nothing else," the pharaoh said, pointing toward the doors, "you may return to your duties."

"There is nothing else." Joseph stood, bowed low, and backed away from the throne.

Once outside, he ordered his driver to return home. He would put the cup in his rooms and then meet Hamid to begin his travels throughout the next city on their itinerary. They'd made the rounds from the Nile Delta to the south of Egypt and were starting over again.

As he rode home, his mind was not on counting grain or building new storage cities but on Pharaoh's words. Would people come from other lands to purchase grain from Egypt? Would his brothers be forced to do the same?

What would he do if he saw them again, this time in need of his aid?

35

HEBRON

Dinah picked up the clay bowl and walked toward her father's tent, her gait slower than usual. Memories flooded her mind every year on this day. The day her brothers had returned to their father with Joseph's cloak, ripped and bloodied. The day her father went into mourning and despite everything had never come out. Most of the camp kept their distance from him on this day, but the man had to eat, so Dinah took him food.

How she wished she was able to bring the light into his eyes again.

She had pleaded every year, surprising even herself at how fast the years had passed. Joseph had been seventeen when he left to find their brothers, and he'd been dead as many years.

A sob lifted her chest, and she stopped, forcing it down. She could not give in to the grief again like her father did. She could not. Hadn't life dealt her enough difficult blows? She'd done her best to care for Benjamin and serve her father, but Jacob's grief only grew with every passing year.

A deep sigh escaped, wavering as she struggled with emotions that should be long past. She lifted her head and continued walking to Jacob's tent. The flap was down, and the sides had not been rolled up to let in the light of day.

Dinah lifted the flap and stepped into the dark interior. "Abba?" She moved into the familiar room and set the bowl near where he normally ate when he wasn't with the family. But he wasn't there. Instead, she found him standing near the center pole, staring into space, unseeing.

"Abba?" she said again. She touched his arm, and he slowly met her gaze. "Are you all right, Abba?" She looked him up and down, suddenly worried that the grief was becoming too hard to bear. She already felt that way and often wondered if he would die of a broken heart. *Please, God, help him.* Her silent prayer came often.

Her father at last turned to face her. "I am well, my daughter." He walked to the cushions and sat. "You brought food. I am not hungry, but I thank you."

"You must eat, Abba. You need your strength." She knelt beside him and touched his knee. "I know this day is hard for you. It is for me as well. But if you will come into the light of day, walk in the fruitful fields, and see how good God has been to us these past few years, surely you will feel better. Joseph would want you to be glad, Abba."

Jacob looked at the food, then at Dinah. His brows drew down, and the telltale signs of sadness filled his dark eyes. "Yes, Joseph would encourage me as you have done." But he did not look encouraged. He picked up the clay bowl and dipped the bread into the porridge.

When he finished eating, Dinah took the bowl and stood. "Won't you come with me to see the fields?" She extended a hand.

He nodded, using his staff instead to help him rise. "We can take a short walk to see the wheat. Bring Benjamin. The boy will enjoy seeing the abundance. If we have as good a crop as we did the past few years, we can sell it for a goodly profit." He walked with her into the main part of the camp, where Leah greeted him.

"Jacob. You are looking well today." Leah took the bowl from Dinah's hands while Dinah went to fetch Benjamin. When she returned with him, she found her parents deep in conversation.

"You are sure you do not wish to go with us?" Jacob asked.

Leah shook her head. "If not for this headache, I would surely come. I thank you for asking me. But I fear I do not feel well. Forgive me, my lord. Another time, perhaps."

Dinah watched her mother move toward her tent and caught the look of concern on her father's face. "What did she say to you?" she asked him.

Jacob stared after Leah, his grief seeming worse after he watched her enter her tent. Her gait had slowed, and her shoulders hunched forward as if her body was too heavy to hold upright.

"She has not been well," he said as if speaking to the wind. He couldn't or wouldn't look at Dinah. She studied him and saw the fear in his gaze. "She should have told me sooner."

Why had her mother chosen this day to tell him? Why had she kept her illness or whatever malady had come over her to herself? Dinah should have been more aware. Should have noticed when they wove together.

But she had noticed. She had seen the taut lines along her mother's mouth and her almost shriveled expression when her head brought her pain. She had shown Dinah that expression often, and Dinah had not seen the significance. How ill was she?

Dinah stood torn between going with her father to the fields and following her mother into the tent to check on her.

"When we return, you should check on Ima Leah," Benjamin

said, answering her unspoken question for her. "She might need some herbs or whatever it is you give us when we are not well."

Jacob turned at Benjamin's words and looked at his son, his face smoothing into a compassionate smile. "Yes, Dinah, you must see that Leah is well. I cannot bear to lose her too."

Dinah walked beside her father and brother to the fields, but her mind was no longer on Joseph or the plentiful harvest to come. How could she have been so blind to what was so plainly in front of her? Her mother was sick. Just how sick, Dinah chafed to hurry home and find out.

ᒐᒐᒐ

CANAAN, 1823 BC

Judah looked about his tent, the silence of the room causing him to dress quickly and leave the place as soon as he could. Though Kaella had been gone now for nearly a year, he could not get used to her absence. Shelah had already left to gather the sheep, and Judah pushed his staff into the earth to hurry himself along. The air was warm, the sun kissing his face. A sense of relief to be free of the tent filled him, and he wondered not for the first time if he should have one of the servant girls who cooked and wove and baked pottery for him make him a new tent as well. He could not imagine marrying again. Though he could not deny that he still battled manly desires.

He caught sight of Shelah calling the sheep and goats to follow him toward the fields. Judah drew up beside him. "You are up early. Did you eat?"

Shelah nodded. "Yes, Abba. Samina made porridge and bread for me. I think she cooks as well as Ima did. She would make a fine wife." He met Judah's gaze, and Judah could not hold it.

"You are meant for Tamar." He turned away, for he knew he could not bear to lose another son to that woman. Would it be so wrong to let Shelah have his subtle request?

But the nagging thought to call Tamar back to his camp had lingered since Kaella's death. Still, how could he go against his wife's dying wish to never allow Tamar near their home again? How could he give his last son to a woman who had been the reason his first two sons were dead?

He couldn't do it. He wouldn't do it. But what was he to do with Tamar? She legally belonged to his household, and he had known from the beginning that sending her back to her father was not the right thing to do. Yassib had shown his anger and frustration with Judah, but he had also given in to Judah's request for the sake of his two lost sons.

There was no possible way he could bring Tamar back now. If Shelah died, he would have no one. Even if he himself married again and his new wife birthed more children, it would be years before they could help him. He would die before he could train them to be better men than his oldest sons had been.

But it was Tamar who had caused this curse to come upon him, not Er and Onan. At first he had not thought so, but now fear rose within him whenever he thought of the girl. He could not go through such loss again.

"What has you so quiet, Abba?" Shelah asked as they came to green pastures and the sheep spread out to eat their fill.

It still amazed Judah how easy it was to go in and out and find lush pastures. God had surely blessed the land, even if He had not blessed him. Was he to do something with this blessing of a land that seemed to drip with milk and honey? Everywhere he turned, everything he touched flourished and grew. Except his family.

What he wouldn't give to have his family again. He glanced

at Shelah, aware of his questioning look. "I'm thinking of your mother and brothers and the bountiful land. I'm thinking of Tamar and you and what I should do." He held his son's wide-eyed gaze.

"I don't want to marry her, Abba. I want Samina." He looked at his feet, his voice dropping in pitch. "And I don't want to die too."

Judah patted his shoulder, then cupped his face with one hand. "And you won't," he said after a pause. "I cannot lose you, and I cannot bring that woman into our house again. I will go to her father and break the contract. Let her be free to marry another."

"No one will want her," Shelah said, his wisdom beyond his years. "Everyone thinks she's cursed by God."

Judah leaned back, unaware of that rumor. He had considered his sons cursed by God. But Shelah was right. Tamar was the one. She was to blame for all the sorrows that had befallen him.

"Then she shall remain a widow," he said, moving away to guide a wayward lamb back to the flock. Yes, let her remain a widow the rest of her life. She really deserved to die for what she'd done to him.

He had assumed that Yassib had raised good daughters. Daughters who could be trusted. He would not pay the price for Yassib's errors. Tamar would never be welcome in his camp again.

⨽⨼⨽

Three months later, as Tamar approached the town well, she saw a group of women standing close together, gossiping, no doubt. What poor soul were they destroying with their words this time?

She lowered her jar into the well and filled it. One of the women approached her, and she faced her after pulling the jar toward herself and holding it against her chest.

"Hello, Tamar," the woman said. "Have you heard the news?" She smiled. "Of course you haven't, for we all just learned of it ourselves."

Normally Tamar did not stand around and listen to their tales, but something in the woman's expression made her curious. "What is it?"

The woman leaned closer. "They say that Judah and his friend Hirah the Adullamite are going up to Timnah to supervise the shearing of his sheep." She tsked her tongue. "I mean, I know the man has to look after his flocks, grieving or not, but sheepshearing is always a festive time. Apparently the man has finished mourning his wife's death."

Tamar stared at her a moment, surprised at the condemnation in her tone. She quickly dismissed it. Judah couldn't grieve forever. But by now he should have given her to Shelah. She could be helping with the festivities if there had been a wedding to celebrate first.

Judah never planned to give you to Shelah.

The thought struck her with more force than she expected. Hadn't she always known it? And now her father-in-law would go to celebrate with his friends while she remained a young woman dressed in black, unable to go out anywhere until she was free of the bonds of widowhood.

"Thank you for telling me," she told the woman, shaking herself from her wayward thoughts. This was information she could use. She wasn't sure how, but as she walked back to her father's house, she knew she must find a way to change her future. She would not remain a widow all her life. She would not allow this man to leave her childless and alone.

36

HEBRON

Jacob woke to the keening sound of the women of the camp, startled by the telltale sign of mourning. He rose as quickly as his aging body would allow, dressed, and hurried to follow the sound. Leah's tent. His heart sank with the realization even before he heard the truth or saw her body. What would he do without Leah?

He braced himself and lifted the flap to find Dinah, Bilhah, and Zilpah surrounding Leah's prone form. Light came from several lamps. Dinah turned, noticing him there, and jumped up and ran to him.

His arms came around her, his only daughter. "She is gone, Abba," Dinah said, hiccupping on a sob. She laid her head on his shoulder, and he patted her back as if she were a small child to be comforted. "I should have known sooner that she'd been feeling weaker for many years. But she never complained, and she kept up with her work . . . I should have noticed."

"Your mother kept many things to herself, my daughter. It is not your fault that she has gone the way of all the earth. We all go there sometime." Still, Jacob struggled to piece together

Leah's actions of late. He had talked with her often, but she had kept her weakness from him as well. She had still made him her best pastries and offered them to him when they were alone. She had still laughed with him even though they talked more about Benjamin than her sons. Leah knew that Jacob held them accountable for Joseph's loss, and she never seemed to fault him for his feelings.

But gone? So soon? He was far older than she was. Shouldn't he have gone to Sheol first?

Now they would travel to Machpelah and Leah would rest with Jacob's ancestors there. Waiting for him until God's time for him on earth was also finished.

If only Joseph could have been placed safely in that tomb instead of torn to pieces by animals. The grief never left him, and now with Leah's loss it simply multiplied. His life was one of much trouble and hardship. Was this how God blessed a man?

He wrestled with the thought nearly as much as he had once wrestled with God Himself, causing his limp. He knew God had blessed him then. He just didn't expect blessing to come with so much heartache and loss.

"Let me see her," he said, gently pushing Dinah aside. He stepped closer to the body, which looked so peaceful, as if Leah were sleeping. "Leave me a moment," he told the women.

When at last he was alone with Leah, he knelt beside her. "Ah, Leah. I never did treat you as you deserved. You gave me fine sons, but I never told you so. You wanted my love, but I couldn't share it with you because of Rachel, and even after she was gone, I couldn't be what you needed. I wish I could have. I wish I had told you how sorry I am before now."

Could the dead hear? Some thought their spirits lingered a moment, but Leah may have died in the night. He had no way of knowing whether she could still catch what he should have said so long ago.

A single tear slipped down one cheek, and he brushed it away. "Goodbye, my love," he whispered as he stood to gaze on her one last time. He must tell her sons so they could build the bier and make the trek to Machpelah. If only it could have been him instead of her.

ມມມ

CANAAN

Tamar rose before dawn, a practice she had fallen into since returning to her father's house. She longed to stay abed and forget her troubles in sleep, but it eluded her after only a few hours. She told herself that she was used to feeling weary. How else was a widow to feel?

Her widow's clothing hung on a peg on the wall beside her bed. With all the time she'd already been forced to wear the drab robes and tunics, she had indulged in making more than one set. Something her father had paid for despite his displeasure with her situation.

She washed with the tepid water left over from the night before, then chose the cleanest garments and dressed. If she hurried, she could get to the well by sunup and perhaps miss the women who had never quite accepted her since her return. Talliya, her best friend, often met her at such times, and today Tamar hoped she would be waiting.

The water jar rested on the floor near the door of the house. Movement in the house told her the family was awakening, so she snatched it up and slipped quietly into the predawn darkness.

Birdsong had yet to break the quiet, the only sounds being

the crunch of earth and stones and a few twigs beneath her feet. She knew the path well and wasted no time in making her way toward the town where the well stood at its center.

Pink light crested the eastern ridge of sky as she approached, and she squinted at a lone figure standing near the well. Talliya had not failed her. How she needed to see this friend once more. They had lost touch when Talliya had moved away with her husband, but after her father died, her husband had returned with their family to take over his estate. Tamar found some small relief in knowing she had one friend in the world besides her sister.

"There you are." Talliya came close, her tone soft so as not to awaken the town, which still lay in shadow. "I hoped you would be here early before the others came." Her eyes were alight with news, and Tamar gave her a curious look.

"What have you heard? Surely you have something to tell me." Tamar set her jar in the dirt and hugged her friend. "At least I know from you the news can be trusted."

Talliya hugged her in return, and the two laughed softly together. "I am so glad we moved back here. I have missed you so."

"And I you. But now you must tell me lest I burst with curiosity!" Tamar rarely cared what went on in the world around her. What did it matter to her, a widow with no one to claim her? But if Talliya thought the news would interest her, it must be important. Might Judah be sending someone even now to wed her to Shelah?

"Your father-in-law is going up to Timnah to shear his sheep," Talliya said. "He's taking his friend Hirah the Adullamite with him."

Tamar took a step back, surprised at her disappointment, and studied her friend. "But this is old news, my friend. I heard it a few days ago. You did not know before?"

Talliya nodded. "Yes. I had heard, but last night Hirah came to our house and told Danel. He invited him to join them because it is a festive time."

"Is Danel going with them?" She thought again that she must use this information, but how?

Talliya shook her head. "Danel has our own sheep to shear, and to mix them together with Judah's many flocks would cause confusion. Besides, after what Judah has done to you, neither one of us likes the man overmuch."

Tamar's expression softened. "Thank you. I try not to bear hard feelings against him, but he has obviously decided that he is not willing to give me to Shelah. And he has not attempted to visit my father to end our contract, so he seems not to care what happens to me. He would keep me a widow the rest of my days."

"You don't sound terribly bitter," Talliya said, smiling. She picked up her jar, tied it to the rope, and lowered it into the well.

"Only a little, I suppose." Tamar picked up her jar as well, waiting her turn. She wanted to be home by the time the other women arrived. "I thank you for confirming this information. Though I don't know what I can possibly do with it."

"Perhaps there is a way you can confront Judah on his way to Timnah. He won't visit your father, and you can't go alone to his camp. But you could meet him on the road. I could go with you if you want me to. If Danel allows it." Talliya placed a comforting hand on Tamar's shoulder. "I will do anything I can to help you, my friend."

A sudden rush of emotion filled Tamar, but she held it back and smiled. "I know you would. Thank you for the offer, but I would not ask you to enter into my struggles. It is enough that you are here to talk to now and then."

"Let's make it every morning instead of only now and then."

Talliya's plain face wreathed in a wide smile, and her dark eyes twinkled in the dawn's glowing light. Sounds of merchants opening their shops and voices of women rousing their children could be heard in the distance.

"Every morning sounds wonderful." Tamar's heart felt lighter at the thought. "But if you do not see me, do not fear. You have given me much to think about. Perhaps confronting Judah on his way to Timnah is a wise idea. I just don't think he will listen to me."

"Perhaps not. But with Hirah there, you will have a witness against Judah for neglecting you. I wish your father would do something." Talliya placed the jar on her shoulder and held it with one hand.

Tamar did the same after pulling her jar from the well. "As do I," she said. "But I know he won't. It is a matter of pride, I guess. Perhaps my father thinks the gossips are right. Maybe I am to blame for the deaths of Judah's sons."

Talliya scowled. "Don't say such a thing. You are a good person, Tamar. Everyone knows it. And everyone also knows that Judah's oldest sons were foolish, immature boys. They died because of their own sins against their father's god, not yours."

Tamar offered Talliya a slight nod and pondered her friend's words. She had thought of little else for two years and truly could not see how she could be to blame for Er's and Onan's deaths. "In any case, I will give your suggestion some thought. If I do nothing, I will remain as I am until I die. And that does not sound appealing."

They parted ways as some of the women from town approached the well.

"Until tomorrow then," Tamar said as she turned toward home.

"You will figure out what to do," Talliya said with confidence. "Be strong and courageous, my friend. Perhaps Judah's god will show favor to you."

As Tamar slowly walked back the way she had come, she wondered if Judah's god saw her or even cared what Judah had done to her. Would his god look down upon her and grant her justice? Even if she sought justice, how was she supposed to get it? Men didn't listen to the concerns of women.

She glanced heavenward, for Judah's god seemed to live above the heavens. She offered a silent prayer. *Will you help me? Do you see me? Will you plead my case with Judah and give my life back to me again?*

She heard nothing in response, but she didn't expect to. Gods didn't speak to people, did they? She knew very little about Judah's god, for no one in his camp seemed to speak of him. Only when Er died did she realize Judah believed in a god she had never heard of, but he had not explained him to her.

As her father's house came into view, she drew in a breath, bracing herself. She set the water jar in its niche and slipped inside to her room, unseen. Suddenly she knew she must act, and quickly. She removed her widow's clothes and donned clothing she hadn't worn in two years, then covered herself with a veil so no one could recognize her. She hurried through the halls of the house, avoiding contact with her family, and started out on a trip with no idea where it would lead her.

ᘓᘓᘓ

Judah walked beside Hirah on the road to Timnah, listening to his friend discuss the latest crop yields. Shelah had gone ahead with his servants and the sheep to where they would be shearing.

"Have you noticed how fat the sheep have grown?" Hirah asked as they came closer to a small village some distance from Timnah.

"It's as though the gods have blessed everything on the earth to make them lush and prospering. We will have plenty for years to come, my friend." He slapped Judah on the back and laughed.

Judah joined the laughter. "We will indeed. I will have to sell more wool than I can keep this year. Of course, I have few needs for new clothes or rugs or even a new tent right now." A few months ago, that thought would have caused him pain, but now he had resigned himself to being alone.

"If you found a wife for Shelah—or for yourself, my friend—you would have plenty of reasons to need your wool." Hirah stopped as they neared the village of Enaim. "Or you could find pleasure in the town's prostitute," he said, pointing to a young woman veiled in colorful scarves who was sitting at the entrance to the village.

Judah stopped as well and looked at the woman. It was impossible to see her features, but he'd seen shrine prostitutes often dressed this way in other villages throughout Canaan. Suddenly the urge for a woman rose within him, and he looked at Hirah. "Wait for me," he said and walked toward the woman without a backward glance.

He stopped in front of her. Her eyes were dark, beguiling, and his desire grew. "Come now, let me sleep with you," he said, surprised at his own boldness.

She searched his face and looked him up and down in a single glance. "And what will you give me to sleep with you?" she asked.

"I'll send you a young goat from my flock," he promised.

She appeared to think over his offer, and he attempted not to show his impatience. She could refuse him, but he realized in that moment that he would give her anything she requested.

"Will you give me something as a pledge until you will send it?" she asked at last.

"What pledge should I give you?" he replied.

Again she paused as if thinking. She lifted a hand, and he caught the scent of frankincense. "Your seal and its cord, and the staff in your hand."

The request was a bold one, and for a brief moment he wondered if doing as she asked was wise. His seal, cord, and staff were his most important possessions. But the scent of her perfume caused his impatience to mount.

"All right," he said and handed each item to her.

She stood gracefully and led him into a small house that stood at the entrance to the city. It appeared to be a place where guards would sleep when they were not on duty, but no one was there, so perhaps this was also where the shrine prostitutes offered their services.

She led him to the bed without speaking and removed all of her clothes except the veils around her face. It would not have mattered, for he could not see her well in the darkness of the room. But he could feel every part of her, and the smoothness of her skin against his reminded him of how much he missed his wife and the need she had fulfilled in him.

When he finished with her, she dressed quickly, and he did as well. He left by the door he had entered and met Hirah, who waited beneath a tree that lined the road.

"Satisfied?" Hirah asked, smiling.

Judah gave him an ambiguous look. "For now," he said, though his heart still beat fast. He knew he probably should look for another wife. His father would never approve of him sleeping with prostitutes.

"She's got my cord, seal, and walking stick," he said as they continued down the road to Timnah. "When we return from sheepshearing, we need to send her a goat and get them back. Will you do that for me?" He wasn't sure he could resist sleeping with her again if he went himself.

287

"I'll be happy to help a friend," Hirah said. "Though she exacted a hefty price to wait for a goat."

"Tell me something I haven't already considered." What could he say? That his urges had won out over reason? But they had. And suddenly he felt the heat of shame fill him. He had given up his most important possessions, all for sex with a woman he did not know. How far he had fallen.

ᒐᒐᒐ

A week later, after the sheepshearing and feasting were finished, Judah walked with Hirah along the road home, the sheep following behind him. At the fork in the road where he could take a different route to avoid coming upon Enaim, he stopped. "You'll go on from here with the goat for me?" He handed the tether he had tied to the goat's neck to his friend.

"Of course! I said that I would, didn't I?" Hirah laughed and waved a dismissive hand at Judah. "Go home, my friend. I will have your things to you by nightfall."

Judah watched him go, relieved to bypass the chance of meeting the woman again. He never should have been so foolish, but there was nothing to be done about it now. He called the sheep to continue on as he led them, with Shelah bringing up the rear of the flock, and at last reached the pens, where he inspected each animal and settled them in for the night. The sheep had eaten their fill earlier in the day along the road, where the grasses were plentiful.

Judah and Shelah reached the camp and were met by Samina and the other servant girls, who offered them food. Shelah followed Samina toward the servants' tents to eat, leaving Judah alone. It was just as well. Judah was too anxious to be good company even to his son. He sat in the courtyard, dipped the flatbread in the stew, and tried to enjoy the taste. If only he could forget the girl and stop worrying about whether she would return his things.

Footsteps and the jingle of bells on the goat's tether caught his attention. "There you are," Hirah called as he approached Judah.

The food turned sour in Judah's mouth, and he set the bread on the clay plate in front of him.

"She wasn't there," Hirah said in explanation. "I asked the men of the village who lived there, 'Where can I find the shrine prostitute who was sitting beside the road at the entrance to Enaim?' They told me, 'We've never had a shrine prostitute here.' I'm sorry, my friend. I can't imagine where she came from. Unless they were lying to me."

Judah's ire rose, along with a feeling of humiliation. He'd truly been played the fool. "Then let her keep the things I gave her," he said. "I sent the young goat as we agreed, but you couldn't find her. We'd be the laughingstock of the village if we went back again to look for her."

"Indeed we would, for I asked everyone in the marketplace and beyond." Hirah handed the goat to Judah.

"Keep him," Judah said, not wanting to touch even the leather rein attached to this reminder of his folly. "It's the least I can give you for helping me."

Hirah offered Judah a slight bow. "For you, my friend, any-thing. But I thank you for the goat."

"Will you stay for some food?" Judah didn't want to talk any further, but it was the polite thing to ask.

"No, no. My wife will have supper waiting. And I should take care of the goat." Hirah waved as he walked away. "I will come again soon."

37

EGYPT, 1822 BC

Joseph rose early and watched the sunrise from his favorite spot overlooking the Nile. After this year, only one more year of God's favor on the land remained. Then the years of famine and hardship would begin.

He rubbed the stubble on his chin, which the barber would shave as soon as he broke his fast. But he needed this time alone with God and His creation.

Would the famine affect the land in Canaan as well as Egypt? Surely God had given Pharaoh the dreams to spare more than just the people of Egypt. Were not the Hebrews, the children of Israel, His chosen people? Abraham and his seed were the ones who were given the promises, not the descendants of Ham. Yet it was to those very descendants that God had given the vision of His coming plans.

Memories of Benjamin, his father, Dinah, and his brothers rushed through his thoughts. How long it had been. Was his father still alive? He could find out, he told himself. He'd argued that very point with himself many a night before falling asleep. But he'd had no peace about seeking out his brothers. They had abandoned him, not he them. He would not return to them and grovel for their acceptance. They would likely not even recognize him now. And what power could he wield in Canaan?

He shook himself as the sounds of servants scurrying through the halls, waking to a new day, met his ears. The sun had crested the horizon now, and though he longed to linger, he dared not. He turned and moved into the house to eat, then went about his routine, allowing his servants to shave and dress him and anoint him with oils. One look in the bronze mirror showed a man he finally recognized but would never be completely comfortable with. He felt as though he put on a new skin each morn.

"My lord." A servant interrupted his musings, which were becoming too close to melancholy. "Hamid is waiting for you in your visiting room."

Joseph nodded. "Thank you." He walked resolutely toward the ornate room where he conducted business with various people of import in Pharaoh's kingdom.

Hamid rose and bowed at Joseph's entrance.

Joseph motioned for him to sit as he took his own seat on the raised dais across from him. "What news do you bring?"

"Potiphar had to put down an uprising in the city of Giza. Some ruffians tried to break into one of the granaries. Apparently they don't want to give Pharaoh his due, but why they wanted the grain now when the famine has yet to come, who can tell?" Hamid rested his hands on his knees.

"I assume Potiphar has handled it to our satisfaction?" Joseph crossed his arms as though warding off a chill. He liked Potiphar well enough, but his memories in the king's prison because of Aneksi, not to mention the things Potiphar had done to the young servant girls who pleased him, left a sour taste in his mouth.

"He has put down the uprising, and the men accountable are

being held in the king's dungeon until they can be sentenced. Potiphar wants to know if you will be doing the sentencing." Hamid rested his arms on his middle, which had grown larger since his marriage to Heba. "Pharaoh has given you that power, my lord. Unless you would rather one of the lesser authorities handle it."

"Pharaoh might want to do so himself," Joseph said, touching the arms of the chair. "But he also might not want to know about it." He stroked his chin, debating what to do. "I will go to Pharaoh and ask him. The men should be executed, but I will not put men to death without his say-so."

Hamid nodded. "There is also the problem of more grain than we can handle. I've ordered the building of more granaries and opened another whole city to house them. I've put more men to the task of building, and they should be done within a week. I did not give them an option to take longer."

"Very good. But I wonder, do we even know how much grain is still coming in? With one more year of plenty ahead, you will need more than one additional storage city."

"I will admit the amount has become impossible to measure." Hamid's expression held defeat. "I have honestly tried to keep track, as I know you like to give Pharaoh accurate accounts, but the amount is truly now beyond measure. Our system of accounting does not reach that high."

"Then stop measuring," Joseph said, smiling. "God has shown us great favor, and His ways are beyond measure, as is the grain He has allowed us to grow. We will focus on storage and make sure the buildings that house the grain are well guarded, protected from mice and other small animals. The air is dry enough here that we should not be in danger of mildew, but make sure the roofs on each building are secure, just in case. If rain or hail does come, it could ruin whole cities of grain."

Hamid sat straighter and looked at Joseph with pride. "You are indeed wise, Joseph. Your God, whom I now believe is the only God, has given you wisdom beyond that of anyone in Egypt. Perhaps you came to us in a way you would not have chosen, but I speak for the people when I say we are grateful that God sent you here. You have saved Egypt. And me."

Joseph glanced beyond Hamid, always slightly uncomfortable with praise. Had God sent him here? Joseph often doubted that fact, though he couldn't deny that God had been with him through everything. "I am very glad you believe now, Hamid. But I haven't saved Egypt. God will do so, as we will see after next year."

He stood, and Hamid did the same, bowing again.

"Thank you, Hamid. If there is nothing else, I must see Pharaoh and find out what he would do with our thieves." Joseph left and climbed into his chariot to speak with Pharaoh. The nagging thought that this famine could bring him together again with the men who had hated him would not leave. And the thought that God had actually sent him here and allowed him to go through so much heartache troubled him even more.

If God cared about him, why would He allow such things? Joseph could not understand it, and he wasn't sure he was ready to accept Hamid's words.

CANAAN

Tamar rose early, hoping to meet Talliya at the well, if she could keep what little she had eaten the night before in her stomach. Three months and a new year had come since she had been with Judah, and she knew now for certain that she was with child. But her mother and sister had managed to remain oblivious to her plight, and she had been too sick before dawn to meet Talliya since their last meeting.

Today she must see her. Would she still come? She had thought her friend would visit her at home, but most people stayed away because of her, and Talliya's husband had not wanted her to come either. The sense of loneliness that brought only added to the fear and wonder that mingled in Tamar's heart.

She hurriedly dressed, managing to keep her stomach calm, hoping that the worst of the sickness had passed. Grabbing the jar from the door, she slipped outside before sunup and walked quickly to the well. She searched the stillness for some sign of her friend, nearly giving up hope. But as the first light of dawn lit the sky, there Talliya was, walking toward the well.

"Tamar?" Talliya rushed closer. "You came at last! I thought I would never see you again. Why have you stayed away? Were you ill? What happened since we last met?"

Tamar laughed softly. "Slow down, Talliya! I cannot answer everything at once."

Talliya paused for breath. "No, of course you can't. But you must tell me how it is with you. We heard Judah had gone to Timnah and returned home, but he stays away from the men of the town and pastures his sheep alone with his son and a few servants."

Tamar set her jar in the dirt and stepped closer to Talliya. "Three months ago, when Judah went to Timnah, I dressed in a robe and veils so he could not see my face except for my eyes. I sat near the village of Enaim and waited. I was not sure how I would confront him, but then he came near with Hirah and stopped to look at me. My heart pounded so hard, I thought he would surely hear it beating. But when he assumed I was a prostitute, as Er once accused me of being, I allowed him to think so. He wanted to sleep with me and offered me a goat for my services." She laughed. "A goat! As if that was all I am worth. Do you know that was part of the price he paid my father for each year that I was forced to wait for Er to grow up? I'm worth the price of an animal to them, nothing more."

She frowned at the thought, for it was the first time she had made the connection in her mind. Was she really so worthless? And if so, what would happen to her now?

"Your brow is furrowed, and I read fear in your gaze, my friend." Talliya touched her arm. "Tell me what's wrong."

Tamar looked at her feet, her cheeks heating in shame.

Talliya touched her chin. "Tamar?"

She looked up. "I let him sleep with me, and now I carry his child," she whispered. "No one else knows, not even my mother. But soon I will not be able to hide it from anyone. And when Judah hears, what will happen to me?"

Talliya's eyes grew wide, and Tamar read in them the very fear that caused a shudder to run down her spine. "He will not be pleased unless you tell him the child is his," Talliya said.

Tamar let silence fall between them. "I kept his personal identification items as a pretense to be returned when he brought the goat. Only I went home and did not wait for the goat, so they are still in my room, hidden."

Talliya brightened. "Then you have nothing to worry about. You have proof the child is his." She laughed softly. "What worries you then?"

Tamar studied her friend as she heard the town waking to another dawn. "It is the shame I feel, I suppose. He owed me a child by his son Shelah, but I forced his hand. Instead of having the courage to speak to him, I let my father-in-law sleep with me. It is not natural to do such a thing."

"It is righteous," Talliya said. "Judah is the one who wronged you, Tamar. You must believe that. He is simply getting what he deserves. And it's not like you will marry him now or sleep with him again."

Tamar shuddered visibly now. "No. Not ever! The very thought makes me ill."

Talliya's brows drew together. "Was he hurtful to you as Er and Onan were? He seemed better than that."

Tamar shook her head. "No. He was not hurtful. He did not say anything, really. We made a transaction and fulfilled it. Then he left and I went home. That was all."

Talliya picked up her jar and tied the rope to it. When she finished, Tamar did the same.

"There is nothing else to do then," Talliya said. "Judah will hear the news and you will prove your innocence. You need not fear, dear one."

Tamar's lip quivered, and she fought the urge to weep. She had grown more emotional of late and knew her fears were not for herself but for the babe growing within her. "You are right, of course. It helps to have shared the news with someone."

They hugged, ready to part ways.

"You will tell your family soon, yes?" Talliya held the jar on her shoulder, her expression concerned. "Your father can protect you."

"I'm not sure my father would do so. I belong to Judah's family. My father has little to do with me." Only her remaining sister, who was soon to wed, and her mother spoke to her, and that was not often. She was a widow in a house of people and yet felt so very alone.

"The gods go with you, my friend," Talliya said, turning to hurry back to her house.

"Thank you," Tamar managed as she slowly trudged the familiar path to her father's house. Talliya was right. She must tell her mother. She could no longer hide the truth. But she wasn't sure she was ready to face that fact.

лллл

Judah headed to the pens with Shelah to take the sheep to the fields. It was the life of a shepherd, but without his wife and sons, he could never shake the feeling of loss and grief. He'd even caught himself thinking of his father and returning home with Shelah. But how could he possibly show up at his father's camp without significant offspring, with nothing to show by moving away except for the additional sheep he now owned?

He should find a wife for his son, maybe the servant Samina as Shelah had requested. Perhaps he could have at least one grandchild. Then he would have a small family to show his father—should he care to do so.

A deep sigh escaped, and when he glanced up from inspecting one of the lambs, he was relieved that Shelah was some distance away and had not heard or seen his struggle. "Come on," he said to the lamb as he led part of the flock out.

As he rounded the bend toward the familiar field, Hirah walked toward him, his stride brisk, his demeanor troubled.

Judah stopped. "What's wrong, Hirah? You do not usually visit me so early in the day." He saw the agitation in his friend's face and felt a sense of foreboding rise within him. "Tell me."

Hirah placed a hand on Judah's shoulder and drew in a slow breath. "I have news you are not going to like." He paused. "Tamar, your daughter-in-law, has acted like a prostitute. And now, because of this, she's pregnant."

Judah stared at his friend, his thoughts jumbled. Tamar had acted like a prostitute? She was to wait for Shelah as a widow, but now, of course, he could never give the girl to Shelah as a wife. The thought brought a great sense of relief to him, for he never intended or wanted to bring her back into his family's presence. Just hearing her name caused his heart to stir with bitterness. But this! She would pay for doing such a thing.

"You are sure?"

"Very sure. The whole town is talking about it, and Yassib said that his wife confirms it. Everyone will look to you as to what to do with her, Judah. What will you do?" Hirah took a step back and studied Judah.

Judah's face grew hot, and rage bubbled to the surface. "Bring her out, and let her be burned!" he demanded.

"You will send a delegation to her father's house then?" Hirah nodded his agreement. "This decision is the only thing you can do to save your reputation."

"You can lead a delegation and bring her to my camp. I will instruct my men to build a fire, and we will tie her to a stake and set her in the flames." Just saying the words made him feel vindicated at last. He would be rid of the girl who had brought such dishonor and grief to his family. He would never have to think of her again.

Like you never think of Joseph?

The thought came out of nowhere, and he felt as though someone had slapped him. No, of course, not like that, he told himself. But as Hirah left to do his bidding, he could not shake the realization that when he hated someone, his reaction was to wish them dead or gone. What kind of person did that make him?

38

The sound of male voices caught Tamar's ear as she sat with her mother turning the spindle and distaff in her hands, trying to keep calm. They had expected the news of her pregnancy to garner some sort of reaction, and now as they waited in the central courtyard of their home, Tamar knew. The louder the voices grew, the more her heart beat with dread and the realization that their presence would not be for her good. She slipped to her room and retrieved Judah's seal, cord, and staff and carried them back to the courtyard with her.

A loud knock came, and Yassib emerged from one of his rooms to answer it. He had stayed away from the fields today, waiting, as they all were, for something to happen or someone to come calling. Would her father have a change of heart and stand in the gap to defend her?

Her father opened the door to Hirah and a group of men encircling him. "Judah has demanded Tamar to be brought to his camp to be burned. She is pregnant by harlotry and must die."

Burned? The normal punishment was to be stoned. How much did her father-in-law hate her?

Her father stepped aside to allow the men entrance into the courtyard. He said nothing to defend her or try to stop the men. Heart sinking, she fought the grief of betrayal and braced herself.

"On your feet, Tamar," Hirah said, his tone holding anger instead of the kindness he had always shown her.

She slowly stood. Hirah gripped her arm and pulled her toward the other men, but she planted her feet, unwilling to go so easily. "Wait."

The men stared, murder in their eyes. Were they enjoying her pain? She produced the staff, pulled the seal and cord from a pocket in her robe, and handed them to Hirah. "The man who owns these things made me pregnant. Look closely. Whose seal and cord and walking stick are these?"

Hirah's face blanched. She knew he recognized them.

"Take them to Judah and ask him," she said. "If he does not recognize them, take me freely."

Hirah accepted the items from her hand and walked quietly from the courtyard. The rest of the men grew silent and followed him.

"Now we wait," her father said, a look of surprise on his face. "You could have told us the child is his."

"I was afraid to tell anyone, Abba." She sank onto the bench to pick up her spindle and distaff once more.

He nodded but said nothing more and walked away.

"You could have at least told your mother."

Tamar looked at her mother, whose scowl showed her need to know before the town found out. "You know now, Ima." She focused on her spinning, its rhythm keeping pace with her heart.

ມມມ

Judah paced the grounds of his camp from one end to the other, bypassing the central cooking fire once, twice, until he'd lost count. He glanced at the fire, then imagined Tamar tied to large branches and set among the flames.

He shook himself. He could not have her killed in the place where they met to eat. He would never get the vision of her death out of his mind. He was walking with brisk steps toward one of the servants to give the order for a separate place to be built, when a commotion came from the path carved out through the trees.

Hirah strode toward him, his face pale, his mouth framed in a frown. He stopped before Judah, who ceased his frantic pacing. "Do you recognize these?" Hirah asked, holding out Judah's cord, seal, and walking stick. The very things he had given the prostitute three months earlier.

He took them from Hirah and placed them where they belonged on his person. "Where did you get these?" But by the look in Hirah's eyes, he knew. He began to shake inwardly as though a cold wind had blown over and through him.

"From Tamar. She said that she is pregnant by the man who owns these." Hirah said nothing more but stood watching him.

Shame heated Judah's cheeks, and he could not hold Hirah's gaze. "She is more righteous than I am, because I didn't arrange for her to marry my son Shelah."

"What would you have us do, Judah? She is carrying your child."

"You don't have to remind me again, Hirah. Obviously I will do right by her. Bring her to my camp. She will not die. But I cannot give her to Shelah either." He rubbed a hand over the back of his neck.

"Will you marry your daughter-in-law then?"

The shock of that thought caused Judah to take a step away from his friend. "Of course not!" The very idea! It would be wrong for so many reasons. He whirled about and stalked away.

"Just bring her home," he called over his shoulder. He would place her in the tent she had shared with both Er and Onan until she could weave a new one. One thing was certain. He would care for her and be a father to her child, but he would never sleep with her again.

⊓⊔⊓

CANAAN, SIX MONTHS LATER

Tamar moved slowly from the well to Judah's camp, carrying the jar atop her shoulder. Talliya had continued to meet with her, though the walk had become harder for Tamar in recent days. She met the servant girl Judah had supplied her and gave her instructions for the day.

"From now on, I need you to gather the water for us, morning and night. I fear I will give birth on the road if I make that trip again." Tamar smiled at the look of fear in the girl's eyes. "You have no need to worry. I will be fine. I simply can no longer handle the long walks."

"Yes, my lady," the girl said shyly, then hurried off to prepare the bread from the grain she had ground, another task Tamar found too difficult to do with the bulk in her middle.

"How are you feeling?" Judah asked, striding toward her, his expression one of concern. "I overheard your comments. Is it time?" His cheeks flushed, and she knew contact with her made him feel awkward. So much ill will had passed between them. How did she make things right with the man who nearly had her burned to death?

"I am tired. Stretched thin. And I think I need to see the midwife soon," she said. She had no sister or friend to tell these things to other than Talliya now and then. Her servant was a child, too young to understand.

"I will send for her immediately." Judah rushed off before she could say "wait" or "not yet," but Tamar realized from the constant pain in her back and the stronger pains that came and went across her middle that perhaps Judah was right to get the midwife now.

She turned to enter her tent and paced slowly, longing to sit but uncomfortable when she did so. Oh, what she would give to sleep through the night! But the child was too active, almost as though he was fighting and she was the target.

She pressed her hands against her sides and breathed deeply. She should have asked Judah to send for her mother and sisters as well. Suddenly she felt so very alone, and the feeling scared her. What if she died giving birth? Her mother should be here to hold the child, to swaddle it and cleanse it with salt. She didn't want only the midwife!

Oh, God of Judah, I need help. She had taken to praying more often to Judah's God, and Judah himself had mentioned Him to her, even thanking his God for each meal.

Those memories helped between the waves of pain that started coming closer together. At last the chatter of female voices filled the air, the distinctive voice of her mother loudest of them all.

"Where is my daughter?" Her mother would have the whole camp in a stir. But Judah's voice calmed her, for she fell silent until she opened the tent flap and hurried to Tamar's side.

"Tamar! My child. Why didn't you call for me sooner?" She patted Tamar's cheek, then placed a hand on her belly. "You are most definitely in labor."

The midwife stepped forward and touched Tamar's belly as well, agreeing with her mother. "Let me examine you," the older, stocky woman said. "Lie down so I can see how long you have to go."

Tamar obeyed, and the woman lifted her tunic to examine her but then looked puzzled. "I see a hand," she said. "Quick, give me a scarlet cord."

Tamar saw her mother comply through another wave of pain as she felt the midwife pull the child's arm and tie the cord around it. "This one came out first," she said. "What! He has pulled back his hand, and another is coming!"

Tamar bit down on a rag, barely able to stand the struggle, when at last the child emerged in blood and fluid.

"How did you break out first?" the midwife asked, her expression astonished. "In all of my years of helping with a birthing, even of twins, I have never seen one break out ahead of the other who came first."

Beads of sweat creased Tamar's forehead as she bore down a second time. A child's cry pierced the air, and the midwife lifted the baby's hand for her to see the cord tied around his wrist.

As her mother and the midwife each held a son up for her to see, Tamar's heart lifted with an instant love for both boys. How was it possible to bear such beautiful sons? In that moment, all of her heartache disappeared and her heart's longings were fulfilled. *Thank you,* she prayed to Judah's God. He had heard her prayers and was not deaf to her pleas.

"Hurry! Wash and bind them," she said. She lifted a hand to touch each one. "I want to hold them close."

The women did as she asked while her sisters cleaned her up and settled her onto her pallet.

Later, when Judah came to the door of Tamar's tent, she said to him, "The one to break out first is Perez." Her mother sat holding his twin. "And the one with the scarlet string on his wrist is Zerah." She lifted her gaze from the son at her breast and met Judah's awed look.

"Two sons," he said in a hushed voice.

Two sons for the two he had lost? She wondered if that was how he saw them.

"They are good names," he said at last, looking from one child to the other. "When they are eight days old we will circumcise them." He met her gaze. "After you are feeling strong enough and the babies have grown enough to travel, we are going home to Hebron where I belong. And their grandfather will hold them on his knee."

Tamar gave Judah a quizzical look but did not argue with him. She was too weary from the birth to think of what moving would mean. But she saw the look of sadness fill her mother's eyes the moment Judah left the tent.

"He can't take you away from us. Not now." Her mother held Zerah closer to her heart. "We just met them."

Tamar lifted Perez from her breast and rubbed his back. "We aren't going yet, Ima." She held her mother's gaze. "I never should have left here. You know that. I have belonged to Judah's house for many years. His children have finally come home."

"They should have been his grandchildren." Bitterness tinged her mother's tone.

Tamar said nothing in response. Yes, they should have been Er's children, not Judah's. But right now, she did not care whose children they were except hers. She kissed Perez's cheek and smelled his newborn skin. She was already in love and silently grateful. Despite the way they had come, they were here safely and were healthy. And they would be good men, for she would raise them to be so.

39

EGYPT, 1820 BC

Joseph sat on a sturdy canopied seat, listening to the lap of the Nile with each dip of the slaves' oars. At the bow, the ship's captain, Jabare, stood watching the slaves' progress, while every now and then he turned to see how close they were to the next city.

A guard stood on a raised platform, Joseph's personal protection during his many trips. Amarna lay behind them, with Hermopolis appearing in the distance to their left. The seven years of plenty had come to an end, and they were now well into the first year of famine, though Egypt had yet to truly feel its effects.

How many times had he made this trip from one end of Egypt to the other? For the local cities, he traveled by chariot, but Egypt was long and narrow, winding like the river that Egyptians considered their source of life. This was his first trip since the years of plenty had ended. He looked out over the calm waters, releasing a slow sigh. How many, if any, uprisings would there be in years to come?

"We're coming upon Hermopolis, my lord," Jabare called to

him from the bow. "Will you be going ashore or meeting with the city officials at the docks?"

Joseph knew the slaves could use a rest from rowing, but he did not want to take the time to enter every city and town to get the answers he sought. He would send his lower officials to check the granaries once the Egyptians began coming to him for help.

"Have the city's governor come to my ship. The oarsmen may go ashore to stretch their legs while we talk. I want to keep moving so we can reach home before the sun rests in the west." He caught the appreciation on the faces of the slaves, whose lives he wished he could improve. His power only reached so far. The best he could do was to treat them with kindness, something he had always appreciated from Potiphar and the prison warden during his own years of slavery.

"Very good, my lord. Prepare to dock," Jabare called to the slaves.

Joseph leaned into the chair as the boat came near the river's edge, where posts emerged from the water. Jabare tossed a rope to a man standing on the pier. The boat was soon tied to the pier, and the slaves climbed from the lower floor and scrambled to shore with another of Joseph's guards following.

The meeting with the men of the city went quickly, and Joseph felt a sense of relief that there had been no trouble there. The attempts to steal grain had been taken down by Potiphar the year before, and so far there had been no more reports of such a problem.

The ship returned to the river sooner than the slaves might have liked, but Joseph had a sense of urgency to get to the next port and back to Memphis so he could report to Pharaoh. Soon he would remain there and hand out grain to needy Egyptians, and while he should enjoy this final trip the length of Egypt, he missed his family more than he would have thought. Manasseh and Ephraim were growing fast, and he missed the warmth of Asenath's arms.

And then there was the nagging thought that this famine would be wider spread than the length of Egypt. If his father still lived, what would he do when they ran out of food? God help him, but Joseph wasn't sure he wanted an answer to that question.

ллл

CANAAN

Judah placed the last tent in the last cart, ready to return to Hebron and reconcile, God willing, with his father and brothers. He had not slept well for many nights, and it had nothing to do with the occasional cries from his sons in the tent next to his.

He straightened his turban and rubbed the back of his neck, wishing he could make his heart calm to a normal rhythm. He'd known he would find himself anxious when this day arrived, but now he could barely keep still. A baby's cry caused him to walk the length of the caravan and stop where Tamar sat with her maid, each holding one of his sons.

"Is everything all right?" he asked, his voice gruff. He found it nearly impossible to speak to the girl in a normal tone. On a rare occasion he could, but only when they were by the fire and darkness covered the land. Never in daylight when his emotions could be exposed. How did one feel such pride in his children yet also such guilt toward their mother?

"Everything is fine, my lord," Tamar said, offering him a slight smile.

She had tried to calm him for days, but he would not be

calmed. She did not know what life would be like in his father's camp. And in truth, neither did he after being gone so many years. Would Jacob accept him with open arms? Or would he be shunned and lose his place in the line of heritage for fleeing his father's house?

"You are worried, Judah," Tamar said, drawing him from his thoughts. Perez nursed at her breast, and her maid offered Zerah a wet rag to suck on while he waited his turn to feed. How did Tamar manage it all?

He shook himself, focusing on her comment. "Yes. I do not know what to expect when we arrive. I do not want you to be disappointed if we are not accepted." He met her gaze for the first time in weeks.

"I will not be disappointed." She smiled at him, then focused on Perez, cupping his head with her hand. "I daresay neither will you, for once your father sees you again, he will be overjoyed that you decided to come home."

"Let us pray you are right. Are you ready to go?" He glanced at the caravan, which included Shelah's new wife, Samina, animals, household items, and his infant sons. Shelah led the sheep at the start of the long line of servants.

"I am ready." Tamar sat straighter and covered herself as she removed Perez from her breast. She had never allowed him to see her as he had the day he thought her a prostitute, and he was glad of it. He dared not even think of her as a wife, mother of his children or not.

He walked away and called to the servants as he headed to the front of the caravan. "Move out!" he shouted, catching Shelah's attention. He still marveled at how accepting Shelah had been of his and Tamar's indiscretion. But he knew that had more to do with Shelah's marriage to Samina and his release from having to marry his brothers' wife.

Shelah turned and waved, his smile wide, then called the sheep to follow.

Judah walked along, moving from front to back to front again, his sense of foreboding growing with each step home.

 JUUU

HEBRON

Jacob leaned heavily on his walking stick as he moved throughout the camp, counting the tents as a matter of habit and watching the servants work. His remaining two wives, the concubines Bilhah and Zilpah, worked with Dinah, spinning and weaving as usual. Benjamin often went with Reuben to care for the sheep, but Jacob did not allow them to travel far, as his other sons did. Reuben had assured Jacob he would keep the boy near and thus far had not failed to keep his word.

One glance at Bilhah, however, and Jacob wondered if he should trust Reuben at all. He shook his head and looked away. A few moments later, footsteps behind him caused him to turn.

"Are you all right, Abba?" Dinah slipped her arm through his and walked with him. "You seem restless today. Or are you still grieving my mother?"

Jacob looked into her eyes and wished not for the first time that life had been kinder to her. She should have a husband and children of her own. He should have been stronger and kept his sons in check. Regret pulsed through him, and a fresh wave of grief added to the many poor choices he had made. If only . . . But looking back and wishing for what could have been never did him any good.

"I do miss your mother, Dinah. Leah became a friend in later years after I lost Rachel. After I lost Joseph." He continued walking. "But today I don't know why I feel on edge. Nothing is right. The crops are not doing as well as they have for years now, and our family is . . . broken."

Dinah kept pace with him as they moved to the central gathering place where stones were placed in a circle and they ate as a family. He thought to sit and rest his weary bones when the baaing of sheep came from a distance. The jangle of wagons and the lowing of cattle grew louder until Jacob watched as a great caravan of people and animals entered the camp.

He stopped, staring, and Dinah gasped. "Judah!" she whispered, and he recognized his son the moment he stepped to the head of the crowd.

"Yes," Jacob said. His legs grew weak, but Dinah's strength held him up.

Judah strode forward, his bearing humble. The closer he came, the more Jacob saw the uncertainty and regret in his gaze. He stopped several paces from Jacob.

"Father. It is I, Judah." He twisted his hands in his belt as if he didn't know what else to do with them.

"Judah! My son!" Jacob opened his arms, not hesitating a moment, and Judah stepped into them, holding him close. "Judah!" Jacob held tight to him, emotion rising within him until he could no longer contain it. He wept against Judah's robe, and Judah's tears mingled with his own.

"I've come home, Father. I should never have left you. I hope it is all right to live here with you again." He held Jacob at arm's length, his tear-streaked gaze holding Jacob's.

"Of course! Did you have to ask?" Jacob shook from head to foot, and Judah helped him find his seat to rest his quaking limbs. "You've come home at last!" How long he had waited for this son to return. He had wondered if he would ever see him again.

Judah sat beside him. "Yes, Father, and I've brought my family with me. You have three grandsons you have not yet met. Would you like to meet them?"

Jacob searched Judah's face. "Grandchildren?" He rose, sudden strength filling him. "Where are my grandchildren?" He followed Judah to the carts and the people who had gathered in a circle near the sheep and cattle. "All this is yours, my son?"

Judah nodded. "Yes. Your God has been very good to me."

Jacob turned to him, searching his face. "You believe."

Judah did not flinch, though his skin flushed as if the subject brought him shame. "It took me a long time to do so, Abba. But I suppose sometimes hardship is what leads us to seek the things we've always known were true. Your God—my God—has taught me much . . . and He has led me home."

Jacob's heart lifted with his son's words. He would never have imagined this day in a thousand lifetimes. Only one thing could have made his life even better than seeing this son and the children who came through the crowd for him to meet—if Joseph had walked into the camp and said those same words. *I've come home.*

But Jacob knew he would never hear such a thing, for his beloved son was dead. Yet this son was alive, and he told himself to be grateful for what God had given.

40

Joseph kissed Asenath and each of his sons goodbye, ready to climb into his chariot and head to the largest granary, where he would preside over the distribution of food. "I may be late tonight, depending on how many people are waiting," he said, looking fondly on each dear face.

"Can I come, Abba?" Manasseh asked, hopping up and down in childish anticipation.

Joseph knelt to his eye level and cupped his cheek. "Not this time, my son." He kissed his cheek and caught the scent of his freshly washed skin. "We will play one of your games when I get home." He stood and looked at Asenath. "Hopefully he will still be awake by then. I don't know how long I will be."

"We know you will do what is best," Asenath said, her smile warming his heart. "God made you for this moment, Joseph."

He nodded, returning her smile, and climbed into the chariot, and the driver took him to the granary. *God made you for this moment, Joseph.* She had often told him so, and by now he almost accepted her words. Yet he had lived with the pain of loss, of feeling abandoned, for so long. He still struggled even now, though he could not deny the gratitude he felt for the wife and sons God had given.

They arrived too soon, and Joseph hopped out of the chariot and climbed the steps to the seat made for him on a platform in front of a long line of Egyptians that had already formed.

"They went to Pharaoh first," one of his guards told him. "Pharaoh told them to go to you and do what you tell them."

Joseph nodded, and the people came forward one man or one household at a time. His servants measured out the amount of grain each family would need for a year, and it was poured into sacks the people had brought with them.

The day moved on, and Joseph's mind drifted as he saw the line grow. Was this what God truly had planned for his life? To oversee the giving of food to people far and wide for the next six years?

Suddenly he did not find his place of importance quite so appealing or even satisfying. But he could not stay home and leave someone else in charge, lest Pharaoh decide he had chosen the wrong man for this position. Then what would happen to his family, to him?

No. He would do the work, mundane as it was, and thank God that he was at least free to come and go as he pleased and no longer a prisoner of his brothers or Potiphar. Though in some ways he felt like he was still a prisoner of his emotions.

᠒᠒᠒

HEBRON

Dinah sifted the grain and handed the flour to Bilhah to make into flatbread. Tamar, Zilpah, and the wives of her brothers all worked together, pooling their resources to feed the seventy people who now made up their camp. But the grain in the sacks was getting low.

"How many more days do you think we can make this last?" Tamar asked Dinah, her brow lined with concern. "If we had known the crops would fail, I'm sure Judah would have saved more than he sold."

"I said as much to our father," Dinah said. "We know this land experiences famine now and then, but I think we all grew too comfortable these past eight years, and now that this year has failed to produce, our supplies are not going to hold out."

"Judah heard that there is food in Egypt," Tamar said. She looked so innocent, so young to be mother to Judah's sons. When Dinah had heard the story, she felt a twinge of jealousy. How was what Tamar did so very different from her own situation with Shechem so many years ago? She could have married him, borne his children. It wasn't right, but neither did it seem right for Judah to sleep with his daughter-in-law.

A sigh escaped her, but she forced the thoughts aside. Tamar deserved some happiness with her sons after all she had lost.

"There is food in Egypt?" Bilhah asked. "Does Jacob know this?"

Dinah met her gaze. "I don't know." She glanced at Tamar, who worked the millstone. "Did Judah tell him?"

Tamar shrugged. She obviously did not know all Judah said or did. She was not his wife, after all.

Dinah set the sieve aside and stood, brushing the flour from her robe. "Then I will ask Judah to do so right now. We dare not wait for them to make such a long trip and get back here in time. We will run out of food before then."

Later that evening Jacob finally got his sons to gather as one. The places to pasture the sheep had grown thin this year, and they were traveling farther each day to keep the animals alive.

"Judah tells me there is grain in Egypt, so why do you just keep looking at each other?" Jacob said as the women set before them a thinner stew and less bread than the previous night. He held up a piece of the flatbread. "If there is grain to be had, we must have it. Go down there and buy some for us, so that we may live and not die." He saw looks of skepticism or perhaps fear pass between his sons but could not figure out why they seemed so hesitant to act. "Egypt is not so far that you could not be there and back again within a week. Do you want your little ones to starve?" He regarded Reuben and then Judah but could not read the expressions on their faces.

"Of course not," Reuben said, looking from one brother to another. "We will leave first thing in the morning."

"Good. And be quick about it," Jacob said, forcing back his irritation. He should have saved the grain during the many years of a good harvest. If he had thought ahead, they wouldn't be in this dilemma now. But he did not stop to think that God might not always bless as He had during much of Jacob's lifetime. How long until He chose to show His favor to them again?

⊓⊔⊓

EGYPT

Joseph's servants lifted palm fronds to cool the air on the platform where he sat governing the allotment of food to the people. The sun's rays had made even sitting beneath an awning difficult in his Egyptian wig and heavy robe and many pieces of jewelry. The fanning helped but a little.

Hamid stepped close to him as another Egyptian family came forward with linen sacks in their hands. "If the sun is too warm, my lord, I would be happy to stay and allow you to return home." He spoke softly lest anyone hear.

Joseph shook his head. "I am fine, Hamid, but thank you for noticing my discomfort. It is all of the added clothing that makes the sun feel warmer than it is. Would that I could strip to the waist as a common man." He laughed at the thought, remembering when he did exactly that in Potiphar's house when he first arrived in Egypt.

"You make a fine prince, my lord. Warm clothing and head-dress or not."

Hamid turned to watch the line of people snaking their way to the main granary where Joseph distributed the food. The line stretched far beyond what they could see, so for a time, Joseph focused on each family as they came.

Several hours later, Hamid stepped close to him again. "My lord, I see a group of men, bearded and wearing the robes of shepherds."

Joseph trained his eyes on the next group coming forward and watched as they bowed before him with their faces to the ground. Their robes, each with its distinct color, would have given them away, but Joseph also recognized their aging faces. Reuben would be fifty-two now, and the others not far behind.

He straightened as he searched their faces, recognizing each one. Except Benjamin. Heart pounding, Joseph again felt like the betrayed younger brother, despite the twenty-two years that had passed since that day.

"Is everything all right, my lord?" Hamid asked softly. "What would you have me say to these men?"

"They are Hebrew," Joseph said, unwilling to admit his relationship to them. "Ask them where they come from." He scrutinized each man, seeing in their eyes a sudden fear of him. As he once feared them.

"Where do you come from?" Hamid asked them in Hebrew.

"From the land of Canaan," Reuben replied, "to buy food."

Joseph listened as each brother repeated the same. Hadn't he wondered, even expected that this moment could come? The famine had stretched far beyond the borders of Egypt, and obviously his family had not been given the foresight to save enough grain to see them through. No doubt they had no idea that the famine would linger for six more years.

Hamid approached Joseph and spoke Egyptian to relay the information. "What do you want me to do, my lord? Shall I sell them the grain as they ask?"

Joseph could not keep his gaze from his brothers, and unexpectedly his mind flashed to the day he'd told them his dreams, that they would bow down to him. Was this what God had been trying to tell him would come of those dreams?

The realization hit Joseph hard, but he kept his expression neutral, even suspicious. They would not get away so easily—not after what they had done to him.

He turned to Hamid. "Tell them, 'You are spies! You have come to see where our land is unprotected.'"

Hamid returned to the men and repeated Joseph's words.

Judah stepped forward and bowed low, and when he rose, he kept one knee bent. "No, my lord. Your servants have come to buy food. We are all the sons of one man. Your servants are honest men, not spies."

Hamid interpreted the words for Joseph, who responded again, "No! You have come to see where our land is unprotected."

After Hamid relayed the message, the brothers turned to each other, distraught. They lifted their hands in supplication, falling to their knees.

Judah spoke for them again. "Your servants were twelve brothers, the sons of one man who lives in the land of Canaan. The youngest is now with our father, and one is no more."

So Benjamin lived, as did his father. The thought jolted Joseph, and he fought to keep back the emotion of a million memories.

Hamid stepped to him and spoke again in Egyptian. "I know you understand them, Joseph, but you obviously do not want them to know that. What more would you have me say to them?"

"I do not trust them," Joseph said, though he could not bring himself to tell this faithful servant and friend why. "Tell them, 'It is just as I told you: You are spies! And this is how you will be tested: As surely as Pharaoh lives, you will not leave this place unless your youngest brother comes here. Send one of your number to get your brother. The rest of you will be kept in prison so that your words may be tested to see if you are telling the truth. If you are not, then as surely as Pharaoh lives, you are spies!'"

Joseph waited for Hamid to repeat his words to his brothers, then ordered his guards to take the men to the king's prison, the very prison he had spent years in while falsely accused.

"How long will you keep them there?" Hamid asked later as he walked with Joseph to his chariot and climbed in beside him.

"Three days," Joseph said. "They need time to think of what they have done. Then I will send one of them back to their father to retrieve the youngest."

Hamid looked at him, his brow raised. But to Joseph's relief, he did not speak again or ask why Joseph was acting as he was. He couldn't tell anyone yet. Not even Asenath. Three days would also give him time to think about how he could force them to bring Benjamin to see him. And how he could eventually bring his father to Egypt as well. But until he knew that his brothers' hearts had changed, he was not sure he could trust them to ever return once they left him.

41

Joseph walked the vast palace halls in the governmental section reserved for him and Pharaoh's advisors. The sun had barely crested the horizon, and he had risen early after little sleep.

The third day since his brothers set foot in Egypt had arrived. He had told himself he would imprison them for three days, but even now he was not sure it was enough. A part of him wanted them to remain captive, to force them to wonder if they would ever be released, to treat them as they had treated him. He did not like this dark side of his thoughts.

The gardens he loved were down a hall to his left, and he followed the inlaid stone path to the steps that led him to their shade. Tall palm trees rose high above his head, and a large pool stretched before him in the middle of the plants, both potted and flowering from the earth. The beauty here always calmed him and gave him a sense of God's goodness, in spite of the images of Egypt's gods that lined every column and statue he passed.

He gazed at the rising blues and muted colors of dawn and sighed. *What would You have me do with them, Adonai?* God knew his thoughts. He did not seek his brothers' harm. Not when he was thinking clearly. It was only in the dark of night or when a memory of past pain emerged that he wished they had a taste of what he had lived through all these long years.

He couldn't keep them here though. He would have to explain to Pharaoh why he would do such a thing with a foreign group of men who had done no obvious harm to the kingdom. Three days was the limit he could keep them hidden without causing a stir or a barrage of questions.

But he could keep one of them. The thought lingered as he walked along the edge of the pool, the scents of the lotus, jasmine, myrtle, and roses adding to the tingle of the cool morning air. One brother could be kept without intense questioning by Pharaoh or even Potiphar. They would assume Joseph had good reason, and Pharaoh might not become aware of the brother at all.

Which one? Joseph pondered that as he turned the corner and made his way back through the long halls to his chambers to dress for his meetings with the lower governors and courtiers. But first he would meet with Hamid and have his brothers brought to the audience chamber intended for his use.

He paused at the door to his rooms. How had he come to this place, this hour? Hadn't God allowed all that had happened to him to save many people? Perhaps even to save his ungrateful kin.

As his manservant dressed him in full royal garb and the headdress again rested on his head, covering most of his dark hair, Joseph was still unable to decide which brother to keep behind. Perhaps God would give him insight when he met with them.

"Hamid," he said moments later as he exited his chambers and met the man in one of the anterooms, "gather the Hebrews from the prison and bring them to the audience chamber. I will deal with them, with you interpreting for me there."

Hamid bowed and left without a word. Joseph strode to the chamber and entered through a side room that led directly to the throne where he would sit like a king. *You are not a king*, he reminded himself. But he was a ruler, and his brothers bowed to him. His dreams of old at last made sense. And life had changed him.

It was time to see whether life had changed them as well.

⌇⌇⌇

Joseph waited on the throne Pharaoh rarely used, his servants milling around him, lighting fires in the braziers along tall columns. Walls higher than the span of several men held paintings and carvings of Egyptian symbols and words and images of the gods they worshiped. The hall stretched out longer than the distance from the door to the Nile, every statue and artifact meant to intimidate all who passed through the great double doors.

Would his brothers feel that intimidation? His impatience grew, though he knew it was a distance from the king's prison on Potiphar's estate to this grand palace. Still, he drummed his fingers on the edge of the chair, wishing he had waited for them to come rather than appear anxious to see them.

He stilled, telling his heart to slow as he heard the doors swing open on heavy hinges. Hamid led ten men on the long walk to him. He searched each face as they approached and saw the fear in their eyes. Good. They would be easier to command if they feared him. And he desperately needed them to obey if he were to ever see Benjamin again.

Hamid climbed the steps to his throne and bowed while his brothers knelt with their faces to the stone tiles.

"Did they say anything on the walk here?" Joseph asked.

Hamid shook his head. "They seemed relieved and surprised

to be released, but they are fearful of what is to come. What message do you have for them?"

"Tell them, 'Do this and you will live, for I fear God. If you are honest men, let one of your brothers stay here in prison, while the rest of you go and take grain back for your starving households. But you must bring your youngest brother to me, so that your words may be verified and that you may not die.'" Joseph angled his head toward Hamid, who turned to his brothers and repeated his words.

"Surely we are being punished because of our brother," Simeon said to the others, wringing his hands.

Judah nodded. "We saw how distressed he was when he pleaded with us for his life, but we would not listen. That's why this distress has come on us."

"Didn't I tell you not to sin against the boy?" Reuben said. "But you wouldn't listen! Now we must give an accounting for his blood."

Joseph stood and left the room, overcome with emotion. He walked far enough away from the anteroom that they could not hear the deep weeping he could not keep in check. *Oh, Adonai. They have not forgotten me.* All of these years later, they still remembered their treachery. But were they truly sorry? They could have searched for him. They could have paid to buy him back . . .

Tears came again, and he quickly shut the door to a small room, where he sank to the floor, his body shaking with uncontrolled sobs. *Oh, Adonai. Adonai. What do I do?* He had not realized until this moment that he carried so much pain. He'd thought God had made him forget his family, when all along they had always been there in the back of his mind. And his heart.

They would wonder what had happened to him, and he had

not even given Hamid instructions to release them. He must return to them, but by now the kohl had surely run down his cheeks. He rose slowly, composed himself as best he could, and called the guard who followed him wherever he went.

"Bring my manservant at once and have him bring the makeup pots," he said, turning aside to hide his emotion.

"Yes, my lord," the man said, hurrying to do his bidding. Another guard replaced him until the first guard and his manservant returned.

The manservant looked at Joseph, his eyes wide, but simply went to work with wet linen rags and applied fresh makeup and kohl to his face and eyes.

"Am I presentable?" Joseph asked when the servant leaned back to examine him.

"As good as you were this morning," he said, putting his brushes and pots back onto his tray.

Joseph looked in the silver mirror to see if he agreed, then left the room and walked back to the audience chamber, two guards following now. He pointed at Simeon and spoke to Hamid.

Hamid called the guards, who took Simeon from his brothers, bound his hands behind his back, and put shackles on his feet. Joseph spoke again to Hamid and made a gesture to show his brothers that Simeon would remain in prison.

The fear he had seen in their gazes upon their arrival in the chamber changed to terror. Through Hamid, he told his brothers to go and collect their sacks of grain. They followed a guard to where Joseph had kept their sacks.

"Put each man's silver back in their sacks and give them provisions for their journey home," Joseph said to Hamid. "Take the side entrance to get there ahead of them."

Hamid gave Joseph a puzzled look but simply said, "Yes, my lord."

Joseph leaned back in the gilded seat and released a long-held breath. Now he would wait and see whether they would do as he had commanded. And the silver would test them to see if they were still dishonest, betraying men or changed men who could be trusted.

ппп

Judah tucked the last of his sacks along his donkey's side and held the reins, leading his brothers on the path toward Hebron. His mind spun with all that had happened since they set foot in Egypt. Why had the governor of the land been immediately suspicious of them? Certainly they stood out as shepherds and foreigners, but the line of people waiting for food came from various lands. Why choose them to blame to be spies?

Was God punishing them, as his brothers had suspected—as he had suspected—for what they had done to Joseph? He trudged ahead alone, not wanting their company, certain he deserved every bad thing that had happened to him. Hadn't it been his idea to sell Joseph to those Ishmaelites in the first place?

His heart stirred as he remembered the boy's cries for help. Had he lost two sons because of his sin? The memories came in waves, and he felt his face heat as the sun rose. Shame filled him, and he mopped his brow with his sleeve and walked faster, anxious to get home to his father and sons.

His brothers walked in silence, the only sounds coming from their footfalls and the donkeys' hooves. They all seemed to be in the same hurry he was to leave the black land. Judah longed to pray to never see that governor again, but the nagging truth remained that Simeon was his prisoner, and in time the grain they had purchased would need replenishing.

They would meet him again, like it or not.

"This looks like a good place to stop," Reuben said, coming up behind him. "It's getting too dark to see, and we will never make it home in one day's journey."

Everything in Judah wanted to argue. They could keep going by the light of the moon and make torches so they didn't stumble. But he also ached to sleep and knew his brothers would feel the same.

He looked at Reuben. "You are right." He stopped his donkey and faced those coming behind him. "We will make camp here tonight." It was the right thing to do if they hoped to stay safe from bandits they might find along the way.

They drew their animals to a stop and formed a circle, building a fire in the center. Hunger gnawed at Judah, and he lifted one of the sacks from the side of his animal. He would gather some grain to toast over the fire and give some to feed the donkey.

The sack seemed heavier than it did when he first lifted it to the donkey's back. He set it on the ground and untied the rope at the neck. The glint of metal caught his eye, and he reached into the mouth of the sack to find his silver—every bit of it that he had used to pay for the grain—sitting atop the grain. His stomach turned over, and fear gripped him at the sight. He looked about him and called out, "My silver has been returned. Here it is in my sack."

He saw the same fear reflected in his brothers' faces. They moved slowly, visibly shaken, and sank to the ground.

"What is this that God has done to us?" Judah said.

"It has to be because of what we did to Joseph," Asher said, drawing a circle in the dirt with his finger. "We never treated him with kindness."

"We were worse than that," Dan said. "We treated him with contempt. Which one among us ever said a kind word to him?"

"I should have been the one the governor imprisoned," Judah

said, sitting beside them in the circle. "If I had said nothing, if I had not had the idea to sell Joseph, Reuben would have rescued him."

"We are all guilty of his blood," Levi said, pulling on his beard. "We should have listened to his cries for help and pulled him out and returned him to our father."

"He would have told Father what we did," Naphtali complained. "We never should have attacked him in the first place."

"Enough of this," Reuben said, taking some of the grain Judah had pulled from his sack and tossing it onto a griddle he'd hung over the fire. "What is done is done. We can't undo what is past. We can only try to be better, do better, in the future."

"What if that man never releases Simeon? If Father won't let us bring Benjamin with us next time, Simeon will remain his prisoner forever," Zebulun said, keeping his voice low. Judah could see how upset his younger brother was.

Why had the man kept Simeon? Why not one of the others? Had Simeon done worse to Joseph that no one knew about? Or was this punishment for Simeon's crimes against Shechem and his whole village because of Shechem's actions against Dinah?

The answers would not come, and Judah felt his head begin to pound. "We can't understand it, so let's forget about it tonight," he said, knowing how cryptic his tone sounded. "Let's eat something so we can get an early start tomorrow. Our families need this food, and there is nothing we can do for Simeon now unless we can convince Father to let us return quickly to retrieve him."

"With Benjamin?" Reuben scoffed. "Father will never agree."

Judah knew that, but a small part of him refused to believe it. He rolled onto his side near the fire, suddenly no longer hungry, and thought about how fractured his family had become. He could not continue to live with this guilt. But there was nothing he could do to rid himself of it.

42

HEBRON

The following day, Judah saw his father's camp a short distance away. What should have been relief to finally be far from the black land turned to angst as he considered what to tell his father.

Reuben and Levi came alongside him as they entered the outskirts of the camp. Their wives and children emerged from their tents and ran to meet them. Judah caught sight of Tamar and her maid holding his sons. A mixture of regret and pride at seeing them filled him. They did not draw close.

A deep sigh escaped him. He leaned closer to Reuben. "Let's not put this off."

Reuben nodded, stepping out of his wife's embrace. Each man took his sack and walked toward their father's tent. Judah called to him, and Jacob limped from the tent and met them in the center of the camp.

"Good, you are back at last," Jacob said. "I worried I would never see you again, considering how long it took you."

"We were detained three extra days." Judah rested his hands on the top of his walking stick, bracing himself for his father's reaction. "The governor of the land kept Simeon until we return again for more grain. He wants us to bring Benjamin with us."

Jacob's brows drew together as he scowled. "What is this you are telling me?"

Judah forced himself to remain steady and relayed all that had happened to them and what they had said to the lord of the land. "We had no choice, Father. The man asked us pointed questions and accused us of being spies. We told him no, we were twelve brothers, the son of one man. We said that the youngest was with his father and the other is no more. But he did not believe us. He kept Simeon prisoner until we return and told us we must bring Benjamin with us or we would not see his face, for he would know we were spies."

Jacob sat staring, looking from one son to another as if searching to see if Simeon was truly missing. He remained silent as each of them opened his sack to present the grain to their father. Gasps came from each man.

"It was not just Judah whose silver was returned to him. Look, every one of us has the money right here," Reuben said, and Judah saw fright fill his father's eyes. Why was the silver in their sacks? How could such a mistake have occurred? Would they now also be accused of thievery?

"You have deprived me of my children," Jacob said, his voice trembling. "Joseph is no more and Simeon is no more, and now you want to take Benjamin. Everything is against me!"

Reuben stepped close to their father and knelt before him. "You may put both of my sons to death if I do not bring Benjamin back to you. Entrust him to my care, and I will bring him back."

Jacob shook his head, his expression adamant, making Judah's heart sink. They would never resolve this if Jacob did not cooperate. "My son will not go down there with you. His brother is dead and he is the only one left. If harm comes to him on the journey you are taking, you will bring my gray head down to the grave in sorrow."

Judah glanced from one brother to the next, then met his father's gaze once more. But there was nothing else he could say. When the grain ran low and Jacob hungered again, they would be forced to speak of this and hope their father had a change of mind. But Judah wondered if such a thing were possible. Their father was a stubborn man, a man who had wrestled with God and lived to tell about it. His limp was a constant reminder to them all.

But this time, Judah was not so sure Jacob or any of them would win this battle against the lord of Egypt. They had met their match, and they were on the losing side.

ᴚᴜᴚᴜ

EGYPT

Joseph strode over colorful rugs in his grand governor's apartments, struggling to keep his mind on his work and not on Simeon, who slept on a pallet in the very cell he had occupied during his years of imprisonment under Potiphar's command. The irony of how he had come to this moment did not escape him. And his heart both acquitted and condemned him for his actions. Had he done the right thing in keeping Simeon behind? Considering what he had done to Dinah, stripping her of any chance of marriage—even one such as she could have had— didn't Simeon deserve to be the one Joseph chose?

And yet, what if his father no longer cared what happened to Simeon because of those very actions, though they happened long ago? If Joseph had kept a son of the concubines, his father might have cared even less. Should Judah, the brother who had sold him into slavery, have been his choice? Or should he have taken his chances that his brothers would be forced to return for food and would have to bring Benjamin with them?

A knock on his door drew the attention of one of his guards, and Hamid entered moments later and bowed low.

"Rise, Hamid. Tell me what you know." Joseph knew his tone was curt, but of late he found himself unable to keep his emotions as tightly in check as he had during the twenty-two years he had spent without a single sight of his family. The anxiety of seeing his brothers made him almost wish they had never come.

"The report from Potiphar's jailer is that Simeon is doing well. He has been given good provisions, as you requested, and despite his confinement has much freedom within the prison walls." Hamid stepped back from Joseph's pacing. "Please, my lord, won't you sit a moment?"

Joseph stopped abruptly and met Hamid's concerned look. Defeat settled over him, and he sank into a plush chair, motioning for Hamid to sit opposite him.

"What troubles you, my lord? Is it the Hebrew you apprehended? Or has something happened?" Hamid leaned forward, his ever-present kindness showing in his dark eyes.

"Yes. I question myself and wonder whether I made the right judgment. Perhaps they were honest men after all." Joseph could not tell Hamid the truth.

Hamid sat in silence a moment, gazing at his hands. At last he lifted his head and looked Joseph in the eye. "I have never known you to do anything without a good reason, Joseph. You have always lived above reproach. So even if those men were honest men, something inside you told you to be cautious. No one would question you on that."

By his expression, Joseph knew Hamid wanted to question

him and his reasons but wouldn't. "Thank you, Hamid. Make sure the Hebrew gets plenty of time outside the prison to move about. He is . . . that is, it is not good for anyone to stay indoors without the light of day for long." He stood, aware that he had almost said too much. *He is used to walking the fields with the sheep.* But only Joseph knew that. "Let us be going. I'm sure there are lines of people already waiting for food, though it is barely past dawn."

Joseph could not neglect his duties simply because his heart and mind distracted him to think about home instead of Egypt. Egypt was his home now. Let Simeon wait and see if their brothers would return for him or betray him like they had Joseph. Then he would have his answer.

ᒪᒐᒪᒐ

HEBRON, 1818 BC

Jacob took the last of the flatbread from the plate Dinah offered him and dipped it into the stew. Sparks from the central fire flew upward as they licked the wood and dung, giving light as darkness fell over the camp.

"This is the last of it, Father," Dinah said, setting the plate on the stone beside him. "We need more grain. As it is, we have very few nuts and will end up having to kill several lambs even if we send my brothers to Egypt this very night. They should have gone weeks ago." Her tone held a hint of accusation, and he did not like her implication.

They blamed him for waiting. Even Benjamin had looked on him with gentle censure. But how could he do what they asked? Yet the lack of food could not be ignored.

He called his sons to come closer from where they sat around the fire. They knelt near him, faces upturned, expectant. Jacob released a deep sigh. "Go back and buy us a little more food," he said, searching each face. He hated the thought of them leaving him. Hated that Egypt had food while Hebron did not. Why had God not blessed this land of promise and instead blessed a foreign land?

Judah shifted and leaned forward, hands lifted in supplication. "The man warned us solemnly, 'You will not see my face again unless your brother is with you.' If you will send our brother along with us, we will go down and buy food for you. But if you will not send him, we will not go down.'"

The words brought a rush of irritation to Jacob's heart, and his voice rose as he asked, "Why did you bring this trouble on me by telling the man you had another brother?"

"The man questioned us closely about ourselves and our family," Reuben said. "'Is your father still living?' he asked us. 'Do you have another brother?' We simply answered his questions. How were we to know he would say, 'Bring your brother down here'?"

Judah crept closer to hold Jacob's gaze. "Send the boy along with me and we will go at once, so that we and you and our children may live and not die. I myself will guarantee his safety. You can hold me personally responsible for him. If I do not bring him back to you and set him here before you, I will bear the blame before you all my life. As it is, if we had not delayed, we could have gone and returned twice."

The rebuke stung, but the look in Judah's eyes was one Jacob had come to recognize since his son's return. He was not the young man who had run away from home over twenty years ago. He was responsible and God-fearing. Of all of the sons looking at him now, Judah could be trusted, though Jacob hated having to trust him at all.

"If it must be," Jacob said at last, "then do this: Put some of the best products of the land in your bags and take them down to the man as a gift—a little balm and a little honey, some spices and myrrh, some pistachio nuts and almonds. Take double the amount of silver with you, for you must return the silver that was put back into the mouths of your sacks. Perhaps it was a mistake. Take your brother also and go back to the man at once. And may God Almighty grant you mercy before the man so that he will let Simeon and Benjamin come back with you. As for me, if I am bereaved, I am bereaved."

Jacob watched as each son rose and went to his tent to prepare for the trip. Why was God asking such a thing of him? Hadn't he suffered enough in his life?

"It will be all right, Abba," Benjamin said, coming to sit beside him. "My brothers will protect me." He leaned close and kissed Jacob's cheek, drawing tears from his eyes.

Jacob clung to the boy and held him for a long moment. When at last he released him, he cupped his cheek. "Be careful. And God go with you."

43

EGYPT

Joseph sat beneath the awning, watching the line of people move slowly closer to his men, offer payment, and receive the grain they desperately needed. More than a year had passed since his brothers had come to Egypt, and Simeon remained in the king's prison. The guilt he once felt for having kept his brother confined no longer troubled him.

Now he worried that he would have to release Simeon without ever seeing the rest of his family, making some excuse that would force him to lie, and would regret he had ever laid eyes on them again. Then again, he had given them enough grain to last a year. Either they had found another way to find food, were killing their flocks to stay alive, or were on their way even now.

Why had they not already come? The grain could not have lasted this long. Surely they were in need. Would they abandon Simeon as they had abandoned him, as he'd expected? His stomach turned at the thought. He had wanted to believe they could change. Had changed.

He shifted in his seat, looking over the city surrounding this distribution center. And then he spotted them. He gripped the sides of his chair, nearly jumping from his seat, and forced himself to remain in control. They came closer and closer, and there, in the center of the group as if to be protected, was Benjamin. Joseph would have recognized those inquisitive eyes and the way he tilted his head anywhere. Besides, he looked just like their mother.

Emotion swelled, and Joseph told himself to stay calm. He could not break down here in front of all Egypt!

"Hamid, come here," he called.

"Yes, my lord. What is it?" Hamid bent one knee to lean closer to Joseph.

He pointed at his brothers. "Take these men to my house, slaughter an animal, and prepare a meal. They are to eat with me at noon."

Hamid turned, and Joseph caught the recognition in his gaze. "Yes, my lord. Right away." He hurried to do Joseph's bidding.

Joseph would arrive later, after things were ready. Let them wonder while they waited. Now that they were here, he was in no hurry.

ᴜᴜᴜ

Holding the reins to his donkey, Judah followed the man who had spoken to the lord of the land while Benjamin walked directly behind him. He sensed the fear in his brothers—fear he could not ignore in his own heart as well.

The walk to the man's house gave them a closer view of Egyptian power and wealth. But when they were led to the king's palace, to a section of the great complex apparently where this man lived, Judah felt his strength fail and a lump fill his throat.

A hand on his shoulder made him jump, but when he turned, it was only Reuben. He leaned close to Judah's ear. "We were brought here because of the silver that was put back into our sacks the first time. He wants to attack us and overpower us and seize us as slaves and take our donkeys."

Judah stared at his older brother, thinking he had surely lost his mind, but one glance at the others told him they were all thinking the same thing. Were they right?

They came to a stop at intricately carved double doors, and the steward opened them and invited the men in.

Judah did not move. He swallowed hard. "We beg your pardon, our lord. We came down here the first time to buy food. But after we left, we opened our sacks and each of us found his silver—the exact weight—in the mouth of his sack. So we have brought it back with us. We have also brought additional silver with us to buy food. We don't know who put our silver in our sacks."

"It's all right," the steward said. "Don't be afraid. Your God, the God of your father, has given you treasure in your sacks. I received your silver. Come." He led them into the house and had them sit on benches near the door, then disappeared through another door.

Moments later that seemed like forever, he returned with Simeon. Judah's heart beat faster. Simeon lived! And by the look of him, he was in good health. Relief nearly stole Judah's breath.

"Here is water," the steward said as servants carried jars and basins and towels for each man. "Wash your feet while I have my servants feed your donkeys."

"If we may, my lord," Judah said before the man could leave, "we have gifts we wish to retrieve from our donkeys' saddlebags."

The steward nodded. "Of course."

Judah stood, and six of his brothers hurried with him to gather the gifts to present to the governor when he arrived. They were to eat with him at noon? The steward's announcement to them before they had begun their trek through Egypt's streets still astounded him. Why would they first be accused of being spies and now be invited to dine with one of the most powerful men on earth? It made no sense.

He had little time to ponder the reasons when guards flanked the very man whose home they now occupied. The man walked into the room and greeted them through the steward's interpretation.

"We have brought you gifts from Hebron, from our father, my lord," Judah said, placing the items at the man's feet. He bowed low, his face to the cool tiles, as did all of his brothers.

The man cleared his throat and bid them rise. "How is your aged father you told me about? Is he still living?" he asked, his voice kind.

"Your servant our father is still alive and well," Judah said for them all. He bowed again, as did his brothers, prostrate before this confusing and intimidating man.

"Is this your youngest brother, the one you told me about?" the man asked, causing Judah to lift his head. The man was looking at Benjamin. "God be gracious to you, my son." And as quickly as he had arrived, he rushed from the room, leaving them alone.

"Where did he go?" Benjamin whispered to Judah.

"I have no idea." Judah touched Benjamin's shoulder. Why had the man left like that? Had they said something to offend him? Would they be in worse trouble than they had been on their first visit?

Before he could think to ask the steward, the steward called them to follow him again. He led them to a banquet hall and sat them in the order of their ages. But the governor did not return, leaving them to wonder how the steward knew their ages and why the governor had acted so strangely.

Joseph nearly ran through the palace halls, searching for
a place to weep, but found nowhere adequately private until
he reached his own rooms. Tears came in rivulets down his
cheeks, and his heart pounded. *Benjamin!* They had actually
brought him with them, and his father still lived. Amazement,
grief, joy, and dismay over the years he had lost all crashed in
on him at once, until he could not hold back the bitter sobs.
All of these years he had held them in check, but now . . . now
he did not know if he could stop and collect himself enough
to eat in their presence.

Great, hiccupping sobs wracked his whole body, and he
fought to take a deep breath. *Oh, Adonai, help me!* He could
not do this. After all his planning for and imagining of this
possible day, he was not sure he could go through with it. But
as surely as the tears began, they ended, and he finally calmed.
He examined himself in the silver mirror and washed his face.
A servant came at his bidding and reapplied the kohl to his eyes.

Smoothing his robe and drawing in a deep breath, he at last
walked the halls to the banquet room and sat at a table some
distance from his brothers. To eat with them would confuse
everyone under his roof, for Hebrews were detestable to Egyptians.

"Serve the food," he said to the servants.

He sent food from his table to his brothers, commanding
that Benjamin receive five times as much as any of the others.
Joseph sensed that at last his brothers had relaxed, and though
he was not yet at ease with them, he felt a sense of gladness
that they could feast and drink freely with him. Perhaps one
day they could truly enjoy each other's company as they never
had before.

When the meal ended, Joseph bid the men to find rest in the guest quarters in his house, telling them they could leave in the morning. He accepted the gifts they had given and told them to thank their father for him when they left the next day.

"Did you find the meal satisfactory, my lord?" Hamid asked once the last man had left the room.

Joseph nodded. "Yes. But now I want you to fill the men's sacks with as much food as they can carry and put each man's silver in the mouth of his sack. Then put my cup, the silver one Pharaoh gave to me, in the mouth of the youngest one's sack, along with the silver for his grain."

"Yes, my lord," Hamid said, his look telling Joseph he now suspected more than he would say.

Joseph longed to confide in his friend, but he could not bring himself to reveal anything until he was sure he could first tell his brothers the truth. And despite bringing Benjamin as he had commanded, they still had to prove themselves to him.

44

Joseph woke with the dawn and immediately called his manservant to dress him. Heart beating too fast, he battled the intense desire to watch his brothers leave mingled with anxiety from a night of fitful sleep. His eyes still felt the sting of too many tears shed in private, and he berated himself for avoiding Asenath and his sons when they could have been a pleasing distraction.

He shoved the thoughts aside and walked the long halls to the balcony, where Hamid met him. "Are they gone?" Joseph asked, keeping his back to Hamid and watching the road they would take. "I had thought to see them off. From here," he added, lest Hamid grow more suspicious than he already was.

"I am told they left before sunup. I should have come to tell you. Forgive me, my lord."

Joseph chafed at Hamid's apology, feeling guilty for causing his friend to think he had offended him. "There was no need. I suspected they might want to be far from Egypt as soon as they could be." He stepped closer to the railing and strained to see, but there was no sign of them. "Go after them at once," he said without turning to look at Hamid, "and when you catch up with them, ask why they've repaid good with evil by taking

341

my cup." Joseph waited to hear Hamid's footsteps, but the man did not move. "Are you waiting for a reason to obey me?"

"No, my lord. Forgive me."

Joseph turned and saw Hamid hurrying away, wishing that he had been less harsh with him. In time he would tell his friend what he could. For now, Joseph needed to put his anxious thoughts to rest. What would his brothers do when they found his cup in Benjamin's sack?

⨆⨆⨆

Judah heard the horses' hooves and chariot wheels coming in their direction. He stopped his donkey and faced his brothers, his fear rising as the Egyptian steward they had met came into view. "Now what?" he asked Reuben. "This is not a good sign."

"No, it surely is not." Reuben's brow furrowed, and as Judah took in his brothers' expressions, he could see the whites of their eyes.

The steward came to a stop a short distance from their donkeys. He climbed down from the chariot and walked toward them, scowling. "Why have you repaid good with evil?" he demanded. "Isn't this the cup my master drinks from and also uses for divination?" Hamid pointed at each man. "This is a wicked thing you have done."

Judah stared at him. What was he talking about? "What cup, my lord? We carry no such cup with us."

"Indeed you do," the man said. "It is missing from my master's table, from the very place where you dined with him yesterday."

Judah paled, then felt a swell of anger. He stepped closer but, noting the man's disdain, thought better of it and took a step back. "Why does my lord say such things?" he asked. "Far be it from your servants to do anything like that! We even brought

JILL EILEEN SMITH

back to you from the land of Canaan the silver we found inside the mouths of our sacks." His confidence growing that none of them could possibly be guilty of such a thing, he added, "So why would we steal silver or gold from your master's house? If any of your servants is found to have it, he will die, and the rest of us will become my lord's slaves."

"Very well, then," the man said, "let it be as you say. But whoever is found to have it will become my slave. The rest of you will be free from blame."

Judah's jaw tensed. He grabbed his sack from the donkey's side, as did his brothers. The man stepped forward and began to search from the oldest to the youngest. How he could tell their age difference still puzzled Judah, but his anger at this audacious accusation overrode his confusion.

"Here it is!" The man pulled an intricately carved silver cup from Benjamin's sack.

Judah felt as though someone had kicked him in the gut. "No!" he said as the same guttural cry burst from each of his brothers, Reuben's voice the loudest of all. Judah reached for the neck of his robe and tore his clothes. The sound of ripping fabric followed as each brother did the same. They silently loaded their grain back onto their donkeys and followed the steward back to the house of the Egyptian lord.

บบบ

Joseph moved to the audience chamber he had used when his brothers first came to Egypt and sat on the gilded throne. That his position would intimidate them mattered little. He wanted that advantage over them now.

A commotion at the door caused his heart to race. Hamid was back, and as the door opened, his brothers followed Hamid closely and literally fell down at the foot of Joseph's throne.

343

"What is this you have done?" Joseph demanded. "Don't you know that a man like me can find things out by divination?" He'd been in Egypt long enough to act the part of a true Egyptian who did believe such things.

Judah's voice carried to him, but he did not lift his head. "What can we say to my lord? What can we say? How can we prove our innocence? God has uncovered your servants' guilt. We are now my lord's slaves—we ourselves and the one who was found to have the cup."

Joseph refused to allow himself to be moved by the words. How often in his youth had his brothers told him things they didn't mean? "Far be it from me to do such a thing!" he said. "Only the man who was found to have the cup will become my slave. The rest of you, go back to your father in peace."

Judah did not hesitate but lifted his head and came to kneel near the first step to the throne. "Pardon your servant, my lord. Let me speak a word to my lord. Do not be angry with your servant, though you are equal to Pharaoh himself."

He paused, and Joseph nodded.

"My lord asked his servants, 'Do you have a father or a brother?'" Judah continued. "And we answered, 'We have an aged father, and there is a young son born to him in his old age. His brother is dead, and he is the only one of his mother's sons left, and his father loves him.'

"Then you said to your servants, 'Bring him down to me so I can see him for myself.' And we said to my lord, 'The boy cannot leave his father. If he leaves him, his father will die.' But you told your servants, 'Unless your youngest brother comes down with you, you will not see my face again.' When we went back to your servant my father, we told him what my lord had said.

"Then our father said, 'Go back and buy a little more food.'

But we said, 'We cannot go down. Only if our youngest brother is with us will we go. We cannot see the man's face unless our youngest brother is with us.'

"Your servant my father said to us, 'You know that my wife bore me two sons. One of them went away from me, and I said, "He has surely been torn to pieces." And I have not seen him since. If you take this one from me too and harm comes to him, you will bring my gray head down to the grave in misery.'

"So now, if the boy is not with us when I go back to your servant my father, and if my father, whose life is closely bound up with the boy's life, sees that the boy isn't there, he will die. Your servants will bring the gray head of our father down to the grave in sorrow. Your servant guaranteed the boy's safety to my father. I said, 'If I do not bring him back to you, I will bear the blame before you, my father, all my life!'"

He paused again, and Joseph could barely move for the emotion welling in him. He motioned with his hand for Judah to continue.

"Now then, please let your servant remain here as my lord's slave in place of the boy, and let the boy return with his brothers. How can I go back to my father if the boy is not with me? No! Do not let me see the misery that would come on my father."

Judah lowered his head again and touched it to the tiles. Joseph looked at these brothers who once would not have cared if he had died but were now willing to give their lives for Benjamin. Judah, the very brother who had gladly sold Joseph into slavery, was now willing to be his slave.

Suddenly he could not hold back the emotion that had overtaken him the moment Judah offered his life for Benjamin's. "Have everyone leave my presence!" he cried.

The servants, the guards, and even Hamid hurried from the room.

Sobs rose in Joseph's throat, and tears streamed from his eyes. He stood and moved down to their level. "Rise, all of you," he said in Hebrew.

They quickly obeyed.

His heart pounded, and he struggled for breath. "I am Joseph!" he said, loud enough for each of them to hear. "Is my father still living?"

He looked from one to another, but they seemed stricken with dread. They didn't believe him.

"Come close to me." He motioned with both hands. Slowly Judah stepped closer with Benjamin at his side, and the rest followed. "I am your brother Joseph, the one you sold into Egypt! And now, do not be distressed and do not be angry with yourselves for selling me here, because it was to save lives that God sent me ahead of you." He searched the faces so familiar to him, yet he knew he looked every bit the foreigner to them. "For two years now there has been famine in the land, and for the next five years there will be no plowing and reaping. But God sent me ahead of you to preserve for you a remnant on earth and to save your lives by a great deliverance."

They stared at him, still clearly unbelieving.

Joseph released a pent-up sob, his voice rising as he spoke again. "So then it was not you who sent me here, but God. He made me father to Pharaoh, lord of his entire household, and ruler of all Egypt. Now hurry back to my father and say to him, 'This is what your son Joseph says: God has made me lord of all Egypt. Come down to me; don't delay. You shall live in the region of Goshen and be near me—you, your children and grandchildren, your flocks and herds, and all you have. I will provide for you there, because five years of famine are still to come. Otherwise you and your household and all who belong to you will become destitute.'"

He stepped even closer to them. "You can see for yourselves, and so can my brother Benjamin, that it is really I who am speaking to you. Tell my father about all the honor accorded me in Egypt and about everything you have seen. And bring my father down here quickly."

Unable to restrain himself any longer, Joseph embraced Benjamin. Their tears mingled and their weeping sounded like that of a wounded animal. Surely his entire household could hear them!

Benjamin clung to him, and Joseph felt as if the years had melted away. He was home again, one brother among many. Wanted. Loved.

He kissed each brother on both cheeks and wept over each one.

"It is really you," Judah said when Joseph's weeping had quieted.

Joseph held Judah's gaze. "Yes."

"I wish I could take back everything I did to you, my brother." Judah's dark eyes filled, and Joseph could see the tearstains on his cheeks. "I could not bear it, nor could I forget you. I left Father for over twenty years, for I could not bear to see the sorrow in his eyes over your loss."

Joseph studied this brother who had once hated him the most. "Where did you go?" What had changed Judah so much that he would give his life for Benjamin's?

"Canaan. I married, had three sons . . . then two more by my daughter-in-law." Judah's skin darkened, and he bowed his head as though he was ashamed.

Joseph clasped his hands behind his back, trying to make sense of Judah's comment. "I don't understand."

Judah looked up. "It is a long story."

"I want to hear it."

"My wife and two oldest sons, the husbands of my daughter-in-law Tamar, had died. By rights, I should have given her to my third son so she could bear a son for my oldest. But I feared she was evil and had caused the deaths of the oldest two. So I withheld my third son from her."

Joseph rubbed the back of his neck. So Judah's life had carried its own hardship. "You have lost much." A sense of sadness filled him, surprising him. Shouldn't he be glad that the one who had hurt him the most had also suffered? But he wasn't.

"You will ask me why I have two sons by my daughter-in-law." Judah interrupted his musings and held Joseph's steady gaze. There was no hint of the disdain he had portrayed in bygone years.

"You do not have to tell me."

"Canaanites do not believe as we do. I thought I could run away from God in their land, but I found only trouble and sorrow." He glanced at Benjamin. "I owed Tamar the right to bear a child, but instead I sent her home. Then my wife died, and a year later on my way to shear the sheep, Tamar dressed as a prostitute and met me at one of the towns along the road. I convinced her to let me sleep with her. When I later discovered she was pregnant by prostitution, I wanted her to die. To pay for the loss of my two sons."

He paused, and Joseph touched his shoulder.

Judah shook his head. "I realized that when I hated someone, I wanted them to die. Like I did you."

Joseph's stomach twisted with the memories. Judah truly had hated him. He was filled with doubt that Judah's love for their father had truly changed him so much.

"But the child was mine," Judah continued, "and she proved it. It was then that I finally saw how cruel I had been to you, to Father, to Tamar, to my mother, to Dinah, and to God."

Joseph stood still, his mind whirling. "I was hurt the most by you, Judah. After my mother died, I thought you cared. But then you didn't."

"I know. There is no excuse for what I did. I hope one day you can forgive me."

A weighty silence fell between them while the conversations of their other brothers went on around them. Did they all have stories like this to tell? But Judah's was the one Joseph had wanted to know the most.

"Did you ever care for me?" Joseph fairly whispered.

Judah straightened. "I would be lying if I told you that I did. When you were born, Father treated you as the only son and the rest of us as his servants. That may not have been what he thought, but it's how his actions felt to us. To me. I was too immature to realize that you did not choose to be favored."

"I was a little spoiled," Joseph admitted, "so likely didn't make myself easy to love."

"Love is something I'm only beginning to understand," Judah said.

"Did you marry Tamar?" The action wouldn't seem strange to the Egyptians, who often married within the family to secure a kingdom or dynasty.

Judah shuddered. "No. Never. She had twins, which is why I have two sons by her."

Joseph smiled. "I would like to meet these twins."

"I would be honored for you to meet them, my lord . . . Joseph." Judah gave him a quizzical look.

"I will always be Joseph to you, Judah, and to all of my family." Joseph glanced at the others, who had stopped talking to listen. Judah's words had shaken him. "You have changed." He looked Judah up and down and could not mistake the deep regret in his gaze. A part of him fought the doubt that any of them could change so much. But hadn't they proven themselves worthy? And didn't God forgive sins? Who was he to question God's ways? How could he do any less than forgive as God had forgiven him?

"I hope so, Joseph." Judah put an arm around Benjamin. "I'm glad I lived to see this day when you could reunite with your brother."

"Brothers." Joseph looked over the group again. They still stared at him as though he were a foreigner. "You must not blame yourself." He smiled. "It is as I said. God sent me here. Though he used your anger to cause you to sin against me, I do not blame you. I know everything happened for a reason. Perhaps to all of us. Now we know what that reason was." He drank in the sight of each one, realizing that he had missed them, despite everything. He had missed them because he loved them.

"Father will not believe you still live," Benjamin said.

"Then you must convince him." Joseph stepped closer and hugged Benjamin again.

"I missed you," Benjamin said softly, and Joseph saw again the baby brother he'd left behind. "I didn't get the chance to grow old enough to know you, and suddenly you were gone. Father and Dinah did not let me forget you, and Father's sorrow kept you always in my mind and heart."

"But now you can come here, and we will have all the time we want." Joseph released Benjamin, then once more met Judah's humble gaze. "You truly would have given your life for his."

Judah nodded. "I could not make Father's life worse than I already had. Benjamin is his life. At least I could have given him that." He glanced down as if he had yet to accept forgiveness from God. Perhaps he was waiting for Joseph to forgive him too.

"I forgive you, Judah," Joseph said softly. "For everything you did to me."

Judah looked up, tears filling his eyes again. "It is more than I deserve."

"You are right. But who among us ever deserves to be forgiven? It is God who pardons our sins, yours and mine." He touched Judah's arm.

Judah nodded and smiled as if in relief, and Joseph saw gratitude in his eyes.

Joseph's heart swelled. Forgiving one who had hurt him so much hadn't seemed possible even this morning. But now that he had, he felt a deep sense of peace roll over him. God had done more than send him ahead to preserve the lives of his family. He had changed the heart of the one who had betrayed him. And He had given Joseph the ability to forgive him. And to love him. To forgive and love them all.

45

HEBRON

Jacob walked the length of the camp, his walking stick barely keeping him from stumbling. They'd been gone too long. Surely something bad had happened to Benjamin. He couldn't bear the thought. The very idea caused such fear to rise in him that he felt his chest tighten, and he wondered if he would fall to the earth and die before they returned.

"Father!" Dinah called, and he turned to see her running toward him. "The men are coming!" She stopped near him, drawing in a breath. Every day for the past week she had watched the road, but there had been no sign of them. "They're truly here!" she cried, coming close to grasp his arm.

Thankful for her steady hold, Jacob gave her an anxious look. "Is Benjamin with them?"

Dinah nodded. "Benjamin is with them, and they look as though they have brought half of Egypt with them! You must come!"

Jacob let her help him walk to the road that led to his camp. He stopped at the sight of a huge caravan of carts, donkeys, men, and so much food and clothing that he could barely make sense of it all.

"Are these my sons or some merchant caravan coming through?" he asked as Judah came toward him.

"We are all here, Father," Benjamin said, rushing toward Jacob and embracing him. "And the best part is—" He stopped abruptly and looked at Judah.

Jacob laughed. Relief filled him that Judah had kept Benjamin safe. "What has you so excited, my son?"

"Joseph is alive," Judah said softly.

Jacob leaned closer, certain he had not heard correctly. "What nonsense is this? Tell me plainly. What did you say?"

Judah knelt in front of him, awe and humility etched in the lines of his face, and he looked much as he had when he returned home after twenty years away. Jacob saw a changed man before him, and he couldn't have imagined a greater change than Judah had already had. "What is it, Son?" he said, placing a hand on Judah's shoulder.

Judah visibly shook at Jacob's touch, as though it surprised him. "Joseph is still alive, Father. He is ruler of all Egypt."

"Joseph is alive?" Dinah gripped Jacob's arm tighter, joy lighting her face.

The words sounded strange to Jacob's ears. He must sit. He looked around for a rock or stump, but Judah led him to rest against his donkey's side.

"Listen, Father," Judah said as his brothers surrounded him. "Joseph was not killed by a lion or wild beast all those years ago. He was captured and sold as a slave to Egypt, but he said it was God who sent him there to keep us alive. He bids you and all of us to come to live in Egypt. The famine is going to last another five years, and Joseph can give us the best of Egypt's land."

Jacob looked about, seeing again all of the extra things his sons had in their possession now—much more than they had taken with them—and allowed himself to ponder their words. Could it be? But the evidence was staring at him. Joseph alive?

"It's true, Father," Benjamin said, leaning his head on Jacob's shoulder. "Believe it and come to Egypt to see Joseph for yourself."

Jacob looked from one son to another, and for the first time in more than half of Joseph's lifetime, he felt his grief lift.

He straightened and allowed himself to smile. "I'm convinced! My son Joseph is still alive. I will go and see him before I die."

ᒐᒐᒐ

EGYPT

Judah rode his donkey along the now semi-familiar streets of Memphis in Egypt to Joseph's residence. Memories of long-ago days filled him. Joseph's dreams. How they had angered him and his brothers. Even their father had rebuked the boy then.

He glanced heavenward as he reached the place where Joseph's servants would care for his donkey. That he was alone troubled him. He should have brought another brother or two with him. But his father had entrusted him to come to Joseph to get directions to Goshen, the land Joseph had promised to them. He was man enough to do the job.

He approached the great doors, and a servant bid him enter. Another servant washed his feet, and yet another offered him refreshment while he waited for Joseph.

The room was simple yet exquisitely designed. He'd paid little attention on their earlier visits, but now he felt small in comparison to all Joseph commanded.

Footfalls caused him to turn, and there was Joseph. Judah fell to his face and bowed before him. He still could not get used to Joseph's Egyptian makeup and clothes.

"Do not bow to me, Judah," Joseph said, taking his hand and helping him up. Joseph embraced him, excitement in his eyes. "Did my father come?"

Judah smiled. The great lord of Egypt still had the heart of a child who missed a beloved parent. How he wished he had not deprived his brother of their father's presence for so long.

"Yes," he said. "He sent me ahead to get directions to Goshen. We are all headed there as soon as we know where to go."

"Come, I will send Hamid to take you there. I will follow shortly." Joseph called his steward, who led Judah outside to his donkey and mounted one as well.

"Welcome to Egypt," Hamid said.

ப௱ப

Joseph waited several hours, hurrying to answer too many questions brought to him, then finally excused himself, climbed behind the driver of his chariot, and headed toward Goshen. He'd asked Asenath to come with the boys, anxious now for her to meet his father and brothers, but she had wanted this day to be just for him to reunite with his father. How blessed he was to have her! Tomorrow he would make a way for his new family to meet his family of birth.

Excitement rushed through him, his heart pounding with every memory of his father, his mother, his childhood. His dreams.

He glanced at the bright blue, cloudless sky, his heart turning to prayer. *I never imagined the dreams meant this, Adonai. It is beyond my understanding that You would allow me to care for my family in this way.* Gratitude swelled at the way God had turned twenty-three years of longing and buried sorrow into immense joy. Despite every hardship, he could never deny that God was good.

At last the chariot came to a stop. Joseph removed his Egyptian headdress, leaving it behind in the chariot, jumped out, and ran toward the camp, where he could clearly see his family. They had grown to many more people than he had left behind. So many he longed to meet and hold close.

But first he searched for one man. His father.

There, at last, he saw him sitting comfortably on a seat Pharaoh had sent for his use. *Father!* What a joyous word. Joseph's throat tightened, and tears streamed down his face as he walked toward his father. He stopped long enough to see how frail Jacob had become, then gently put his arms around his aged frame. Their weeping filled the entire camp.

"I never want to leave you again, Father!" Joseph clung to him, surprised at his father's strength when he found himself encased in his arms.

Jacob cupped his veined hands over Joseph's smooth cheeks and gazed into his eyes. "Now I am ready to die, since I have seen for myself that you are still alive."

Joseph wiped the tears from his eyes and took his father's hand in his. "Tomorrow you will meet my family and dine with me. And may our God grant you many more years so that you can hold my children's children on your knees." He kissed him, then told his brothers what they should say to Pharaoh when they met him. They could not live near him at the palace because Egypt's people had such an avid disdain for shepherds, though he had never understood why.

How he wished he could live among his family instead of so far away in a house too grand for him. But he was where God had placed him. Looking at his brothers and his father once more, he realized that not only had God fulfilled his dreams, but He'd given him the greater blessing of reunion and reconciliation.

In all of his life, he would never consider anything better than the peace he had right now. The past was forgiven and the future bright. He had been restored as a beloved member of a family he thought he would never see again. He belonged in a way he never had. And they belonged to him. There could be no better feeling as long as he lived.

END NOTE

Then Israel said to Joseph, "I am about to die, but God will be with you and take you back to the land of your fathers."

Genesis 48:21

Four hundred and thirty years later, Joseph's bones left Egypt with Moses as he led the people of Israel back to the land of their fathers, just as Jacob had said.

Then [Jacob] gave them these instructions: "I am about to be gathered to my people. Bury me with my fathers in the cave in the field of Ephron the Hittite, the cave in the field of Mach-pelah, near Mamre in Canaan, which Abraham bought along with the field as a burial place from Ephron the Hittite. There Abraham and his wife Sarah were buried, there Isaac and his wife Rebekah were buried, and there I buried Leah. The field and the cave in it were bought from the Hittites."

When Jacob had finished giving instructions to his sons, he drew his feet up into the bed, breathed his last and was gathered to his people.

Genesis 49:29–33

NOTE TO THE READER

Joseph's story doesn't end where I ended this book, but that's simply because it's an epic tale and the rest has mostly to do with blessings and burials. And though I did not include those details, which can be found near the end of Genesis, Joseph's life was also one of blessings and burials.

He was blessed to be the firstborn son of the favorite of Jacob's wives. You can read more about that love story in Genesis 29–35 and my fictionalized version in *Rachel*, book 3 in the Wives of the Patriarchs series. Some of Joseph's story carries over from hers, but they can be read independently.

Joseph was also blessed with two separate dreams from God. In a way, that was the greatest of his blessings, because those dreams gave him a glimpse of what God had for his future. Unfortunately, he couldn't see it then. Just like we cannot tell when our present is going to turn into great blessing in our future.

Joseph probably spent more time, as Jacob did, feeling as though he had been cursed and ended up in a horrible place. Slavery had to feel that way to a young man used to privilege. To anybody, for that matter. No one is so low or so poor that they deserve to be another person's slave. But too often man's inhumanity to man wins out, as we see with what happened to Joseph. His brothers let their jealousy explode into murderous hatred, and Joseph paid the price.

One thing that struck me most in the telling of this tale is the truth we see in Galatians 6:7–8. God declares through the apostle Paul, "Do not be deceived: God cannot be mocked. A man reaps what he sows. Whoever sows to please their flesh, from the flesh will reap destruction; whoever sows to please the Spirit, from the Spirit will reap eternal life."

Judah fled from his father's house, and while the Bible does not give us his reasons, we do know that it happened right after his bright idea to sell Joseph into slavery and lie to his father afterward. The shame and guilt had to have followed him, because eventually he knew the only way to feel right again was to make things right with his father. Judah was a classic case of the prodigal son. He reaped what he sowed, but like the prodigal son, he realized his sin and returned to his father, repentant.

Though Joseph was also a sinner—no one escapes that fact— he was the exact opposite of Judah in his behavior. Some consider him a type of Christ. In truth, we can't really fault Joseph for much as we read Scripture. He was spoiled, yes. But he was humble too, and that is where he seems to mirror the character of Jesus. And he mirrors that character best when he forgives Judah, the ringleader betrayer, along with every one of his brothers.

Isn't that what we love about a story? We want a happy ending. We don't always get one in this life, but when we find true redemption, reconciliation, and restoration, we find the best story there is. We see this in Joseph's life, which ultimately points us to Jesus.

May we see the contrast between the prodigal brother and the princely one. They each have a lesson to teach us if we are looking for it.

In His Grace,
Jill Eileen Smith

ACKNOWLEDGMENTS

This book will always carry with it the fact that it was written during the unprecedented year of 2020. You might think that having more time on my hands—as in, there were few places we could go—meant that this book would have been written with ease and ahead of schedule. The truth is, this is the first time I had to ask for an extension to finish all of my drafts. (I edit a book many times.) And for some reason I also needed prompting, which is a strange feeling for someone who has always been highly self-motivated.

So my first thanks go to my dear friend and fellow author Hannah Alexander for meeting with me daily for months to "time-write" in order for both of us to get our books done. I don't think I could have made my deadline without your support and motivation.

Special thanks also go to my editor Rachel McRae for giving me a few extra weeks to turn in the manuscript when a family need arose and took me away from finishing on time. I am so very blessed to work with everyone on the Revell team, including Jessica English, Michele Misiak, and Karen Steele. We've worked together a long time now, and I am most grateful for each one of you.

Wendy Lawton, as always, my thanks to you for taking me on and being so supportive throughout this adventure called publishing.

To my dear friend and fellow author Jill Stengl, thank you for brainstorming, chatting, and reading so many of my manuscripts ahead of time. I am so grateful that God brought us together as friends.

It is hard to list all of the people who have covered me in prayer through the years. One friend, whom I've never met in person because she lives in England, entered my life a few years ago. Avril Hooper and I pray for each other and share a love for Jesus and a love of writing. I often thank God for her and friends like her. She specifically prayed for this book, for which I'm most grateful.

To the rest of my friends—2020 was a hard year to stay in touch, but I thank all of you who worked to do so. We have a new appreciation for talking over a computer.

To my family—I love each one of you. We welcomed a new granddaughter the year this book was birthed, so now we have two granddaughters to love.

Randy, you will always be my best friend and true love. We made it through the toughest year to date, and I'm so glad we get to do life together.

As always, my deepest gratitude goes to the Lord Jesus, Messiah, Savior. Joseph's story reminds me once again just how much I desperately need Him.

Jill Eileen Smith is the bestselling and award-winning author of the biblical fiction series The Wives of King David, Wives of the Patriarchs, and Daughters of the Promised Land, as well as *The Heart of a King, Star of Persia: Esther's Story*, and *Miriam's Song*. She is also the author of the nonfiction books *When Life Doesn't Match Your Dreams* and *She Walked Before Us*. Her research into the lives of biblical women has taken her from the Bible to Israel, and she particularly enjoys learning how women lived in Old Testament times. Jill lives with her family in southeast Michigan. Learn more at www.jilleileensmith.com.

Meet

JILL EILEEN SMITH

at **www.JillEileenSmith.com** to learn
interesting facts and read her blog!

Connect with her on

f Jill Eileen Smith
𝕏 JillEileenSmith

LOVE. DUTY. FEAR. COURAGE.
In the court of the king,
which will prevail?

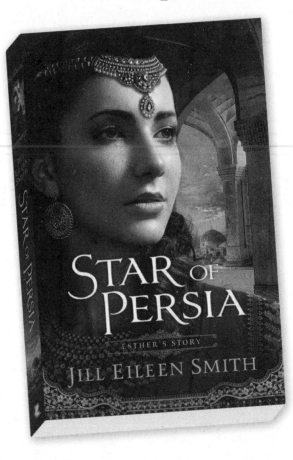

Esther is poised to save her people from annihilation. Relying
on a fragile trust in a silent God, can she pit her wisdom against
a vicious enemy and win? With her impeccable research and her
imaginative flair, Jill Eileen Smith brings to life the romantic,
suspenseful, and beloved story of Esther, queen of Persia.

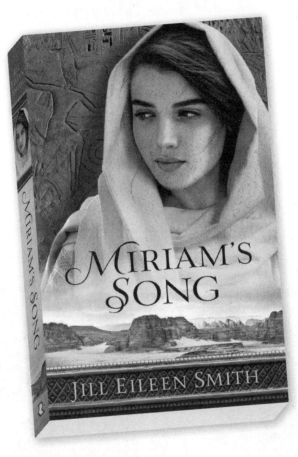

Against the Backdrop of
OPULENT PALACE LIFE, RAGING WAR, AND DARING DESERT ESCAPES
Lived Three Women . . .

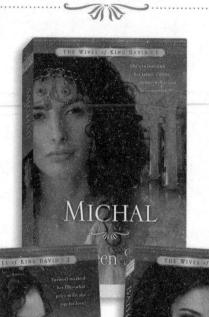